Viva Violetta & Verdi

A Novel

Howard Jay Smith

HISTORIUM PRESS

First Edition published by Historium Press

Images by Shutterstock, Imagine, Promeai, & Public Domain
Cover designed by White Rabbit Arts at The Historical Fiction Company

Visit Howard Jay Smith's website at
www.beethovaninloveopus139.com

Library of Congress Cataloging-in-Publication Data on file

Hardcover ISBN: 978-1-962465-88-5
Paperback ISBN: 978-1-962465-87-8
E-Book ISBN: 978-1-962465-86-1

Historium Press, a subsidiary of
The Historical Fiction Company
New York, NY / Macon, GA
2025

Carlos, Aida, La Traviata, Ernani, Rigoletto, Otello, Lusia Miller, I due Foscari, Simon Boccanegra, MacBeth, Un Ballo in Maschera, Falstaff, Il Corsaro, and *The Requiem.* He also had lead roles in *Carmen, Tosca, Madame Butterfly, Turandot and La Bohème.*

Viva Violetta & Verdi would not have been possible without Eduardo's friendship and his contributions to my understanding of Verdi's works and the very nature of opera performances. And though I will miss his laughter and friendship, his memory lives on inside this novel *as Il Torino*, the Little Bull, a barrel-chested singer with a warm and well-rounded voice and sharp intellect who was renowned throughout Europe for performing regularly in many of Verdi's operas.

Advanced Praise:

"Smith's writing on music, culture and history is rich, lush and drenched in knowledge. It is nothing less than a gift. His latest novel on Verdi, his two wives and the Risorgimento is a stunning, significant book that compels readers to reflect upon the turmoil of our own times and how we must continually fight to protect the freedoms and relationships we hold so dear. I dearly hope Viva Violetta & Verdi gets the major NYT review attention it so richly deserves." – **Sheila Weller, author, *Girls Like Us & Carrie Fisher, A Life on the Edge***

"In VIVA VIOLETTA & VERDI, Smith delivers a breathtaking rendering of Verdi's musical genius, his loves, friendships, and stunning role in Italy's struggle to become a democracy in the mid-1800s. With thrilling authenticity, this historic drama embraces universal themes of class and religious persecution, and weaves gorgeous language with an intimate knowledge of Italian food, music, and political hypocrisy that contemporary readers will find irresistible." **– Jessica Brilliant Keener, author of Strangers in Budapest, an Indie Next pick and SIBA bestseller**

"Viva Violetta & Verdi is a well-researched love letter to Verdi, opera fans are sure to love." – **Leslie Zemeckis, author, actress, & award-winning documentarian, *Grandes Horizontales; Here; Polar Express***

"Howard Jay Smith is a master at story telling. Every single magnificent detail of Viva Violetta & Verdi - from the small - an ancient brass mezuzah - to the smell and taste of pieces of music and the power of music… To the French Revolution, democracy, liberty, and equality … to every single luscious nuance on the page. Perfection. You are right there, inhaling and breathing in the words, the smell, and each piece of music. It is both a love song and a love letter. The irrefutable power of a muse, Violetta. Researched to perfection, it is a must read. Especially now. Yes, especially now. Bravo, Mr. Smith, Bravo!" – **Amy Ferris, author, *Mighty Gorgeous; Marrying George Clooney***

"As complex and rich as a Verdi score and an aged Brunello. By deftly combining music, food, romance and politics, Smith serves up a compelling history of Italy's wars for independence, and the men and women – composers, waiters, opera stars – who believed in freedom above all else." – **Patricia Morrisroe, Author of** *The Woman in the Moonlight*

"To travel back in time and meet our heroes as they lived their lives is a fantasy of many an individual, and in the case of Giuseppe Verdi and his muse Violetta, how their lives in context led to the timeless art that emerged from those circumstances. To fulfill the fantasy of bearing witness to creation of art that would affect the entire world, is being one step closer to God and the mysterious way in which they create. Howard Jay Smith brings us into this fantasy beautifully, and his very present voice brings us as close as one might get to the miraculous act of creation." – **Hershey Felder, Musician, writer, director, & producer,** *George Gershwin Alone; Beethoven; Violetta; Mozart & Figaro in Vienna*

"Howard Smith's latest novel, which follows Giuseppe Verdi and his exquisite Violetta against the backdrop of Italian political history of the Risorgimento, shares and celebrates la bella vita. In fine fashion, Smith captures Verdi's love of opera, his passion for freedom that he carried in his bones, and finally his love of love itself. Viva Violetta & Verdi is a triumph, at equal turns fiery and informative, joyful and tragic, but above all else, his latest novel is exceptional storytelling. Bravo." – **Kerry Candaele, Author, Filmmaker:** *Following The Ninth*: *In The Footsteps of Beethoven's Final Symphony; Love & Justice: Beethoven's Rebel Opera; & Beethoven's Last Will & Testament: The Late Quartets*

"Once is good, twice demonstrates more than a lucky start, but three times a winner cements an author's oeuvre as really outstanding. To be consistently at the top of one's game is incredibly hard, so the plaudits to Howard Jay Smith on the triumph with his third novel — Viva Violetta & Verdi — bespeak a level of excellence that few writers attain. Following on the heels of Beethoven in Love, Opus 139, and Meeting Mozart, Smith as a maestro has once again used the language of music to conduct a beautiful story that keeps the reader engaged, so that after the last act, the response is universally, 'Encore!' Bravo!" – **Fredric D. Price, Founder & Publisher of Fig Tree Books LLC.**

"In prose so beautiful it borders on poetry, Howard Jay Smith has created a riveting story cleverly weaving historical fact and fiction. In the opening pages, we are suddenly at Verdi's funeral with Toscanini on the podium conducting hundreds of thousands of people in one of the most famous choruses ever written, Va, pensiero. From Verdi's Nabucco, an opera about the Babylonian captivity, this deceptively simple choral work had come to symbolize the Risorgimento, the unification of Italy, and everyone in attendance not only knew it but understood its deeper meaning. Smith's bountiful explication of this time period is never boring or pedantic. He weaves his story of the real and imaginary characters in this tumultuous time period through skillful and involving storytelling. Without giving away any of the plot, I can tell you that it's a fascinating piece from beginning to end, impossible to put down until finished." – **Joanna Barouch, Contributing Reviewer, *Broadway World***

"With his latest novel, Viva Violetta and Verdi, the established writer Howard Jay Smith turns his attention to the truly tortured and tempestuous life and times of Giuseppe Verdi, a man who in many ways came to symbolize the spirt of nineteenth century Italy. Smith has already penned two gems of musical historical fiction in the shape of his accomplished and much praised works Beethoven in Love and Meeting Mozart. Here, in his latest work, Verdi comes to symbolize the struggle in this crowded century to transform Italy from a mere 'geographical expression' into a proud and free independent nation in its own right. Often embroiled at the very heart of the events of this epic story of a young nation seeking its own united destiny, Verdi, with his towering works and in particular his passionate and powerful Operas, comes to epitomize the undaunted spirit of the Italian Risorgimento. Here, using a broad palette with both sweeping brush strokes and a fine and delicately probing eye, Smith unrolls for the reader also a fine and sensitive profile of Giuseppe Verdi, a very human being with his life and loves. He emerges from these pages as a living, breathing person with his own loves and passions, of food and wine and good company, trapped in a love triangle and against a vivid historical backdrop panorama of passion and politics, reversals and triumphs" – **Julian De La Motte Harrison, author, *Senlac, Books 1 & 2***

"If you consider opera to be stuffy and antiquated, think again. In his latest novel, Viva Violetta & Verdi, Howard Jay Smith deftly brings times past alive with a rich tapestry of political intrigue, revolution, romance and the power of music, all with one of opera's greatest composers at the center of it all." – **John Scheinfeld, Filmmaker, *The***

U.S. vs. John Lennon; Chasing Trane: The John Coltrane Documentary; & What The Hell Happened To Blood, Sweat & Tears?

"Bookended by the grand funeral in Milan for the great Italian operatic composer Giuseppe Verdi, Viva Violetta & Verdi reveals the secrets of two lifelong friends from the small town of Busseto, one, Dario, an Italian Jewish partisan, the narrator of Howard Jay Smith's intriguing novel, and the other, Verdi, a fallen away Catholic. As the composer's music inspires the Risorgimento – the three wars for independence that dominated the 19th century Italy, with songs of defiance, Smith's graceful and effortless prose, weaves the untold story of Violetta, the leading opera diva of Italy who opened the door to Verdi's future successes, with the history of those of partisans who fought for freedom. A Five Star read by an award winning author." – **D.Z. Stone, journalist and author,** *No Past Tense - Love and Survival in the Shadow of the Holocaust*

"Howard Jay Smith does it again with Viva Violetta & Verdi, his historical drama that embraces both his devotion to Verdi and his love of music. As a professional musician, I find his writing to be consistently thought provoking while creating an exciting arc of storytelling as it unfolds. Bravo, Howard Jay Smith!" – **Pamela Kuhn, Operatic Soprano & Host of "Center Stage with Pamela Kuhn" WGCH Talk Radio, Greenwich, CT**

"An elegantly penned romantic drama that captures the time, place and ambience of 19th century Italy, like few others. You can smell the pasta cooking, taste the delicious red wine, and hear the Verdi playing in the background. Howard Jay Smith has penned an excellent read for the beach, the bedroom, or the living room. Highly recommended." – **Alex Simon,** *The Hollywood Interview & Venice Magazine*

"Howard Jay Smith paints a breathtaking panorama of history, politics, food, and music at the time of the great Verdi and his contemporaries. Viva Violetta & Verdi is so meticulously researched and so vividly describes in every small detail his subjects and their lives that I felt swept away as if I was myself participating in the Risorgimento and enjoying the delicious Sachetti at Tartufo at the Ca' Dario restaurant in its rowdy atmosphere of intrigue, romance, and of course Italian music. For any connoisseur of the period or an aspiring history buff, this is a page turner which keeps you spellbound by the power of love and music in Verdi's world, long after you finish reading. BRAVO!" – **Elena Klionsky, Concert Pianist**

"From the very first, Smith's captivating historical novel, *Viva Violetta & Verdi*, regales the reader with rich details of the atmosphere and ambiance of the period… and the extraordinary love affair between Verdi and Giuseppina - the unsung hero of their story… Not one page of this adeptly wrought, all-important saga disappoints… Clearly Smith has done his research and then some as he places the reader in prime position, making them feel like they in the thick of the events and creating an atmosphere that bristles with Italian authenticity. One imagines with great anticipation what Smith might have up his sleeve for his next project." – **Erica Miner, author, *The Julia Kogan Opera Murder Mystery Series* & former Metropolitan Opera violinist**

"Howard Jay Smith has written another tour de force historical novel of the life and times of a great composer--this time Giuseppe Verdi—with its tragedies, passionate love affairs, marriages and musical triumphs, all brilliantly woven against the dramatic story of Italy's period of unification, or Risorgimento. Narrated by Dario Conegliano, a Jewish friend of Verdi, a sometime opera singer and an innkeeper, the book is full of derring-do, of spies and revolutionary activities as these men and their friends and families, all secret supporters of a unified Italy, fight against the hated Austro-Hungarian Hapsburg soldiers. Read this lively and fast paced novel and immerse yourself in the food, the politics and the music of 19th century Italy. The descriptions of Verdi's music may send you, as they did me, to listen to the arias described so beautifully by Smith and leave you humming the familiar strains of Va' Pensiero, from Verdi's opera Nabucco, the unofficial anthem of the newly unified Italy." – **Florence Reiss Kraut, author, *Street Corner Dreams & How To Make a Life***

"Giuseppe Verdi - We know the history of this, the most beloved of Italian composers, the genius behind many of the greatest world operas, the young revolutionary fervently supporting the Risorgimento, the liberal supporter of the nationalist cause, champion of Italian unification, and ultimately hero of the new Italian state. The 'figurehead of Italian pride' whose death drew some 400,000 to his funeral procession in the streets of Milan, to the sounds of Va, pensiero, sull'ali dorate – Fly, thought, on wings of gold - an anthem to the new Italy's freedom from foreign domination.
But what lies beneath this history? What was Verdi's true inspiration throughout his entire life? Who was Verdi's muse, guiding him to glory

on his artistic and political journeys? Now, Howard Jay Smith gives us a glimpse of the real story behind the man - a story of revolution and triumph, love and joy, a story of the brotherhood of man. This is the story of Verdi and his Violetta, living the joys and sorrows of life in this world, the drama and compassion of life and love, the heart and soul of being human that brought his nation into a new century and his Italian compatriots into a new world." – **George Konstantinow, Ph.D., Board of the Santa Barbara Symphony & ETC, the Ensemble Theater Company**

"Nothing is as treasured to me than music, the arts, and the grandeur of all that complements the worldly gifts they bestow upon us all. Howard Jay Smith's astonishing Viva Violetta & Verdi, is one such remarkable achievement. In this, his third novel about composers, Smith again demonstrates that he has simply the most perfect, eclectic and encyclopedic voice to write about not only the tragedies and romances of Verdi's life but also riots and revolutionary acts that led to the creation of a new Democracy in Italy. The gravity of that struggle mirrors the fault lines of our own conflicted era. This is a rare gift, and no one writes better with such quintessential gravity and beauty. A perfect must read!" – **David Marks, Book Reviewer, Author**

Table of Contents:

"That which comes next is not always progress."

— Alessandro Manzoni

Author's Notes

The events of this novel take place during the lifetime of Giuseppe Verdi, between 1813 and 1901, in what is now the nation of Italy. The process of Italian unification is referred to as the Risorgimento. Between 1848 and 1866, there were three successive Wars of Italian Independence. Prior to 1813 and dating back to the demise of the Roman Empire, the Italian peninsula did not exist as a unified state. Different regions were occupied and controlled by an ever-changing cast of foreign rulers. In fact, when Verdi was born in the town of Busseto in the Duchy of Parma, his birth was recorded in the town hall records in the French language as most of the Italian peninsula was controlled by Napoleon and the French Army. A year later it was back under the control of the Austrian Hapsburg emperors. In the south Sicily and Naples were under the thumb of the Spanish Bourbon kings. Rome and central Italy, the so-called Papal states, were dominated by Pope as both a secular and religious ruler. Parma was a Duchy beholden to the Austro-Hungarian Empire – the Hapsburg family – along with Venice and Lombardy where Milan is located. The rulers of Savoy controlled the northwest corner of Italy along with the contiguous regions of what is now southeast France. The removal of most foreign occupying powers through military force and the formal establishment of the Italian nation under King Victor Emanuel II of Savoy finally occurred in 1861 but was not completed until nearly ten years later.

The Prologue:

Oh, My Country, So Beautiful And Lost

Milan, February 27, 1901

On the morning of Verdi's funeral, I awoke well before dawn. After a double shot of espresso and a *cornetto*, one freshly baked and served up by my daughter-in-law, Luisa, I dressed in my black mourning suit. At my age, this was an exercise I engaged in with an all too familiar regularity.

Then with the necessary assistance of my silver-handled cane, I left my bedroom suite and headed down the marble stairs to the entryway foyer of our home, *Casa di Trevi,* on the Via Vittorio Veneto. Tap, step, step. Tap, step, step – a rhythm and beat that had been my companion for over three decades. Tap, step, step.

There, waiting by the coat rack was Luisa, whom I had known since she was thirteen. A pugnacious and steely eyed woman, she greeted me with a warmth that never flagged, *"Buongiorno papà."*

I nodded and thanked her for the coffee. "And Tre?" I asked referring to my son, whom we all called by his nickname.

"He left an hour ago," she replied as she helped me into my black overcoat and then handed me my top hat.

As I settled the hat onto my head, Luisa stepped back and gave me that "look," that glare, the one which every man who has ever been married, knows only too well.

"What?" I asked as I glanced in the hallway mirror. Save for a few flecks of grey in my otherwise neatly trimmed beard, the reflected image of my hair came back to me as black as the night I was about to step out into. Despite my age, I was fortunate that my hair, save for a few grey streaks, still retained its natural color.

"Just this," she said. From a pocket buried in the many folds of her housedress, Luisa pulled a patch to which she had already added a tri-colored ribbon of red, white and green. She pinned it to the band of my top hat and then kissed me on both cheeks. "Now you are ready, *papà*. Viva Verdi."

"*Viva la rivoluzione,*" I replied as I looked in the mirror and nodded my approval.

"*Viva la rivoluzione,*" repeated Luisa as she opened the front door.

I stepped out into the chill of that February morning. The streets of Milan were still deserted at this hour. Later, though, news reports would hold that some four-hundred thousand mourners would gather along the funeral route to view the carriage carrying Verdi's coffin along with that of his wife, who had preceded him in death by some three years. The procession would travel the two miles from the *Cimitero Monumentale* to the Piazza Michelangelo Buonarroti and their final resting place at the *Casa di Riposo per Musicisti*.

One reporter from *Corriere della Sera* would even remark that the crowd for Verdi's funeral procession was the largest gathering of humans in a single place since Napoleon invaded Russia in 1812. That event some 89 years ago occurred a year before Verdi and I were born just days apart in Busseto, a small village in the Duchy of Parma some 65 miles southeast of here. And although today Verdi is considered not only the quintessential Italian composer but the quintessential Italian, our birth records in the Busseto town hall archives are written in French, for they ruled our home territory.

Yes, *liberami*, save me. There is no one else alive today who has known Giuseppe Verdi longer than I. Today it is time to put my friend to rest in the soil of an Italian nation that did not exist when we were born and to remember all the sacrifices our beloveds made in blood to achieve those victories.

Tap, step, step. Tap, step, step. With great intention I decided to detour past La Scala, the great opera hall where I'd witnessed the success of Verdi's career as an opera composer solidified in a single night, that of March 9th, 1842, with the production of *Nabucco*. The opera starred the then reigning queen of the stage and the woman that would later become known as one of the greatest loves of Verdi's life. And you must trust me when I tell you his life was filled with many a romance.

By the time I reached the piazza separating the theater from the Galleria Vittorio Emanuele II, the winter sun had begun to rise behind the spires of the Duomo just to the east. The shadows of those spires fell across the empty square as if they were the fingers of a god. They all pointed to a portrait of Verdi draped in black that hung between the doors of La Scala.

The main entryways were shuttered, and the entire portico was draped in black bunting. Hundreds, if not thousands of bouquets of flowers – primarily red and white and laced with greenery – lay piled against the stucco walls, all dropped by a populace mourning Maestro Verdi's death.

In contrast to the still and reverent façade of La Scala, the side doors on the service alley were wide open. Light from backstage spilled out onto the cobblestones. I paused a moment and watched as an irregular but nonetheless steady procession of musicians from the La Scala orchestra and singers from their chorus entered the hall in preparation for the funeral concert to be held later that day at the *Cimitero Monumentale* under the baton of Maestro Toscanini himself.

Though Toscanini, a frequent diner at my restaurant, Ca' Dario, was young, a mere thirty-four or so, he well understood the somber yet historical significance of the funeral and subsequent procession. He had told me himself the other night of his concerns about having the orchestra play to what he expected would be a noisy sea of humanity out in the open air where the power and solemnity of the music – all Verdi compositions - would be easily dissipated. To that end he nearly doubled the size of the orchestra and put together what was perhaps the largest choir ever assembled in the history of Milan, some eight hundred and twenty singers.

But enough dawdling, I thought. It was past time to head over to our trattoria to check on preparations for the gathering there tonight after the funeral, when I was startled by a shout. It was a deep and resonant tenor one at that.

"*Ciao,* Dario! *Anche tu?"*

Turning back around, I was blinded for a moment by the sun, now rising in the eastern sky above the Duomo.

"You're singing with the chorus too?" The tenor continued.

Shielding my eyes, I at last recognized an old friend coming out of the light, Eduardo Villa, whom we all knew as *Il Torino*, the Little Bull. He was a barrel-chested singer with a warm and well-rounded voice and sharp intellect who was renowned throughout Europe for, in his younger days, performing regularly in many of the Maestro's operas. Verdi loved Eduardo, noting that our *Il Torino*, always understood not only his role in an opera, but all of the roles, including the conductor, the musicians and the composer. Eduardo, if I recall correctly, hailed from a little town in California - Santa Barbara. Now in his late 60's, he worked for Maestro Toscanini, serving as a mentor for the younger singers at La Scala.

Before I could respond, Eduardo wrapped me in a bear hug. "Toscanini's a genius, for adding your voice to the choir. We're going to need your bass-baritone if we're to project over the noise of the crowds," he said.

"No, no," I said. I explained that I was only pausing here on my way to check in on Ca' Dario. Our trattoria was a few blocks further west in the old Porta Nuova district. And though it's true that I was once a singer and a graduate of the Conservatory myself, that was nearly seventy years ago, and the world was a very different place. Toscanini's choir had no need for an aging restaurateur.

After Eduardo confirmed that he and his latest love, a mezzo whose voice he said I should adore, would be joining us at the Maestro Toscanini's table that evening, I left him and headed into the warren of cobblestone streets that lead to Ca' Dario. Tap, step, step. Yes, Eduardo, bless his heart, our *Il Torino* was never without a woman.

I arrived at the back door to the kitchen. As I entered, I kissed my own forefinger and then touched it to the ancient brass mezuzah on the doorpost. My son, Tre – so named because he was the third

Dario in the family – was already in the kitchen with our staff and overseeing the preparations for the evening's celebratory feast in honor of Maestro Verdi. In truth, it had been ages since I had been involved in actively managing my restaurant, but I loved the place so dearly that Tre often had trouble shooing me away.

I hail from a family that for many generations prided itself upon being restauranteurs, chefs and cooks. My long-deceased grandfather, Dario Conegliano, had originally immigrated to Busseto from Ceneda near Venice to open and run, Figaro, a *salumeria*, a sort of delicatessen, that served up simple meals of sliced sausage meats, wine and bread to the farm workers and laborers who needed the calories, protein and alcohol necessary to endure their bitterly hard lives. My grandfather named his *salumeria* Figaro after the French writer, Beaumarchais's play, *Le Mariage de Figaro*, which Napoleon himself considered to be the first shot in the French Revolution for its mocking of the aristocracy. Both my father, Jacopo and his twin brother, my Uncle Roberto, worked at Figaro and were proud to do so for many reasons, including both politics and food.

In 1796 Napoleon invaded the territories of Savoy, Lombardy and Parma and defeated the armies of the Austro-Hungarian Empire that had controlled these regions for over a hundred and fifty years. As the French army liberated each town and village, they brought with them the ideals of both the American and French Revolutions: democracy, liberty, equality and fraternity. In the spirit of those revolutionary movements, Napoleon ordered the walls of each and every Jewish ghetto torn down and all restrictions upon the lives and movements of all Jews eliminated. The impact of those gestures upon my people was profound.

Soon thereafter Uncle Roberto, perhaps the more independent and secular of the twins, set out for Milan – where there were no Jews - to make his fortune. And he did. Ca' Dario, the trattoria, and I were both named in honor of my grandfather. And when Roberto, who never married, passed away more than half a century ago, Ca' Dario became mine.

"A che ora aprirete stasera?" I asked Tre. "What time will you

open tonight?"

"*Alle sette, papà.* Seven o'clock."

"And we'll have enough of everything? Wine? Meats? Cheese? Bread?"

"*Si, nonno. Stasera sarà perfetto.*" Tre reassured me that everything would be perfect. "We will have enough food and drink to last us until dawn. It will be a night worthy of the Maestro Verdi himself."

It was after all a menu that Verdi had not only suggested, it was one he had insisted upon when we last dined together only days before he had passed away. In addition to endless *salumi* platters heaped high with miles of sliced meats and exotic cheeses, Tre had specialty ordered barrels of wine from across the breadth and depth of our still new nation that Verdi loved: Nero D'Avola from Sicily, Brunello from Montalcino, Sangiovese from Tuscany, Barolo and Barbera from the Piemonte, Taurasi from Naples, Prosecco from the Veneto, and Cagnulari from Sardinia. But the centerpiece of the evening, the specialty dish Verdi had specifically asked for was one he had enjoyed at Ca' Dario for nearly seventy years, our *Sacchetti al Tartufo*, a satchel shaped dumpling filled with ricotta cheese and black truffles that was served in a delicate parmigiano white sauce. In Verdi's own words, not only was it the most delicious dish that ever graced his palate, it was the one he most associated with the *Risorgimento.* To be Italian is to be passionate about food, opera and *l'amore stesso* - love itself. Verdi, the quintessential Italian, had his first taste of our *Sacchetti al Tartufo* on the night the revolution to birth a free and democratic Republic of Italy began. And his honor, for tonight only, we added a garnish of fresh basil and finely chopped bits sweet red peppers to the *Sacchetti's* white sauce to echo the tricolors of our national flag.

After leaving Tre in the kitchen, I walked leisurely through all the main rooms of the restaurant, inspecting each to see if they were indeed ready for the hundreds of guests who would be showing up later that night.

First of course, was *Il Nord,* the North, our primary dining room, a convivial place where only our best food and wine was served by neatly uniformed waiters. Yes, I saw that each table was covered with a crisply ironed white tablecloth and for today only, a special cloth runner patterned with those colors of Italy, red, white and green. The chinaware settings featured elegant matching dishes, silverware and crystal glasses.

The walls of *Il Nord* were painted with classic scenes, ranging from the canals of Venice and the Piazza San Marco on the eastern flank, to the castles and spires of Turin on the west, with the Lake District and Milan's La Scala and Duomo in the center. And who did those paintings? My Uncle Roberto was not only a generous man with an oversized heart, he was more importantly, an admirer of all the arts. I convinced him to employ some of the finest painters in all Italy whose names will remain anonymous. After all, the work was done when those artists were down on their luck and needed a meal – and sometimes a bed in Ca' Dario's attic loft - to get them through their days and nights of poverty.

Off to the Turin side of *Il Nord* was a small bandstand and stage area where most evenings, young singers, students from the Conservatory anxious to show off their talents to the elites of the city, would sing opera *canzoni* and arias accompanied by equally young musicians. Our staff had already draped the piano with tri-colored bunting that Luisa had made herself. On the back of the piano on the side facing the audience, they hung a portrait of Verdi. Tonight, long after the funeral crowds would have dispersed, the music would be nothing but those of the Maestro.

On the southern side of *Il Nord*, I passed under a small archway into the bar, the Tuscany room. Did I forget to mention that Ca' Dario was shaped much like the peninsula of Italy? Even the floor was painted with a map that that stretched from the Alps to the Calabrian boot. It had been Uncle Roberto's dream to create a space that echoed his personal politics without being too obvious to our then Hapsburg overlords who controlled all of Lombardy as part of their Austro-Hungarian empire. Roberto and I were covertly members of *Giovine Italia* - Young Italy - a secret society led and inspired by Giuseppe Mazzini, that sought to throw out all the foreign rulers and then unify our Mediterranean peninsula into a single democratic republic. As an intentional consequence the map painted on the floor had none of the political boundaries that had divided up *Il nostro Paese* – our country – since the fall of Rome, just rivers, mountains, towns and cities. Membership and support for the outlawed *Giovine Italia* was in the tens of thousands in the northern provinces alone. Had Roberto's politics been known to the Austrian officers who frequented Ca' Dario and controlled Milan with a brutal fist, my uncle would have certainly been jailed for treason, if not summarily executed in the streets. Punishment was swift for all who challenged the dominion of the Hapsburgs who ruled Lombardy with the support of their allies, the highly conservative Roman Catholic clergy.

Perhaps needless to say, from behind the elegant oak bar that dominated the length of the Tuscany room, our servers offered up the finest wines as well as any of those hard liquor drinks or cocktails that had become the latest fashion. Here too the walls were splashed with visions of the Arno, the Ponte Vecchio, the Cathedral of Santa Maria del Fiore, Michelangelo's David and the Pitti Palace. Even the bar itself was also draped in more of Luisa's handmade tri-colored bunting.

A second archway, this one framed by fresco paintings of the Trevi Fountain of Rome opened into the next dining room, one we called, *Il Colosseo* – the Coliseum. Here, the murals depicting crowds of ancient Romans overflowing the stands of *Il Colosseo*, made anyone sitting or dining inside that space, feel as if they were in the ring of gladiators facing off against lions, tigers, bears or dragons whose images surrounded them. The tables in *Il Colosseo* were bare wood, the chinaware and utensils were a mixed lot, and the wine – which was less expensive than that served in *Il Nord* - came in unmarked glass *caraffe*. These young vintages were more suited to the wallets of the office workers and clerks of an ever growing urban middleclass. The menu was also priced accordingly and though the dishes served lacked the exquisite presentations of our main room, they were still heavenly and divine. You must remember that with we Coneglianos, every morsel was prepared with love and affection – and that affection was repaid to us with a loyalty by our customers who came day after day and decade after decade to dine here. Uncle Robert would be the first one to tell you that it you wanted to succeed in any endeavor, you needed the three "p's:" *passione, passione e passione.* Yes, at Ca' Dario everyone was treated as family, and we all respected each other as such. And when one of those customers asked me, their host, why the room was made to resemble *Il Colosseo,* I answered thus, "Never forget that my people were first brought to Rome as slaves by the Emperor Tito after the fall of the Second Temple in Jerusalem, where they were forced to build *Il Colosseo.* Then, later, the successive generations of our tribe were compelled to fight and die there with swords or tridents in their hands. It is those *antichi Ebrei*, the ancient Hebrews, we salute."

Continuing my inspection, I crossed through *Il Colosseo* to another archway on the far side, the entry to the third dining area, *Lo Stivale* – the Boot. This arch was painted to resemble *Monte Vesuvio* all afire with smoldering red-hot lava. *Lo Stivale* was a place where laborers could fill their bellies on rice, polenta, pasta and other simple foods at rough benches set beside long wooden tables. The inexpensive wine, often a first year's vintage, came from barrels lining the walls. The barrel spigots flowed freely beneath murals depicting the rustic hills and towns of southern Italy such as Abruzzo, Puglia, Basilicata, Calabria and Campania.

Yes, for a century now each of our many loyal customers was made to feel at home by entering from the street a dining room most suited to their nature. Embracing the democratic notions of liberty, equality and fraternity as well as the traditions of my faith, I made sure that at Ca' Dario no one left hungry. Just outside a small door at the far end of *Lo Stivale* there was a short archway that connected it to Sicily, the first of two outbuildings. Inside and surrounded by murals depicting the ruins of the innumerable Greek temples that marked the Sicilian countryside, there was a *Cucina gratuita*, a free kitchen to feed the poor, no questions asked. All one had to do was to appear at a service window where a server would fill a wooden bowl with whatever surpluses or leftovers were available that day. Yes, at Ca' Dario, we lived the spirit of *la rivoluzione* every day.

It was now daylight as I walked outside and around Sicily. I glanced over at the other outbuilding, Sardinia, which was our storeroom. Downstairs were the rooms where we kept all our reserves of wine, wheat and such, while upstairs was the loft where, in the past, many a poor artist slept. Tre was there at the storeroom door, unlocking it for one of the chefs. Satisfied that all looked well, and confident that Tre had all the preparations under control, I called out to him.

"*Ciao, a dopo*, I'll see you later."

"*Ciao, papà*," he shouted back at me.

I left the back courtyard and headed out the alley to the avenue. The streets were just beginning to fill with mourners. I picked up my pace with a tap, step, step; tap step, step and crossed one of the small bridges over one of the many canals that linked the Porta Nuova district of Milan to the distant Adriatic Sea. I then passed by the San Marco parish church, where back in 1874, Verdi conducted the premiere performance of his *Requiem* for his favorite writer and modern Italy's first literary lion *Signor* Alessandro Manzoni. Manzoni's writings, particularly his novel, *The Betrothed,* were as much an inspiration for the unification of our Italy as were Verdi's operas. I remember the performance that day all too well: Teresa Stolz singing, Verdi conducting, and his wife, *Signora* Verdi, squirming in her seat next to me, asking, "What's next?" Only after giving a nod towards the opened doors of this classically styled thirteenth century cathedral, did I hasten over to the *Cimitero Monumentale*.

By the time I reached the *Cimitero* all manner of humanity had begun to fill the streets in every direction. A young Italian cavalry officer, a regular at my restaurant, recognized me and called out with a hearty, "*Ciao*, Dario." No doubt spotting the tri-colored patch on my hat, he took me by the arm and led me to the very first row of seats that had been set up in front of the orchestra for dignitaries. Amongst all the guests from far and wide, princes and prime ministers, composers and countesses, who were milling about, I spotted Teresa Stolz, standing alone and seemingly perplexed. Stolz, a superb soprano who had premiered the role of *Aida* for Verdi, had unfortunately paid the price with the press for being the last of his lovers. Nearby was Enrico Guastella, a cousin of mine by marriage, a veteran of the wars and one of the founders of Milan's *Risorgimento* Museum. Beside him was Arrigo Boito, who wrote the libretti for both Verdi's *Otello,* which I loved and for *Falstaff*, which I, seemingly alone among operagoers, found insufferable. They were both chatting with Maestro Toscanini and several members of the Ricordi family, who had been Verdi's publishers for four generations.

As soon as Toscanini spotted me, he came running over. *"Ciao*, Dario!"* he exclaimed as he hugged me. In turn, so did Guastella, Boito and the Ricordis, each also shouting out my name as well with such enthusiasm, as if, *"Ciao*, Dario," was the new greeting that had replaced *"Buongiorno."* It's true, throughout all Milan, I was perhaps the only gentleman of this fair city of ours who was always called by his first name, "Dario." No *Signor* Conegliano was I. Though normally a man such as myself would always be addressed as *"Signor* So & So," I took it as no measure of disrespect to be known to all as simply, "Dario." Indeed, for all my countrymen and women, my name was as ubiquitous as my trattoria. Indeed, Ca' Dario was my house, my restaurant, and my identity.

Toscanini pulled me aside, "Dario," he said. "I'm concerned about *Signora* Stolz. Have you seen how pale she looks? I fear she's not well."

I agreed with the Maestro, for although Stolz was twenty years younger than Verdi, the strain of his convalescence had clearly taken its toll on her.

"Will you accompany her as she follows behind the hearse? She'll need a friendly and familiar hand, or she'll never last the entire route, yes?"

"Certo! Of course," I answered. I had made a solemn promise to Verdi himself when he talked about how he wanted his funeral procession to proceed, that I would escort *Signora* Stolz. Despite my dependence on my cane to get about, I was still generally hale and hearty. My plan was to live well at least until I turned one hundred. I travelled as easily on my "three legs," as most others did on two.

"Bene, va bene," Toscanini answered. He then turned and noted

the ever-growing masses of mourners, which were rapidly filling every space in the *Cimitero* plaza and the procession route. Off to the side of where the orchestra and choir members were beginning to assemble, was the horse drawn hearse that held the coffins of Verdi and his wife. The honor guard, a troop of mounted cavalry officers with plumed helmets, waited nearby, their horses snorting with impatience. "It's as if our entire country came here today, Dario," he said with a measure of disbelief, "If not the world. And I dare say, there would be no Italy if it were not for Verdi. Wouldn't you agree? You've known him the longest of all."

I shook my head and then spoke to the maestro in a slow and measured pace, "You're asking if the *Risorgimento, la rivoluzione* would have succeeded without Verdi? *Chissà?* Who knows?"

"But wasn't it his songs that inspired those three wars of independence and our final unification? Didn't they bring us together as one nation fighting for freedom and democracy?"

I studied Toscanini's eyes, his face. Though brilliant, he was still young, still naïve. And he, like so many of our countrymen, had no notion of our true history. The mythmakers had succeeded. Few knew that the heroes of the *Risorgimento,* Garibaldi, Camillo Cavour, Giuseppe Mazzini and King Victor Emanuel II, all hated and fought with each other. Or that success, that is the initial unification of Italy as a single nation had only come through repeated failures on the battlefield. Only Italy could win through losing and walk backwards into nationhood. Toscanini was merely a toddler when the last battles had occurred. Why, he was even younger than the Austrian bullet that was still lodged in my right hip.

"While it's true we stormed the ramparts with better music than most revolutions," I pointed to the other dignitaries filling the front rows of seats, "Half of those people here – the Briscolas, the Trombas, the Pietras, the Giulianis - would have stood in opposition to Verdi's politics and *la rivoluzione.* Who amongst us can decipher the past and decide what should have been? If you insist upon giving Verdi credit for his contributions to the *Risorgimento,* then you must also heap praise upon the woman who rests in that other coffin."

My remarks puzzled Toscanini. "Whatever do you mean?" Clearly, to him, *Signora* Verdi was a woman of no worthy consequence. He sounded like every other typical "Italian gentleman" who could never grant any woman the respect and equality these types of men demanded for themselves. In this regard, I seemed alone among my male peers. Our conductor was too young to have ever known her in her prime when she was strong, beautiful, smart, independent, and possessed of a truly superior and agile voice. In the world of theater, *Signora* Verdi was known as *La Generalina*, the Little General. She was a commanding presence, a star whose brightness in the firmament clearly outshone a youthful Verdi.

Finally, I stated with a firm resolve, "Maestro, if you want to praise Verdi, let us not debate whether or not there would have been an Italy without him. *Chissà?* Perhaps Verdi and *la rivoluzione* made each other. But there is one truth of which I can assure you: without *La Generalina* there would be no Verdi."

"I still don't understand." Toscanini shook his head again, "What does she…., *La Generalina*? You must tell me," He practically begged.

"*Certo*, but not now. Afterwards though, you must salute *Signora* Verdi. She deserves our respect. She is the unsung hero of their story, one far too long and too important to be rushed in the telling." I pointed to the podium where my friend, Eduardo Villa, was laying out the conductor's score, "But aren't you supposed to be up there now, Maestro?

"*Si*, yes, it is almost time to begin. But you will tell me? If it's about Verdi, I must know. Tonight, perhaps?"

"Yes, of course. Tonight," I reassured Toscanini.

At Ca' Dario?"

"*Si,* definitely at Ca' Dario. And although historians may disagree with me," I added, "The *Risorgimento* that our Verdi championed began at Ca' Dario sixty-eight years ago."

"That's twice my age, sixty-eight years."

"Yes, twice your age. Tuesday, July 16, 1833. A day I will never forget, a day that changed our Italy – and the world forever."

"*Grazie*, Dario, I want to hear more, to hear it all." Toscanini moved toward the orchestra and was soon chatting up Eduardo, no doubt confirming last minute instructions for the musicians and choir.

I took my seat in the front row, just to the right of *Signora* Stolz.

"*Ciao,* Dario," she said with more than a hint of exhaustion in her voice. She squeezed my left hand with such ferocity that I could measure the pain and emptiness she must have felt in the month since Verdi's actual death. "Help me through this day. I don't know how else I'll make it."

I patted her back and as I leaned over; I whispered in her ear. "Have no fear. I'm here for you to lean on for as long as you need."

She sighed deeply and grasped my hand ever tighter. Tragically *Signora* Stolz had often been cast as the "other woman." I alone perhaps, as a lifelong intimate of *la famiglia* Verdi, knew the peculiar truth of that *terzetto*, that triangle, the one the journalist and gossipmongers often distorted for their own, often cruel, purposes. As we all know that sad truth: salacious stories always sell.

Finally, the moment we had all been awaiting: Toscanini stepped up to the podium with baton raised. Arrayed before him, the full orchestra of some one hundred and twenty or more players was poised to begin as was the massive chorus that surrounded it on three sides.

On the downbeat of Toscanini's baton, the La Scala symphony musicians began the prelude to the one piece of Verdi's music from *Nabucco* that had its premiere at that theater some sixty years earlier, *Va' Pensiero*. This melody, so poignant and pure, had become the unofficial anthem of our newly united country. Nonetheless, how could I not note with supreme irony that in this most Catholic of all nations, *Va' Pensiero* was a song that was about my people, the Jews of Israel, exiled to Babylonia after the fall of the First Temple who yearned for freedom. "*Oh, my country so beautiful and lost!*"

And if you recall anything at all about *Va' Pensiero,* you will know that the instrumental introduction lasts for almost a full minute. It begins with powerful violin riffs, then a teasing melody by the flutes, which is then followed by three grand orchestral *tutti* stings. And in those fleeting sixty seconds, the melody was steadily picked up and hummed by the entire crowd surrounding the *Cimitero*. First by those nearest to the stage and then gradually, block by block and street by street, everyone joined in and began to hum. By the time those eight-hundred and twenty singers began the first lines: "*Va, Pensiero, sull'ali dorate;* Fly my thoughts on golden wings," they were joined by the entirety of the other four-hundred thousand who had crowded around and filled every possible space for blocks around.… Can you imagine a crowd that size not only singing, but singing their hearts out with a passion, a distinctly Italian passion, that came from the depths of their souls? Certainly, never before in my life – and I have seen and heard a lot in my many years.

This unexpected wave of sound cascading over the *Cimitero* was so all powerful, nearby buildings shook, windows rattled, cavalry horse bucked and whinnied. And poor maestro Toscanini? The tidal wave of voices almost knocked him off the podium.

Yes, I knew then that tonight at Ca' Dario over glasses of Brunello and platters of *Sacchetti al Tartufo* I would share the true history of the *Risorgimento*, of Verdi, of Stolz, and of *Signora* Verdi - *La Generalina* - for all to hear, perhaps understand, and hopefully remember. Truth is a hard commodity to preserve. Even now, the dark clouds of Fascism, authoritarianism and anti-Semitism hover on the horizon. Our Republic is young and frail, its fate unknown. If Democracy is to survive the storms that will surely come in this Twentieth Century of ours, then we must nurture and tend it with the same passion one would a lover, for as Verdi's favorite novelist, *Signor* Alessandro Manzoni, so prophetically wrote, "That which comes next is not always progress."

But for now, we sing.…

Fly, thoughts, on golden wings;
Go, settle upon the slopes and hills,
where warm and soft and fragrant are

the breezes of our sweet native land!
Greet the banks of the Jordan,
the fallen towers of Zion ...
Oh my country so beautiful and lost!
Oh so dear yet unhappy!

Oh, golden harp of the prophetic seers,
why do you hang silent from the willows?
Rekindle the memories within our hearts,
tell us about the times gone by
Oh, similar to the fate of Jerusalem,
play the sounds of a sad lament;
or let the Lord inspire a concert
That may strengthen us to endure our suffering.

Chapter One:

Tell Us About Times Gone By

Ca' Dario, the night the Revolution began, July 16, 1833

A thunderbolt rattled the walls of Ca' Dario just as the door to *Lo Stivale* opened. In walked Verdi. But he was not the man we were expecting. Verdi, who was drenched, shook the rain off his coat like an old sheep dog. We had a full house that night, each of the dining rooms was packed. The rain helped. Once anyone entered, they were reluctant to head back out into the storm. Verdi maneuvered his way past the stonemasons, carpenters and peasants there and found a seat upon a bench in the back corner of the dining room. He pushed his equally soaked suitcase under the table. When he finally looked up, his eyes met mine, he forced a smile on an otherwise distressed face. I headed over.

Mind you, back then, Verdi was not the famous man we see in his classic portraits. No top hat, no wool overcoat, no silk scarf and no gentleman's cane. He was merely a poor student seeking shelter and a probable meal of inexpensive polenta. Oh, and his trademark beard? Well, he had started to grow it out so as to look older than his twenty years, with the yet as unrealized hope that he and his compositions would be taken far more seriously than they were. Perhaps it was needless to say that his beard was still as sparse as his hopes.

Though we had known each other from our childhood spent in Busseto, I saw him only rarely now that we were both living in Milan. I had left home a few years earlier so as to study at the Conservatory as a singer. I had paid the tuition by working part time at Ca' Dario as a jack-of-all trades for my Uncle Roberto and saved money by living in one of the bedroom lofts above our trattoria's storeroom. Verdi, who had not been as fortunate as I, had failed to gain admission to the school, a slight he never forgot or forgave.

Verdi would have never been able to leave the musical backwater of our village for Milan, the grandest city in all Italy for opera, if not for the intercession and monetary support of a benefactor back in Busseto, Antonio Barezzi. In addition to being a wealthy merchant of our hometown, Barezzi was an impassioned music lover, who believing in Verdi's inexhaustible talent as a composer, was willing to assist him financially. As an aside, I should add that Barezzi also had a talented, witty and lovely daughter, Margherita. She had a fondness for Verdi and vice-versa. The presumption of all in Busseto was that one day, the two would marry. In an ideal world it would have been hard to image a better or happier match for either of them.

So, in the end, it was Barezzi who both arranged and financed Verdi's studies in Milan with a private tutor. He also arranged for his housing. While in Milan, Verdi stayed with the family of one *Signor* Seletti, a business associate of Barezzi. And Verdi – who was even poorer than I was - took most of his meals there as well. That arrangement left Verdi just enough pocket change so as to be able to afford tickets to La Scala and some of the other opera houses in the city.

Occasionally I'd run into him at the theater. But tonight, I had more pressing matters to deal with, matters of the utmost secrecy and danger. Uncle Roberto had gotten word that a senior member of the leadership of *Giovine Italia*, who was on the run, was supposed to show up, incognito, at Ca' Dario. That leader was codenamed, "Renzo," after a character from *Signor* Alessandro Manzoni's recently published novel, *I Promessi Sposi, The Betrothed.*

It is only now, decades later, that I must reveal to you one of the best kept secrets of the *Risorgimento*: how we communicated information and secret plans. There were many techniques used over the course of our three wars for independence to avoid our dispatches from being intercepted, but the method that we preferred and later perfected, was one in which the secret messages were coded into musical scores. These our leader, Giuseppe Mazzini had nicknamed *Canzonatinis.* He chose that term to honor the spirit of the French Revolution and Napoleon. While the word meant "little jokes" in Italian; in Corsican, Napoleon Boneparte's native tongue, it meant "little songs." Although the details are extremely complicated, the basic concept was very simple. Secret information necessary for the advancement of our political and military objectives was woven through codes into musical scores that could be easily transported and circulated without attracting the attention of the Austrian police. As highly trained musicians, we were often tasked with writing these pieces of music, anonymously of course. The works might be little piano romances or folk dances or waltzes or whatever – all of which had a motif from the *Marseillaise* woven somewhere into the fabric of the *Canzonatini.* The precise location of the motif in the composition would then reveal to the recipient of that piece of music where and how to begin to translate the coded instructions.

By using *Canzonatini* the leadership of *Giovine Italia* was therefore able to coordinate with our partisans and revolutionaries secretly and efficiently. Thus, we knew Renzo would be in disguise and wearing a blue fedora and in need of our assistance. Roberto had put a plan in place to ensure that *Signor Renzo* would make it to safety as an exile in Switzerland. And the man I was waiting for when Verdi surprised me by entering *Lo Stivale?* Well, that should have been Piero Lusardi, a local trader and smuggler I had also known since childhood. Lusardi was an essential cog in the plan to assist Renzo to escape, as he knew every dirt road, mountain pass and backwater village in the province.

Verdi's unexpected appearance was a distraction that I needed to deal with and quickly, less Roberto's plans unravel. In fact, the last time Verdi and I had seen each other was two months ago at the Teatro alla Canobbiana back in May. We had watched the premiere of Donizetti's *L'elisir d'amore.* Afterwards, as often as not, we'd engaged in a lively discussion about the merits of the work, the musical score, the libretto, and the singers - especially the two sopranos. By the end of the evening, over a pitcher of cheap wine in *Lo Stivale,* we then moved on from discussing the artistic merits of the opera, to which of the divas we'd most like to have taken to dinner and whose company we would have loved to enjoy right through a champagne breakfast. In that regard, our prospects were as empty as our pockets.

Given his relative poverty, I was surprised to see Verdi at Ca' Dario, even if it was just for a bowl of polenta. And the suitcase? What was that about, I asked him.

"*Liberami,* save me," he muttered. "I have been blessed with doubly bad news."

"Worse than this thunderstorm?"

"Yes. Do you remember Father Abbondio?"

Father Abbondio Briscola was a priest posted to the church of San Michele in Busseto, known more for his girth and obesity than any saintliness. Born into one of the ruling clans of the region, Abbondio was a typical hypocritical prelate whom we as kids often called Father *Abbandonare Dio* – the one who abandoned God.

"Unfortunately, yes. In fact, he's sitting up in *Il Nord* right now with Bishop Giuliano Giuliani. They're well into their second bottle of Barolo and the Bishop just ordered them both a full rack of lamb roast." As with Father Abbondio, Bishop Giuliani was also connected to one of the rulings families of Lombardy and owed his power and position more to patronage than any pretense of piety.

"Hardly surprising, the pigs, aren't they? And gloating, no doubt." Verdi reached into his coat pocket and pulled out a letter, which was also drenched from the rains. It veritably fell apart as Verdi unfolded it. And what was left was little more than ink stains on soggy shreds of paper.

"*Porco Zio,*" cursed Verdi. He crumpled the paper up. "Father Abbondio brought me this letter earlier today. From my father. They want me home. My little sister is dying."

Verdi had great affection for his younger sister, Giuseppa, who we all knew as *una ragazza ritardata,* a retarded child, and one who also was frequently ill. Before I could respond and express my sympathies, Verdi continued. "But as if that tragic news was not brutal enough, Father Abbondio arrived when I was supposed to be tutoring the Seletti's daughter at the piano in their music salon, but…"

From the expression on his face, I guessed the rest and said as much. "But your lessons with this girl… They were of… of an amorous nature?"

"*Si*, when *Signor* Seletti entered the salon with Father Abbondio and saw the two of us embracing, he threw me out of the house – for good. Gave me ten minutes to pack up and depart while ranting that he was going to report every detail to *Signor* Barezzi. And Father Abbondio was verily laughing as I tossed everything into my suitcase and left."

It was no secret, even back in Busseto, that Verdi had no love for the clergy and vice-versa. This mutual animosity dated back to when Verdi had been an altar boy at the Church of La Madonna dei Prati. One of the priests, a man of questionable ethics, especially around young boys, smacked an eight-year-old Verdi and knocked him down during a communion service when my friend spilled some of the wine. Even at that tender age, Verdi did not tolerate such abuse. He cursed the Father and declared – in what became known in local lore as *La Maledizione*, the Malediction, that lightning would strike the priest down. And sure enough, a few years later, while that priest was ringing the church bells, a thunderous bolt blasted the church steeple. That gift from heaven fried the cleric as crisp as a Roman artichoke.

"And here you are, homeless, eh?"

"Yes, and when Seletti reports to Barezzi, I'm ruined."

"*È vero*. It's true," I nodded agreement, but with no time to worry along with Verdi if the incident would destroy his relationship with Barezzi or his daughter, Margherita, I hurriedly explained that we had a full house tonight, and that I was preoccupied with some urgent work on behalf of my uncle. I pulled a set of keys to out of my waiter's uniform and handed Verdi the one to the Sardinia's loft. "But you, you're practically family." I suggested he head up to the loft where there was an extra bed. He could dry off, unpack his bag, and then come back down later when I would be able get him something to eat. "You're welcome to stay as long as you need."

"*Grazie mille. Sei un vero amico*, you're a true friend," Verdi offered up that he just needed a bed for the night. He would try to catch the first coach of the morning to Busseto. He was desperate to not only see his sister before she died, but to also meet with Barezzi and get his blessing to propose to Margherita before Seletti's letter arrived. Though Verdi was never one to rattle easily, he was terrified that the life he had imagined – a career as a composer and a marriage to Margherita - would crumble into ruins because of his grievous mistake.

Verdi thanked me again, then headed out into the storm to reach the shelter of Sardinia. I walked the other way. I passed under the Vesuvian archway and through *Il Colosseo*, hoping to spot our operative, Lusardi, but he was still not there. Was he delayed by the rain or was there trouble?

I continued on into the Tuscany bar. Pausing at the counter, I could just barely hear a soprano singing off in the next room, *Il Nord.* When the house was full and the crowds boisterous, sound hardly traveled from one room to the next. Abruptly another flash of lightning illuminated the bar. It was followed by a blast of thunder that rattled the windows. The noise drowned out the singer and her accompanist, not that any of the patrons in the bar would have been paying attention. No, the Tuscany room was the sanctuary of hard-core drinkers and card players, many of them Austrian soldiers, who were so engaged in their games that the roar of summer thunderstorms meant little compared to the cannon fire most had faced in their careers.

Something felt off though and it wasn't just the weather. When you work restaurants as long as I have, your unconscious mind catches these anomalies. Maybe it was just my own nervousness or a touch of paranoia. Uncle Roberto needed me to put the next step of his plan into action, but my sixth sense noted that too many other eyes were studying the room. And those eyes belong to men with guns and swords. I gave our bartender, a man who knew nothing of our plans, specific instructions to overfill the glasses of every Austrian soldier in the bar as a gesture of respect and friendship. Yes, Roberto and I wanted them all as drunk as possible.

I then moved slowly into *Il Nord* and lingered by the arch so as to discreetly study the crowd. Although the room was full, I recognized many of the patrons. Off in one corner was Father Abbondio, drunk of course, his round face as red as a full moon at sunset. He and Bishop Giuliano Giuliani ripped apart their lamb roast bare-handed like two wild boars shredding a carcass. Blood covered their fingers and knuckles right up to their wrists. Nothing unusual there.

A few tables away sat the Comandante of the local Austrian army barracks, Field General Matteo Gaetz and three of his officers. Though Gaetz was a frequent customer who always ordered the best of everything and left our waiters generous tips, he had a reputation as a brutal-by-the-books-type commander. Word on the street was, that if you crossed up Gaetz, he'd not hesitate to put a bullet through your head with the silver handled pistol he carried. In contrast to the gluttonous clergy, the soldiers, in their starched grey dress uniforms, the ones with the red and gold trim, sat upright. They cut and ate their schnitzel with a Germanic precision that could only be deemed mechanical. No joy there. They listened politely but unmoved as our soprano segued into Mozart's *Porgi Amor* from my favorite opera, the revolutionary, *Marriage of Figaro.* But when one of our waiters leaned in to refill Commander Gaetz's glass of prosecco, the Comandante covered his glass with his hand and demurred with a polite but firm, *"Nein, danke."* I took careful note when the other three officers followed suite. *"Nein, danke."* That never happens, not with soldiers at Ca' Dario unless they were actually on duty. Something was afoot.

The soprano, a girl really, not more than seventeen, had a superior *bel canto* voice. I did not know her name, as she had joined the Conservatory as a legacy and scholarship enrollee just as I was approaching graduation. Seems her father, now deceased, had also once been at the school as a composition student. She was petite, pretty with large dark grey eyes that bespoke a depth of intelligence and garbed tonight in a high waisted Directoire style violet gown. A matching broadbrimmed chapeau titled at a jaunty angle, rested on her chestnut hair. Draped over her shoulders was a soft purple silk shawl. Pinned to the gown was a clutch of violets.

Apparently, her wardrobe choices that evening were to highlight her next song. She followed the Mozart with a Ladino *canzone. Adío Querida* or *Violetta's Lament*. It was a song I knew from childhood, Ladino being the patois of the ancient Jews communities of the Mediterranean world that blended Hebrew with Spanish, Portuguese, Italian and even a little Greek. The sad but poignant stanzas told the apocryphal tale of Violetta, a much beloved and admired daughter of King Solomon who had the power to charm one and all through her *canzoni.* Much to the dismay of her retinue and family, our princess falls in love with a wandering troubadour who had a gift for crafting arias that were as intoxicating as the most potent wines. Over the objections of King Solomon, who fears that her marriage to such a minstrel would cause Violetta to lose her own powers, our princess – very much in love - weds the troubadour. At first, blessed by the powers inherent in their mutual affections, the amorous couple experiences greater glory as everyone is besotted by her singing of her troubadour's songs. But there are dark powers at work. As the troubadour's fame grows, he composes ever more magical – but difficult - arias for Violetta to sing, ones that strain the very limits of her capacity. Violetta does all she can to keep up until, alas, one day she opens her mouth to sing and naught, but silence emerges from between her lips. Her voice forever gone; her troubadour pushes her aside for another. Violetta begs for death wishing only to perishes in a flood of her own tears, *"Adio, my love, I do not want to live…"*

Staring intently at this whisp of a girl, one in my mind's eye that I dubbed "Violetta," was none other than Alessandro Lanari, the most famous opera impresario in all Italy if not Europe. In front of him was an oversized platter of our *Sacchetti al Tartufo*, which he ate with a relish perhaps equal to the delight he took from observing our soprano.

Sitting to his right, her hand resting under the table on the impresario's thigh, was the red-haired diva I had admired in her role as Adina in *L'elisir d'amore*. Tonight, though, and despite her caresses, Lanari only had a taste for our *Sacchetti al Tartufo* and eyes and ears for our Violetta.

Flanking Lanari on his left side was Bartolomeo Merelli. Beside him sat the other soprano from *L'elisir d'amore*. These two men each separately dominated our world of opera. Bartolomeo Merelli ruled over La Scala and the Vienna opera house back in the Hapsburg's capital. Lanari controlled or held the contracts of not only the elite divas and tenors, but many of the composers and musicians as well. Careers rode the tide of their whims. With a tip of their hat, or a tap with their cane, and a deal was done or worse, unmade. And for an aspiring diva? The toll for success was paid in the bedroom. Would it be the redhead tonight? Or the brunette? Or our little Violetta? Or *chissà*, who knows?

Another massive bolt of lightning struck the monastery just up the street from Ca' Dario. The boom and rumble of thunder shook the windows of our trattoria so much so it elicited shouts of surprise from the soldiers behind me in the bar. As I turned around, I could see back through the arch into *Il Colosseo*. There, sitting by himself, I spotted Lusardi. He was a big man with shoulders like an ox and arms like fenceposts. Lusardi was wiping the rain off his face with a handkerchief and breathing heavily, as if he'd just been running. Yes, it was time to put our plan into action. I left my spot and headed through *Il Nord* and into the kitchen, there to meet Uncle Roberto.

At the rear of the kitchen, beside a window that looked out back toward the Sardinia storeroom building and the outhouses, was a small nook that Roberto used as his office. I found him sitting at his desk, flipping through the pages of a deluxe, leather bond edition of *Signor* Alessandro Manzoni's novel, *I Promessi Sposi, The Betrothed*. Underneath the book and half hidden from sight was a *Canzonatini* score.

"He's here," I said. Given that the members of *Giovine Italia*, such as my uncle, operated strictly on a need-to-know basis, I always made it a point to remain as ignorant as possible. "What now?"

"Give Lusardi this," he said referring to the book. "Let no one see what you are doing." Roberto then explained to me that *Signor* Renzo will come with another exile, a woman code-named, "*Signora* Lucia," also from the novel, and sit at Lusardi's table in *Il Colosseo*. The *Signore* will have an identical copy of *The Betrothed* with him, which is how they will recognize each other. When their dishes arrive and the table is crowded with platters of food, Lusardi and Renzo will discreetly switch copies, exchange a few words, and then, separately, leave.

There had to be more, I thought - but I did not ask.

But just as Roberto nodded, one of our waiters came running back through the door to *Il Colosseo* and towards the office in a panic.

"Come quick, Boss. Trouble!"

Uncle Roberto got up, hurried to the kitchen door but sensing danger on the other side, he abruptly stopped. Through a safety window set in the portal, we could see Commander Gaetz's soldiers dragging Lusardi out of the *Il Colosseo* and into the street. But Lusardi would not go quietly. He wrestled with the guards, throwing one to the cobblestones and another into a wall as his screams pierced the night.

"Salvatemi! Aiuto!" "Save me! Help!"

We watched helplessly. There was nothing Uncle Roberto could - or would - do. Not with Gaetz's soldiers all over the place. As the soldiers beat down on Lusardi, he thrashed wildly, continually trying to twist away from his captors. *"Aiuto! Salvatemi! Aiuto!"* Suddenly, he broke loose and began to race away down the avenue.

"Go!" I thought, "Run!" But then, a single pistol shot rang out from Gaetz's silver handled pistol. Abruptly, save for the sounds of the rainstorm, everyone and everything fell silent. Though I must confess that seeing Lusardi shot down made me sick to my stomach, I knew even then in my heart of hearts, that he had been the first casualty of our revolution. Just as the American Revolution began at the Battle of Lexington and Concord, the match that triggered the *Risorgimento* was lit that night on the streets outside Ca' Dario.

Stone-faced, Roberto turned around and walked slowly back to his desk, his mind filled with thoughts as he recalculated and considered what to do. I followed.

It was then, with the aid of another flash of lightning, I saw Verdi through the rear window, coming down the back steps from the

Sardinia. Knowing my friend shared our same political sentiments, I said, "Don't worry," to my uncle, "I've got a plan."

I grabbed the copy of *The Betrothed* and tucked it inside my waiter's coat before striding confidently back out into *Il Nord*.

As everyone in the room was still in a state of shock from the arrest of Lusardi, I hastened over to the soprano. In a whisper I told her that Lanari and Bartolomeo Merelli were sitting there and not only did we need to calm the room down and change the mood as quickly as possible, but that this was her chance to impress the impresarios. I then asked this Violetta if she could sing "*Madamina,*" – the Catalog Song from *Don Giovanni* - and could she do it with comic impact even though it was written for a male baritone?

Violetta giggled but did not have to be asked twice. She was a smart girl, instantly perceptive. Understanding exactly what was needed, she immediately jumped in. Affecting a deep and husky male voice, she sang as powerful as she could:

> *Little lady, this is the record*
> *Of the beauties my master has loved.*
> *It's a catalogue that I myself compiled.*
> *Come closer, read it with me.*
> *In Italy six hundred and forty,*
> *In Germany two hundred and thirty-one,*
> *One hundred in France.*
> *In Turkey ninety-one,*
> *But in Spain already one thousand and three!*
> *One thousand and three,*
> *One thousand and three,*
> *One thousand and three…*

By the time she hit that third repetition of "*One thousand and three,*" calm had been restored and all eyes, especially those of the impresario, Lanari, were on our Violetta.

I used that momentary peace as my own cue and hustled through the restaurant. I met Verdi just as he returned to his spot inside *Lo Stivale.*

"Lusardi? That's dreadful," said Verdi after I told him only as much of the story as prudence would allow. "That's why you were so busy earlier? And you want me to sit here and wait for a man in a blue hat?" Verdi asked, "And in exchange for my swapping books with him, you'll feed me a bowl of polenta? I heard that gun shot. You're kidding, right?"

"No, no peasant's polenta," I answered, "I'll feed you an endless supply of *Sacchetti al Tartufo* and our best Barolo wine, but you must relocate to a table in *Il Colosseo* and wait there."

"Are your *Sacchetti* worth an Austrian bullet in my back?"

"You won't know unless you try...."

"But in your opinion?" Verdi asked.

"Would I have asked my oldest friend to do this, to put his life on the line in exchange for a bowl of pasta? *Si.* "

"Why do I trust you? All I want to do is get home to Margherita – alive."

"Of course, you will. Would I ever let you down? You are my best friend."

Verdi rolled his eyes. "And the book, what's the book?"

"*Signor* Alessandro Manzoni's *The Betrothed.* I slipped it out of my coat pocket and placed it on the table.

He grabbed the novel and began thumbing through the pages. "How is it you knew I've been dying to read this... Yes, even if it kills me. *Viva la rivoluzione.*"

****

It was about an hour later that *Signor Renzo,* accompanied by *Signora Lucia,* entered *Il Colosseo.* His blue hat was pulled low across his face. The *Signore* was of average height, perhaps thirty years of age, with a receding hairline and a bushy goatee. The features of the woman were harder to distinguish as she wore a long black cloak with a deep hood, but she did have a thin gold band on her left ring finger. Slung over each of their shoulders were oversized carpet bags.

Once more our trattoria was bustling, noisy and crowded - the incident with Lusardi now just a memory. Most of the soldiers had gone – but not all. In the front room, Commander Gaetz had joined Father Abbondio and Bishop Giuliano Giuliani at their table. The three men lingered over Sambuca and our finest sweet dessert, our Sicilian *crostata al pistacchio* – a pistachio tart made from my own mother's secret recipe. Lanari and Bartolomeo Merelli had moved on to coffee and cigars while the two opera singers sipped our homemade limoncello. And our Violetta? Well, between breaks our soprano continued to impress the *Il Nord* crowds. Even Verdi – who could not see her from where he sat - took note of her voice when she reprised, *Violetta's Lament*.

"Who is she?" he asked when I passed by his table.

"Violetta, perhaps?" I replied with a shrug. "*Chissà?* Who knows?"

"Well, viva Violetta… Her trills, her articulations, her dexterity, in a hundred years you'll never hear a voice with such range, power and emotion. Just spectacular." How Verdi, even at the tender age of twenty, knew all that, *chissà*? His perceptions and his ability to distinguish subtle sounds were beyond the range of us mere mortals. "But what language is she singing? It starts to sound familiar and then, not."

"Ladino." I explained to him about how when the Jews living under the Bourbon rule in Spain and Sicily were expelled during the inquisition of 1492, they migrated to the northern half of the Italian peninsula and central Europe, bringing their Ladino culture and songs with them. And *Violetta's Lament, Adio Querido*, was popular as the lyrics were in truth a metaphor for the endless expulsion of Jews from one country to another.

"Sad," said Verdi, "But beautiful and haunting."

"Si," I said, "It is the fate of Jews to wander endless in search of home and safety."

And *Signor* Renzo*?* He had no trouble finding Verdi at a small square table set for four that was tucked against the wall of *Il Colosseo*. My friend was so engrossed in *The Betrothed* that he almost took no note of the *Signore* and the *Signora* when they sat down at his table.

"*Piacere, Signor* Lusardi*,* Pleased to meet you, Mr. Lusardi," said Renzo barely above a whisper as he extended his hand towards Verdi.

Verdi glanced up from his book and, ignoring Renzo's outstretched hand, he stared directly into his eyes. He also spoke softly, less anyone else hear, but he did not mince words. "The gentleman you seek is dead. Shot right outside by the Austrian police not an hour ago."

"Oh my God, they know," the woman gasped involuntarily before catching herself.

Verdi watched as Renzo hugged her. But even as he said, "It's all right, Lucia," Verdi read her face and realized she was no timid flower. Nor was he. Their steely resolve was etched as firmly onto their faces as Donatello's statue of David.

"If not for the rain, Lusardi's blood would still be on the cobblestones, but we should eat," said Verdi with a touch of cynicism as he waived me over. He ordered the requisite *Sacchetti al Tartufo* and the promised several bottles of Ca' Dario's finest Barolo wine to wash it all down.

"Grazie," replied Renzo as he pulled his copy of *The Betrothed* out of his coat. "And so, tell me, how are the roads in and out of Milan? Have the rains washed them out?"

"Wait, say nothing" said Verdi as he noticed Father Abbondio staggering through the bar towards them. "A donkey from my hometown of Busseto is about to join us… He's a prized bit of livestock with big ears…"

"Who brays loudly, eh?" whispered Renzo.

"*Si*, his mouth is the source of much evil," Verdi nodded as the priest came over to his table.

"A Si… Si… *Signor* Ver… Ver… Verdi." Abbondio could not help but slur his words. "You are… are… still… still here?" The priest barely able to stand, leaned heavily upon the back of the fourth chair at the table.

"Would you have me travel home in this storm?" replied Verdi, now dreading the prospect of Abbondio joining them.

"What is rain… but the tears… of our Lord… come to wash… to wash you clean… clean of your sins… And you… you Verdi… *La tua Maledizione*, your Malediction, you have sinned…," insisted the priest. "And when… and when I return from the latrine… your confession, your confession I will hear…"

The priest turned away and then staggered out a side door to the latrines situated behind the Sicily building.

Verdi laughed as he watched Abbondio drag his robes through one puddle after another. "My Malediction? If only there was enough lightning in heaven to rid us of all these priests who have corrupted the church." Much as Verdi despised the priest, he feared that Abbondio would be only too gleeful to share his gossip with Barezzi… Or worse, with Margherita.

Renzo started to speak but Verdi held a finger to his lips, once more urging the man to hold his tongue, as I returned with their food and wine. Only after I had placed their platters of *Sacchetti al Tartufo* on the table, filled their glasses with the wine, and left, did Verdi nod towards Renzo.

But Lucia spoke first, calmly and assured to her husband, "They know. If Lusardi's dead, they'll discover us too unless we change plans."

Their fears and concern were all too apparent on their faces. Verdi discreetly swapped books with Renzo.

"*Mangiamo.* That donkey will be back all too soon, and we all need to eat before, before it's too late." Verdi bit into his first taste ever of our *sacchetti* and suddenly exclaimed, "Oh heaven! Oh my God, this is unbelievable." He took another bite, closed his eyes and savored every flavor that verily exploded onto his tongue as he swallowed. "Heaven."

Renzo and Lucia followed his example. In moments the three of them were all smacking their lips and practically swooning over the *sacchetti*, just enough so that for now, they could ignore their troubles. Yes, our *Sacchetti al Tartufo* were that good, as good as a mood changer as a wizard's magical wand. And in truth, every morsel on our menu was just as memorable. When it came to running Ca' Dario Uncle Roberto had a few simple ethical principles, his mottos, if you will, which were inscribed over the bar, *"Perché essere banale, quando, con passione, puoi essere monumentale? Qui in Italia è sempre una questione di cibo.",* which translates very simply into "Why be mundane, when with passion, you can be monumental? Here, in Italy it is always about the food."

"I do not want to know who you are, where you have come from or where you are going, said Verdi. "Tell me nothing. But whatever route you had planned to take with Lusardi; don't. Men with guns will be watching and waiting."

"And you" asked Lucia, "You are going to Busseto, yes?"

"*Si,*" replied Verdi.

"And how will you get to Busseto? By coach?" she asked. "Is that safe?"

"Busseto?" Renzo started to query of Lucia, "Busseto is south, not…" But Renzo stopped himself when his Lucia gave him that look that freezes a man cold.

Lucia continued. "As the esteemed *Signor* Alessandro Manzoni wrote in the novel you both seem to hold so dearly, '*events come at us sometimes by our own causation and sometimes from purely external, but where they come from is less important than the fact that we must deal with them, nonetheless.*' So, I repeat my question, Is it safe to take a coach to Busseto?"

"For me, yes," replied Verdi, who quickly added as he looked from Lucia to Renzo and back again, "But for you? *Chissà?* Whereas it may be safer to go south first in order to go north…. Or east…. Or west…., there are no coaches until the morning and even those may well be watched leaving the depot. No, that won't work."

"What might you suggest then?" asked Renzo.

Verdi was about to answer but paused when he saw Father Abbondio returning from the latrine. The priest was staggering, worse than even than on his way out, as he entered *Il Colosseo*. I hurried over quick as I could to be ready to assist, if necessary, but not before Abbondio wagged a threatening finger, first at Verdi and then at Renzo.

"Youuu…. Youuuu have sinnedddd… Repentttt," he yelled. "You must pay for your Malediction!" The priest grabbed a bottle of the Barolo off the table. He took a deep long swig that drained the bottle. He belched, then collapsed onto the floor.

Before anyone else could react, I grabbed the priest under his arms and dragged his limp body into the bar. Then, finding an empty table in a corner, one that was out of sight of the Bishop and Comandante Gaetz, I propped the priest up in a chair.

Verdi, for his part, thinking quickly, said to Renzo and Lucia, "You both need to leave here immediately. And not by coach." Verdi went on to explain that before they arrived at Ca' Dario, he was reading in *The Betrothed* and noted how the fictional Renzo, the hero of that romance, followed the canals out of Milan at night when he needed to escape. It gave him an idea. "We can find a canal boat a few blocks from here, one heading south and vanish just as Renzo did." He suggested that the three of them could travel together on one of the boats that goes southeast away from the city center. They would use the waterways to reach the city of Lodi. At Lodi, Verdi continued to explain, the couple can switch to taking a canal boat back northeast to Bergamo or Lecco, thus circumventing Milan. From there they could pick their way north until they reached the safety of Switzerland or wherever else they might be fleeing towards. They should leave Ca' Dario separately. In half an hour they would rendezvous at the San Marco parish church, which stood beside the canal in the Porta Nuova district.

In order to create a distraction for them, I returned to *Il Nord*, and once again pulled our Violetta aside. "Do you know *Là ci darem la mano* from *Don Giovanni*?"

She did. I told her I would sing Don Giovanni's baritone part and that Violetta would sing as Zerlina but with a twist. We were to sing our duet parts to members of the audience. I'd sing to the women in the room and she, the men. Once more our Violetta was game.

And I began by singing to a teenaged daughter out to dinner with her well-dressed father, *"There I'll give you my hand, There you'll say yes: See, it is not far, my love, let's leave from here."*

Violetta sang to the father, *"Should I or shouldn't I, my heart trembles at the thought, it's true, I would be happy, He could still make fun of me!"*

And then, when out of the corner of my eye, I saw Renzo and Lucia leave by the front door, I turned away from Violetta and sang directly to the red-haired soprano I had once fantasized about, *"Come, my beloved beautiful!"*

Violetta chose to seduce Lanari with her voice – and the impresario was decidedly pleased that she did. He was riveted by her performance, *"It makes me pity Masetto."*

I became worried though, when I overheard Gaetz and the Bishop expressing concern about Father Abbondio. "Where was he?" And so, I nudged Violetta to go over and sing directly to Commander Gaetz. I switched over to the brunette and sang to her in my deepest bass-baritone, *"I will change your fate."*

Violetta was a quick study. When Gaetz made a move as if to get up from the table, Violetta stopped him cold by sliding onto his lap and planting a kiss on his cheek. *"Soon ... I am no longer strong enough to resist."*

I was beginning to really admire this young diva. Yes, viva Violetta!

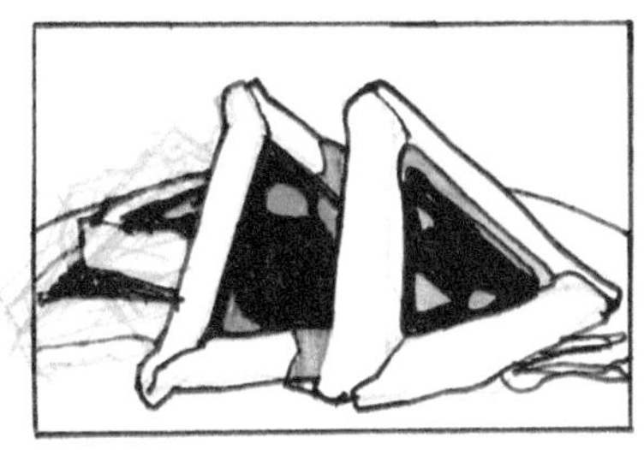

Chapter Two:
The Fallen Towers Of Zion

Ca' Dario, Later that night, July 16, 1833

Verdi and I first met when we were little boys and though you might imagine it was music or even politics that brought us together, the singer and the composer, you would be wrong. It was a passion for food, *salumi* in fact to be more precise, that linked two boys from Busseto, one a Jew, one a fallen away Catholic. My father, Jacopo Conegliano, had not only taken over Figaro from my *Nonno* Dario, Grandfather Dario, he also was the chief merchant in Busseto for the importation and resale of *salumi*, pasta and wheels of cheese from the far corners of the Italian peninsula. Every Sunday, while most of our Catholic neighbors were at mass, my father would load his delivery wagon with fresh supplies to be delivered on contract with many of the outlying estates and other inns and trattorias. Our farthest delivery would be to the largest and most prosperous estate in the region, one called *La Corte degli Angeli*, the Court of Angels, owned by the Duke of Mantua, Domenico Briscola and his family. Fortunately, in a town as small as Busseto, where the gates of the old ghetto had been torn down long before I was even born, we Jews had comparatively few issues with our Christian neighbors. Though some of our customs differed, we looked alike, dressed alike and since Roman times, we spoke alike. For the most part, we also lived and worked side by side in relative peace, probably because we were an insignificant minority.

I was probably no more than five when *papà* first had me help him make those deliveries. For the next ten years, until I left for the Conservatory in Milan at age fifteen, I joined him every Sunday morning. My initial job was to hold the horses' reins while *papà* unloaded those crates filled with long rolls of *salumi*. We had a pair of old *cavalli da tiro*, draft horses, named Abramo and Isacco, that were as calm as meditating saints and needed no tending – but at that age, I knew nothing and therefore undertook my responsibilities with the utmost seriousness. If I did my job well, *papà* would then reward me at the end of the day with some of *Mamma*'s freshly baked Hamantaschen cookies. And if you had ever tasted *Mamma*'s cooking, you would know that I was well paid – and most happy – and looking forward to the next Sunday as well.

Given that *La Corte degli Angeli* accounted for more than half of our orders, we usually went there first. We always avoided the elderly *padrone* of the Briscola clan, Domenico Briscola, the Duke of Mantua, a mostly absentee landlord whose reputation as an arrogant and cruel man earned him the sobriquet *Il Diavolo*, the Devil. Fortunately, we only dealt with their kitchen staff. Remember poor Piero Lusardi, the collaborator whose blood now stained the streets outside Ca' Dario? He grew up at *La Corte degli Angeli,* a member of one of several peasant families that labored there, people so poor, their lives were barely better than slaves. Lusardi, who came from one of the few mixed-marriage families, was a few years older than I. His father was a Catholic whose second wife, Sophia, was Jew from an old Busseto Hebrew family, the Benedettos. It was Sophia, Piero's step-mother with whom my father dealt with. She kept all the kitchen records and had a huge collection of books, including some in Hebrew. Together there must have been eight or ten children in total. Whenever I was there with the horses, the youngest and most precocious of the little girls, Isabella, would rush over to pet Abramo and Isacco and beg for one of mother's cookies. Even though I was just a few years older than her, she'd look at me with her adorable eyes and I'd surrender to my little girlfriend. She would repay me with a kiss on the cheek.

Lusardi later rose up the ranks and became a foreman, *Il capo*, that is until he was fired. As with most of us from the working classes, his political views gleaned from the French and American Revolutions were deemed far too radical by Father Abbondio Briscola and his uncle, *Il Diavolo*, Duke Domenico Briscola, who not only owned this estate but many others. The Briscolas were also related by blood ties to many of the great ruling families of Lombardy, Parma and the Veneto, including the d'Estes, the Sforzas, the Borgias, the Farneses and the della Roveres. The entire Lusardi family, the children including Isabella, and her elderly grandparents were thrown off the estate with nothing to show for their years of hard labor. Unemployed and homeless, Piero Lusardi turned to smuggling. As careers go, it was a perfect fit – until the Austrians murdered him in cold blood with what I still consider the first gun shots of the *Risorgimento*.

It was on the return trip from the estate that we would pass through the outlying Busseto district of Roncole where Verdi's parents had a small inn that catered to travelers, traders and merchants. They too purchased some of their supplies from *papà*. And it was there that one day when I was holding the reins, that a young Verdi, also five or six, came out to see the horses. Verdi, who had an apple in one hand, started to pet Abramo when suddenly Isacco snatched the apple and swallowed it in two quick gulps. Verdi was distraught and I thought he might even begin to cry. I quickly found a bag of my *Mamma*'s Hamantaschen cookies that *papà* had stashed under the wagon seat and gave one to Verdi. Thanks to momma's baking – and a lifelong love of good food - we've been rock solid friends ever since. Years later Verdi would delight in retelling this same story, no doubt embellishing it more and more as the years wore on, "Yes," he would declare, "Isacco may have stolen an apple from the Tree of Good and Evil, but when I bit into one of *Mamma* Conegliano's Hamantaschen cookies, I verily escaped the gates of Babylon and the clutches of Hell, to find myself in Heaven."

So yes, we both grew up in and around restaurants and came to relish great recipes and as such over the years we both came to know many of the merchants, suppliers and more importantly, the smugglers who would travel up and down the Po River Valley, that watery highway which linked every neighborhood and city in our region. I mention this because on that night in question, July 16, 1833, the day the revolution started, Verdi had a pretty good idea which boatmen he might very well find at the Porta Nuova canal.

And more importantly, he knew which ones hated the Austrians enough that they could be trusted with *Giovine Italia's* precious cargo – Renzo and Lucia.

Verdi was late, more than forty-five minutes late before he finally arrived at the church of San Marco. Yes, the rains were still falling as if in preparation for Noah's flood. He found the exiled operative from *Giovine Italia* and his lady sheltering themselves from the storm in one of the back pews. The ancient church was bathed in candlelight.

"Are you sure no one followed you?" Renzo asked Verdi.

The question irritated Verdi "How can I be sure? Lusardi's dead, Austrian soldiers are everywhere and you want guarantees?"

Lucia interceded, "It's been a difficult journey. Your help is valued."

"Yes, it is, very much so," added Renzo. "What do we do next?"

Verdi studied the faces of these exiles in the flickering light. Much as he wondered who they were, he was determined not to ask any questions or hear any more answers, less he knew too much. He explained that he was delayed by trying to locate a boatman, a smuggler, who would take them directly to Lodi, one who was willing to leave immediately despite the thunderstorm. He found one but said it would cost them dearly.

"How much?" asked Renzo.

When Verdi told them the price in Austrian gold, Lucia gasped.

"We don't have that," she said.

"Maybe we do," said Renzo. He pulled out a pocketknife and then sliced open the spine of that deluxe leather-bound edition of Signor Alessandro Manzoni's book. Out tumbled six gold coins – enough for a month of barge rides up and down the Po – and various maps, charts and a *Canzonatini.*

Lucia picked up the papers and looked them over. "With Lusardi dead, these are useless." She used a candle to set everything but the *Canzonatini* on fire.

Verdi meanwhile picked up one of the coins. "Come and come quickly, we have passage to negotiate."

They hurried outside, and through the pounding rain, they made their way over to the canal towpath, which was slick, muddy and crisscrossed by numerous little rivulets. Up ahead was a small barge with a sheltered cabin that had a lantern burning inside.

"Wait here," said Verdi, "While I secure the deal." Dodging the mud puddles, Verdi hurried as best he could over the slippery surface and went on ahead to the smuggler's barge, leaving the exiled couple to wait on the towpath in the pitch-black stormy night.

They watched as Verdi entered the barge's cabin. Through the window they could see him talking with the boatman.

"We're going to make it," Renzo said to his wife as he gave her hand a reassuring squeeze. Another flashing of lightning followed by another peal of thunder, shook the sky.

"*Nein*," declared a voice coming from the shadows. "*Hände hoch!* Hands up! *Wo sind deine Papiere?* Where are your papers?" It was Commander Gaetz stepping out of the darkness, his silver handled pistol aimed directly at Renzo's head. Standing behind Gaetz was Father Abbondio, his collaborator who appeared far less drunk than he had an hour earlier. Together, the two men represented everything we all hated about that unholy alliance between the church hierarchy and our foreign oppressors.

"*Ich verstehe kein Deutsch*, I don't understand German," said Renzo as he and Lucia complied immediately and raised their hands skyward.

"*Eine Schande, du Narr.* A pity you fool. Your papers?"

But when Renzo reached for his coat pocket, Gaetz knocked his arm back up into the air and then shoved the gun into his gut. On Gaetz's command, Father Abbondio reached into Renzo's coat and pulled out his identity documents. These he handed to the Commander. As the rain continued to fall, soaking the papers, Gaetz studied the documents and then declared, "By the authority of the Hapsburg Emperor, you are now mine. *Komm mit…* Come with me."

With the utmost calm Renzo replied to Commander Gaetz. "You can jail me, kill me, silence me, but you cannot kill an idea."

"And what idea would that be?" laughed Gaetz. "Tell me and I will use this pistol to expunge those thoughts right out of your head."

"Go ahead, turn me into a martyr and a thousand more will rise up to fight for liberty, justice, democracy."

Gaetz snickered at Renzo's bravado. "You're pathetic."

"You and your Godless rabble will always be on the losing side of history," added Father Abbondio.

Just then, Verdi emerged from the barge's cabin. In the darkness of that stormy night and as yet unaware of Gaetz's or Abbondio's presence – he called out to Renzo and Lucia, "Come quick! We have a deal!"

In that instant Gaetz's eyes shifted to look towards the canal boat. Lucia, who truly was one tough partisan, spun round and swung her carpet bag hard as she could at Gaetz's gun hand. She knocked his pistol away. As the gun tumbled onto the muddied pathway beside Abbondio, she and Renzo raced towards the barge.

Like two circus clowns, Gaetz and Abbondio kept bumping into each other as the Commander tried to recover his gun. Annoyed, Gaetz finally pushed the priest out of his way and grabbed his pistol. Abbondio slipped on the mud and to prevent himself from sliding into the canal, he grabbed onto Gaetz's leg. Just as the Commander lined up for a shot at Renzo's head, the heavens rumbled and spit out a flare of lightning that danced across the night sky…

"Oh my God," muttered Abbondio as he watched the lightning explode out of the heavens...

****

I was cleaning up the Tuscany Bar at closing time when the impresario, Alessandro Lanari, approached me. Behind him I could see through the open door to the street, where the rest of his party, Bartolomeo Merelli, and the women, were dodging the rain drops as they each climbed into a waiting coach.

"Would you rather sing here or at La Scala and the grandest

opera houses in the world?" he asked.

I was dumbfounded by the question. Opera's most important impresario was asking that of me? Like a dumb mute, I stared back at him blankly

"You are Dario Conegliano, the bass-baritone, Yes?"

"Yes, yes," I replied, wondering how he even knew I existed.

"The Conservatory speaks highly of you. And your *Don Giovanni* tonight, not bad."

Those comments puzzled me even more. Yes, I had graduated the Conservatory last month, but I was hardly their best student. I was no star, not with a voice that even I had to admit was better suited for the chorus.

Lanari pulled his business card out of his pocket. "If you want a job, come see me first thing in the morning. And don't be late."

I took the card, thanked him profusely and said I would be there. My first professional opera role? La Scala?

****

Verdi was so exhausted by the events of the day, that he fell asleep clutching his suitcase not minutes after the smuggler's barge pushed off and headed south. Curled up between sacks of rice and dried polenta, he did not rest peacefully. Thunder and lightning flashes punctuated the sounds of the endless summer storm, so much so that even his dreams were filled with terrors, both real and imagined. And woven into those nightmares was the plaintiff voice of his beloved Margherita crying out in disbelief, "You did what? You did what?"

Distorted images of his dying sister's face, once so kind, so innocent, and now stricken with pain, floated through his consciousness. And *Signor* Barezzi? Verdi saw his benefactor's eyes gone teary with disappointment at his protégée's failings. Even in the dream, he wondered if Barezzi, a man he adored and admired more than his own father, would abandon him. And if Barezzi yanked his support, would he prevent Verdi from marrying his daughter, Margherita?

And what of Margherita, would he lose her love? A love he had counted on and perhaps, shamefully, taken for granted? Had he been a fool? Was life so frail that a single failure could upend his entire future? In his nightmare, he saw Margherita's beautiful dark eyes, eyes that now haunted him. Her cascading red hair tumbled about her face like scorching flames as she again howled like an injured soul teetering at the gates of hell itself, "You did what? You did what?"

Our home village of Busseto was a small place where everybody knew everyone. Verdi and I were only seven months older than Margherita and thus all through our school years the three of us were always around each other. Her father, Antonio Barezzi, was the head of the town's *Società Filarmonica* – the Philharmonic Society – and often hosted their performances in the grand salon of his town home in the heart of the village. Barezzi was also a skilled musician who expressed his passions through his personal favorite instrument, the flute. Margherita shared her father's and Verdi's love of music. She was a pianist possessed of lean and agile fingers who could also sing with a sweet and rich soprano voice. Verdi himself had been her principal instructor on the keyboard. Although he could not remember when he first became aware of Margherita's existence, Verdi knew the exact moment they fell in love with each other. And that love was his lifeline to the domesticity and happiness he had envisioned for their future.

The *Filarmonica* had gathered at the Barezzi townhome for a party to kick off the new performance season. Even as teenagers, Verdi and I were key members of the company. We even had uniforms. I sang with their chorus, while Verdi's compositions became an integral part of their repertoire. Still, Verdi remained a shy, reserved young man who was decidedly uncomfortable in large social gatherings. Rather than mingle with the guests, he had busied himself with the task of pouring punch for some of the older women who seemed wedded to their chairs, until one of them urged Verdi to go mingle with the younger people there. He hesitated as this was not something he was inclined by nature to do – that is until he caught Margherita's eye from across the room. Hers was a friendly, familiar face he could trust. Verdi realized he had never seen her dressed so elegantly. She wore a full-length turquoise silk gown with matching kid leather gloves. Margherita's long thick red hair was pulled up in a stylish French knot and she was wearing make-up and a red lip stainer for what might have been her first time ever. She smiled at him and he decided to head over to her. He carried a glass of punch in each hand. As Verdi handed her a glass, her fingers brushed against his. A wave of energy – a pleasure he had never experienced before – shot through his body.

And when Margherita informed Verdi that she had a surprise for him that day, he asked what it was. Margherita blushed. She looked at him with a warmth and regard that caught him unaware. "Just wait," she had told him, "It is a special gift." She took his hand in hers and brought it to her lips and kissed it gently. "I hope you like it."

Verdi had never not liked anything about Margherita and this little kiss practically had him spinning. He found himself talking nervously about the weather, noting the rain the previous week and how it would impact planting the next wheat crop. She sipped her punch and smiled in response, happy to be chatting with him about anything, even the weather, silly as that was.

When it was time for the entertainments at the party to commence, Margherita took her place at the piano. Barezzi stood beside her with his flute. Her father then announced that the two of them would begin the evening's performances with none other than the premier performance of a romance for piano, flute and voice. As Margherita sang in a pure, angelic tone, her fingers – long and graceful - danced across the keyboard. Verdi could not take his eyes off of her. He watched every movement of her face and body, her expressions of joy and ecstasy, the lines of her arms, the curves of her chest and hips. So distracted was Verdi by Margherita's appearance that she was a dozen bars into the piece before he realized the surprise she had promised. The composition was one he had written himself but had never before been performed. And Margherita's performance, the depth of her musical stylings brought the romance to life better than anything he had ever imagined when he first wrote it. And she knew it. They both knew it. And when their eyes met again across the piano, he felt that passion, one he had never known before. Yes, this was the woman he wanted to share his heart, his life, his music and his soul with until the end of their time on this earth.

But in this nightmare aboard the barge all Verdi could hear was Margherita's angry questioning, "You did what? You did what?" Verdi was desperate to reach home before that damnable letter from Seletti arrived in Barezzi's hands.

****

The next morning as I headed over towards Lanari's hotel in the Porta Nuova district the incessant rains from the thunderstorm had finally let up however the skies over Milan were still overcast and grey. But no, I was not going to let the depressing weather darken my mood. Lanari had promised me La Scala and in that elated frame of mind, I verily flew across town. I crossed over the canal bridge near the San Marco parish church and knowing that the towpath would be a shortcut to his hotel, I turned onto it. The trail was muddier than I had expected and, in some places, I had to jump over the rivulets that crisscrossed it. I had not gone more than fifty paces when I spotted a blue fedora wedged into the bushes that ran alongside the canal. Examining it, I realized without a doubt that it was the same hat that Renzo had been wearing the previous night. Not knowing what else to do with it, I took it with me as I continued on to Lanari's. I could not help but wonder what had happened to Renzo, Lucia and by extension, my friend, Verdi. Had they escaped? Were they safe?

A few minutes later I found Lanari's hotel. The impresario's penthouse rooms were on the fourth level and so I headed up the stairs, the blue fedora tucked under my arms. Just as I neared his floor, I heard a door slam shut and a woman in a full-length hooded cloak that covered her face raced past me and headed down the steps. I turned and watched her descend. Trailing beneath the hemline of her cloak I could very clearly see the gown belonging to the soprano who had been singing at Ca' Dario the evening before, the one I called, Violetta. Knowing the corrupt nature of our business, I had no doubts our little soprano had spent the night auditioning for her future roles in Lanari's bed.

Fortunately, the impresario had a different contract in mind for me. When I knocked on the door, a servant answered and led me to the salon where I was asked to wait. Lanari, dressed in a morning suit and robe, entered minutes later, at the same time the servant returned with a tray of *cornetti*, a pot of espresso and two cups.

"Are you free to travel for the next few months?" he inquired whilst pouring the richly aromatic coffee into our cups.

"I've nothing to hold me here," I replied while wondering, what about La Scala.

"Good." Lanari wasted no time. He quickly detailed how he had a troupe heading out on the road shortly but that their bass-baritone singer had turned up ill and could not travel. He needed a replacement immediately. Did I want the role? He gave me about thirty seconds to decide.

"Where is the tour headed?" I asked.

"America," he replied, "New York first."

"The Italian Opera House?" I asked. It was not La Scala, but I was excited nonetheless.

"*Si,*" replied Lanari with some surprise. "How do you know about the Italian Opera House? It just opened this past year."

"My cousin built it."

"Your cousin?" Lanari was completely taken aback. "Who is your cousin?"

"Emanuele Conegliano. He's actually my grandfather's first cousin. You may have heard of him by his Christian name, Lorenzo Da Ponte."

"Lorenzo Da Ponte, the priest who wrote the libretti for Mozart's greatest operas is your cousin? My, my…."

"Yes," I said. I told Lanari how the entire Conegliano family here in Milano, Busseto and Ceneda in the Veneto, had been receiving and sharing his letters and stories from the New World since before I was born and that I grew up learning to sing his operas, *The Marriage of Figaro, Don Giovanni*, and *Così Fan Tutte*. The prospect of singing for *mio cugino* in New York was even more thrilling than opening at La Scala.

"Then you need to get yourself down to Genoa immediately," was Lanari's reply as he handed me a contract to sign along with my first payment and a set of instructions for the trip. "The troupe sails out of Genoa for New York on Monday next."

"And Violetta? Is she coming too?" I asked, but it was Lanari's turn to stare back at me blankly.

"Who?"

"The soprano from last night? *Violetta's Lament*. She was leaving just as I arrived. Is she coming too?"

"Her?" Laughed Lanari, "No, Merelli and I have other plans for her. Now get moving. You need to be in Genoa by Sunday night."

I raced out of Lanari's apartment and practically danced down the stairs. New York. I was going to New York. The Italian Theater. Emanuele Conegliano's theater. Wow!

Thrilled beyond my own imagination, I left the hotel just as the rains started up again. I made my way along the towpath in the direction of Ca' Dario. At first it was a drizzle, then it changed into a steady downpour. Though I had mixed feeling about wearing Renzo's hat – especially not knowing his fate - the torrential rains made wearing it essential. And it fit perfectly.

I had gotten about halfway home when I saw a crowd of boatmen up ahead gathered around a section of the towpath that had practically slid into the canal. They were talking and gesticulating wildly. Only when I approached did I understand what all the commotion was about. Lying at their feet were two entangled bodies that had been pulled out of the canal. Both were badly burnt and disfigured from what had to have been a direct lightning strike.

Was it, as I suddenly feared, Renzo and Lucia? The corpses were so charred that they were completely unrecognizable. Despite the downpour, I took the hat off my head. Had it belonged to this dead man?

"You're drenched," was Uncle Roberto's first words to me when I finally reached his office at Ca' Dario. He pulled a bottle of absinthe out of his desk and poured us both shots. As we sipped the warm green liqueur, I told him all that had happened that morning. Roberto was both thrilled for me but apprehensive about the fate of Renzo and his wife. "When you get to Genoa, you must go to this address…." He then leaned in close and whispered it into my ear so none of the cooks in the kitchen could hear that he had given me instructions to the secret headquarters of *Giovine Italia*. "Bring the hat as proof Renzo made it this far. Show it to Giuseppe Mazzini if he is there or to one of his lieutenants. They will know what to do. But above all, go in secret. Make sure you are not followed. Tell no one. Do not write down the address or anything else. Many lives and perhaps the future of the *Risorgimento* is at stake."

Three days later I found myself in the port city of Genoa. The rain seemed to follow me. By now, not know what else to do with it, I wore the blue hat on my own head. Before connecting with the opera troupe heading to New York, I made my way to the address I had been given. The front door was solid oak and heavily reinforced. I knocked twice. And waited.

Moments later a peephole slot in the door opened at eye level and a woman's startled yet challenging voice demanded to know my business.

"I have news of *Signor* Renzo for *Signor* Giuseppe Mazzini," I replied. I waved the blue hat in front of the peep hole.

The door opened slowly. Behind it was a remarkably beautiful young woman with waist length raven black hair and hazel eyes. I was so taken in by her appearance that I stared at her like a dumb ox. Those eyes – almond shape set above high cheekbones - drew me in as none had ever done before. She, however, was having none of this. Without saying another word, this young woman used instead, a pistol in her hand to wave me inside and toward a second door directly opposite.

I obeyed as if under a spell.

The inner door suddenly opened and I was dragged inside by a powerfully built man in his mid-twenties with reddish-blond hair, a scraggly red beard and a faded red shirt. The man, whom I took to be some sort of sailor or merchant marine, thrust a gun into my stomach.

"*Mani in alto!* Hands up! Who are you and what do you want?"

And that is how I met Giuseppe Garibaldi, a future hero of the *Risorgimento.*

Garibaldi listened intently as I – with my hands still held high in the air - told him the story of what had happened at Ca' Dario, including the killing of Lusardi; the arrival of Renzo and Lucia; the exchange of Signor Alessandro Manzoni's books with my friend Verdi; and my discovery the next morning of the hat on my way to Lanari's apartment. I told him about the job offer and how on my way home, I saw those two unrecognizable bodies fused together along the canal. I concluded by sharing Roberto's instructions that I should come to this apartment before I met up with the opera troupe and sailed for America. Only after all of that did Garibaldi lower the gun and replace it back into his belt.

He was actually a kind man who then apologized for the extreme caution that he and the members of this now outlawed *Giovine Italia* were compelled to take to protect themselves in the wake of a recently failed uprising against their ruler, the king of Savoy. And then to my surprise, Garibaldi grabbed my hand and shook it enthusiastically. He thanked me for all I had done as a soldier on behalf of what he called, "*la rivoluzione* – the revolution."

I did not know I had joined the revolution but maybe I had, *che sa?*

Finally, he picked up the hat. After examining both the inside and outside with great care, Garibaldi handed it back to me. "Yes, it's his, but keep the hat."

"Keep it? Why?" I asked, surprised they would turn a compatriot's hat back over to me, a mere nobody.

"It's raining out there, isn't it? You'll need a hat."

"Yes, but…."

"And it rains in America too. Look," he said, "regardless of whether Renzo is dead or safely in Switzerland, he won't need this anymore. And by wearing the hat you will continue to honor the man and the cause you tried to help."

"Honor? I don't understand."

"Is it correct for me to assume you really do not know Renzo's true identity?"

"No," I said before repeating Uncle Roberto's advice that it was always safer in times of upheaval to be as ignorant as possible.

"Your uncle is a wise man," said Garibaldi, "But since we are both sailing to the Americas on the morning tide, there is little harm in my telling you that the exiles you tried to help were none other than Giuseppe Mazzini and his lover Giuditta Sidoli."

I was stunned. "Giuseppe Mazzini himself?"

"*Si*," replied Garibaldi, "The King and his court have put a price on all our heads. Giuseppe Mazzini and I and most of the other leaders of *Giovine Italia* have been condemned to death in absentia."

"*Liberami*. A death sentence?"

"*Si.*" Garibaldi grabbed a canvas duffle bag that had been lying on the floor and slung it over his shoulder. "Come on. I will take you to the port." He ushered me out the door and, past the young woman with the hazel eyes. Oddly, her face was frozen, as if in shock. I stared at her or at least tried to as Garibaldi led me back onto the street. My heart fluttered. I was in love – or at least wished I were. You may think me a fool, but yes, she was that beautiful, an angel.

As Garibaldi and I walked toward the harbor district, I was already wondering how I would juggle knowing a wanted criminal onboard the same sailing ship with Lanari's opera troupe.

"And so, you're fleeing to New York?" I asked "We're on the same boat?"

"The same boat, yes. New York? No. We travel together only so far as Lisbon. From there I'm off to South American, Brazil, that's where the battle for freedom is going on now. *Viva la rivoluzione, my friend, viva la rivoluzione!"*

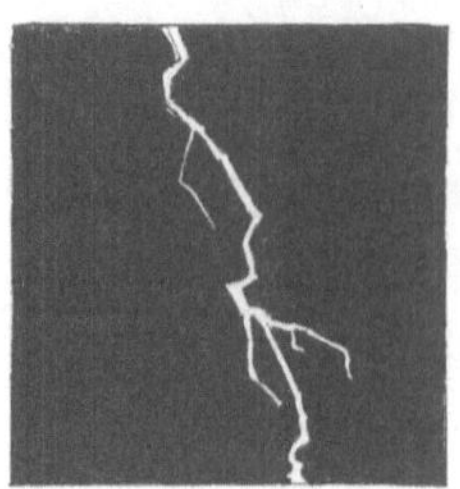

Chapter Three:
Let the Lord Inspire a Concert

The Palazzo Modignani, Lodi, October 1834

My tour of the Americas lasted fifteen months. And unlike communications today with daily newspapers, trains and telegraphs, news then simply did not travel. I knew nothing of events back in Europe and even less about Verdi's fate or the revolutionaries from *Giovine Italia.*

Our trip to America began at the Italian Opera House in New York City with multiple performances of *Don Giovanni* under the stage direction and guidance of our Conegliano cousin, Lorenzo Da Ponte. Due to a shortage of capable singers, I was quickly pressed into service in the title role for this and many of the other operas we performed. I may not have had the best voice, but I was a fast study and versatile. And on occasion, the only sober male singer available. America, that land of freedom and democracy that we all admired from afar, had lots of whiskey back then but no wine. My fellow Italians on the tour, men and women alike, had no experience with such hard spirits and well, need I say more? The results were often not pretty. Me, though? Having grown up around restaurants and bars, I knew my limits. While other fell victim to inebriation, I prospered on the stage.

If they needed a tenor, for say, Donizetti's *L'elisir d'amore* to play opposite our diva, I faked being a tenor. And in Boston I even had to play a young page, Cherubino, from the *Marriage of Figaro* in the highest male range, a counter tenor. You might say, I left Milan an amateur and returned a seasoned professional. There was nothing I could not do, especially if I wanted to eat, stay employed and have shelter over my head.

Da Ponte, then in his mid-80's, was as thrilled to meet me as I was him and his family. I would often take dinner with them, meals heavy on overcooked steak and half-dead vegetables chased down by raw whiskey. To say Americans had their own cuisine would be an oxymoron but I was always grateful for their kindness and good intentions. In response to Da Ponte repeatedly telling me *La famiglia è importante*, the family is important, I prepared a feast centered around a dish that had long been a Conegliano clan favorite, the ironically named *Carbonara Gemelli Ebraica,* for him and his friends. After devouring this pasta dish that featured smoked bits of pork and silvered almonds, Da Ponte lit a smile in my soul when he declared it the best meal he had had since leaving Venice as a young man half a century ago.

While Da Ponte and I were walking near an open field where a group of young men were playing a game then called Rounders – and now known as Baseball – he also expressed deep concern about the future of religious freedom in our homeland. His specific worry was what would happen if there was an Italian revolution akin to the American and French revolts against the ruling class. Were all the foreign rulers booted out, would the Pope and his army of cardinals and bishops slip into the power vacuum and exert ever more civil control? Would the church's power be unchecked? Having once been a part of the Catholic clergy, Da Ponte knew firsthand and far better than most, just how corrupted its bureaucracy had become. How, he demanded to know, would those who supported this *Risorgimento*, prevent the return to power of these clerics who despised Jews? I had no answer. When it came to politics, I was still a novice, that is to say a naïve young man. But I understood his fears, ones that every Jew harbored, if not openly, in the secret recesses of their heart.

All this became ever more apparent when on one night in September, Da Ponte met me at the theater after we had finished our performance. In secret he then took me to small, non-descript building over on Mill Street. Entering, we heard voices in prayer, Hebrew voices celebrating Rosh Hashanah, the Jewish New Year.

The building?   New York City's first and at the time, only synagogue, Shearith Israel. The interior, decorated in the style of Sephardic temples, was as ornate as the exterior was bland and nondescript. Women prayed up in the loft, their beauty and allure hidden from the men *davening* downstairs. This segregation of the genders, well, it was something I never understood even though I grew up with it in Busseto.

But why did we go there in secret? Although Da Ponte had lived his professional life as a Catholic priest, none of Da Ponte's business associates had the slightest idea that he was born a Jew. He was a converso on the outside only. If those people knew he was a Hebrew, it would have meant instant ostracization. In that regard, the New World differed little from the old. People feign liking Jews until they find out you are one.

Here however, inside Shearith Israel, my cousin could be himself. All the other members of the congregation knew him only by his Hebrew name, Emanuele Conegliano. Within the walls of this synagogue, Da Ponte, the man ordained as a Catholic priest, did not exist. And when Emanuele Conegliano came to up to read from the Torah, he used a simple brass *Yad* as a pointer so his fingers would not actually touch the scrolls. The *Yad*, he had told me, was the same one had had since his own Bar Mitzvah in Ceneda some seventy years earlier. When it was my turn to ascend to the *bemah* and read from the Torah, he passed the *Yad* to me. But when I was done and went to return it to him, he told me, "No. I want you to deliver the *Yad* and my secret diaries to Ceneda when you return home to Italy." He then gave me the original copy of his secret diaries about his life as a crypto Jew and asked that I carry them both back to our family's hometown, not far from Venice. I was to personally hand these secret diaries back to Rabbi Yael Spinoziano, another cousin, who would hopefully be able to ensure that his journals would be published. Although all the world knew Da Ponte as a Catholic, he wanted his people – our people – to know that such garb was merely the mask and costume their true cousin, Emanuele Conegliano, had donned to survive and ultimately prosper in a Christian world he saw as an essentially hostile place for Jews.

Before we left Shearith Israel, I vowed that I would fulfill his request to deliver the *Yad* and the diaries back to our ancestral home, a task that I considered a sacred honor.

After the service, he walked me through an equally obscure Hebrew Cemetery that was tucked around the corner from the synagogue and near the field where we'd seen those young men playing Rounders. He led me to an empty patch beneath an elm. There he told me in the greatest confidence that after his death, he had given his closest friends instructions to have the coffin of Lorenzo Da Ponte surreptitiously removed from the Catholic Cemetery at St. Patrick's Cathedral and reburied at this spot with a headstone for Emanuele Conegliano. Despite having worn the collar of a Catholic priest for much of his adult life, he had no intention of spending eternity sleeping in the company of Christians.

Our company played New York for three months, then made similar stops in Boston, Philadelphia, and Havana. During those long days at sea and in-between performances I busied myself reading a series of booklets on politics and revolution Garibaldi had given me before he left our ship. True to his word, when we took on supplies in Lisbon prior to crossing the Atlantic, Garibaldi boarded another vessel heading to Brazil. The papers were written by the man whose blue fedora I continued to wear, Giuseppe Mazzini. These works included *The Manifesto of Giovine Italia; On the Superiority of Representative Government;* and finally, *Rules for the Conduct of Guerilla Bands.* Yes, these were serious books for serious people who were determined to overthrow the domineering power of the foreign kings, emperors and aristocrats and their church allies who held the entirety of the Italian speaking world in their bloodied fists. I cannot say we Italians weren't influenced by these ideas and by the experiences I learned in America about democracy. These concepts that grew out of both the American and French Revolutions had a direct bearing upon the *Risorgimento.* In those Democracies, we saw their leaders work to find unity and common ground for the benefit of all. Their policies contrasted sharply with the aristocratic and theocratic tyrannies of Europe where the rulers sought to divide and conquer their subjects through campaigns of hatred and alienation. By creating false enemies, these tyrants distracted their subjects from the real threat – their own rapacious rulers and the clerics that propped them up through their perverse interpretations of scripture. Consequently, Mazzini's works had a life-altering impacts upon not only me, but our Maestro Verdi and the Risorgimento. They are, as you might well imagine, at the heart of tonight's narrative.

After playing Havana the troupe returned to our homeland via the port of Venice, which the Austrians of the Hapsburg Empire ruled over with a fist squeezed tighter than the one that held Milan in its clutches. Before we passed through customs, I made sure to shred and burn all of Giuseppe Mazzini's pamphlets, less I be caught and arrested for being a member of *Giovine Italia*. Unlike the America I had so recently toured, an America that had thrown off the dictatorial rule of an English king, the Hapsburg Empire offered up no illusions about inalienable human rights or a free and uncensored press – all the more reason we needed a revolution.

In Venice, the troupe performed several operas at La Fenice for a month before Lanari sent word that I alone was to meet him at the Palazzo Modignani in the town of Lodi to showcase a new prima donna that he was about to introduce to the opera world. Why me? I don't know, but it was a job, one that paid well and would bring me ever closer to home, my friends and my family. After leaving Venice, I made a quick overnight detour to Ceneda where I delivered Da Ponte's diaries and his *Yad* to our cousin, Rabbi Yael Spinoziano. But even he, along with the other Conegliano family elders, fearful of censorship and retribution by the Catholic Hapsburg authorities, doubted that they would be able to have the diaries published at this time. In that regard, Da Ponte's fears proved correct; the world, including America, was a hostile place for Jews, a lesson I swore to never forget.

From Ceneda I caught a series of coach rides to Lodi and found my way easily to the gates of the Palazzo Modignani. And yes, I still wore Giuseppe Mazzini's blue fedora.

No sooner than I had introduced myself to the guards as one of the singers for today's concert, than I heard a sweet and familiar voice call my name from the street behind me.

"Dario! Ciao, Dario." It was Margherita Barezzi, whom I had seen only rarely since I had left Busseto for the conservatory. In those intervening years she had grown ever more beautiful and striking.

I turned away from the guards and went back into the street to greet her.

"What are you doing here? When did you get home?" she asked.

We embraced warmly. I quickly explained that I had just arrived from the Veneto and was to sing back up to some new young diva Lanari was presenting that afternoon.

Margherita had known about the concert and in fact had come up from Busseto the night before with both her father and Verdi.

"Where are they now?" I asked, "I would be thrilled to see them. It's been so very long," I said in earnest, for I had not heard any news of Verdi – or Giuseppe Mazzini - since that fateful night at Ca' Dario fifteen months earlier. Truthfully, until that moment I did not even know if my own parents, Liliana and Jacopo, much less Verdi, were dead or alive.

"They have been trying to arrange a meeting with your *Signor* Lanari for weeks now but without success. Our dear Verdi has completed a score for his first opera and frankly," she admitted with some distress in her voice, "He's been desperate for someone, anyone to read through it. Coming here was a last resort. Truly, Verdi would do anything to get the score into Lanari's hands."

"I'm sure it will happen. His compositions are always brilliant. But why so desperate?"

Margherita waved her left hand past my eyes. The sun glinted off a tiny diamond chip mounted on the thinnest of gold bands, a symbol of a very poor man's honest pledge of love – and an indication that my guilt-ridden friend had been forgiven for his transgression with Seletti's daughter.

"We're engaged, but Verdi admits he'd be embarrassed to go through with the marriage until he is certain he can support us."

"But surely a man of his talent and abilities?" Verdi was one of the smartest, most knowledgeable and wisest people I had ever known, not just in music, but in all fields – and Margherita was certainly his equal. All through our school years they were both always at the top of our classes.

My comment only made Margherita grimace even more. "Verdi won the concertmaster job in Busseto over a candidate put forward by Bishop Giuliani and that should have been enough. We could have managed on that salary. But the Bishop Giuliani was livid that Verdi had won the post. He wanted someone under his thumb, someone the fathers could control readily."

"And that's not our Verdi," I interjected.

Verdi would never submit to following orders, particularly by someone he not only considered a mediocre fool, but one he considered an apologist for the ruling aristocracy. And we all know that those who don't follow, by definition, lead. And those that lead in opposition to Bishop Giuliani become his enemies. Verdi was near the top of that list.

Margherita knew this all too well. "No," she said, "And in revenge, Bishop Giuliani decreed that the *Società Filarmonica* was forbidden from conducting any concerts or choirs in any of the parish churches so long as Verdi was its concert master."

"Revenge for the Malediction?"

"Worse than that. By restricting performances, the Bishop Giuliani's action effectively cut Verdi's salary in half. After Father Abbondio passed away last year, the bishop…"

"Wait. Abbondio is dead?"

"Yes. The stories have Abbondio getting drunk and drowning in his own…" Margherita cringed. "He's gone and though I wish I could say there's one less leach in the pond, the church fathers just sent us another friar, Father Cornetti, to replace him who's as equally nasty. But you're right about our Verdi. He won't kowtow before any of them. So unfortunately, even with him doing extra teaching lessons, there's not enough for us to marry."

"It appears the church fathers are doing all they can to keep you miserable and apart," I added, "Just as they did to Renzo and Lucia in *Signor* Alessandro Manzoni's book."

"*The Betrothed*, you mean?"

"Yes."

"I've yet to read it, but Verdi has – three or four times. He loves that book and quotes lines from it to me all the time. He's even composed choral pieces based on *Signor* Alessandro Manzoni's other writings, including an *Ode On the Death of Napoleon.*"

"I'm not surprised. No one seems to have captured the state of our beautiful but lost country better than *Signor* Alessandro Manzoni.

"True enough," she said, "But Verdi and I have no intention of letting our oppressors win."

Less anyone gets the wrong impression about the spiritual nature of my friends, I should reiterate here that they were neither atheist nor anti-Christian. Like so many of our countrymen however, they were fed up with the corrupt nature of the church hierarchy that supported the exploitation of the poor in favor of rich landowners. One needs to understand that back then, before the *Risorgimento*, the majority of the Cardinals and Bishops who dominated the church, were not religious people. They were the sons of the leading aristocratic families who garnered their appointments because of their political connections and not for any spiritual prowess – if they even had any. Thus, the church's militant support of the foreign – but Catholic - dynasties and rulers and aristocrats that had sway over the Italian peninsula and kept our peasants in perpetual poverty, was absolute. And we all know the cliché, that power corrupts, and absolute power corrupts absolutely. And that was the state of the Italian peninsula in the 1830's. Sooner or later something had to give. Back then we did not know it would take three Wars of Independence over four decades to create our Italy.

"But even if the money Verdi earns as head of the *Filarmonica*, were sufficient," Margherita continued, "You and I both know it's not the career Verdi wants – and I'm determined to see that he gets what he deserves. No one has worked any harder than he."

"I am so sorry. Yes, composing opera is all he ever really wanted to do. But nothing is easy in the music world, even for a genius."

"But can't you help? You know, with *Signor* Lanari? Verdi's desperate to get that score into the right hands. He needs someone, an impresario who can help launch his career."

I had to explain to Margherita that I barely knew the man, having met Lanari only that once before going off on tour. "But of course," I reassured her, I will do all I can to help," while knowing sadly and in truth that I had no clout whatsoever. Nonetheless, Margherita's support for Verdi and her determination to help him progress in his career was most admirable - as was the depth of their love and support for each other.

"You will read through his opera score, won't you? You know how he respects your opinion."

"Of course. To read a Verdi score is an honor, one I value."

"Will you be able to join us after the concert? I will have him give you a copy. Perhaps for dinner?" she asked. "Verdi would so love to see you and my father would too."

"It would be my greatest pleasure to dine with the three of you and spend hours in the company of my oldest friends," But I went on to explain to Margherita that after the concert I was to a catch the evening coach to Milan. Apparently, Bartolomeo Merelli, Lanari's close friend and the director of La Scala, had an immediate vacancy for a bass to play Dr. Bartolo in the *Marriage of Figaro.* And the letter of instructions Lanari had sent to me in Venice, warned me not to be late or I'd lose the assignment. "I'm sorry to say no to dinner," I finally said to Margherita, "But if Verdi can come up to Milan soon… Well, you know, we'll talk, and I'll see how I can help."

"*Grazie mille*, Dario. Thank you. But you do know I am going to hold you to your promise, eh? You must read his score."

"Yes, yes," I reassured her. Margherita was nothing if not determined. Her support and energy were fully aligned behind Verdi. My friend could have had no better allies than Margherita and her father. With a quick kiss on each cheek, I bid her goodbye and headed back inside the palace gates.

As was typical of an aristocrat's city palace, the grand salon where the concert was to be held, opened out into an inner courtyard filled with gardens and fountains. This arrangement created an effective bandshell for musical performances. The town's elite sat inside and under the building's shade, while the rest of the attendees were out in the garden, either sitting or standing in the warm October sun. As I entered, I found servants placing plush chairs in every available space. Moments later I located Lanari in a room off the Palazzo's main salon. He was pacing anxiously back and forth. The impresario was in a nasty mood and I apparently, yes, I was the cause.

"You're late," he said with a displeased growl. "I was expecting you yesterday in time to rehearse. It's too late now. We start in half an hour. You are just going to have to wing it. You can do that, can't you?"

Absolutely," I said, as I apologized. I dared not mention I was a day late due to my detour to Ceneda. Nor was I fool enough to say a word about Verdi. "Don't worry," I finally said, "Over the last year I've had to improvise more than you can even imagine. Why in Philadelphia alone, when one of the other singers passed out in his dressing room, I played both Don Giovanni as a baritone and Leporello, his servant as a bass, simultaneously."

"You did what? Both roles? How? Don Giovanni and Leporello are in almost every scene together."

I tapped the blue fedora on my head and said to Lanari, "Whenever Leporello sang, I wore this blue fedora. And whenever Don Giovanni had to respond, I turned back around and doffed a tricornered hat with a feathered plume and played as a baritone. The audiences loved it. Granted they were opera virgins. Few had ever seen Don Giovanni before, much less any opera. Nor had any of the local theater reviewers. They adored my double role, believing it was part of the original fabric of the opera. The reviews were over the top and we sold out the rest of the run in Philadelphia."

Lanari began to laugh uncontrollably. "*Perfetto*, Dario! That's perfect. 'Opera virgins,' indeed! Dario, a man of many talents. God bless the Americans. I am glad I trusted my instincts and hired you for that tour."

Whatever I said must have pleased Lanari or at least impressed him enough to let me go on stage. Before running over the program, he reiterated to me in no uncertain terms that after the concert I was to a catch that evening coach to Milan. Though it meant passing up dinner with Verdi and Margherita, I assured him I would be on that wagon. After all, Lanari was paying the bills and I was in no position to argue or disagree. And it was La Scala, I was finally going to play at La Scala, the most famous opera house in the world. No, I was not going to miss that coach.

Lanari's notes were easy enough to follow. When we finished, he said, "Time to introduce you to our diva. Are you aware, Dario, that she did ask specifically for you. Said you worked together before."

Lanari's comments surprised me. I could not imagine who this diva was unless it had been one of the whiskey-addled sopranos from the American tour – which seemed unlikely – or one of my fellow students from the Conservatory. Lanari knocked on the door to an adjacent room. When it opened, there, standing before us in a gorgeous diaphanous full-length gown of lavender silk was none other than the young singer I had once dubbed, Violetta. With her hair coiffed and her face made up exquisitely, she looked every part the *Bel Canto* era heroine.

"I believe you two know each other each other, eh?" said Lanari.

"Dario of Ca' Dario. You're here at last. What a pleasure." The young diva extended her hand to me. "Thank you for backing me up to today." There was genuine warmth and gratitude in her voice, traits not typically associated with a prima donna.

While executing a slight bow, I took her hand in my own and kissed it. "Viva Violetta," was all I could say.

She laughed. "You don't know my real name, do you? But why should you?"

"I'm embarrassed to say you are correct."

"Strepponi, Giuseppina Strepponi," she said. It was a name none of us would ever forget or worse, take for granted. Without her, *La Generalina*, the Little General, who knows if our revolution would have ever succeeded?

****

The concert, which lasted a little more than two hours, was a huge success. When not joining *Signor*ina Strepponi for one of the three duets we performed together, I sat quietly behind her. I studied the crowd, hoping to spot Verdi. It took some time, but I finally spied my friend along with Barezzi and Margherita standing way far away in the very back of the gardens. It saddened me to think that although the physical space from Verdi to the stage was hardly more than thirty meters, the professional distance was as wide and as tempestuous as the two Atlantic crossing I had endured. How, I wondered, would I ever be able to help him across that great divide?

Strepponi began with an aria from *The Marriage of Figaro* and two hours later concluded with yet another reprise of *Violetta's Lament*. In between she performed cavatinas from Bellini's *Norma*, and several others from Donizetti. The biggest applause came when we performed *Là ci darem la mano* together; and the greatest laughter when she teased the crowds by singing "*Madamina,*" – the Catalog Song from *Don Giovanni* – in the same affected husky male voice she had used at Ca' Dario.

In the end, the audiences at the Palazzo Modignani in Lodi, Strepponi's hometown, were thrilled by her coming out performance. Throughout the concert, I could not help but wonder how my friend Verdi would judge her voice and stage presence, qualities that already surpassed those of any other soprano I had ever heard. Each aria was met with enthusiastic applause and at the conclusion she received three standing ovations. It was clear to all who heard her that night that Strepponi was destined to be one of opera's most illustrious stars.

And afterwards, when the concert and the greetings and meetings were all over, *Signora* Strepponi, pulled me aside and whispered in my ear, "Dario, thank you. Not only for tonight but for helping me out at Ca' Dario last year. If not for that evening, *Signor* Lanari would have never taken me on. I owe you. Whatever favor you may need, is yours for the asking."

"Ah, thank you," I said back to her, "But you – and your voice -

have won this honor all on your own. And I wish you all the success possible. But as for that favor," I quickly added, thinking of my friend Verdi's opera score, "One never knows. That day may yet come."

Yes, *Signor* Lanari had indeed launched the career of the opera world's next greatest diva. He had that power. Could he, would he do the same for Verdi?

Today, however, was not the day to ask either of them for a favor. As soon as the concert ended, Lanari urged me out the door and off toward the stagecoach depot. Yes, La Scala was next. My destiny awaited – provided I could stay out of trouble and the revolution did not get in the way.

****

Ca' Dario, Milan, A week later, October 1834

"Is that Renzo's blue hat?" asked Verdi, a constant and keen observer of all that passed before and around him.

It was after my third performance as Dr. Bartolo when I returned to Ca' Dario for quiet dinner in *Il Colosseo*, that Verdi finally caught up to me. He was alone, and although his face revealed a tired if not haggard and desperate man, his blue eyes sparkled with the joy we both shared at seeing each other again. His clothing and manner of dress however were another matter. As head of the *Società Filarmonica* in Busseto, Verdi now dressed the part; a clean black suit, a neatly trimmed beard, a starched white shirt and a freshly pressed necktie. Stated more simply he was becoming the Verdi that all the world now recognizes from his portraits.

We embraced each other as two long lost brothers from different mothers who had found their way home.

"Yes, it is – or was - Renzo's." I told him about finding it on the tow path the next morning. "Come, sit down. Join me. This is great. We need to celebrate." I turned to one of our waiters and asked her to double the platter of *salumi* I had ordered and to bring us,

"Prosecco! And lots of it." But then I stopped and started in again and said to our waiter. "This is a special occasion. Instead of a *salumi* platter, bring us both the *Milanese Verdi* and the *Polenta con Pomodorini.*

"Grazie, amico!" said Verdi with great anticipation as we both sat down, "But what are these dishes? *Milanese Verdi* and *Polenta con Pomodorini?"*

"New specialties of the house from the fertile mind of Uncle Roberto," I replied. "The *Milanese Verdi* is our classic veal *schnitzel* to which we now add to the breading, some finely ground pistachios and herbs. You'll love it. And the *Polenta con Pomodorini?* Well, that too starts with our basic polenta. We add certain herbal seasonings and then, the tiniest of tiny tomatoes, ones about the size of a blueberry. They go in whole and uncut so that when you eat the polenta, these juicy little tomatoes explode inside your mouth with a burst of warm, intense flavor."

"Fantastico," said Verdi who was already savoring the meal in his mind's eye. *"Grazie,* Uncle Roberto! Count me in." Even then Verdi was already the epicure you all knew him to be later in life. He just did not have the money to indulge his tastes back then. Later, oh yes, indeed. Truly, if you want to understand the Maestro and his life, then you must know it actually revolves around his passion for food. And when you are the quintessential Italian as Verdi was, it's always about the food.

As we waited for dinner to arrive, I asked him to tell me what had happened on the canal towpath with Renzo and Lucia.

Verdi began as if conducting the heavens with great animation, "Just when I called to them to hurry onto the boat, a massive bolt of lightning struck the towpath. Picture this enormous explosion. And then a fireball! And out of the flames, Renzo & Lucia come running. The barge is already underway. They jump on board just in time, but the hat, your hat, goes flying off his head. Renzo grabs for it, but too late. We're floating into the channel and there's no turning back."

I stopped Verdi right there. "So, you're saying Renzo made it on to the boat safely?"

"Yes, both of them, he and Lucia. Why do you ask?"

"Until now, I thought them both dead."

"How so?" he asked.

I told Verdi about finding the two bodies the next morning near where I had discovered the hat. He had no idea whose corpses they were or might have been, nor at that moment, did I.

Just then Uncle Roberto, who had heard us talking, came over to the table with our bottle of prosecco and two glasses. These he filled as he spoke. "Those two bodies? I though you already knew, but yes, I guess you were away on tour. Those two bodies were so badly damaged they were impossible to identify, save for one clue, the remnants of Commander Gaetz's silver handled pistol. Seems that burst of lightning struck Gaetz's gun, which exploded. Between that, the lightning and the resultant fire, the bodies of Father Abbondio and the Commander were welded together and dispatched to hell."

"Good riddance, Uncle Roberto," said Verdi, whose affection for my uncle was such that he too considered Roberto as family. "Lusardi's Revenge, *si?*"

"*Si,*" said my uncle. "More than we even knew. Not only was Father Abbondio a member of the Briscola clan, he was a collaborator in Gaetz's service all along. Abbondio got wind of the escape plot from a parishioner's confession and fed that information to the Austrians."

"A fitting finale and one that further confirms the evil conspiracy between the Pope and the Hapsburgs," said Verdi. He then reiterated that Renzo and Lucia had succeeded in escaping. As soon as were safely on board, Verdi left them alone in the cabin while he went down below to the forward cargo hold and fell asleep. The two exiles stayed topside until the barge reached the canal junction just outside of Lodi. There they hooked up with another boat heading northeast and eventually to Switzerland.

Verdi was not surprised when I told him about Renzo being none other than Giuseppe Mazzini. Recently he had seen a sketch of a man very much resembling Renzo in *Le Figaro*, a Paris newspaper. Apparently, the Swiss authorities were not happy sheltering the leader of *Giovine Italia* and soon after his arrival there, they escorted Giuseppe Mazzini to the French border. While in Paris

Mazzini began organizing the *Giovine Europa* movement to help spread his ideas across the entire continent. And although Verdi confessed to also having read copies of the same treatises I had burnt before landing in Venice, we both agreed the political climate did not, at the moment, favor a revolution. Best, we acknowledged equally, it was the season to duck down and stay quiet and away from trouble. There were enough stresses in our own lives without taking on the burden of a new nation conceived in liberty… Not now anyway.

Still, given the ever-worsening political climate and the distrust manifested by both factions, it was reassuring to me that Verdi and I stood on the same side of the divide. We each agreed that the best way forward was the path Giuseppe Mazzini had described in his paper, *On the Superiority of Representative Government.* Its essence? The unification of the several states and kingdoms of the peninsula into a single republic was the only true foundation of Italian liberty. Out with the divine right of kings; in with Democracy and let all power reside in the voice of the people through their voting. The new nation had to be: "One, Independent, Free Republic".

As Verdi and I refilled our prosecco glasses, a waiter delivered our *Milanese Verdi* and *Polenta Piccoli Pomodorini.* Not only was presentation splendid, the aroma of the two dishes wafting up, had both our mouths watering. We paused our conversation and dug in. Each bite of the *Milanese Verdi* was heavenly with the taste and crunch of the pistachio adding a divine spark to the veal dish. And the explosion of flavor from those hot blueberry sized tomatoes was just extraordinary.

Over what was probably way too many rounds of prosecco, we continued to catch up with the stories of our respective lives and adventures the way old friends often do as if we'd never been apart. And Verdi, recalling his panic at the thought that Seletti's letter might reach home before he did, described how when the smuggler's barge reached an isolated cove in the Po River near Busseto, he left the boat and practically ran the five miles back into town. He did not want to stop until he could once again wrap his arms around Margherita.

He then went on to tell me about his life in Busseto, his apologizes to Barezzi and Margherita, his engagement and about all of the problems with the church fathers, Bishop Giuliano Giuliani, and the *Filarmonica*.

For my part I described my adventures in the free and democratic land of America, including not only meeting Da Ponte and many of his famous friends, but cooking that feast for them as well. These included Clement Clark Moore, who read to us a poem he was working on called, '*Twas the Night Before Christmas;* James Fenimore Cooper, known for his novel, *Last of the Mohicans*; William Cullen Bryant who reviewed theater and opera for the *New York Evening Post* and last but certainly not least, Joseph Bonaparte, Napoleon's brother. The man who once embodied the spirit of the French Revolution and later held the crown of Naples and Spain, had been living in America in exile.

"Can you imagine the thrill," I said to Verdi, "of what this poor boy from Busseto experienced since we last met? Giuseppe Mazzini's hat, Garibaldi's gun, and Bonaparte's hand in friendship? Not to mention the women! Do you have any idea what it is like to be treated as an opera star in a foreign land?"

"No," Verdi smirked. "No, but I am sure you're dying to tell me, eh?"

I went on to describe how members of the company were hosted and toasted as if we were the demi-gods and heroes we portrayed in our operas. And how frequently I found myself invited into the quarters of some adoring coquette who had just watched me perform in *Don Giovanni* or *Così Fan Tutte*. Their expectations were high. Did my performance match? What can I say? Although I have been more inspired by the passion and love I shared with my wife as an equal partner, I must confess I learned more about the art of *Amore* in those fifteen months than in all the decades since. Suffice to say that education has served me well.

We finished off our dinner with demi-tasses of limoncello and Hamantaschen cookies made, of course, according to my mother's recipe.

When I asked Verdi his impressions of Giuseppina Strepponi's Lodi concert, his eye lit up again. With even greater excitement than before, he went on to praise every aspect of her singing, from her trills, articulations, and dexterity to her range, power and emotion. He pronounced her, the best, most perfect singer he had ever heard, one whom he would have loved to compose for. Nothing more, nothing less.

Eventually though, between all the laughter and liquor, our conversation came around to his score, *Oberto*. I had never seen my friend so upset. Frustrated. Depressed. Disillusioned. What could I do? I glanced at the first few pages of the copy he gave me. The overture was, of course, brilliant, inventive and melodic. But when I told him that, it only seemed to increase his despair.

"To know I can do this," he said, "And yet no one is even willing to look at it, the work of a nobody, a peasant from Busseto." He begged me to deliver it into the hands of either Lanari or Bartolomeo Merelli at La Scala.

I confessed that though I worked for these two men, I knew neither of them well enough to make such a gesture on his behalf at this point in time. To them I was just a peasant too, a waiter at Ca' Dario who sang.

"But you have spoken with them, yes?" he asked.

"Of course," I replied, "But more often than not it was to suggest a wine to go with whatever dinner they chose, a Chianti, a Barolo, a Barbera."

"And did they listen? Did they take your advice?"

"Yes, they heard me out, and yes, they accepted my recommendations."

"And were they pleased with your suggestions each time?"

"Yes," I answered. "Of course, I always found the right wine to complement their dinners. I know wine better than I know opera."

"And did they ever complain about the wine you suggested?"

"No," I said. "In fact, they'd usually order a second or third bottle."

"Well, then, my friend," Verdi concluded, "You're halfway there.

They say all our troubles vanish with wine. You've already got the two most important impresarios in Italy saying 'Yes,' to you. Now all you need do is deliver *Oberto* into their hands along with a bottle – no make it a case of whatever wine you recommend for reading my score. I'll find the way to pay for it all. Perhaps a Dolcetto, a red with a sweet but bold temperament, eh? And if that does not work, your mother's Hamantaschen cookies should seal the deal, yes?"

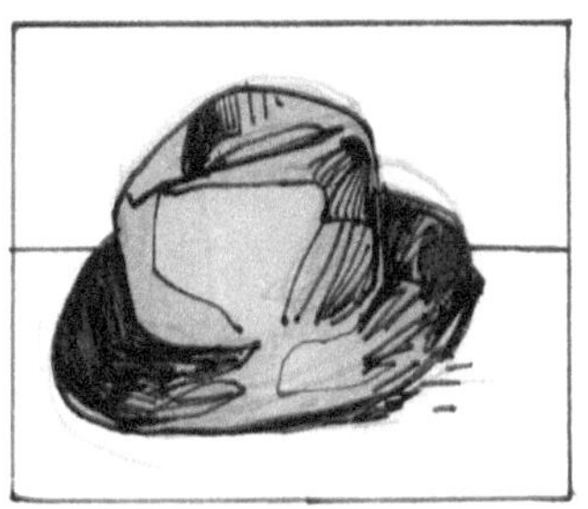

Chapter Four:
Our Sweet Native Land

Ca' Dario, April, 1839

Passover and Easter had both come a week earlier to Milan, bringing on their heels, an early spring along with hopes for renewal, rebirth and the *Risorgimento*. When not on tour I had continued to sleep in the loft above the storeroom and work at Ca' Dario. My dream was to save the money I had earned singing so as to eventually be able to buy a home of my own in the Porta Nuova district. I had my eye on one not far from La Scala and just around the corner from the writer, *Signor* Alessandro Manzoni's lovely three-story home. It was the only residence on Via Vittorio Veneto, an alley so short that its address was longer than the street itself. Locals simply called it *Tre V* – the three V's, which in the Milanese dialect sounded like Trevi, as in the Trevi Fountain in Rome.

This particular Sunday, I woke early, dressed quickly and then headed downstairs and over to the Ca' Dario kitchen. Once inside, I grabbed a fresh *cornetto* that our cooks had just pulled out of the oven. As I nibbled on that soft, moist, buttery roll, I whipped up a double shot of espresso for myself. As with most every other item on our menu, our espresso was unique and a coffee confection to love. Early each Sunday morning, long before the restaurant would open for lunch, we would roast and grind our own coffee beans with exacting perfection. And to that rich dark blend we would add a carefully measured hint of cardamon and a few other spices too secret to name even here in this narrative about Verdi, Violetta and our *rivoluzione*. The aroma of roasting beans would not only waft through the trattoria but also outside to the street as well. The allure of our espresso was so enticing, that I have even been told by a sleepy-eyed friar from a monastery up the block that the scent of our beans wafting through their chapel made their dawn prayer service ever more inspiring. "Even God needs a good jolt in the morning," he had said.

Thus, it was of no little surprise that when I walked from the kitchen into *Il Nord* that I would find Verdi sitting alone at the piano, an espresso cup by his side. Although the restaurant was closed and empty at this early hour, my Uncle Roberto, who also believed in Verdi's inexhaustible talents, had long ago not only given Verdi carte blanche to come in and use the piano any time before we opened each day, he also made a point to feed my friend for free whenever he was struggling.

"Verdi," declared Uncle Roberto to me one day, "Verdi embodies the three P's of success, "Passion, passion and more passion. He will go far if we, like Barezzi, give him support."

Verdi was staring out into space and did not seem to notice me enter – or anything else – except the musical score for *Oberto* on the piano. Truth be known, Verdi, when working, often appeared catatonic to outsiders, especially when he would be sitting alone, lost deep into thoughts about his musical creations. I knew better than to interrupt his contemplations. It was as if in the stillness, he was able to reach into the inner recesses of his genius, which was vast and incalculable, and see before him the masterworks he was then creating. Yes, to him, our espresso was like a welcomed drug that had a profound effect upon his consciousness. Indeed, without so much as moving a muscle to shift his eyes, Verdi would reach for his demi-tasse, lift it to his lips, sip gently, and then, sigh. His eyes would blink as if waking from a coma before he would turn and look at me.

"She is coming, yes?" he asked.

I nodded as I took off my hat and set it on the piano, "Yes, she promised." 'She' being Giuseppina Strepponi.

"Ah, good," said Verdi. He took another sip of espresso, closed his eyes, and returned to whatever thoughts were deep inside his own mind, before speaking again, "What did you put in this espresso?"

"Why, whatever do you mean?"

"It's addicting," he declared. "This is my third cup and I am still craving more. That's not natural – even for an old addict like me. Are you using opium?"

"No, just cardamon," I said.

"That's all? I don't believe you. It must be opium."

"And a pinch of ginger, if you must know."

"Ah, yes," Verdi mused, "So now you've gotten me addicted to ginger. I should have known not to trust your innocence. You're a devil when it comes to food and sustenance. And you are sure your diva is coming?"

"Yes," I reiterated. Quite some time had passed since I had made my solemn commitment to Verdi to have his *Oberto* score read by people who mattered, people who could ensure that his work would be produced. And much had happened in all of our lives since *Signorina* Strepponi's coming out concert in Lodi.

First off, Verdi had returned to Busseto to run the *Filarmonica*. Fully determined to make his life as a musician work, he not only continued as the group's full-time leader, he took on as many students as possible to supplement his income. And on top of this, he continued composing. He wrote non-stop; choral pieces, marches, solemn hymns, romances and of course opera. Despite his struggles, Verdi was quietly confident even at that age in his own abilities. No, it was not bragging, just an inner certainty that was well justified. He had no doubts that sooner or later his absolutely passion for opera would find a way to break through all the obstacles that stood between him and success, including those posed by his enemies in the church hierarchy such as Bishop Giuliani. If anything, Giuliani's hostility, strengthened Verdi beliefs in the need to take down not only our foreign oppressors but our clerical ones as well.

Although Verdi's earnings were never quite enough, Margherita convinced him that they should nonetheless stop waiting for a future that may not arrive in a timely fashion. She firmly believed that that life was indeed short, and they should marry now and set up their life together. Verdi's love for Margherita was so deep and profound, he needed no further persuasion.

After the wedding, which of course my father's *salumeria,* Figaro, catered, the determined couple moved into an apartment in the heart of Busseto. To help with their finances, Margherita insisted upon her also teaching piano to music students. By and by they were able to manage their life. And soon enough their first child, Virginia, was born. I cannot tell you the immense joy her birth brought into the life of my dear friends. All one had to see was the sparkle in their eyes to know the depth and truth of their feelings. Fifteen months later their son, Icilio, was born, but instead of their happiness being doubled, a month later Virgina suddenly died. Margherita's words about life being short were all too prophetic.

Ever wonder where all the mournful music in Verdi's operas originated from? They were born that day, the day they buried that tiny coffin holding Virginia in *il Cimitero di Busseto.* Even now I can still recall our little Busseto marching ensemble, the wail of trumpets and horns, the deadly drum beat and the tears of women lining the streets.

****

As for me, both my opera career and my work for *Giovine Italia* took a few unexpected turns as well. After my run as Dr. Bartolo at La Scala ended, I went back to work at Ca' Dario. It was there one night a few weeks later that Lanari approached me once more, with yet another job offer. He was about to launch Strepponi's career with an extended tour of some of the great Italian opera houses, but he wanted, no, needed an insider – someone he could trust, such as me - to journey with her in support, a sort of traveling secretary who would represent his firm and ensure that everything everywhere went smoothly for his young star. In exchange, Lanari promised me both a base salary and the opportunity to have a singing role in every opera in which Strepponi performed. Sometimes in the chorus, Lanari offered, and sometimes in a supporting role and with luck, maybe even a lead role every now and again as a stand-in.

Of course, I agreed. A singer with my fair to middling talents, took what came and turned nothing away. Lanari paid me well. I wanted that house and the life that came with it.

When Lanari asked for a recommendation for a good champagne to toast our new arrangement, I suggested a wonderful prosecco from Ceneda, a fine Conegliano.

That selection pleased him thoroughly. Presuming Lanari was in a great mood, I brought up the prospect of him reading Verdi's score.

"Frankly, Dario," he replied, "Our agency now only represents singers. That's where the money is. Impresarios who manage theaters, who stage operas and who negotiate with composers, will go grey or bald and die young. Not my style. If this Verdi fellow has a credible opera score, bring it to Bartolomeo Merelli. He has the contract with the Hapsburgs to oversee both La Scala and their Vienna Opera House."

"But," I pleaded, "After we closed *The Marriage of Figaro*, you know Bartolomeo Merelli left for Vienna."

"So much the better," said Lanari. "Bring the score with you as *Signorina* Strepponi's tour will eventually wind right through his stage in Vienna, the *Kärntnertor* Theater. You will have Bartolomeo Merelli all to yourself there."

And so, it began. A week later *Signorina* Strepponi and I were on the road. All I can say is that once our young diva began her tour, she never stopped. Our premier in Trieste was at the Teatro Grande. There she stunned audiences with her brilliant performance in Donizetti's *Anna Bolena*. True to his word, Lanari had me join the chorus for that production.

Then, in rapid succession we performed operas in Udine, Gorizia, Verona, Mantua, Piacenza, Cremona, Bologna, Florence and Venice. Strepponi went from being the "New Voice," the rising star that would re-energize the entire opera world, to the dominant soprano of that era. Her fame and wealth grew rapidly, as did mine – at least the money part. Fans applauded her everywhere and tickets to her performances were usually sell-outs. Unlike other stars I've known, Strepponi was a delight to travel with. She was always upbeat, always pleasant, and always kind and appreciative of the effort all of us put in, in support of her.

In Ancona, Strepponi sang in a command performance before the Hapsburg Emperor, Ferdinand I and his wife, the Empress, Maria Carolina. I backed her up and performed several duets with her, much as I did for her in her coming out performance in Lodi. Afterwards the royals showered us both with gifts. Strepponi was presented with diamond bracelets, while I got an exquisite gold pocket watch. Yes, although it was flattering and profitable to be so recognized by the Emperor and Empress, I was also deeply troubled. There I was, singing for the very rulers we, the people behind *Giovine Italia*, were seeking to liberate our county from. I knew from my contacts within the Hebrew community of Ancona that the Emperor had ordered the destruction of the local Jewish neighborhood – the old ghetto – and the local synagogue, so as to build out new estates and palazzos for their family. The Emperor's political stance, built upon the purported divine right of kings, was antithetical to my own beliefs in the equality of all, as my American cousins had shown me. He had also put a price on the heads of Giuseppe Mazzini and Garibaldi, the earliest leaders of the *Risorgimento*. Were Garibaldi there with me, would he have assassinated these rulers and declared a Republic, one for and by the people? I did not know. This contradiction was one I could not resolve in my own mind, at least not then.

The tour continued. As the now leading diva of the Italian Opera circuit, Strepponi was in constant demand for this role and that. Her bookings were non-stop. When I asked her why she was pushing herself so hard, she reminded me of her song the night we first met, *Violetta's Lament*. Strepponi confided that she knew the course of any diva's career – much like Violetta's was short. Her fame and resultant fortune were an illusion, she declared, akin to a rainbow arching across the sky. Eventually, when the light changes, the colors vanish. She was determined to pour enough gold into that pot at the end of that rainbow so as to support herself well into the future. The prime of a diva, she declared, lasted only so long. It was a sentiment I completely understood, for my own career as well.

Over time our entourage also grew along with her successes. She added first a maid, and then later a dresser, who would both travel with us. My role when not performing in an opera became ever more administrative. I handled much of the correspondence, contracts, hotel bookings and payroll for Lanari's touring groups – while saving every penny I personally earned. And, as Strepponi's fame grew we also had to be more discreet in our bookings so as to maintain her privacy. I would often register her under the name, "Violetta Lamentina." And now and again, just to keep my hand in the food game, so to speak, I would stop in one of the local markets and then prepare a sumptuous feast for our little troupe or some of our fellow cast singers.

Eventually we arrived in Vienna, the capital of the Hapsburg Empire, where Strepponi was to sing at both the Kärntnertor Theater and the Theater *an der Wein*. Our stage coach delivered us to the depot and livery stable on *Kärtnerstrasse*, mere blocks from the theaters. Upstairs was the *Wilden Mann Gasthaus*, where we took several rooms for our entourage. The *Gasthaus* was the very same hostel that my cousin, Lorenzo Da Ponte, had stayed at some fifty years earlier. Downstairs, occupying one half of the ground floor, was the Café Venezia where Da Ponte had met his future wife, Celestina, who was also its owner. Da Ponte often took his meals there with Mozart when they were writing *The Marriage of Figaro*. What could be more inspiring than to dine in their shadows in the very café where the music for that first shot of the revolution was composed? And although that might have seemed like ancient history, it was only a decade before we arrived, that Beethoven, yes, the immortal Beethoven himself premiered one of his very last works, his *Opus 132 String Quartet* in the Café Venezia. Strepponi and I made a point to dine there with her staff as often as possible during our stay, if only to soak in the history and the food – which was nearly as good as that back home at Ca' Dario. I also made a pilgrimage to the Theater *an der Wein* where Beethoven lived while composing his only opera *Fidelio* – one of the few existing operas until Verdi's that actually spoke of freedom, democracy and of overthrowing corrupted oppressive regimes. For those of us in *Giovine Italy*, and for Verdi, the politics of *Fidelio* was a guide star, a precursor to our own uprising.

Though I had obviously never been to Vienna before, I had read Da Ponte's secret diaries over and over many times before delivering them to Ceneda. The diaries not only described his decade worth of adventures in the city, they also painted in vivid and at times gory details, a picture of about how horribly Jews were treated and abused under the Austrians. They were our oppressors and would remain so until we broke the harness these aristocrats used to constrain us all.

As a city, and the capital of a vast empire, Vienna was a wonderfully beautiful and fascinating place. Nonetheless, I could never feel comfortable there. That discomfort helped me understand why my cousin had used his identity as Catholic priest, as a costume to hide the fact that he was a Hebrew. To do otherwise simply did not feel safe. If you had read Da Ponte's accounts of how he, along with Mozart and Baron Wetzler, another *Converso*, visited the underground site of the Vienna *Gesera* massacre below the modern city's *Judenplatz* where in 1421, fourteen hundred Jews were burnt alive, you would understand why this city of smiling, pleasant Austrians terrified me.

Before Strepponi and I began our run of performances in Vienna, I sought out Bartolomeo Merelli at his offices at the *Kärntnertor* Theater, only to discover that he had returned to Milan weeks earlier. Any thought of having him read through Verdi's score for *Oberto* had vanished.

On the other hand, Strepponi once more wooed both the musicians and aristocrats of the capital. At one point she dated the concertmaster of the opera orchestra and then later, Donizetti himself when she did a reprise of her role in his *Anna Bolena*. On more than one evening I dined alone with our staff while Strepponi was out and about.

There were other times Strepponi would encourage me to date one of her lady friends, typically other singers or chorus members she thought would match up well with me. I'd go out with them, but much like my experiences in America, I considered such affairs a distraction from my goal of finding a true partner to love, marry and have a family with. I appreciated Strepponi looking out for me, but what can I say, these assignations always felt empty.

We performed several operas in Vienna over the next month and though I had great opportunities covering a number of major roles, I was never so glad to leave a city and get back on the road. And so, after Strepponi's triumph there, our tour resumed at the same breakneck pace across the northern Italian cities.

Eventually we reached Turin, the capital of Savoy. With the future King of Italy, Victor Emanuel II, in the audience, Strepponi took to the stage of Teatro Regio to perform as the young ingénue of Donizetti's *Lucia di Lammermoor.* But a problem arose for which there was no simple solution. No matter how the costume mistress dressed *Signor*ina Strepponi, there was, unfortunately, no way to hide the fact that our diva was at least seven months pregnant.

Who was the father?

In her rise to stardom Strepponi's social whirl had spun ever faster. Like a queen bee anointed in honey perfume, she found suitors swarming around her. And most were rich. Most were aristocrats. And most were already married. But they all wanted to bed her, this impassioned diva, whose voice intoxicated them. Or so these lotharios all would claim. But Strepponi was no innocent fool. In fact, I still regard her as one of the smartest, most well-studied people I have ever known. Her intellect was right up there with Verdi himself. In addition to her native Italian, she could banter with the best in fluent French and Spanish and she even had a rudimentary knowledge of English, sufficient enough to read Shakespeare's plays while we were traveling. This wise woman saw no reason not to take advantage of these affairs and relationship and use them to benefit her career. If the men of the opera world could do that, so, she determined, could she.

And though Strepponi confided that she did her best to take precautions, the inevitable happened. The father? Strepponi acknowledged that it could have been Lanari, Donizetti, her Vienna violinist or anyone of the leading men she had an affair within in the recent the course of our travels. In the end, it turned out to be an associate of Lanari, Camillo Cirelli, a minor impresario more than twice her age who had occasionally joined us on tour. Cirelli took some responsibility for the child, but in the end, not enough. After all, he too was already married and not about to divorce a wife of many decades.

Despite her noticeable pregnancy, Strepponi performed right up until her January delivery date. She had a boy, who was quickly given up for adoption.

But there were consequences.

In the rarified world of Italian society, it was one thing to be a goddess desired and taken by men, but another to advertise those affairs by becoming pregnant. On one side of the scale, the scandal was great for the box office as her bookings continued at a frenetic pace. The downside was that invitations to high society salons fell off ever more rapidly. In each city we toured, the diva had suddenly become a social pariah. Among the aristocracy, wives were scandalized, but their husbands, well, they kept calling. Of course, they did.

Never more than a thin whisp of a girl, the constant touring, the non-stop performances, the demands upon her voice, were often too much of a demand upon Strepponi's stamina and her overall constitution. I urged her to slow down, but she would not listen. The pregnancy and her rush to get back on stage as soon as possible, added to the negative impact on her health. Though she was only twenty-three – yes, only twenty-three - there many were nights when she simply could not go on stage. She began to miss and cancel performances, which raised ever more concerns among the managers that ran the opera houses in each city we toured.

Strepponi was a realist. She tried to continue on as if nothing had happened but in her heart of hearts, she knew the world around her had begun to change, both brutally and permanently. In the self-righteous, male dominated society of the 1800's she had become "the fallen woman," "the one who has gone astray," or as they say in the Milanese dialect, *"La Traviata."*

This pained her but such was the way of the world back then. Of course, none of her male lovers suffered any consequences. Call it unfair – it was – or consider it one sided – it was – but such was life for a woman in the theater back then. Ironically, this new and undeserved reputation as a fallen woman, a woman little better than a courtesan, now made Strepponi even more attractive to lovers who sought her out in private.

And so, her tour continued so she could continue to fill up that pot of gold. And, yes, the affairs continued. A year later she was pregnant again. And the father this time? *Chi lo sa?* Who knows? Once more, there were too many suspects. She performed right up until the day she delivered. After she gave birth, I was the one tasked with bringing the poor infant – in secret - to the foundling orphanage, the *Ospedale degli Innocenti,* in Florence. I placed the baby in the little revolving door outside the orphanage and when it closed, that child entered another world, one none of us would ever know or experience. The impression that experience left upon me was as deep as witnessing poor Piero Lusardi being shot down by the Austrians in cold blood. I never wanted to be in that position again.

When the season ended, we all returned to Milan to rest and recuperate. Strepponi had taken on a grand and spacious apartment only a few short blocks from La Scala. It was replete with servants that she could now well afford. And me? I went back to the loft above the Sardinia storeroom, biding my time until I could afford to buy that house I wanted on Via Vittorio Veneto.

Around the same time Verdi decided it was now or never for him to launch his career. Aided by his father-in-law Barezzi's financial assistance, he, Margherita and their baby, Icilio, moved to Milan. Uncle Roberto also helped by insisting that Verdi and his family dine regularly at Ca' Dario in the *Il Nord* room. My uncle instructed him to bring is wife and son as often as they liked, whenever they liked. There would always be a table for the Verdi's and there was never be a bill. Their poverty was offset by the joy of being a loving couple out with their beautiful Icilio. Though to this point my opera career had been far more successful than my friend's, I was the jealous one. Being on the road for so long was antithetical to building up a true relationship. Yes, the audiences' applause and multiple standing ovations were wonderful experiences, but where, I had begun to wonder, was my wife, my child, my home? These were the gems I wanted. Not a gold watch from a tyrant.

In fulfillment of my vow to Verdi, I was finally able to bring his score to Bartolomeo Merelli at La Scala. The impresario glanced over it but was not convinced. I kept pleading until he finally came up with an option that seemed workable. Strepponi, he told me, was committed to doing a one-time benefit concert for him later that season for the Pio Institute of Milan. If she approved of the score, he would consider using Verdi's work.

I left Bartolomeo Merelli's office knowing that now was the time to call in that favor from Strepponi. When I visited her apartment a few days later, I found her exhausted, sick and taken to bed. Though I was hesitant to place yet another demand upon her, the *Signorina*, grateful for all that I had done for her, she agreed.

"Two days hence," she said, "On Sunday morning, after I have had a chance to rest more, your Violetta Lamentina will meet you both at Ca' Dario and read through the score with Verdi.

****

"You're certain she'll come?" Verdi asked me again.

"She promised," I said. "And in all the years I have known her, she has always been true to her word. She is a woman you can trust," again, words not normally associated with a prima diva.

Verdi took another sip of espresso – his fourth cup of the morning - and the effect was immediate. His eyes lit up and his face became animated. And sure enough, as if on command, *Signorina* Strepponi walked in the door.

But she was not well and that was clear from the moment she entered. Her face was pale, her eyes sunken and watery and she moved with the strained effort of one who was exhausted. She barely held up through the introduction to Verdi before abruptly excusing herself with the need to take a seat and rest.

Verdi immediately jumped in to assist her. "Dario," he asked, "Can't you get her something to eat? Some meat, some bread, something solid and some of that strong espresso?"

While he continued to comfort her, I nodded agreement and headed to the kitchen.

There, one of the cooks said he would whip up something for her and have it brought out in a few minutes.

I poured an extra-large cup of espresso and returned to the dining room, where I found Strepponi and Verdi both laughing over some little joke one of them must have told the other. Despite her exhaustion, Strepponi was in a good mood. She had actually been looking forward to this day, inspired she confessed, by all the stories I had told her about Verdi and his music.

When I asked what they were laughing about, Verdi spoke first while Strepponi refreshed herself with sips of our espresso.

"*Signorina* Strepponi was just telling me about the time you nearly starved to death in Bologna, yes? Seems, your show ran hours late because of a rainstorm, and you had no dinner?"

"*Si,*" I replied. It was true. We had not eaten before the performance and were famished by the time the last curtain call had dropped. When we left the theater, all the restaurants were already shuttered. Dawn was not far off.

"Yes, we were starving" interjected Strepponi. "So, what did this magician, our Dario do? He sends me back to the hotel alone with instructions to stoke up the fireplace. Which I did. An hour later he comes back with groceries along with a bottle of an exquisite Chianti – from where and how at that hour I have no idea – and then somehow over that fire he manages to whip up *Bistecca alla Fiorentina* with this astonishing black mushroom sauce. *Liberami*, it was one of the best meals I have ever enjoyed."

"Food is the only reason I stay friends with this rascal," laughed Verdi. "He's always coming up with something unexpected. At our wedding in Busseto, when Margherita and I calculated what we could afford to serve all our guests, we settled on platters of *salumi*. 'Keep it simple,' I tell Dario and don't go over budget. Of course, he ignores our request. Dario not only had one of their servers, an elderly woman, a deaf-mute, everyone in town called *La Sordomuta*, deliver the *salumi*, he also prepared a *rouladen* of beef, bacon, ham and chicken with a side of risotto for each and every one of our guests – a wedding gift he called it. And knowing you've eaten his cooking," Verdi says to Strepponi, "There is no need to tell you how this meal thrilled and delighted our guests."

Strepponi raised her cup in a salute which Verdi joined, "Viva Dario, *Il re della cucina*! – the king of the kitchen. Why be mundane, when with passion you can be monumental?"

"*Si,* and when the revolution comes," said Verdi, "Dario will be the caterer," a declaration that turned prophetically true.

"*Grazie, amici*, I am humbled by your praise," I replied just as the door to the kitchen swung open.

In walked a waitress, one I did not initially recognize as I could not see her face nor recognize her profile. She carried a plate of *Tournedos, Bianco e Nero*, toward Strepponi. As she passed by Verdi, he waved his hand as if to draw the aroma of that dish ever closer. The smiles on his face and on Strepponi's told all. Of these twin filet medallions, one was smothered in a white truffle sauce and the other swam in a sea of black truffles.

"*Liberami*," said Strepponi as the waitress, who had her shoulder length black hair pulled into a pony tail, set the plate before her. "I cannot believe this, oh my God. Dario, what have you done?" She turned to the waitress, "*Grazie*, my dear."

"*Prego, Signorina,*" said the young woman. However, as she passed by and I got a glimpse of her face. There was something familiar but I struggled to place where, when or how? Suddenly, the young woman grabbed my blue fedora off the piano. She popped it onto her own head and disappeared into the kitchen.

It was only after the door swung closed, that it hit me. I blurted out much to the confusion of Verdi and Strepponi, "That's her! Garibaldi!"

It was the woman with the hazel eyes. My shock at seeing this vision from years past, caught Strepponi's attention.

"Dario? What is it? Who is she? I've never seen you react to any other woman that way."

And she was correct. What was this woman from Genoa doing here?

I looked at Strepponi and shrugged, "I don't know."

She laughed and said, "Go after her while I eat."

I could not move.

"Go on," she insisted, "Go. I want to savor these *Tournedos* and I can't do it with you sputtering and stuttering like a school boy. Go on."

I did. I stood up and started towards the kitchen as Verdi questioned Strepponi, "What's that all about?"

She laughed again. "Every time I would arrange a date for Dario, a date mind you with some of the most beautiful, talented and spirited women Italy has to offer, Dario would inevitably compare her to this beauty he saw for five seconds in Genoa when he met Garibaldi. Now I know why. If that's her, she's stunning. A face like an angel and there's genius in her eyes."

Verdi nodded in agreement.

I entered the kitchen and looked around for this woman with my hat. She was nowhere. I could not find her. Uncle Roberto was standing in the middle of the kitchen. He noticed my puzzlement, which for some reason made him laugh as if I were the sole target of some joke.

"What?" I asked.

He smiled and then pointed toward his office area. I stepped around the corner and saw the young woman sitting behind his desk. My hat shaded her beautiful hazel eyes and her lips formed a wry smile. Even with her formerly exotic waist length hair cut short, she still appeared absolutely stunning. Yes, an angel – with my hat!

A string of half formed question fell out of my mouth as I tried to understand what was going on. "Who are…, What are you…, My hat…, What's going on?"

With great care and calmness, the young woman, bemused by my confusion, stated very simply and clearly, "Giuseppe Mazzini wants his hat back. The revolution needs you."

"What? Who are you? What are you doing here?"

"You don't remember who I am, do you?" She asked.

"Of course, I do," I insisted as I stared at her face. It wasn't that I could only think about how absolutely gorgeous, she was – and she was. It was this. Over the course of my now very long life, I've come to believe that when each of us is birthed, we arrive in need of another to balance us. And the image of that "other," is planted deep inside our consciousness. Thus, in life, our souls remain restless until we find that person, that lover, that partner. "You were the one who opened the door to me when I came to meet Garibaldi in Genoa."

"No, before that? You don't remember?"

I was dumbfounded. "Before that?" I had absolutely no idea who she was or where I had ever seen her other than that one time, but my heart was pounding… I had been dreaming about that face, those eyes, this woman forever.

"How could you forget?"

Was she mocking me?

"I, I… I…"

"A clue perhaps?"

"Please…"

"You used to come to our home every Sunday morning with your father, his wagon and those two horses, Abramo and Isacco. "

"I did?"

"Yes, I loved you," she said, "Well, at least it was a school girl's crush."

She loved me? This woman of my dreams loved me? But still, I had no idea who she was.

"In Busseto?" I mumbled.

"Of course, Busseto. My mother was the chief cook at *La Corte degli Angeli,* and every Sunday we'd wait for the wagon to come with all of those wonderful supplies you and your father would deliver."

She saw the still blank look on my face and then continued.

"Piero Lusardi was my big brother, my step-brother. And when you came to the estate, you would let me pet the horses and you would give me one of your mother's…"

And then it hit me, "Isabella! My mother's Hamantaschen cookies. It's you, Isabella!" I had not seen her since I had first left Busseto for the Conservatory in Milan. She couldn't have been more than a skinny little twelve-year-old back then, but those eyes, those hazel eyes. "Oh my God, you remembered. I love you," I blurted out.

"When you were six? Or sixteen?" she laughed.

"But why didn't you say something in Genoa?"

Abruptly her expression changed from one of joy to one of extreme sadness. She took the hat off and placed it on the desk. Tears were trickling down her cheeks. "I was in shock. I could not speak. When I heard you tell…" She choked up and took a moment to compose herself before continuing. "When you told Garibaldi about what had happened in Milan…. That is how I learned that my brother, Piero, had been murdered by the Austrians."

"I am so, so very sorry, "I said. "Had I known… Had I recognized you sooner, I would have… I would not have blurted it out so."

"Well, it's okay." Her mood shifted back and lightened, "It was seven years ago and if I recall correctly Garibaldi did have a gun pressed against your stomach."

"And you were waving one as well."

"Oh, that. Yes."

"So, Garibaldi, Giuseppe Mazzini, *Giovine Italia*, how, how do you fit in and what do you mean he wants his hat back?"

Isabella turned serious, "It is a long story, but the quick of it is this. I worked for them. I still do. We're reorganizing. The revolution is coming and that single thought is stronger than an army. Giuseppe Mazzini wants to know if you are in or out. And if you are out, he wants his hat back, if you are…"

I took the hat from off the desk and put it securely on my head. She nodded approval. My heart fluttered again, even if those beats were forever making my head its fool. Not wanting to break off this conversation but aware I needed to get back to Verdi and Strepponi, I asked Isabella, "Can we, can we talk later, maybe dinner after your shift? I need to…"

"Of course," she exclaimed. "I suppose I owe you that much. You were the first boy I ever loved."

"Ay, *è vero*? It's true?" I asked.

"Si. È vero. There are some things that are beautiful and handsome, even when they are imperfect, and one of these, I am sure, is you."

"Then, please, one last question before I go."

"Si?"

"Do you still love me?"

"Ah, Dario, don't be silly. I don't know you, you the grown man."

"Okay, fair enough. Then one more last question before I go back inside?"

"Certo, certainly."

"Mi vuoi sposare?" I asked, "Will you marry me?"

I dreamed her answer came with the most magical, wonderful kiss of a lifetime, but in truth all she would say is, "Later, we'll talk… Now, go sing with your friends. Go."

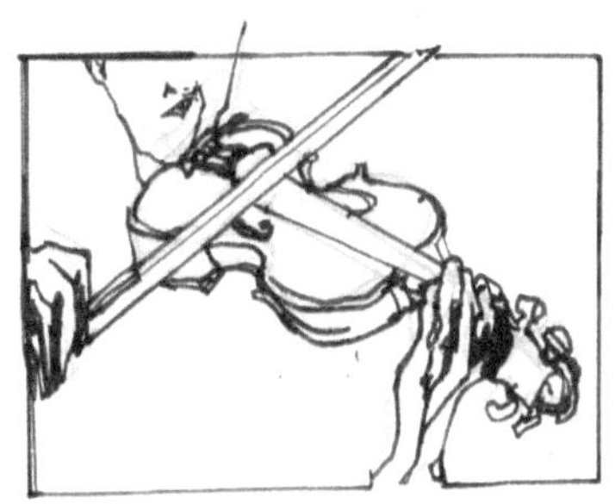

Chapter Five:
The Fate Of Jerusalem

Busseto, late August 1839

If you asked back then what my role in the *Risorgimento* was, or how I earned the right to keep that blue fedora, I would have just shrugged my shoulders and feigned ignorance.

Yes, every day, we, the members of *Giovine Italia* were preparing for a revolution that needed rifles, ammunition, supplies and most importantly, information. Although the various leaders of the movement, such as Garibaldi and Giuseppe Mazzini remained in exile, their followers still numbered in the tens of thousands. Uncle Roberto, Isabella, Verdi and I were among them. We had become part of a vast but invisible ghost network of traders and travelers across all of the northern Italian states. Hidden behind the guise of our everyday lives, we became smugglers, gunrunners, messengers and when necessary, guerilla fighters.

And yes, we even refitted our old wagons, such as the ones my father and I used to bring supplies to all of the outlying estates and farms of Busseto, with well camouflaged false bottoms. Beneath cases of wine, or cheese or under sacks of flour and rice, we hid rifles, muskets, pistols, which were covertly passed around to our fellow countrymen and women in advance of uprisings.

And yes, Verdi and I also perfected the art of writing those *Canzonatini* with which the leadership of *Giovine Italia* was thus able to coordinate with our partisans and revolutionaries secretly and efficiently. In accordance with the strategies laid out in *Rules for the Conduct of Guerilla Bands*, our fighters had taken on the onerous task of raiding Austrian soldiers and their military outposts. We were after all, soldiers in what became a series of three wars of independence and freedom. Now I call share the truth, a truth that might inspire future generations here and abroad to do the same when faced with oppression.

Nonetheless, I did not earn the right to keep my blue fedora until after my first date with Isabella – a carefully calculated and executed ambush of an Austrian military patrol. I joined Isabella and her squad of a dozen partisans on a woody hillside overlooking a narrow stretch of highway between Milan and the Duchy of Parma. Each of us carried a musket and two handguns. Our goal was to pick off the officers and scouts in the front and back of each column, which we did with surgical precision after Isabella – our best gunner - gave the signal. Then, rather than engage the full force of the army, we immediately vanished like ghosts back into the hills.

Not only did this regularly repeated tactic minimize our risk of causalities, these lightning-fast partisan ambushes rapidly spread fear and terror throughout the Austrian army. No one wanted to lead, no one wanted to be in the rear guard. To serve in those positions usually meant death from a nearly invisible enemy. This strategy quickly furthered our goal of demoralizing the enemy troops, most of whom were poor conscripts who had little desire to fight in the first place.

The Austrian commanders had no good answer for our continual assaults except to throw more troops out into the countryside. But when they did that, other partisan units would switch tactics and raid the patrols inside the cities. We, the ghost fighters of *Giovine Italia* disappeared at will, only to strike again when and where we were least expected.

Our little victories did however create complications. In August, right after the *Ferragosto* holiday, Verdi, Margherita and Icilio were attempting to return to Busseto to visit their families and more importantly to attend my wedding to Isabella in our town's little *sinagoga ebraica* – the Jewish synagogue. During this trip, Verdi was required to make adjustments to his opera score. Based on Strepponi's recommendation, Bartolomeo Merelli had agreed to use *Oberto* as the opera for his fundraiser for the Pio Institute benefit concert to be held at La Scala in mid-November. Strepponi herself, however, had to bow out due to health issues of her own, thus compelling Verdi to adjust his score to fit the voice of Antonietta Marini, the soprano hired to replace her.

When the coach carrying Verdi and his family approached its border with the Duchy of Parma, they were met by three Austrian soldiers, a young private, an older sergeant and their commander, a handsome Lieutenant who had his left arm bandaged and in a sling. In fear of our guerilla activity, the Austrian military had set up guard posts throughout the entire southern region of Lombardy. As these were tense and often violent times, every stagecoach was stopped and searched.

The young Austrian Cavalry Lieutenant snapped out orders in both German and Italian as he opened the door to the stagecoach transporting Verdi, his family and several other passengers.

"Bitte alle raus aus der Postkutsche. Please, everyone out of the stagecoach. *Hände hoch, bitte.* Hands up, please. *Schnell Bitte;* Quickly please. Leave everything inside," he added as the private and the older grizzled sergeant began to search the outside of the wagon. "Men over there, woman and children," he said as he waved the coachmen down with a sword he held in his right hand. Using his saber as a pointer, he indicated which spots he wanted everyone to stand during the inspection.

Verdi put away the musical score he had been working on and slipped the papers into his leather portfolio. There was reason for concern. Not only was Verdi transporting a *Canzonatini,* just a few days earlier, our partisan squad had assassinated two soldiers in a skirmish near this very border post. While discreetly studying the Austrians and wondering if the Lieutenant had been wounded in that assault, Verdi assisted Margherita down the steps of the wagon. She held Icilio tightly to her chest. Out of an abundance of caution, Verdi said nothing to the soldiers as he joined the other men standing beside the road. Verdi knew back then these Austrian conscripts far from home were often unpredictable when dealing with we Italians whom they viewed with suspicion. Margherita, likewise moved quietly while gently rocking Icilio and stood with the other women.

The lieutenant inspected everyone's travel documents while his men first scoured the outside of the coach and finding no contraband, they then searched the inside.

"Ah, we'll eat well tonight," yelled the sergeant as he pulled back the cover of a large picnic hamper belonging to the Verdis and waved it out the open door of the wagon. He had rifled through the contents, which included wine, bread, sausages, cheese, some fruit and fresh vegetable.

"That's for my son," pleaded Margherita, "That's all we have to eat on this trip."

"Not this *Liebfraumilch*," The sergeant roared with laughter as he sabered the top off one of their wine bottles and began to drink.

"Lieutenant, sir! I found something!" Yelled the private. He had Verdi's portfolio containing his opera score and the *Canzonatini*. These he hurried over to the Lieutenant. "This might be it," said the private as he flipped through the pages. "There are pictures of fortresses, an attack on a castle and notes in Italian."

Clearly disturbed and agitated by these remarks, the Lieutenant sheathed his sword and grabbed the portfolio. He rummaged through the papers closely, "Whose are these? Step forward."

Verdi was concerned. The *Canzonatini* contained very specific instructions about how the arms and ammunition stored in the basement of the *sinagoga ebraica* were to be distributed to our partisans. Not wanting to aggravate the officer further, he complied at once, "They're mine."

After examining the papers more closely, the Lieutenant's demeanor abruptly changed and a smile appeared on his face. "This is an opera, yes? You're composing an opera entitled *Oberto*?"

"*Si*," replied Verdi, who was definitely relieved by the Lieutenant's shift in attitude. "It's going to open at La Scala in November – if I ever finish it."

"And these little songs here?" the Lieutenant began to hum as he sight-read the notes. "They're lovely and these bars here, why that even echoes the *Marseillaise.*

Verdi began to sweat profusely. "Those are just some little *canzoni* – songs - for a wedding march. Is there a problem?"

"Where are you going now, *Signor* Verdi?" The Lieutenant asked.

"Home to Busseto with my family. I'm to conduct the music for my best friend's wedding."

"Congratulazioni al tuo amico," said the Lieutenant as he handed the portfolio back to Verdi. "I used to be a violinist at the Emperor's *Kärntnertor* Theater. The great impresario, Bartolomeo Merelli, himself, hired me as First Violin for the opera."

"È vero?" asked Verdi, grateful that a random Austrian cavalry officer, a musician at that, had failed to realize that the *Canzonatini* was actually a secret dispatch.

"Yes, concert master for the opera. But now I am Lieutenant Samuel Kreisler, of his Royal Majesty's Dragoons at your service." The officer extended his right hand to Verdi, "Yes, Mozart, Rossini, Donizetti, I performed them all. But Beethoven's *Fidelio*, and its cry for freedom from despots, that was my favorite."

"What happened? How is it you now wield a sword instead of a bow?" asked Verdi

"A woman."

"A woman?" repeated Verdi.

"Ah, yes," began the Lieutenant wistfully, "A woman, a beautiful woman, a prima diva. An affair, a sublime one. But alas our Emperor Ferdinand had his eyes on her as well. Certainly, you must have heard of her; Giuseppina Strepponi."

"Strepponi?" Though taken aback by this, Verdi stayed stone-faced. "Yes, indeed, a fine singer. What happened?"

"When I was younger, my father wanted me to follow in his footsteps and become a doctor. I wanted to be a violinist, and the Emperor? He just wanted me gone. My orders came the next day. 'Trade your violin for a sword and lance.' And, so here I am, rummaging through food hampers with one arm to stop smugglers while the Emperor proclaims his divine right of kings to do whatever he wants. Hardly seems fair, but orders are orders. And given this wound, who knows if I'll ever be able to ever play my violin again?"

"May I wish you good fortune," said Verdi. "It would be a blessing for us all to have you away from here and back in the orchestra pit."

"Thank you."

Verdi nodded.

Finally, after reviewing everyone's travel documents and passports, the Lieutenant decided that no one on the coach presented a threat. He ordered everyone back onboard, but not before instructing his Sergeant to return the food basket to Margherita. "These are good people. We're going to let them pass."

This did not please the Sergeant but he did as ordered.

"*Grazie*," replied Margherita who also knew the danger they had faced. "You are too kind." She rummaged through the hamper until she found a small package inside. "Here Lieutenant. For you and your men."

As Lieutenant Kreisler unwrapped the package, his eyes lit up with delight when he saw it contained, "A dozen *Cannoli al pistacchio*?"

"From Ca' Dario," added Margherita.

"Ca' Darío? Ah, bless you, *Signora*. I love Ca' Dario. Bless you all," added Kreisler as shared them with the other soldiers.

A few hours later Verdi and his family finally arrived in Busseto. They settled in at the Barezzi residence, where they would be staying for the next few weeks. Exhausted from the trip and needing to calm his nerves after the encounter at the border, Verdi set out alone on a walk through his hometown. August always delivered the most extreme heat and on this particular afternoon it was still uncomfortably warm in the village. Windows everywhere were open to catch what little breeze came on the heels of sunset and with that came the sounds of households going about their usual summer routines. As Verdi neared the *Via Giudecca*, the Street of the Jews, where my parents lived, he could hear a choir of voices singing off in the distance. He followed the sounds right to the wide-open doors of the little two-story house that passed for our synagogue in Busseto. Stepping inside, Verdi found himself a bench in the back and listened.

Upstairs was a loft where, according to Sephardic tradition, women would not only pray separately from the men, they were hidden behind wooden lattice screens. This tradition was maintained by the choir as well. The women sang from above, while down below the men's choir would respond. With the High Holy days – Rosh Hashanah and Yom Kippur - as well as my wedding all happening in the next few weeks, the choir along with several musicians, were rehearsing a wide variety of psalms, songs and dances under the guidance of our cantor, Dr. Elia Segré, who also doubled as Busseto's only physician.

The congregation at our temple was so small, never numbering more than thirty families at most, that we relied upon visiting rabbis from other nearby towns to lead our services. And for my wedding, that visiting rabbi was going to be none other than our cousin from Ceneda, Rabbi Yael Spinoziano.

Verdi was entranced. Though he knew most of the singers and musicians, many of whom also performed for him in the town's *Filarmonica*, he had never heard any of them sing in Hebrew nor did he recognize any of the Ladino melodies with the exception of *Adío Querida, Violetta's Lament*. At this time of year, when the Jewish calendar was coming close to the end of its annual cycle, most of the psalms were inspired by the fifth and last book of the *Torah, Deuteronomy*, in which Moses leads the Hebrews to the edge of the Promised Land and Jerusalem. The songs were exotic and so different from all Verdi knew. Some were poignant and tragic, others joyful and uplifting. Nor had he ever heard a clarinet which one of our musicians whose family was originally from Budapest, played in the Klezmer style, one that drove the dance music into a frenzy similar to the wild peasant and gypsy rhythms of eastern Europe. Verdi was particularly taken with our Cantor Segré's profoundly deep bass voice, a voice so rough and gravely, a voice that seemed to come from the bowels of the earth itself, that it could raise the bones of the dead and set them happily dancing.

What impressed Verdi the most however was when Rabbi Spinoziano lifted up and practiced blowing the *shofar*, the ram's horn, used to call in the Hebrew New Year at Rosh Hashanah. The powerful trumpet-like blast of the *shofar* which rattled the very walls of the *sinagoga*, reminded Verdi of the *Canzonatini* that Lieutenant Kreisler had missed: there was enough ammunition and arms hidden beneath his feet in the basement to blow up most of Busseto. Yes, Jews fight too; the revolution was everywhere and we were all prepared for our part.

After sitting and listening quietly for the better part of an hour, Verdi slipped back out the door and headed into town where he was due to join Margherita, Isabella and me at Figaro, my father's *salumeria*.

Isabella and I had arrived in town a few days earlier than the Verdis. Both my parents who were well aware of the tragic history of the Lusardi family, had welcomed Isabella in as the daughter they never had – a gesture most gratefully appreciated by my bride. Instead of taking the public coaches, we had driven one of the larger wagons my uncle normally used for delivering supplies to and from Ca' Dario. And as you may have guessed by now, not only did I have a number of *Canzonatinis* in my possession, our wagon also had a false bottom. Beneath crates of produce, cheese and wine, were new rifles which were to be transferred and hidden prior to their being distributed to partisans who were scattered throughout the Duchy of Parma.

As restaurants went, Figaro was about as basic and simple an eatery as Ca' Dario was sophisticated and grand – a distinction that also could be applied to my father Jacopo and his twin, my Uncle Roberto. Nonetheless, both facilities were equally beloved by their patrons. Figaro served one dish and one dish only, a *salumi* platter of meats and cheese accompanied by chunks of freshly baked bread and local red wines served exclusively in bowls. The only question patrons ever had to signal to our server, *La Sordomuta*– who was both deaf and mute - was not "what they wanted," but simply, "how much?"

The three of us had just seated ourselves when Verdi arrived. *La*

Sordomuta came over to the table, Isabella smiled at her and raised four fingers. *La Sordomuta* smiled back, gave a nod, before returning our order to the kitchen.

Verdi, still bubbling over with enthusiasm over what he just heard at the *sinagoga,* asked, "Dario, why have you never told me about the music at the temple? It is marvelous, unique, tuneful, and yet, each melody is so poignant and soulful – ever more so than anything in the Catholic Mass. And though the music is exotic, especially with that clarinet playing in that Klezmer style, the emotions behind those Ladino melodies feel as if they emerge from the very soil of the earth itself."

Clearly the sounds of our *sinagoga* had made a surprisingly deep musical impression upon Verdi, one that you will find echoes of throughout his many works.

"Exotic?" questioned Isabella, "Only if you haven't sung them since infancy."

"I thought you grew up at *La Corte degli Angeli* and not off the *Via Giudecca*?" Margherita asked of Isabella.

"I did," replied Isabella as *La Sordomuta* delivered our food and wine, "But my mother was Jewish and she sang to me every day, all day as she worked in the kitchens there."

"How sweet," replied Margherita.

"Well then, on that note, let's toast," said Verdi lifting up his wine bowl and paraphrasing a line from Da Ponte's libretto for *Così Fan Tutte*, "Blessed be Dario and Isabella, his lovely bride. To your wedding, to your happiness. May a kindly heaven smile upon you both and in the way that hens and roosters are, may you be prolific with progeny equal to you in beauty and sweetness!"

"*Grazie mille,*" I declared as we all clinked our bowls together and drank heartily.

"What about your family, Isabella? Will any of them becoming to the wedding? Asked Margherita.

"Only my mother lives, the rest..." Isabella's voice petered out and the light in her eyes went dead.

Margherita sensed something was wrong, deeply wrong here but tread lightly. "Oh, your mother, where is she?"

Isabella pointed to *La Sordomuta*, who by now was leaning peacefully against a wall in the back of the *salumeria*, her eyes keenly surveying all that passed before. Although she was grey-haired, *La Sordomuta's* face had all the beauty of a classical Greek goddess.

Margherita was taken aback and a bit embarrassed, "The deaf mute? *La Sordomuta*? She's your mother? But I thought you said…."

"*La Sordomuta*," replied Isabella very slowly and with a measured but strained tone. "*La Sordomuta* – a deaf mute is what she became, not who she is. *La Sordomuta* is what they did to her. Her name, my mother's real name is Sophia, Sophia Benedetto Lusardi and she is one of the most brilliant and scholarly women Busseto has ever known."

Sensing my fiancée's discomfort at having to repeat a story so painful and tragic, I put a supportive arm over her shoulder as she continued to share her family's bitter history. "I was only fifteen when our family, the Lusardis, were evicted, sent into exile, without any warning or notice by *Il Diavolo* of *La Corte degli Angeli,* the old Duke of Mantua and by his even more diabolical son, Cesare."

"Father Abbondio's uncle?" asked Margherita.

"Yes, the same," replied Isabella. "There were seven of us still living there and I was the youngest. Some of my older step-brothers and sisters had already grown up and, desperate to find work, had moved away. Those of us thrown off the estate were two step-brothers, including Piero, both my parents, and two very elderly and frail step-grandparents, Beppo and Aurora. My father's parents were both in their late eighties and they were, well, you know, too old to understand what was happening. Both been born at *La Corte degli Angeli*, and neither of them had ever known another home. We had no place to go, no shelter from the winter, and no idea what to do next. Gathering up what little possessions we had, we started walking. My mother, Sophia, was a very learned woman who assembled a great a wall of books in the kitchen storeroom at *La Corte degli Angeli.* She surrendered them all, carrying away only a single unbound leather volume, *Una Festa d'Amore*, - *A Feast of Love* - that might have been the finest and most exhaustive collection of recipes in all Italy. I wore almost everything I owned to stay warm. Where to go, no one knew. We needed shelter and we needed food and we needed work, but one by one we found the gates of all the other estates in the region were closed to us."

Isabella took a deep breath and swallowed hard as she reached back into the dark recesses of her memories. "It had been a drought and a particularly bad harvest that prior Autumn. Every farm in the region was struggling. All over the Duchy of Parma, the padrones were discharging their part time farm workers or those too weak to carry full workloads. The roads were filled with the homeless, the penniless and the starving. First Beppo, and then Aurora became sick and disoriented. On the morning after our third night on the road, we awoke to find my grandparents frozen in each other's' arms, dead from exposure. When we carried their bodies to a church in a nearby village to plead for a paupers' burial, we were turned away and called troublemakers by none other than that pig, Father Abbondio, who was, after all, a Briscola himself. He yelled and chased us off, declaring that we as "Hebrews and half-breeds had no right to salvation in the Holy Mother Church's consecrated soil."

"Oh, my God," said Margherita. She reached across the table and took Isabella's hand in her own in a gesture of simply compassion. The two young women locked eyes with each other before Margherita added, "How cruel. What could you do?"

"Yes, we were desperate," said Isabella, nodding with appreciation at being heard and her pain understood. "We waited until nightfall. In a sheltered patch of woods on the edge of some grand estate, my father and my brothers dug a pit, into which we buried poor Beppo and Aurora. Our efforts did not go unnoticed. The next morning a gang of thugs, at least five of them, including two of the Duke's sons, Cesare and Dante and their henchman, Rocco Pietra, attacked and beat us with sticks. *Mamma* tried to shield herself from Cesare's blows with her cookbook, but he nevertheless repeatedly smacked her about the head and left her to die. Blood gushed everywhere. My father and my brother, Marco, who tried to protect Sophia, were beaten to death. Dante Briscola threw me to the ground with the intent of raping me. While that bastard struggled to rip off the multiple layers of clothes I had been forced to wear, Piero swept in and slit his throat from behind, baptizing me in Dante's blood. Cesare, seeing his younger brother fall dead, was enraged. He dove towards Piero, but my brother quickly spun around and slashed Cesare across the face, leaving a wide scar. With that, the bastards fled, but not before swearing to get their revenge."

"All this here in our Parma," muttered Verdi, shaking his head in disbelief. "Such barbarity. And no justice. Not what one what's to believe about their homeland, but I know this brutality is all too real. At least their cousin, Father Abbondio was roasted on the spit for his own savagery."

All four of us nodded in agreement.

Isabella took a deep breath and sighed before she could continue, "Piero was certain the Briscola thugs would return with guns and knives and more allies. With no time to lose, we quickly bandaged my mother, and carried her away. We had no choice but to leave the bodies of my father and brother behind… Imagine, *la mia famiglia,* a feast for the wild boars."

Margherita gasped, "And you were only fifteen? To know such horrors, as a child."

"*Si,* it still gives me nightmares when I picture them lying there on the ground, blood everywhere. Still, I don't know how Piero did it. Somehow, he led us cross country through the woods and fields until we were able to sneak into Busseto at night. We got *Mamma* back to the Jewish community here. Mercifully she was taken in and sheltered by our cousins from the Guastalla family. Can you imagine," she said, "My mother, this once beautiful and vibrant woman, who used to sing me to sleep with her gorgeous voice, was left a deaf mute by these pigs. And now, she's unable to hear or speak a single word."

Isabella sighed and took another deep breath. And then another. And then a third. This was not easy, but she continued, "And Piero, knowing that *Il Diavolo* would put a price on our heads, insisted we escape from the Duchy of Parma immediately. We left *Mamma* and her cookbook behind and before sunrise, together we fled Busseto. We traveled only by night through the mountain passes and over the border to Savoy. I can't tell you how hard that was but we eventually made it to the port at Genoa. From there we hoped to catch a boat to America. In Genoa, while trying to beg, borrow or steal enough to pay for our passage, we met and ultimately fell in with Garibaldi, Giuseppe Mazzini, and the partisans of *Giovine Italia*. When we told them of our misfortune, they listened with great compassion. Afterwards Garibaldi remarked that they had heard similar tales hundreds, if not thousands of times from all over the Italian states. Giuseppe Mazzini told us that wealth and power are ultimately the same element, and that since the wealth of a nation remains relatively constant, the only variables are who controls that wealth and what percentage of the population holds that power? In our Europe, he explained, it is the aristocracy, a mere one percent of our population, that controls upwards of ninety percent of the economy. The only way these horrors we described would ever stop was when the aristocrats and land barons were overthrown by a democratic revolution for and by the people, the peasants of Italy. Just like the French and Americans had done. *'Viva la rivoluzione!'* he declared and we, Piero and I signed on."

By the time Isabella finished telling this bitter history, Margherita, who was in tears herself, was hugging and consoling my bride. "How do you endure all of this?" she asked.

"I sing," replied Isabella.

"She has a lovely mezzo voice," I quickly added in.

"Singing?" questioned Margherita, "You mean singing prayers and hymns?"

"No," Isabella laughed. "No, not hymns, not prayers. This."

Isabella stood up and without fanfare or introduction she began to belt out at the top of her lungs, Figaro's Aria, the *Largo al Factotum*, from Rossini's, *The Barber of Seville: "Make way for the factotum of the city. Hurrying to his shop now that it is already dawn..."*

As soon as she started in, everyone else in the *salumeria* stopped whatever it was they were doing and joined in to support her with rhymical clapping. Obviously, this was not the first time someone had sung *Figaro* there.

From across the room, her mother, Sophia, who could clearly see what was happening, smiled a smile that was broad enough to span the River Jordan. She too joined in the clapping.

And as Isabella came to climatic moment, those famous calls of "*Figaro, Figaro, Figaro,*" my *papà*, Jacopo, joined in with his deep bass voice and together as a duet they continued to sing.

And when they finished, every single patron in the *salumeria* stood up and gave Isabella a rousing salute, with the grandest applause of all coming from her mother.

"You have more courage than any woman I have ever known." Margherita embraced Isabella, a gesture of acceptance, support and if you will, sisterhood that my bride, a poor peasant girl, not only deeply appreciated, it was a kindness she swore to honor and would never forget.

"No, not I, *Mamma, mia madre*, she's the one," Isabella replied as she not only blew a kiss across the room to Sophia, but also communicated to her mother using some sort of sign language. Sophia signaled back to her daughter and then sent a kiss to her. "We will win. For every Briscola, for every padrone, for every brute, there are a hundred of us. The aristocrats may have the army, they may have the clergy, but we have the people and the people will never be defeated. Like our ancestors driven into exile by the Babylonians of old, we shall return and reclaim our land and our country from those parasites. I will not stop until we put a stake through the heart of those vampires at *La Corte degli Angeli* who have sucked every drop of blood from our veins."

"You're certain of that?" asked Verdi, deeply impressed by her passion and the depth of her commitment.

"*Assolutamente!* Never again will we allow ourselves to be victims. Never again. Of that I am certain or I will die trying. Cesare Briscola and the others who murdered my family will pay along with all of their allies and thugs. This is one young Jewess who knows how to load a musket and shoot a gun. And I am not afraid to use it," concluded Isabella. And it was abundantly clear to all that evening that she meant it. Yes, and need I tell you, that after dinner Isabella and I would devote ourselves to transferring the rifles we had smuggled in from Milan to a smaller wagon destined for the peasants at *La Corte degli Angeli?*

That is the woman I married - *La Sordomuta's* daughter - in *La Sinagoga di Busseto.* After that first date, how could I marry another?

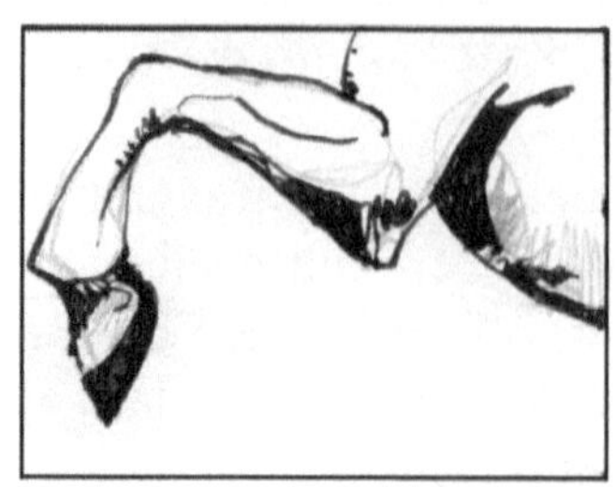

Chapter Six:
Play The Sounds of a Sad Lament

Milan, November 17, 1839

On Sunday evening Giuseppe Verdi and I headed over to La Scala for the premiere of his first ever opera, *Oberto, Count of San Bonifacio.* As we crossed the square in front of the Duomo, Verdi was characteristically tight-lipped. I could sense he was staring inward, nervously scanning every corner of his thoughts, as if trying to remember what, if anything, he had forgotten. Had he given all his notes to the singers? Would the conductor remember to pause after the crescendo? Had they fixed the oboe's score where the copyist had put a sharp instead of a flat? I said nothing. This was his day, one Verdi had earned through endless years of persistence, talent, and passion. And tonight, we would learn if the world – or at least the two thousand people in the audience – admired Verdi's musicianship as much as we all did.

We entered the theater from the artists' entrance on the side of the hall and quickly found Bartolomeo Merelli in his office.

"Nervous?" the impresario asked Verdi, who only shrugged in reply.

"Did you get the box we requested?" I asked.

"Of course. I had to evict Bishop Giuliani and his lover, but it is my theater," relied Merelli, "Second Tier, Stage Right, Box Thirteen. Did you expect anything less for our Maestro here on his virgin voyage?"

"Perfect," I said, though from the scowl on Verdi's face I could see he did not appreciate being considered an opera house virgin –

but he remained tight-lipped. And to hear that Merelli pushed Bishop Giuliano Giuliani out in favor of Verdi, now that was heavenly justice.

Regulars at La Scala know that the theater is essentially six horseshoe shaped tiers of seats stacked one upon the other. Many patrons believe that the best seats are either those on the main floor or the handful of luxury boxes that are closest to the stage. Still others would place high value on those reserved boxes clustered around the Royal enclosure in the center and back of the theater, reasoning if the Emperor sat there, the seats must be the very best. All of them would be wrong.

And here is why: sight and sound. To fully enjoy and appreciate great opera, you need to have those two elements in perfect balance. Seats on the main floor, close as they may be, lack the necessary height to be able to fully view the depth and complexity of the sets on stage used for most big operas. The close in boxes are also troublesome as they are essentially perpendicular to the stage. Although they may be wonderful for impressing the grandees and gossips sitting in those boxes opposite and across the way, one always has to strain one's neck to actually see. And hearing? Forget about it. Those seats are plagued by sound dead spots. And those regal boxes in the back surrounding the two-story tall Royal encampment, well, they offer a great sightline, but are simply too far away from the stage to actually see the faces of the singers or comprehend the emotions they are expressing.

No, for my tastes, the best seats for anyone actually interested in watching and listening to an opera are those midway around the curve of the horseshoe. And the best one of those at La Scala is Box Thirteen on the second level. First off, you are high enough up – but not too high - to see the full depth and breathe of the performers on stage. Next, you can also observe the conductor and musicians in the pit and, most importantly, in this part of the theater, the sounds of the orchestra and the singers blend perfectly and with the greatest clarity.

As Merelli handed me our seat tickets, he said, "Oh, and Dario, this package just arrived from a Rabbi Spinoziano in Ceneda. It's addressed to both of you."

"What's the good Rabbi want?" Verdi asked, breaking his silence. The two men had gotten to know each other during the preparations for the wedding. "Or maybe, do you think he is sending me a prayer for the success of *Oberto*?"

"Well, my friend, you did impress the Rabbi," I said to Verdi as I put the package under my arm, "He likes your music very much, and he appreciates your political sentiments, so, yes, maybe it is a blessing on your behalf. He knows opera like great food, is about passion, human passion. And the rabbi comprehends its ability to move and inspire people. Everybody in Ceneda does, especially the Jews. It is after all, Da Ponte's hometown. Rabbi Yael's father, Baruccio Spinoziano, was Da Ponte's, that is to say, Emanuele Conegliano's rabbi. Come, let's go up to our box. I'll open it there."

Tense as he was, Verdi could barely even manage a hint of a smile – but I knew it was there. Who doesn't like the prospect of a surprise gift?

In the first few weeks following his return to Milan from our wedding in Busseto, Verdi could not have been happier nor more content with the promises of his life. He was in love with Margherita, thrilled at being a father to Icilio, and ecstatic to be residing in a city synonymous with opera. With his first score, *Oberto, Count of San Bonifacio*, finally scheduled to premiere at La Scala, Verdi finally felt that he had knocked at the right door, one that would open up to a life as an opera composer.

And we, his loyal friends, were equally thrilled for him. Looking back to that time from the prospective of the old man I have become now, it was "*Era un momento più semplice, più naturale* - It was a simpler, more natural time." Yes, even when we radicals, revolutionaries and partisans fought, we shed blood for the right to have nothing more complex than a good and happy life.

The crisp air of autumn had replaced the stale and oppressive heat of summer and for those first few weeks everything seemed right in the world. My bride and I moved into that three-story house I had purchased, which Verdi immediately nicknamed *Casa di Trevi*, after the alliterative rhythm of the three "V's" of "Via Vittorio

Veneto." Together Isabella and I spent many a day wandering through the markets and used furniture stores, purchasing this and that for our new home. Remember that my bride grew up so poor at *La Corte degli Angeli*, that she never really owned anything beyond that which she could wear or carry. Shopping was a new experience. Though Verdi and Margherita were still struggling financially, they would occasionally join us on these ventures. The two women had by now become inseparable friends. But yes, even on the eve of his first opera, the Verdis were still living month to month on loans from his father-in-law, Antonio Barezzi, and an advance from Merelli against the eventual gate receipts for *Oberto*. Oh, and clearly, Verdi and Margherita knew that their future depended on the success – or failure - of *Oberto*.

On October 10th, the occasion of Verdi's twenty-sixth birthday, we two couples along with fourteen-month-old Icilio, had gathered at Ca' Dario for a small celebration. I treated the Verdis to his favorite dessert, a *torta al pistacchio*, and several bottles of Conegliano Prosecco which I retrieved from Uncle Roberto's private stash in the wine cellar, yes, the same cellar where we hid our weapons-in-transit. Yes, for whenever war came to Lombardy, Uncle Roberto insisted we be prepared.

In turn, Verdi congratulated us for buying our *Casa di Trevi* and then he presented us with a housewarming gift that he found in one of our local flea markets. It was a fanciful painting of the Trevi Fountain in Rome that was identical in style to the murals on the walls of our *Il Colosseo* dining room at Ca' Dario. He declared, "May your joy and happiness flow as freely as these waters." The painting was signed by one of the formerly impoverished but later highly respected artist whom my uncle had once supported, Barbarina Francini. Even after all these years, her painting still hangs over the fireplace at our *Casa di Trevi*.

In addition to all I had just mentioned, there was much to be joyful about. Isabella, who by now was bouncing Icilio on her knees, went next.

"I'm pregnant!" she announced.

This caught everyone, including me, off guard. But I could not have been happier. Dreams can come true. The lives we had all wanted, were beginning to unfold. After I hugged my bride for what seemed like an ungodly long time, the four of us clinked our glasses in salute.

"May our child grow up in a free and democratic Italy!" I declared.

"Here, here!" added Verdi clinking my glass once again. "*Viva l'Italia!*"

Viva la rivoluzione! But," continued Isabella, "Here I am, I love opera. I am now married to an opera singer, and toasting an opera composer but I have never ever seen a real opera. *Oberto* will be my first one."

This surprised Margherita, "You have never seen an opera?"

"What peasant child from *La Corte degli Angeli* could afford La Scala? Not this one. Not even the cheap standing room tickets on the top floor. And what would I wear? I have only the clothes of a poor farm girl from Busseto."

"I can help you with that," said Margherita, who, as the daughter of an affluent merchant of Busseto always had a closet full of gowns. "We'll find you something perfect for the premiere."

"Something perfect," mused Isabella, "I would love that. Thank you, Margherita."

"Yes, I can see you wearing this lovely blue turquoise one, yes, that's the one, and there's a jacket to match."

"If you have never seen a performance," asked Verdi, "How do you know you love opera? Is it the music, the songs? Do you know them?"

"Of course, the music, everyone knows the music. As I told you before, my mother always sang to me, but...."

"What then?" asked a puzzled Margherita, "What is it you love about opera?"

"The hair!" laughed Isabella as she ran her hands through Icilio's golden locks. "I love the hair."

Her remark puzzled us all.

"The hair?" Margherita asked.

"Yes, the hair," insisted Isabella.

We were all dumbfounded.

"The hair?" Verdi and I asked again in unison.

"Of course, the hair," she argued again. "Everyone wears a wig. How do you think I have supported myself all these years? I have been selling my hair to the costume designers and wigmakers since I was a child."

This set Verdi laughing, "I had never thought of hair as a crop to be harvested."

"Then, my dear Icilio," replied Isabella as she nuzzled and kissed the boy on his cheeks, "There is much your *papà* still has to learn of about the lives and labors of our people. My parents, slaving away for *Il Diavolo* and the Briscolas, barely earned enough to keep us alive. If my sisters and I had not sold our hair, we would have starved to death."

"Amen," said Margherita. She reached across the table and put a hand on Isabella's. "I have faith we will change the world, but thank God you are here with us now. Such a blessing…"

Isabella, however, suddenly turned serious as she put her hand on Icilio's forehead. "He's burning up. Your son has a fever."

****

After Verdi and I settled into our seats in Box Thirteen, I opened the Rabbi's package. Inside, wrapped in a blue velvet cloth bag was a letter, a silk scarf and the very *shofar* Verdi had admired in Busseto. I handed Verdi the ram's horn and said, "This is a gift to you from Rabbi Spinoziano."

Verdi was stunned. He held the *shofar* in his hands as delicately as if it were a sacred relic. "I can't believe he gave me this. What do I do? How do I play it?"

"Oh, there are instructions," I told him and then reading from the note, "The Rabbi writes, 'Consider your destiny in this era of travail.

When the time comes to destroy the walls of our enemies and bring down the emperors who oppress us, put your lips together and blow. If we are fortunate, your clarion calls will succeed. And if you fail, let's hope reinforcements arrive in time to save us all.'"

"That's it? That's all? Your rabbi is quite the politician, isn't he? And a comedian too. Yet when I was at your *sinagoga* I had the impression, that the *shofar* was only used for sacred rituals?"

"Sacred?" I laughed, "Rabbi Spinoziano is much like Giuseppe Mazzini, both are first and foremost humanists. To him, the only truly sacred things are those actions which serve to uplift and support people: love, truth, justice. Objects and rituals are not sacred. A horn is just a horn. It had one purpose when its first owner, the ram, lived, and another purpose when it was transformed into a musical instrument. According to the rabbi, only two types of people imbue these objects and the rituals surrounding them with purported magical powers. The first are the superstitious and weak-minded, and the second are the dictators and tyrants who exploit the fears of the first group so as to rule over them."

"Your rabbi is a bit of a revolutionary too, eh?"

"Of course, being an outlier is the essence of being a Hebrew in a Christian world. Remember, fundamental to Judaism is our belief in the rule of law and equal justice for all – concepts that don't exist when emperors, kings have some made up divine right to rule as they please. Our very existence is a thorn pricking the hand of the aristocracy and the clergy. And when it comes to taking up arms against the empire, trust me, the Jews of Italy are there."

"Ah, I see, but doesn't the *shofar* have a special place in your High Holidays?

"Yes, of course. But it's not magic. It's a horn, just a horn used to call the congregation together in an age before clocks or brass trumpets came into existence."

"How very different from our churches where you cannot help but trip over one holy relic or another, bought and sold by the clerics. Does the good rabbi at least give any detailed instructions about how to play it?"

"Beyond putting your lips together? No. It takes some practice – just like we all learned to shoot rabbits with a hunting rifle growing up. That's all."

"And what's that he sent you?" Verdi asked.

I pulled the scarf out of the package. It was a hand woven one made of pure white silk with some blue line running horizontally near the two ends. "It looks like a *tallit*, but it's not," I said as I put it on. The blue even matched that of my ever-present fedora. I looked further in the note to see if there was an explanation.

"What's a *tallit*?" Verdi asked. "Is it that prayer shawl I saw the rabbi wearing at your wedding?"

I nodded, then read aloud from the rabbi's note. "Dario, an apple does not fall far from the tree whence it came, but being round like a matzo ball, it can roll far away before being eaten by some beast. So, my friend, when in the silk weavers' market of Ceneda, I found this scarf, one which reminds me of a *tallit,* but is not, I thought of you. May its gentle cloth keep you warm throughout your many travels while always reminding you of your roots."

"You get a scarf; I get an enigma. That's it?"

"There's nothing more in here about the *shofar*. The rest of his letter is about our American cousin, Emanuele Conegliano, Mozart's librettist, the one you know as Lorenzo Da Ponte."

"Da Ponte? Is he still around?"

"No, apparently not. That's what the letter reports. It seems that my cousin, the former *Abbé* Lorenzo Da Ponte, passed away in August of a year ago and was buried beside his wife, Celestina, in the graveyard of St. Patrick's. He was eighty-nine, and had outlived Mozart by nearly fifty years. Imagine that."

"Remarkable, what a life he led," said Verdi. "Our opera world is deeply indebted to him and sadly few today recognize his genius. Without Da Ponte, there'd be no Mozart. Da Ponte's home in Ceneda ought to be a shrine."

"Truly, I added, "But not only did he create the libretti for Mozart's best operas, he is the man who also introduced opera to America and started the first two theaters there in New York City.

But there's more here. Listen to this: The rabbi's letter goes on to say that a month after his Catholic funeral, the Hebrew friends of Emanuele Conegliano and his family, secretly and out of sight of authorities, removed those coffins from St. Patrick's and reburied them in the shade of an elm tree in the Jewish Cemetery of Shearith Israel. There, Emanuele and Celestina Conegliano will spend eternity in the company of their fellow Hebrew brethren in a land where the rule of law prevails over kings and their conspirators."

This news about the secret reburial stunned Verdi to the core, even though I had long ago described to him all about Da Ponte's life as a crypto-Jew.

"They did that? They actually did that? They reburied him? And in secret?"

"Yes, it was what he wanted. He told me that himself when I was there. He even showed me the spot he had picked out."

"So, Da Ponte really did live a life behind masks and capes?"

"Yes, it was his solution to living in a world that is hostile to Hebrews."

"And only in death could he return to himself?"

"Yes. It is true. He had to die to become a Jew again."

"That's tragic and a story worthy of an opera in and of itself. One I'd call *The Secret Life of Lorenzo Da Ponte*."

"Yes, indeed. But he will be a Jew for eternity," I said.

"Eternity?" Verdi laughed for the first time that day. "I don't believe in that Heaven and Hell nonsense. When you're dead, you're dead, there's no turning back."

Verdi lifted the *shofar* up to his lips, but when he blew into it, naught came out except his sputtering. His eyes watered, he tried again, nothing. And then the tears began to flow. Verdi dropped the *shofar* onto the floor and then began to sob uncontrollable.

"Icilio!" he wailed, "Icilio! Why? Why?" Verdi buried his face in his hands and the tears flowed as wildly and fierce as those once portrayed in *Violetta's Lament*.

****

When the first act of Oberto ended with its curtain drop and a smashingly good round of applause, Verdi looked at me, his face a wild map of emotions. "Wait here. I have to see Margherita."

Verdi scrambled out of our box and raced down the stairs until he reached the exit doors. He left La Scala at a gallop and then ran the half-dozen blocks all of the way back to his apartment on Via San Simeone. There, breathless, he found Margherita in the company of my Isabella, who was of course wearing that blue turquoise gown and the matching jacket.

Since the sudden death of Icilio four weeks earlier from a mysterious fever, Margherita had been inconsolable. Her grief had been so intense that not only was she unable to join us for the premiere, she had scarcely left their home since the funeral. And my Isabella, whose innate sense of empathy and compassion was unrivaled, insisted on staying by her side. If anyone understood, tragedy, it was my bride. She knew when to speak, when to be silent, when to listen and when to simply share tears. It went without saying that Isabella, who understood better than most what was truly important in our lives, would easily surrender the prospect of seeing her first opera to be in support and to be able console, Margherita.

Verdi hugged his wife in a long lingering moment of shared grief and then whispered, "It's going well. A success, so far."

Margherita could only manage the tiniest of smiles before collapsing again in tears.

****

Yes, the audiences and critics of Milan enjoyed *Oberto* sufficiently that Bartolomeo Merelli extended its run for a full fourteen performances, thirteen more than expected. Not only was the impresario pleased with the gate receipts, which he shared with Verdi, he also handed my friend a contract for three more operas, all to be staged at La Scala at eight-month intervals. In the midst of intense personal grief, Verdi had finally found his first small success along with a bit of a new cash flow to pay off his debts.

Additionally, Merelli introduced Verdi to the Ricordis, who in turn bought the publishing rights to *Oberto.* Through their efforts *Oberto* would soon appear on stages from Genoa to Trieste. Verdi's association with the House of Ricordi would continue uninterrupted for sixty-one years, that is until this afternoon, when all of us walked together behind the Verdis' funeral cortege from the *Cimitero Monumentale* to their tombs at the *Casa di Riposo per Musicisti.*

But I digress and must tell you that the road between there – six decades ago - and here today, was neither easy nor without even greater trials. Three wars, many deaths and much travail, most of which came at Verdi both as fast and fierce as the demonic Furies of Greek and Roman mythology. All of this began benignly enough when he was handed his next libretto to score, a comedy.

Bartolomeo Merelli asked Verdi to prepare the music for a lighthearted romance by Felice Romani, *Un Giorno di Regno.* As was his habit, Verdi immediately plunged into composing but uncharacteristically he found it unusually difficult and challenging. That had more to do with his own life and Margherita than the material at hand.

His wife's depression over losing both of her children was deep and profound. Even when Verdi suggested that they were still young and could have more children, Margherita declared in no uncertain terms that she was simply not ready to, as she described, "to move forward." Verdi, being a good husband and an intuitively sensitive soul, did not push or prod or provoke Margherita. He was as haunted by their deaths as she was and so he simply stood by her side. Verdi stayed compassionate, always sensitive to her pains and wishes. But none of this made Verdi's task of writing music for a comedy any easier.

Merelli, ever the business man, had scheduled the premier of *Un Giorno di Regno* for September. As the months began to slip away, Verdi, preoccupied with the weight of his family's personal tragedies, found that being "light-hearted" did not come naturally and his efforts to compose became an endless struggle.

Only when the blossoms of spring in Milan casted off the ferocity of winter, did Margherita's mood begin to lighten. Perhaps it was being around my Isabella, who had a May due date, and was ever more showing off her well-rounded belly, that helped pull Margherita out of her depression. The two had been almost inseparable through the dark months, each supporting the other through their respective trials. At last, Margherita began to go out more, see friends, and take a greater interest in the score her husband was composing.

Margherita even came to *Casa di Trevi* regularly, as everyone began to call our home, so as to assist Isabella in preparing a nursery room for our child. And the four of us set aside time to attend an opera together. Isabella's first and a perfect choice for a political partisan, was a revival at Teatro alla Canobbiana of Mozart and Da Ponte's, *The Marriage of Figaro*. She was fascinated to see why Napoleon considered the play's mocking of the aristocracy to be that first shot in the French Revolution.

Awaiting her first opera with the anticipation and awe of a child, Isabella could not help but smile. "*Viva Figaro! Viva la rivoluzione,*" She declared as we entered the theater. Yes, there was power in the politics of opera. And that was not an insignificant concern for the Austrians ruling Milan and Lombardy where our network of armed partisan grew exponentially each year.

Naturally, we procured a favorite box, Teatro alla Canobbiana's equivalent of La Scala's Box Thirteen for the performance. Margherita found another gown for my Isabella, one with purple highlights and lace that was tailored for a very pregnant mother to be. The audience scattered below us on the main floor was the usual mix of local Milanese citizens and Austrian soldiers in their starched grey dress uniforms. The private boxes were filled as well for this popular opera. Even the two upper most balconies – the standing room only areas that allowed entry for a handful of *pfennigs,* were packed tight as pickle barrels – and those "common folk" were in a boisterous mood long before the overture began.

As we settled into our seats, Verdi discreetly nudged my elbow and motioned towards the Royal Box. "There it is, the evil triumvirate, the Church, the Hapsburgs and their henchmen."

Much to my dismay I spotted Field Marshall Joseph Radetzky, the new commander of all of the Austrian forces in Lombardy sitting there. Radetzky's reputation for brutality exceeded that of his predecessor, the now deceased Commander Gaetz. Sitting in the box with the Field Marshall was Bishop Giuliani along with *Il Diavolo*, the Duke of Mantua, and his son, Cesare Briscola, Cesare's very pregnant wife, Duchessa Carlotta, and Rocco Pieta, one of their allies who also had a murderer's blood on his hands. I had heard that due to the Duke's declining health, the family had made their urban Milan mansion their primary residence instead of the far more remote *La Corte degli Angeli*. For fear of upsetting my pregnant bride, I said nothing to Isabella.

Radetzky was also no man's fool. His goal was to crush our *Giovine Italia* - and ours was to chase him out of Italy. The Field Marshall knew that most Lombards, who hated our Austrian overlords, were sympathetic to our movement and would voice their support anytime and anywhere if given the opportunity, including inside the opera houses of Italy. You need to understand that back then opera was not only the most popular of all entertainments in the Italian speaking world, it was the universal language that united us all. Every city and town had a theater and everyone, from peasants to the Pope, knew the songs and knew the stories.

And consequently, Radetzky was aware that opera houses which massed crowds into a single venue, would easily become sources of political combustion if not constrained. Therefore, as a means of inhibiting audiences from becoming overenthusiastic or out of control, the Field Marshall had imposed a ban on all encores as well as any other political display. But the tighter the Austrians squeezed, the more the citizens of Milan chaffed.

Just as the conductor walked onto the stage, Isabella turned and spoke to Verdi and me in a calm and controlled voice just above a whisper, "You needn't worry. I see them. I know *I Diavoli,* the devils, are there. I see them in my dreams, I see them in my nightmares. I see them every day. That they live without punishment is a crime against my family."

"And that they live," added Verdi, "That the Briscolas live in honor and glory in the eyes of the Emperor and the Pope is a crime against all humanity."

"Their judgement time will come. And when it does, we will end their rule," said Isabella. "We will end it."

"Come," said Verdi reaching out his arms until the four of were able to link our hands together, and then he repeated Isabella's words, "We will end it."

"We will end it," all four of us vowed in unison.

As soon as the orchestra began the now famous *Marriage of Figaro* overture, the audience – one noticeably more raucous than usual - began to clap and cheer. Every now and again from different quarters of the theater you could hear shouts of "Viva Figaro!"

And of course, as soon as the curtain rose, Isabella was quick to point out the singer's wig, "I wonder if she's wearing my hair?"

The first act began well enough with Susanna, Figaro's bride to be, expressing her fears for her virginity on her wedding night because their licentious boss, Count Almaviva, insists on sleeping with her first. The overly enthusiastic audience applauded everything, that is until the servant Figaro, launched into *Bravo, signor Padrone*. In this aria, Figaro proclaims his intention to outwit his boss, Count Almaviva. His goal? To prevent the lord from exercising that ancient right that would allow Almaviva to bed Susanna before their wedding. Just as the singer declared, *"Figaro has spoken!"* in the middle of his aria, a veritable snowstorm of confetti made up of red, white and green paper – the colors of the Italian flag - showered down upon the main floor from across the breadth and depth of the two upper balconies. The entire theater went wild as shouts of *"Viva Figaro, Viva l'Italia,"* drowned out the rest of the aria. The people of Lombardy were speaking up loudly and in public.

Field Marshall Radetzky did not hesitate. With loud blasts from his police whistle he ordered his soldiers into action. The opera was stopped and the theater ordered closed.

As everyone was pushed and shoved out onto the streets of

Milan under the brutal eye of his army, Verdi leaned into Isabella and said, "I hope you enjoyed the opera, but they're usually not this short."

Isabella smiled, "*Viva Figaro! Viva l'Italia!*"

As our group of four exited the crammed hallways into the lobby and then and out onto the night, horse mounted Austrian cavalry soldiers lined both sides of the street. Given the size of the crowds exiting the theater, there was hardly sufficient room for people to squeeze through and past the mounted guards and any number of audience goers were crushed or injured in the stampede that followed.

Exiting just ahead and to the right of us, was the Briscola clan. The old knife scar on Cesare's face had grown ugly and now marred the entire left side of his features. Cesare led his devil of an elderly father, through the masses by rudely pushing people out of his way. Some stumbled and fell toward the nervous horses – which in turn bucked and neighed dangerously. Rocco Pietra was doing the same for Cesare's pregnant wife, Duchessa Carlotta, pushing commoners beneath him to the left and right. As we started down a short series of steps toward the street, I instinctively put a protective arm around my Isabella when she bumped into the Duchessa. That got Pietra's attention.

Rocco Pietra stared back at Isabella, "You?" he blurted out as if perhaps recognizing her from their past encounter in the woods of Parma. But suddenly, and seemingly out of nowhere, Rocco Pietra tripped over someone's foot and fell face down the stairs. The crowd however kept pushing forward with a pressure that one could only deem as relentless. When Pietra struggled to get up, someone else in that stampeding mass of humanity booted Pietra from behind. That shove propelled the thug directly at one of the stallions of the mounted guards. The horse reared up high and threw its rider. The Duchessa screamed in panic. Cesare and his father turned around, only to see the horse's hoofs crashed back down and deal a fatal blow to Pietra's skull. And if that had not killed him, the crush of humanity that followed certainly would have.

We four hurried away and only when we were safely clear of the crowds, a disconcerted Margherita asked, "What just happened?"

"Count Pietra is dead," I said. "The horse killed him."

"I saw that," said Verdi. "But it looked as if he was intentionally tripped and kicked first."

Isabella turned and looked at the rest of us. "Pietra recognized me. He and Cesare are the ones who murdered my family?"

"God, no," uttered Margherita.

Isabella nodded. What she said next with utter calmness and clarity stunned us. "I killed him. I did that. I pushed him into the horses. I did that for my mother, my father my brothers and for my child. That scum of the earth deserved nothing less."

****

A few weeks later, on the morning of May 20th, my beloved Isabella went into labor. Margherita was with us at our *Casa di Trevi*, supporting my wife all the way through the delivery of my infant son, Tre, who finally arrived just before midnight.

But then, out of nowhere, a darkness fell over all our lives, a darkness so deep and all-encompassing that not even a glint of light escaped.

In early June, just three weeks after the birth of our son, Margherita was stricken with encephalitis. Verdi immediately sent word to her parents in Busseto to come right away.

On June eighteenth, surrounded by Verdi and the Barezzis, Margherita closed her eyes and passed from this world.

And *il mio amico* Verdi? Blind-sighted by the unexpected, he was devastated.

Chapter Seven:
Strengthen Us to Endure Our Suffering

Milan, March 9, 1842

Once more, from the comfort and security of Box Thirteen, Isabella and I watched as Verdi entered the orchestra pit from the wings. The applause from the frequently critical La Scala crowd was polite but restrained for this virtually unknown conductor. How Verdi had the courage to even do this, I am not sure. The journey for him from Margherita's death a year and a half earlier to the conductor's perch at La Scala would be unfathomable to anyone other than those who had experienced their lives derailed by immense personal tragedy.

Now dressed formally in a black suit with tails, Verdi shook hands with the concertmaster and then stepped up to the podium. With a half-turn he acknowledged the audience, which had filled La Scala to the last tier. What terrors Verdi hid behind his eyes would be impossible for any of us, his close friends and supporters, to comprehend or name.

When at last he raised his baton to begin the overture to his opera, I stared at that little stick in his hand and wondered how my friend had found the strength to lift it up, so staggering was the weight and pressure it must have represented for him.

Yes, after Margherita's passing, a darkness had fallen over my friend that was so deep I feared he would never survive, much less recover his former bravado and self-confidence. His dreams, his love, his family, his partner, had all been ripped from him. He was alone. His energy, his motivation, his zeal, all crushed. He wanted to simply surrender. He wanted to crawl back to Busseto and hide in some dark room where the light of day never penetrated. What did music, what did creativity, or even the revolution mean, if one's life suddenly lacked focus or even purpose? In the weeks that followed, Verdi was akin to an untethered boat swept downstream in a tempest of roaring tides. He wailed, he moaned, he cried out and he cursed the darkness. At night when he tried to sleep, he'd hear the ghosts of Margherita and his children screaming at him, "Where are you? Where are you?"

And in the middle of this, Bartolomeo Merelli, ever the impresario, held firm. After allowing Verdi many weeks to mourn, he reminded my friend that there was a contract to fulfill and an opera score that needed completion.

"A comedy about love?" Verdi would respond whenever questioned. "How can I possibly write music for a romance, when every joy has fled from my soul?"

In those early months, months filled with pain, Isabella and I stayed as close as possible to Verdi. I arranged with both Merelli and Lanari to only book me for local performances so I would not have to leave Milan. We fed Verdi, drank with him, sat with him, spoke with him. Each day a challenge. I would often despair of knowing what to do or what to say to my friend next, but my ever-sweet bride always seemed to know what words of commiseration to speak – or not speak. And what to do – or not. Some days she would just appear at his apartment with our maid carrying groceries so he would have something to eat. They'd clean his rooms, bring flowers, or make him coffee. There was no one better at this or more empathetic than my Isabella.

Though Verdi was decidedly appreciative and respectful of all we did for him, there was little we could actually do to help him compose. And Merelli still needed a score for *Un Giorno di Regno*, which was due to be staged on September 5th.

Slowly but with his eyes on the calendar, Verdi forced himself back to work. But his heart was never in it. How could it have been? Those three p's? Passion, passion and more passion? Verdi simply could not manifest any enthusiasm at all. And when the night came for the initial performance, Verdi, as stipulated in his contract, took his place as a conductor at La Scala for the very first time.

To say it was a disaster would have been an understatement. The boos and hisses began before the overture had ended and aside from a few moments of respite, the displeasure of the audience never ceased. And my friend Verdi, exposed as he was on the podium in front of the orchestra, had no choice whatsoever but to endure torrents of abuse from the audience. Among those joining in the chorus of hostility were Bishop Giuliano Giuliani, Cesare Briscola, plus many of their allies such as Barons Silvio Banno, Primo Tromba and Father Cornetti, their new spy in Busseto. When it was mercifully over, Verdi was as shaken as a dying leaf caught in the tumult of Autum winds. Isabella and I gathered him into our arms and brought him home.

After Bartolomeo Merelli wisely cancelled all future performances, Verdi did in fact flee back to Busseto to hide. He stayed for months with the Barezzi family. But eventually, he snuck back into his apartment in Milan like a wounded dog. That is where we found him, gaunt, underweight and decidedly depressed. Verdi begged us to help him pack up his belongings and leave.

"Why did the audiences at La Scala abuse the opera of a poor, sick young man? Couldn't they understand, I was harassed by the pressure of the schedule and heartsick and torn by horrible misfortune? They did not need to applaud, by oh, could then not have borne their displeasure in silence?" he cried out.

Instead of joining in his despair, we took him out to dinner at Ca' Dario – where else? And we ordered for both ourselves and Verdi, his absolute favorite from our menu, the *Sacchetti al Tartufo*.

At first, he resisted, picking at his plate, seemingly unable to eat anything ever again. Sustenance meant life and life had little interest for him now.

"*Dio mio* - oh my God," said Isabella after she swallowed her first bite and her face lit up like a spiritual novice finding enlightenment. "I'd forgotten how good these were."

Verdi was unmoved.

Isabella speared a *sacchetto* off of Verdi's plate, bathed it in that delicate parmigiano white sauce and brought it to his lips as if spoon feeding Tre, our young son. *"Mangia!"* she insisted. "Eat!"

And like a child, Verdi opened his mouth and took in the *sacchetto*.

Slowly, yes, ever so tediously, he chewed the dumpling. And then, again steadily as a full moon rising, his eyes began to brighten, until at last an expression of sheer and total joy swept over his face.

"Thank you," he said as he let a smile escape from his lips. "Yes, *anche io*, I'd forgotten how good these are. *Grazie, amici.*"

Ah, *Sacchetti al Tartufo,"* I declared, "Best medicine in the world."

"Bartolomeo Merelli came by to see me yesterday," said Verdi. "I almost threw him out."

"What did he want?" I asked.

"For me to compose again."

"Another opera score?"

"*Si,* but I told him, 'No, I just can't do it. I am done. I am going back to Busseto to be a farmer.'"

"A farmer?" I grabbed Verdi's hand and made a mock exam of his hand. "Not a callus in sight. You are not a farmer, my friend. You are a composer."

"No."

"*Si!"* I insisted.

"Tell me," Asked Isabella, "What is it about composing, why do you – or why did you begin to write music in the first place – that is before you decided to join us peasants shoveling the Duke of Mantua's manure? It seems an odd profession, though I suppose somebody has to put all those notes down on paper so people can sing? I really don't understand."

"Composing? You want to know about composing?" asked Verdi.

"No, not composing. I don't care about that," answered Isabella. "What interests me, is what did you feel about composing, especially for operas. Why? What was it?"

"Ah," said Verdi, sitting back in his chair. "What I felt?"

"Yes, what you felt."

"Have you ever been to a play? At a theater?"

"Once only," replied Isabella. "A drama by Shakespeare."

"We saw *Otello* last month at the Teatro alla Canobbiana," I added in quickly.

"Good," said Verdi. "And Isabella, you read, don't you, books that is?"

"Of course, since I was three," She replied instantly, "We Hebrews are people of the book, you know. My mother built a library of books at *La Corte degli Angeli*. That was the dowry she brought to *mio papà*. Of course, I can read. Her library was my window to the world; the Torah, Socrates, Petrarch, Cesare, Shakespeare, Voltaire, Schiller, Victor Hugo. And now? And now I could recite by heart everyone of Giuseppe Mazzini's exhortations from his books.

"Excellent," said Verdi. "But novels, do you read novels?"

This question set Isabella off laughing. "Do you recall exchanging copies of *The Betrothed,* with Mazzini? That was my idea and so was the use of Renzo and Lucia, as their code names. Or would you have preferred Otello and Desdemona?"

"*Va bene!*" replied Verdi. "So, when you ask about composing for an opera, let me say that it is much like the work of a novelist or a playwright. Our art is about the drama all humans experience."

I quickly interrupted. "You mean to say, you used to tell stories. That is before you decided to plant wheat or is it going to be rice?"

Verdi nodded in my direction before continuing his explanation. "A play, such as *Otello*, that you watched, is about what people say about their lives which is then expressed through dialogue. A novel, such your *Betrothed*, is similar but it is about what people think. For example, *Signor* Alessandro Manzoni's authoritative narration brings us inside the inner consciousness of his protagonists, Renzo and Lucia, as well as all of the people they meet during their odyssey. An opera, such as *The Marriage of Figaro* that we all saw bits of together, is about what people feel expressed through song.

Music, emotional passionate music, then is the language of opera. And in a truly gifted score, such as those composed by Mozart or Bellini or Donizetti, every note exists to express the emotions of the moment and to drive the story forward."

"Oh, it's not just about the wigs?" chided Isabella. "Or scribbling a lot of pretty notes on paper? Even I've done that."

"What do you mean, 'you've done that too'"? asked Verdi, very much surprised by this claim. "You've written songs? Music?"

"Canzonatini," said Isabella.

"You composed *Canzonatini*?" This startled Verdi even more as crafting one was no small feat, even for a professional musician.

"I invented them," she replied most matter-of-factly. "Too many of our messages and messengers were being caught. Giuseppe Mazzini needed a better method. I gave him one."

"Dario," said Verdi, "Your bride is full of surprises."

"Why?" I replied, "You didn't think a peasant girl could read, write, compose and know literature? These are all requisite skills for the farmer you want to be."

"So," said Isabella, "Back to those pretty notes you were scribbling that drive the story."

"Ah, *va bene*," Verdi continued to speak with an energy and zeal we had not seen in months. "Yes, every element counts; the wigs, the costumes, the acting, but most of all the notes, those squiggly lines on a page. In the process of its creation, an opera score requires an alignment between the composer – me - and the nature of the story to be told. My inkwell is akin to the pool of all human emotions bottled up in a little jar. When I dip my pen into that well and then write, what I am actually doing is searching the depths of my own experiences so as to capture those feelings and that energy I need to flesh out the storyline of my opera. The actual plot of the libretto may be completely different from what I may have undergone in my own life, but by tapping into my own feelings, I can bring them to bear in the score I compose."

"Every note?" asked Isabella.

"*Si*, every note. And in order to do that, I must fully comprehend each and every aspect of the libretto, the story. An opera might be, say, two or three hours long. But what's the story? What are we trying to share with our audience? What do we want them to think, them to feel? In that regard, the composer is akin to a skillful lawyer. Through the music I can induce the audiences to feel what I want them to feel, to experience what I want them to experience and to come to a conclusion that I want them to reach. Therefore, the story must engage listeners. The way to do that is through conflicts that reflect life as we live it and in the resolution of those issues, we hopefully inspire people to create a greater world, one better than what they and we have now."

"And the language you speak is the score? The notes you write?" she asked.

"Precisely. The notes are my alphabet, the tools I use to weave them into sentences, paragraphs, chapters, except we call them overtures, interludes, arias, duets, trios, scenes, or acts. But the glue that holds them all together is passion."

"And this is what you work on when you compose? Getting every last note correct? You don't just throw notes on a page?"

"No, just like a *Canzonatini*, the message has to be spot on correct. Think about the possible difference between two people who are painters, one does houses and the other portraits. The house painter who slaps on many coats of whitewash on the outside of your house without regard to subtlety, meaning or emotions, is similar to a mediocre composer whose work is undistinguished, unemotional and boring. A great opera composer, a Donizetti or a Rossini, is more the portraitist who strives to capture a moment, a mood and a feeling or atmosphere with each tiny brush stroke."

"And those are the notes. *Certo*, okay, I get that, but then you have to conduct the opera and tell everyone how you actually want the work performed, yes?"

"You're catching on. Take Dario here for a moment. He's a bass-baritone. His voice has certain qualities."

"My voice is my instrument," I interjected.

"Wait," said Verdi. "Yes. Dario's voice, all the singers' voices are their instruments, but for me the conductor, all the singers and all the musicians, they are my instrument. When I compose, I have in my head a notion of how my work shall sound. When I conduct, I am not just waving a wand and keeping time, I am in fact using all the orchestra and the chorus under my control to be the expression of my original thoughts, of the notes I wrote down and of the score I composed. And in a perfect world, what they give me back is the best possible version of what I created."

"So, what are going to grow on this farm of yours?" asked Isabella.

"Manure," confessed Verdi, finally admitting to himself and the world that he was not going to be farmer.

"What is the libretto Bartolomeo Merelli wants you to score?" I asked.

Verdi pulled a manuscript out of his satchel, "Just this."

He handed me the libretto for *Nabucco* by the poet, Temistocle Solera, which was a melodramatic love triangle set against the backdrop of the destruction of the First Temple in Jerusalem and the subsequent exile of the Jews to Babylon. I flipped through the libretto until I came to the page that Verdi had folded down and dog-eared.

"What's this? *The Chorus of Hebrew Slaves?*" I asked before reciting the lines of what we have all come to recognize as *Va' Pensiero*.

Oh, my lord," exclaimed Isabella when I had finished, "That's is so beautiful, especially that last line *'endure our suffering.'*"

"*Si*," said Verdi. "You won't believe this but after Merelli left, I threw the libretto onto my desk and it opened to that page, the one you just saw. I couldn't stop reading it over and over again."

"Why was that?" asked Isabella. "What was the attraction?"

"After watching three coffins leave my house in as many years, you have to ask?"

"Yes," persisted Isabella. "Yes, I am asking. I am asking what it meant to you. Was it the line about suffering?"

Verdi nodded. "In an instant I understood the entire story, the pain, the longing, the anguish, of how a people, a nation, and even a young couple, all felt in exile from that which they loved. I could hear their voices singing even before I finished reading. I thought of Margherita, and my children, Virginia and Icilio. I remembered you, Isabella, your family's eviction, the cruelty of the Briscolas and of the longing of the starving peasants back in Parma. I heard Cantor Segré voice calling out to the Hebrews about the Promised Land and I felt the *shofar* of Rabbi Spinoziano crack the walls of the Emperor's castle. I saw Giuseppe Mazzini escaping from Commander Gaetz and Father Abbondio and in that moment, I understood his dreams of uniting all Italians in a free and fair republic. All this came to me in a perfect expression of its glory and solemnity. Ah, and then the melodies began to swim inside my head."

"And you knew you could do this," I added quickly.

"Yes, *certo!*" Verdi answered. He could do this and he did. All he had needed was that little push from Isabella, a gentle shove – in the right direction - that brought Verdi back into himself again. Spreading manure on the fields could wait.

In the months that followed, Verdi put pen to paper. He wrote in a fevered pitch, not stopping until he had completed the score on schedule. After the first few rehearsals there was a buzz about town about this purportedly fabulous new work. Unlike *Oberto*, which Verdi wrote with his head, with his intellect, *Nabucco* was written from the depths of his soul – and it showed. Even the stage hands building out the sets would stop their work and listen to the singers rehearse. Tickets to the premiere sold out in advance and such was the anticipation that on opening night, it was standing room only at La Scala.

And so, on that March night, Verdi overcame all of his fears, all his terrors and mounted the podium at La Scala for the second time. He raised his baton before the audience and made history that night.

The passions in the overture instantly hooked the skeptics of La Scala. It began with muscular, bold and powerful movements yet, when necessary, Verdi used the oboes and flutes to turn it elegant and sweetly nostalgic with light, floating notes. A stunning choral work followed, one which thrust us into the personal drama surrounding the first act's Fall of the First Temple in Jerusalem. By the time we hear the bone rattling cries of the Jewish high priest Zacheria dominate the stage, the audience had no doubt about Verdi's skills as a master of composition. His intellectual genius, now honed by the fire and forge of personal tragedy, demonstrated a mastery that was revealed in every note.

As the rest of *Nabucco* rocketed along, I could hear echoes in the music of our past life in Busseto: the funeral marches, the call of the *shofar*, Barezzi's sweet flute playing, and the longing of all our people for freedom and peace, not just the Hebrews of *Nabucco*, but all the peoples of the Italian peninsula. And yes, those of us who knew Verdi well could see how he had transformed his own personal horrors into the seamless beauty of a nearly perfect opera.

What precisely the audience felt that night, I will never know with certainly, but *Nabucco* was a triumph of the highest order. Verdi had not only touched the very core of his own being to compose the music, he had touched the soul of a nation, a nation that was just about to experience the explosive violence that comes with birth. And *Va' Pensiero*? What can I say? Overnight we Italians embraced it as the emotional heart of our country, one so beautiful but lost. After every song, the audiences at La Scala applauded thunderously. And damn the Austrian police rules; we got our encores. When the curtain dropped at the end of the fourth act, their applause demanded an endless number of curtain calls. How many, I could not even count. No one wanted to leave the theater. And why not? They had witnessed in Verdi the creation of a new star that would lead the way to our Promised Land, the *Risorgimento*.

But I would be negligent if I did not tell you that the true hero of *Nabucco*, Abigaille, was the woman whose personal demons drove the libretto. Played by a soprano, Abigaille was a warrior princess, the step daughter of the Babylonian tyrant. She was also a woman scorned in love, a woman passionate and hungry for power and dominance. Yes, the role of Abigaille was the tale of a woman who wanted what she wanted but one, who in the end discovers she cannot succeed. The vocal demands upon the singer were so extraordinary that it took a prima diva at the very height of her talents to sing this epic role in all its necessary range and subtlety. And that diva, that woman who dominated the stage for nearly three hours, that woman who came back into all of our lives was none other than the young girl I had once nicknamed Violetta, the Little General, *Signorina* Giuseppina Strepponi.

Truth be known, that even though Verdi had written Abigaille's part specifically for the nuances of Strepponi's voice, she almost did not get the role. It had been some time since either of us had last seen Strepponi during which her frenetic concert life had not changed a whit. Whereas I wanted to stay close to home after the birth of my son, Strepponi kept going and going. She toured non-stop, which included her continually having affairs and paying the resultant price for them. Twice she miscarried and she birthed at least one, if not two more babies, which of course were immediately given up for adoption. Although Strepponi was still only twenty-seven years old, the combined strain of her pregnancies and her non-stop work caused her health to decline precipitously. Often, she was compelled to cancel performances at the last minute. Whereas in the past, theater managers and impresarios were delighted to have her name on the marque, now they increasingly considered her unreliable, and Bartolomeo Merelli was no exception.

Verdi desperately wanted her to play Abigaille and she was equally anxious to do it as well. He had asked me to help him with all the singers during the rehearsals, which naturally meant spending a fair amount of time working with Strepponi again. She confided in me that she knew her days as a prima diva were nearing an end, so much so that she was seriously considering an offer of marriage from an unnamed aristocrat in Lodi as a graceful way to exit the stage forever. I assured her I would do all I could to get her through this, even if it meant spoon feeding her my mother's chicken soup between every act.

"I'd love that," she said. *"La Zuppa della Mamma. Fantastico."*

Verdi and Strepponi genuinely liked and admired each other. My Isabella might have been the only one who noticed but, as she pointed out to me, there was always a spark of light in each of their eyes whenever the other was in the same room. I said nothing. Individually, their lives were too complicated at the moment for it to go any further. I saw them each as a wounded bird. They both needed every ounce of strength and resolve their souls could muster, just to be able to lift off and put the wind under their wings if they were to succeed in the work at hand. Romance? No. Verdi still had too many ghosts screaming at him every night. If love was to ever arrive and bind them as one, it would have to wait until they each had their wounds staunched and healed.

Still Verdi knew her talents and considered her the finest singer in all Italy – when she was healthy. And she sensed in him a depth as a composer few outside our small circle of friends would have understood.

I did not tell Strepponi that Merelli was also taking no chances. Unbeknownst to both her and Verdi, our impresario kept an understudy waiting in the wings for the entire time, just in case Strepponi were to bail out again. Together though, Verdi and I coaxed her through the initial run of eight performances and she not only made it, she succeeded brilliantly and to some of the greatest acclaim of her career. *Mamma's* soup helped.

The instant success of *Nabucco* was also historic. Bartolomeo Merelli who was so completely and overwhelmingly thrilled with the success that he not only scheduled a second run for the summer – a run that lasted over fifty performances – he further arranged with the Ricordis to have *Nabucco* performed in many of the leading opera houses of Italy over the next few months. And much to the annoyance of our Austrian authorities, orchestras bowed to the wishes of the audience and thus *Va' Pensiero* was frequently encored - performances I considered the next perfect gun shots of the revolution.

Invitations for Verdi to attend parties and salons flooded in from the wealthy families of Milan. He became *la celebrità del giorno* – the celebrity of the day, a distinction that as we all now know, lasted for another six decades. Men wanted to dress like him and have a beard trimmed like his. And women? They simply wanted him. The most important of these seductions and the one that would have the most impact upon my friend's future life came after the last performance in March from the Countess Clara Maffei.

The Countess, who was just a year younger than Verdi, and her much older poet husband, Andrea, had hosted for many years, what was perhaps the most famous and influential *salotto* – salon - in Milan. It was favored by many of the most prestigious artists, writers, musicians, and politicians, particularly those supporters of the *Risorgimento* who were aligned in their disdain for our Austrian overlords. Inside the Maffeis' grand casa at the Piazza Belgioioso these intellectuals would come and spend the evening wining, dining, playing cards and discussing the latest events of the day, be they about the theater, politics or, of course, the latest gossip. Who were these people? Some we've already met, such as Lanari, Merelli, Donizetti and the Recordis. Others, such as our future prime minister Camillo Cavour, the partisan writer, Carlo Tenca, and *Signor* Alessandro Manzoni himself, the writer of *The Betrothed,* we'll encounter in due time. But if you would know anything about the salon, let it be said clearly that there could not have been a better or more important place for Verdi to be in the furtherance of his career.

And Clarina, as Verdi would come to call her, had her eyes on him from the start. Know that her marriage to Andrea was one of those upper-class classical clichés, that is to say, one of convenience. Their divorce that came years later was amicable and in much the same spirt. Minutes after Verdi finished his bows on stage opening night, the Countess had wrestled a pledge out of him to attend her *salotto* when the run of eight performances was over, one that would be staged in his honor.

When Isabella and I found Verdi backstage in his dressing room after that final show, he pulled me aside and said, "Merelli just handed me a new contract. He revised the old one and told me to fill in how many *Lire* I am to be paid going forward."

"He left it blank?" Even I was surprised. Merelli was many things, but being uncommonly generous was not one of them.

"What do I do?"

I shrugged. I truly had no idea what to say.

"Perhaps I should ask Strepponi," Verdi said, "She's been around long enough to know what everyone else earns, eh?"

I shrugged again.

Verdi stepped out into the hallway and then knocked on Strepponi's dressing room door. We found our soprano sipping from a warm bowl of *Mamma's* chicken soup.

"*Grazie*, Dario, you saved my throat and maybe my career."

"*Piacere mio* – my pleasure," I replied.

After the usual exchange of congratulatory pleasantries Verdi explained to her about the contract and how he was stumped by not knowing what to do.

"Bellini was paid 8,000 Austrian *Lire* for *Norma*," she told us, "That's the most any impresario has ever paid to any composer. If you believe you are worth that, ask for the same… Or more."

Upon hearing this from Strepponi, Verdi did not hesitate. I watched as *il mio amico* scribbled 9,000 Austrian *Lire* before signing his name with a great flourish. He placed the contract back in its envelop and handed it to me. Clearly, he had a true measure of his own worth – and from then on, he got it. Not only was Verdi poised on the cusp of great artistic success, he was also on the road to becoming an extraordinary wealthy man.

"Dario, would you please return that to Merelli?" he said while politely gesturing for Isabella and me to exit the room. "I'll join you both at the Countess's *salotto* later. There are matters I would like to discuss with *la nostra cara Violetta in privato.*"

Isabella and I immediately left, closing the door behind as we did so.

"What was that's about?" Isabella asked. "He's never called her Violetta, before. Are they….?"

"I don't know, but I sense trouble."

"You're thinking Verdi wants to invite her to the *salotto?* And more?"

"Si," I said shaking my head. "Yes, that's what I've been dreading."

"Why? Isn't that a good thing? Margherita's been gone for almost two years. Don't you think it is about time for Verdi to enjoy a little romance?"

I shook my head, knowing full well that neither of them had healed enough to salve the others wounds.

"But why not Strepponi? They'd be a good fit," insisted Isabella.

"Why? Because Strepponi had me book her a private coach in the name of Violetta Lamentina. Right now, at this moment, the driver is waiting out in front of La Scala to take her directly to her aristocrat in Lodi."

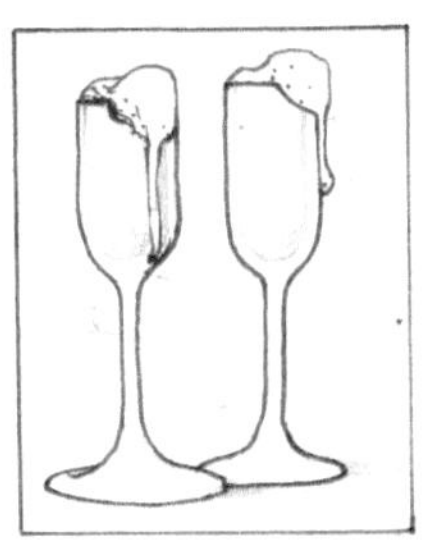

Chapter Eight:
Let's Drink To Love's Warm Kisses

Paris, July 27, 1847

When Verdi first arrived at his hotel suite in Paris, *Le Jardin de la Beauté Tranquille*, he was not surprised to find a letter from his French publisher, Léon Escudier, waiting for him on the piano next to a chilled bottle of champagne and a silver platter piled high with *hors d'oeuvres*. After a two month long stay in London to produce his opera, *I Masnadieri*, Verdi was exhausted from the journey and in no mood to read. He left the envelope there while he unpacked. Clothes here, boots there. Papers, coins, keys, wallet and his passport quickly found a home in the desk.

His drawing room overlooked a secluded Oriental style garden filled with roses, night-blooming jasmine and *camélias* and where a muster of peacocks nested beneath a statue of *Kwan Yin*, the Chinese Goddess of Compassion. Verdi opened the windows and let the night breeze carry the scent of the flowers into his chambers. What a sweet contrast their aroma was to the stench of the road and the coal fired smog of London he had just escaped. Still, it had been a good trip. The English audiences responded well enough to *I Masnadieri*, which had been based on Friedrich Schiller's play, *The Robbers*. Even Prince Albert and Queen Victoria, who came to the opening at the appropriately named, Her Majesty's Theater, applauded enthusiastically. Verdi's opera, however, starred the only queen he cared about, a soprano considered northern Europe's reigning Queen of Song, Jenny Lind. Also known as the Swedish Nightingale, Lind gave a performance Verdi considered exquisite. The libretto, also well received, was written by his now good friend, and Clarina's soon to be ex-husband, Count Andrea Maffei. Overall, *I Masnadieri* was Verdi's eleventh opera and his eighth in the five years since the success of *Nabucco*. It was no wonder he was exhausted. After his successes at La Scala, every theater impresario from Venice's La Fenice to Naples' Teatro San Carlo, wanted a Verdi opera. Each of his premiers had been successful, including ones at the Teatro Argentina in Rome and Florence's Teatro alla Pergola. And, despite the wildly different stories, settings and plotlines that characterized these works of his, all of them had a similar underlying patriotic refrain that linked them to not only the spirit of the times, but the *Risorgimento* itself. Each featured heroes, and heroines such as Macbeth, Ernani and Joan of Arc, fighting against the depredations of tyrants and oppressors. It was those patriotic themes that endeared Verdi and his operas not only to the Italian speaking world, but to the under trodden everywhere across Europe. Yes, Verdi was not only living the spirit of his politics through his art, his audiences were in turn making him a very rich man. Yet, he was so exhausted by the work necessary for his career, that all he could think of was quitting.

Money, fame and new commissions came flowing towards him, as did the attention and sweetness of women – especially Clarina Maffei. She was the first among her friends – but by no means the only one - to bed the up and coming composer. Clarina however set limits and rules, rules Verdi quickly came to appreciate; sex at night, friendship by day, but nothing more. Though it was not his nature to pursue multiple affairs, he quickly applied Clarina's rules to all his relationships with the very many society women who wanted to seduce or be seduced by him.

Frankly, I will tell you that following the death of his two children and the bitter loss of his beloved Margherita, Verdi was terrified of getting any closer than a causal relationship with any woman. Those tragedies gnawed at him constantly and kept him awake at night when he'd hear the ghosts of his children crying out in pain. He came to believe that the best of life was stolen from him and that the world was essentially cruel. These sentiments never left Verdi and opera dramas plumbing the depths of tragedy came to characterize much of his later work. Even though it was in his nature to be a loving, kind and affectionate man, he was simply not willing to fall in love and risk that enormity of loss again. Simply put, Verdi reckoned that if he did not put his hand into the fires of passion, he would never suffer more burns. Thus, his affairs were to remain just that, trysts in the bedroom that never lasted past sunrise.

He opened the champagne and poured himself a glass, letting the bubbles come right up to the top of the lip. Verdi sat himself down in an overstuffed chair by the open window and inhaled the night air. The natural perfume of the flowers worked their magic, chasing the scent of the road and the rural countryside from his nose. He needed a day, if not weeks and months of rest. The world could wait. Paris could wait. And Escudier's letter – which he knew was certainly about more work – could definitely wait. Though he would have much preferred to have gone straight home to Milan from London, the weight of his obligations in Paris pressed in on him. War was coming and he knew it, everyone knew it. Only this time it would not be the struggle of one country versus another but rather, the fight for freedom by citizens everywhere against the oppressions of an aristocracy, which, from Moscow to Madrid and Palmero to Paris, was connected by blood ties and wealth, staggering wealth. The disparities so extreme, that the aristocrats of Europe, who comprised a mere one percent of our population controlled more than eighty to ninety percent of the total wealth.

The tension in France, the plight of the workers and farmers had been palpable on his ride into the capital just as it had been back home in Lombardy and Parma. At a stagecoach rest stop midway between Calais and Paris, and just outside the town of Beauvais, Verdi had been admiring the skills of three gypsy blacksmiths who sang in Romani while hammering in unison to repair a plow when a wild-eyed peasant woman clutching a swaddled baby close to her chest, confronted him, begging for a handout. The desperation in the eyes of this woman, who reminded him of the character Azucena from the play *El Trovador* by a Spanish playwright, was genuine. Remembering the suffering of Isabella's family when they were evicted from *La Corte degli Angeli*, Verdi obliged this Azucena by turning over the remaining food he had brought for the journey and by placing a few additional francs in her hands, probably enough to buy bread for a month. He was at first embarrassed when the poor woman fell to her knees in front of him to kiss the hem of his jacket, but then horrified when she started to offer up a prayer of thanks and the baby fell from her arms. It was dead and had clearly been so for days.

Poverty was everywhere and the tension? Yes, the sickening, disquieting mood out there on the streets felt like the air before a thunderstorm – one that everyone presumed would explode across the continent one day with unfathomable violence. What day, he did not know but he suspected that Giuseppe Mazzini did. He had met the man himself again in London where the leader of *Giovine Italia* and *Giovine Europa* was now living in exile. A calculating and incisive man, Mazzini knew well the heartbeat inside the workers and peasants of Europe. Mazzini believed that a popular uprising would create a unified Italy, which in turn would inspire a European-wide revolutionary movement. Nothing would change until nations embraced democracy and shredded the notion that the current ruling aristocracy had a divine right to rule. For his part, Verdi had agreed to compose a patriotic battle hymn and take on a few other tasks for Mazzini on behalf of the *Risorgimento*. The music was easy, it was those other tasks – writing and passing along several complex *Canzonatini* that laid out sophisticated battle plans and tactics – those were the dangerous ones. And indeed, that risk also preyed on his mind. But they too, those *Canzonatini* – critical as they were - could wait. He was profoundly tired. Verdi sipped the champagne, noticing how perfectly dry and smooth it tasted, which made him suddenly think about Giuseppina Strepponi.

The prior year Strepponi had relocated to Paris for a fresh start. She now worked as a teacher and coach of young opera singers wanting to learn our Italian performance style. Verdi had dined with her in Paris two months earlier when he was on his way London. They had shared an equally dry champagne that afternoon in a meeting that did not go well. They'd both so been brittle and tense that neither could have said a word without upsetting the other. But thoughts of her, no matter how insistent they were, no matter how much they refused to be settled inside his mind – they too could wait. He finished his glass in a gulp and quickly poured another. He was alone. It was quiet. The air was as scented as paradise and all he wanted to do was find a night of peace in *Le Jardin de la Beauté Tranquille.*

Verdi let his mind go blank – a rare feat for him – and continued to sip his champagne. It was not until he had finished his second glass and began a third that he returned to Escudier's letter. Inside was a long note, an invitation actually, to join Escudier and one of his friends, Nestor Roqueplan, a Parisian opera impresario, for dinner at a salon held at the city estate of Princess Marguerite Gautier, occurring Thursday evening, two days hence. According to Escudier, Roqueplan was desirous of staging a Verdi opera in Paris and hoped to negotiate a deal with the composer as soon as possible. Escudier made a point of stressing that this was to be the last salon of the season before the denizens of Paris' *Beau Monde* fled the city for the cool of the countryside – and those were the good folk he insisted Verdi meet during his stay. It was their money that kept opera alive. Among the attendees, Escudier told Verdi he could expect to see at Gautier's were fellow composers, Hector Berlioz, Gioachino Rossini and the consumptive Frédéric Chopin; the writers Balzac, Victor Hugo, Alexandre Dumas fils and the androgenous George Sand, Chopin's mistress, who insisted on dressing as a man. Also, there would be Count Armand Duval; the painter Eugène Delacroix, famous for his portraits of Napoleon and *Liberty Leading the People*; as well as the Barons Rothchild and de Varville. Princess Gautier routinely hired Rossini to organize all the entertainment for her salons, including singers, musicians, jugglers, mimes and dancers, and though it was not required, Rossini himself so enjoyed these parties that he often spent the entire night at the piano accompanying anyone and everyone till dawn, so long as there was always a fresh glass of wine within arm's reach. Though the inherently shy Verdi, who despised making small talk, knew he had much to gain by these events, it was his nature to dread them and detest being there, especially given his state of exhaustion.

All of this weighed upon him. Why even Giuseppe Mazzini had instructed him to attend such events in Paris in order to make contact with an unnamed secret ally of *Giovine Italia* and deliver a critical *Canzonatini.* Verdi had accepted the request despite the dangers, something he considered as a duty in furtherance of the *Risorgimento*.

He also wondered if Strepponi would be there. And if so, how would they each react to seeing the other? But most of all, he wondered, why did he even care? Why could he not escape thoughts of her? What was the hold she had on him? Yes, he did care, but, their interactions these past five years since *Nabucco* and been volatile and unpredictable to say the least.

After that last performance at La Scala, Strepponi had indeed rebuffed him to flee to some purported fiancé in Lodi. That stung, as he had presumed their attraction was mutual. Only months later did we all learn that her story of an aristocrat waiting for her on bended knees was simply a fiction, one Strepponi had invented. And that made her rejection ever more bitter. Yes, only later would she confess that the little lie she told was an act of desperation. She needed to escape from the unbearable stress of her opera driven life. Though her performance in *Nabucco* had been well received, Strepponi knew it was only a matter of time before her voice deserted her. The signs were all there; the notes she could no longer reach, the trills she could no longer sustain, the throat that hurt and the breaths that were now too shallow to give power to her arias.

After *Nabucco*, Strepponi was too exhausted, depressed and despairing to see how different her life had turned out than what she had first expected after graduating from the conservatory. She retreated to her mother's house in Lodi, the place where she had grown up. For the first months there, Strepponi was so desperate to save what was left of her voice, that she declined to speak, much less practice singing or continue with her daily vocal exercises. She'd simply nod or shake her head. Only, when necessary, would she communicate further by handing her mother or sister scribbled notes. Mostly she spent all her time in solitude, be it staring out the window, reading, or taking long walks, lost in a web of her own thoughts.

Early on Strepponi dreaded sleeping because she couldn't. And she dreaded waking, counting the hours before she could suppress the sad thoughts overwhelming her head and slink back to bed again. It was a hopeless cycle. In the morning she'd bolt down espresso to shake the gloom off and then by mid-afternoon, she'd be into the wine to calm down the agitation the coffee had triggered. In that unsettled state, reading novels and plays were the only thread of activity that let her escape the storm racing around inside her own mind.

How was it that none of the men in her life, especially those she suspected of fathering the children she birthed, suffered any of the consequences that she did? Although she had once believed she could play the romantic field as equally aggressive as men, she learned the cruel truth in the most bitter way that they go off scot-free. And she, she had to suffer for a lifetime the burdens of their mutual actions. "How unfair," she would often write in notes to her mother, her sister or anyone who cared. Many were the nights she spent sleepless, alone and in tears, crying over the children she'd surrendered to others and mourning those that she could never have. Her last miscarriage had rendered her sterile, a cruel fate for a still young woman who had always expected to have a husband and a family when her singing days were over.

Now, fearing her voice was nearly gone, she faced a future where none of her dreams, simple as they were, remained possible. Much as men craved taking her to their beds, none of them wanted to welcome her to their homes nor be the father of her children. What was left? She had become a social pariah, the *Traviata*, the wanton woman. Yet, true intimacy was something she felt incapable of handling. The scars on her soul were so deep that she was actually terrified after her run as Abigaille had ended, that Verdi would have wanted to get close to her. She understood all too well that he was still recoiling from the death of Margherita and his children. And how could she possibly care and attend to another when she could barely hold herself together each day.

Ironically it had been her greatest strengths, her drive and determination, that had caused Strepponi to push herself too far, far beyond what she could handle. She's been so strong for so long but ultimately the frailties of her body betrayed her. Physically, she was a wreck. Her youthful verve and innate resolve had been beaten down by an overwhelming work schedule and her all too frequent pregnancies. With her voice now in obvious decline, she saw the end of her career as a highly paid diva rapidly approaching. "What then? What's next?" She would constantly ask herself. She had no answers, none whatsoever. Frankly, she was terrified.

She found it impossible to imagine working again, much less actually singing in public and demurred every offer that came her way out of fear she'd be exposed as a fraud. Still however, she hoped beyond hope that those roles would magically reappear when she was ready to perform again - if she ever performed again.

Even the notion that she must have a career to survive, depressed her. In truth all she wanted was a quiet and peaceful life, a life she could share with a good man, but what man would want her, a burnt out shell of a diva who was not yet even thirty?

Nonetheless, after nearly nine months of seclusion in Lodi, she finally grew weary of her own nightmares and inactivity. There were only so many novels she could read before that distraction became a bore as well. Yes, just as a thunderstorm eventually burns itself out, so too was it with her depression. Beneath the layers of exhaustion, Strepponi began to discover herself again. At her core, she found bedrock and stability. She was too wise, too determined, too vital not to do so. She started to eat again, her strength returned, and bit by bit, so did her confidence.

When she heard rumors that the *Nuovo Teatro Ducale* in Parma was going to produce *Nabucco*, Strepponi wrote to Verdi. Included with the letter was a small portrait of herself attired in her violet Violetta gown offset with a gold necklace with a pearl drop and matching earrings, one that had been painted a year or so earlier just before she had performed in *Nabucco*. She opened with, "My Dearest Verdi, I hope you have not forgotten me the way the rest of the world has." Without mentioning in her note that she desperately wanted – no needed - to play Abigaille again, she asked him to meet her for dinner in Milan. She imagined it as a first step back into the world with an opera she knew and a man she trusted. Yes, despite their difficulties, she knew Verdi to be a sincere man, always honest and true. And so very few men in her world were.

Verdi had just premiered *I Lombardi alla Prima Crociata - The Lombards on the First Crusade* – at La Scala and was already starting in on his *Ernani* score for La Fenice in Venice when he received and read Strepponi's letter with a mixture of fear and longing. The truth was simple. He had fallen in love when he had first heard Strepponi sing *Violetta's Lament.* Back then, Verdi ever loyal and faithful to his wife, dismissed all romantic thoughts. But Verdi also recognized his own inner truth; he could not deny their mutual attraction. He considered Strepponi to be a remarkable woman well beyond her talents as a singer. There was an affinity between them, one of mutual admiration and ultimately, trust. Verdi knew her to be smart, personable, well-schooled, wise, easygoing, kind, considerate and with considerable charm. She knew the worlds of literature, philosophy and drama as well if not better than anyone else he had become acquainted with since leaving Busseto. And such was the harmony he experienced whenever their eyes met, that Verdi felt as if they had always known, trusted and respected each other. Much like Isabella and me, they were two bookends who belong together. So why couldn't they get along?

In response to her letter, he had agreed to meet her at Ca' Dario. When he arrived, Isabella, working as the hostess that day, greeted him with her usual warmth, but asked, "You're late. What took you so long?"

"Late? I'm not late," replied Verdi, a bit flustered. He checked his pocket watch, "In fact, I'm ten minutes early."

"Not by my calendar. You should have stopped at her home a year ago. You do remember it's half way between here and Busseto, eh?" chided Isabella.

"Oh, I must have missed that *Canzonatini.*"

"Nonsense. Don't blame *la rivoluzione.* You know damn well what I mean. Come, I'll take you to her now." Isabella escorted Verdi over to Strepponi's table, a quiet one off in a corner of *Il Nord* and then left them alone.

When Strepponi looked up, her eyes met his. Their gaze was that of two old friends delighted – no, relieved to be in each other's company. Strepponi was sipping a glass of Barbera d'Alba. Before her was a bowl of *La Zuppa della Mamma.* To Verdi, she was as alluring as ever, dressed just as she was in her portrait - Violetta in her silk gown offset with the same gold necklace with a pearl drop and matching earrings - which he was quick to compliment.

She immediately rose to meet and embrace Verdi. Though their polite kisses were meant to land gently on each other's cheeks, instead, as the corners of their lips brushed each other's, they both let their kisses linger. And when Strepponi slowly, yes, ever so slowly began to slip away, Verdi pulled her back into his arms to kiss her full on. Her lips met his willingly and their very first kiss ever, lingered – that is until Isabella returned to their table with a bowl of *La Zuppa della Mamma* and a glass of Barbera for Verdi.

"Ah, excuse me," Isabella chided, "There's a room in the loft for that."

Verdi went beet red. "Now what?" Verdi looked at the bowl, "Did I order this?"

"Yes," said Isabella. "Now sit down and start talking."

"*Basta! Basta!* Enough!" said Verdi, affectionately shushing Isabella away with a sweep of his hands. "I can handle this."

"*Va bene!* I was counting on you doing just that," said Isabella, walking away.

After sitting back down Verdi turned to Strepponi, "Where were we?"

"Making up for lost time," she answered.

"*Certo!*" replied Verdi with relief that she felt the same as he did. "Dario tells me you've been resting and in retreat back home in Lodi, yes?"

Strepponi nodded affirmatively.

"And you're singing?" Verdi asked.

"I did order *La Zuppa della Mamma,"* she replied while pointing to her throat.

"I'll take that as a 'yes."

She nodded again.

Verdi continued. "We're casting now for *Nabucco* in Parma. Are you ready to become Abigaille again?"

Strepponi reached across the table and took Verdi's hand in her own, *"Assolutamente,* I accept,*"* she declared. "But if you hadn't asked, I would have fallen to my knees and begged."

****

As Verdi continued to sip the champagne Escudier had sent over, he recalled how the reprise of *Nabucco* brought out the best in them, but also revealed them at their worst. Yes, the opera with Strepponi playing Abigaille did open at the *Nuovo Teatro Ducale* in Parma that April. Verdi's contract called for him to oversee rehearsals and to conduct the first two performances.

He and Strepponi had each booked separate rooms at their hotel, the Albergo Corona, just a short walk to the theater. After their first dinner together, Strepponi invited Verdi up to her room. Once inside, they began to kiss. The outcome? Not as expected, at least not at initially. And to understand that, you need to understand that what bonded them was their deep compassion for the tragedies the other had suffered.

After that opening embrace, they each began to cry - first, Strepponi and then Verdi, both shedding deep heartfelt tears. It was there, in each other's grasp they both found the courage to let loose the pains they had carried on alone and in silence. For Verdi, he had never truly allowed himself to grieve for his lost family in the arms of someone whom he trusted implicitly.

Only later, much later that evening, did their passions for each other take over as if it had been preordained from birth… Verdi stayed for a breakfast of *un cornetto* and an espresso, a repast they shared together each morning for the next seven weeks. As Strepponi was particularly fond of those that were crème filled and sprinkled with pistachios inside, Verdi made certain those were delivered fresh to their room daily. Those were the good days.

But although what started as compassion for each other's pain and the blissful release it brought, their time together soon ended in anger and recriminations. Though pain was the glue that bonded them, their respective wounds were so deep, that the salve they each needed to heal appeared to be mutually exclusive. Suffice to say neither was ready for the other. Strepponi wanted more than Verdi could give and, in the end, he, reciting "Clarina's Rules," and unable to commit, bolted back to Milan. There Verdi fell back into the casual but undemanding arms of Clarina and her kind.

Frustrated and heartbroken but always a realist, Strepponi moved on. Determined as ever to control her own path in life, she performed here and there until she ended up signing a long term contract at the Palermo opera house in Sicily. Though her performances started well, her voice soon deserted her. It was there, before half empty houses, that her career finally crashed, never to be revived again.

Surrendering to her fate, she decided to leave the Italian opera world behind. The idea of reinventing herself in a new world had great appeal – and a large part of that appeal was that it meant escaping the mud and mess of all of her past lives and lovers – Verdi included. That's when she decided to forever give up her singing career to become a vocal instructor. And she deigned to do it in the best city in Europe for music, Paris, far from the madding crowds of Italian opera houses.

And Verdi would have probably never seen or encountered her again had the impresarios of Her Majesty's Opera not paid him huge sums of money to create and conduct the premier performances of *I Masnadieri* for the English stage. And to get to and from London from Milan, Verdi inevitably had to pass through the Scylla and Charybdis that Strepponi represented in Paris.

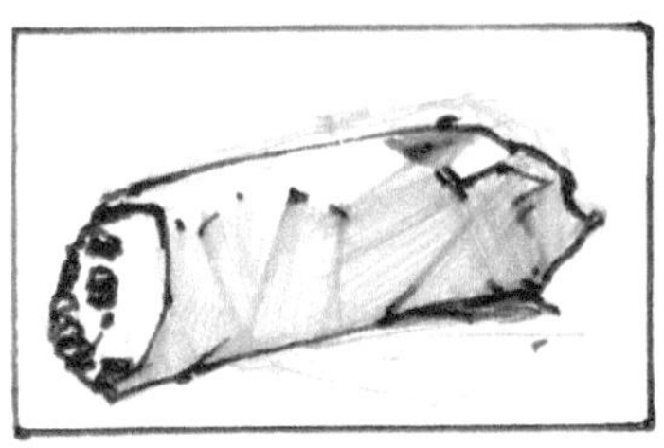

Chapter Nine:
All the World is Folly

Paris, Two Days Later, July 29, 1847

Nothing in Milan had ever prepared Verdi for the whirling, swirling, twirling Dervish of a salon that was unfolding in the mirror lined halls and banquet rooms of Princess Marguerite Gautier's glimmering palace – nor was he prepared for the dangers inherent with him even being there. Every foyer was filled with dancers, music, mimes and magicians. Champagne flowed from fountains and food, endless platters of exquisite French foods - fondues, crepes, creme brulé, hors d'oeuvres, escargot, quiche and *les fromages* - appeared here and there and everywhere on silver trays carried by uniformed servants. Society women bedecked in gold and diamonds, mingled with courtesans in their brilliantly colored garters and gowns. Princes and poseurs alike dressed in tuxedoes and top hats to play poker or pacino while in other corners philosophers and poets argued over plays and politics. Yes, the entire *Beau Monde* of Paris that Escudier promised Verdi he could expect to see at Gautier's was there, from Berlioz and Balzac to a Baron Rothchild or two. And yes, the excesses of wealth and food displayed here could have feed the dispossessed of Paris for a month. With the disparity between rich and poor growing ever wider, Verdi knew Giuseppe Mazzini was correct to predict uprising and revolts were just around the corner. And spies? Spies for every faction were everywhere. Verdi knew to trust no one.

Verdi sat in an alcove on the veranda ringing the grand salon where below two orchestras – one on either end of the hall – alternated playing a perpetual stream of the latest Viennese Strauss waltzes. As soon as one band finished a dance tune, the other ensemble would start up. Thus, the melodies never, ever stopped and those entwined couples, ever so addicted to pleasure, let dancing be their nightly drug of choice, one that blinded them to what was happening out on the streets. With Verdi was Léon Escudier, his French publisher and Nestor Roqueplan, that French impresario so very anxious to get a Verdi opera on to the stages of Paris.

"Over there, you see him?" asked Escudier as he pointed to pianist down below who also conducted one of the orchestras.

"Yes," said Verdi as he recognized the man presiding of this maelstrom of mayhem and mischief was none other than Gioachino Rossini himself. Verdi had met the older composer not long after his successes with *Nabucco*. The two men had taken a genuine liking to each other, particularly after Rossini, a fellow *oenophile*, shared a story about a gift of grapes from Baron Rothchild's vineyards. Crates of those freshly picked fruits unexpectedly arrived at Rossini's home after the Baron attended one of the composer's operas. Rossini, however, sent them back to the Baron with a note: "I do not take my wine in pill form. Eating, loving, singing, and digesting are, in truth," he declared, "The four acts of this comic opera we know as life, and they pass by as quickly as the bubbles escaping a bottle of prosecco. Whoever lets them pop without having first enjoyed them, is a fool." The ever astute Rothchild had the grapes replaced with crates of his finest wines.

"Ever since Rossini retired from composing operas," said Roqueplan, "Our Maestro takes great delight in producing all the chaos you see before you. It's great fun and nobody can pull it off as well as Rossini can, but I miss his operas on our stage."

"We all do" said Escudier, pointing his finger at Verdi, "And that's one of the many reasons there's such great opportunity for you here."

"Opportunity? That's hardly the first time someone has said that to me." Verdi opened up the leather satchel he always carried and pulled out a sheath of papers, his grand *Canzonatini* that secretly detailed Mazzini's instructions for the uprising that was expected. "Yes, thank you. But do you think we can ask Rossini to perform this?"

"Oh, one of yours?" asked Roqueplan, clearly excited.

"No," replied Verdi, "It's just an English waltz in the Italian style a friend handed me as I was leaving London. I'd love to hear how it sounds. And if it's as pretty as I believe it to be, those dancers downstairs should love it as well."

"Absolutely," said Escudier. He snapped his fingers. His valet, who had been standing nearby, came hurrying over. Escudier handed him the score and instructed him to bring it down to Rossini.

What Verdi did not tell his two companions was that this *Canzonatini* he had prepared with Mazzini was destined for the unknown secret agent of *Giovine Italia* who was purportedly at the salon. As Verdi wondered who it was going to be, he also could not help but wonder if somewhere in the swirling masses of humanity that seemed to crowd every space in the palace, would there be that Italian woman, that new transplant to Paris, that teacher of opera, that woman who bedeviled him, Giuseppina Strepponi.

As the valet worked his way through the crowds and down the stairs, the conversation of the three men returned to the business at hand.

"Well," said Verdi, "You expect me to conjure up a new opera by November? Do you think I am made of magic? Impossible."

"But our Parisian audiences are craving a Verdi opera," insisted Roqueplan. "Please don't disappoint us. We're prepared to pay you for your efforts most extravagantly."

"You think it's about the money? It's not," countered Verdi. "Though I take it on principal that you will pay me what I am worth for whatever operatic effort we might agree upon, it is not about the money. All the gold in Paris will not buy me what I need most, which is time to rest, relax and recover. Do I not look like an exhausted man, a galley slave?"

"Free men row harder," chided Escudier.

"Even if they're too dead tired to lift the oars?" Verdi shot back. Just then, out of the corner of his eye, he spotted Strepponi down below waltzing with a handsome young gallant, one that seemed vaguely familiar. "Who's that?' he asked, pointing to the man.

"The one dancing with Strepponi?" asked Escudier.

"Yes, that one."

"Ah, that would be Doctor Samuel Kreisler," answered Escudier. "He's a Jewish physician from Vienna who showed up in Paris after a falling out with Emperor Ferdinand I."

"Half of Paris believes him to be infatuated with Strepponi," added Roqueplan, "The other half wagers on whether he'll succeed in storming her castle."

"She resists?" asked Verdi as he realized he did know the man. It had been Kreisler, who as the wounded Austrian Cavalry Lieutenant searched their wagon at the Parma border crossing years earlier. And now, had the former violinist and soldier become a physician, as Kreisler's father always wanted?

"What does it matter that some Jew is dancing with Mademoiselle Strepponi?" questioned Roqueplan, changing the subject again, "Isn't there some way you can give us a Verdi opera we can produce?"

"Yes," Verdi relented. "For November, but it's not something new. If you agree and you pay my full fare, I have a plan. I will rescore *I Lombardi* to a French language libretto and add in a ballet sequence. We change over the roles from Lombard Crusaders to French knights and rename the opera *Jérusalem.* All you need do is find me a poet who can rework the libretto and do it quickly."

"Perfect," insisted Escudier, "Don't you agree?" he asked of Roqueplan.

Just as Roqueplan sat back to consider this option, Rossini's dance orchestra began playing the *Canzonatini.* As soon as Verdi heard those notes, he immediately shifted his attention to the Grand Salon below. Rapidly scanning the crowded dance floor, he wondered who, if any one would react. In so doing, he could not help but notice that Strepponi was still dancing with Kreisler. Was that why she'd been so brittle when they'd met before he went on to London? Another man, was that it? Had she finally found another partner?

Verdi was contemplating that possibility when right on cue the orchestra played the motif from the *Marseillaise* that he had woven into the fabric of the *Canzonatini.* Verdi waited. Who would it be? Who was the secret agent? What happened next however stunned him. Kreisler, that purportedly lovesick puppy, abruptly broke off dancing with Strepponi. Leaving her alone and dumbfounded on the dance floor, he headed over to Rossini's piano. Was Kreisler the secret agent? Or worse, an Austrian spy who had recognized their code? And the *Marseillaise?*

"Excuse me," said Verdi to his two companions as he hastily stood up to leave, "I need to run downstairs. Léon, do the deal and work out the details."

Strepponi was still standing alone in the middle of the Grand Salon when Verdi verily slide into her arms.

"May I have this dance?" he asked as he placed one arm around her waist while entangling the fingers of his other hand into hers.

"*È strano,* it's strange your suddenly being here," stated Strepponi with surprise as they began to dance in time to the waltz. One, two, three; one, two, three…

Verdi loved nestling his hand into the small of her back. It felt so natural, as if it had always belonged there. "By your side I always feel myself reborn."

"Seriously? You're hardly a new born babe. And if I said, 'No?' would you go away?"

"Are you asking me to leave?"

"No, not yet."

"Good, then."

"Why? Did you imagine your love was fatal to me?"

"If it is your desire that I should leave, I would. Is that your wish?"

"Is it?" she asked. "You destroyed me in Parma with your Clarina's Rules… And that still hurts," she retorted. "But if you're suddenly thinking you're the only salve for my troubled heart, know my escort is right over there." Strepponi motioned with her head towards the piano where Rossini was leading his orchestra. Kreisler was hovering over him. "He'll be back any moment."

"No, he won't."

"He will, he's madly in love with me. Ah, maybe he's the one who lit up a new fever that aroused my love! He's modest and vigilant and you know he'll be back to climb the steps to my door once again."

"He won't. He may be infatuated, but he doesn't love you," Verdi replied with utter assuredness as he stared directly into her eyes to ascertain what truths hid there.

Strepponi could not help but wink back at him with a look, a satiric and bemused one that could have only passed between two old lovers quarreling on stage in a comic opera. And the more they each tried to one up the other, the more their repartee took on the air of a duet orchestrated by the very waltz they were dancing.

"You are just jealous," Strepponi said. "Of course, he loves me. All Paris knows it."

"Ah, all Paris," repeated Verdi, "Escudier makes the same claim, which makes it certainly a lie. Shall we wager your doctor has other priorities?"

"How would you know that?"

"Escudier is a publicist, an impresario, ergo, everything he says is a lie."

"And ergo," she responds, with a tone mocking his use of the word, *ergo,* "The opposite must be true? You returned from London just to tell me this? No thanks. Did you sleep with the Queen? Did you bring joy to her troubled soul?"

"Victoria. Not a chance. Prince Albert never left her side,"

"Not that queen. Lind, Jenny Lind, the Queen of Song. Did you sleep with her too? I read the reviews. You were gushing over her performance."

"Gushing? I don't gush."

"You do. You did."

"I don't."

"You did. You said she was exquisite."

"She was." Verdi continued to watch Kreisler, unsure what to expect and unsure what he should do, especially if the former Lieutenant was a spy for the other side.

"I'm a woman, damn it. I know what it means when you grade her as exquisite."

"I didn't come here to fight."

"No?"

"No. And I did not sleep with her. Nor the Queen. Nor anybody. I came to apologize."

Just then the *Canzonatini* waltz ended and the second orchestra on the opposite end of the room started up a new dance.

"For what? Demeaning my lover? Would a serious affair be a misfortune for me? He's coming back, you know."

"You think so? Shall we watch?" Verdi shifted their waltz positioning so they could both look down the length of the room toward Rossini's piano. "I still say he won't return."

"And I say he will. I'm a woman. I know what intrigues the good doctor."

"A bet?"

"A bet."

Together they both watched as Kreisler lifted the *Canzonatini* score from the piano. He folded it over and then tucked it inside his coat. Kreisler then scribbled a note, which he handed to Rossini. After that, he made to leave the palace altogether.

This stunned Strepponi. "And you knew he was going to leave because Escudier said he would stay? Is that it?"

"I knew he would leave because he has a job to do – be it for good or evil."

"Other than being my escort? Leaving a poor woman, alone, abandoned in this crowded desert they call Paris? What suddenly took precedence? What am I to hope for now on? What must I do? Have fun? And perish in this vortex of pleasure!"

"I can't say."

"You can't? Or won't?" She asked.

"Those that speak, do not know. Those that know, do not speak."

"*Merde*. Nonsense." She replied.

Out of the corner of his eye, Verdi saw Rossini discreetly wave him over. "War is coming. As Dario so often advises, safety lies in letting secrets sleep."

"Yes, but Kreisler walked out - abandoned me. At least tell me where he's going."

"Vienna," he answered as he gradually maneuvered them ever closer to Rossini's piano.

"Vienna?" Strepponi was puzzled. "Why Vienna.?"

"Because those are his instructions."

"This is your doing, isn't it?"

"Perhaps, but there's nothing more I can add.

"Why must all these radicals be so rude?" demanded Strepponi.

"I'm not sure he's one of ours… he might be one of theirs. He is - or was - an Austrian officer."

"Kreiser hates the Emperor. He blames Ferdinand for the wounds that ended his career as a violinist."

"So, he says. If he's a spy, that's an excellent cover story.

"Yes, he says."

"But I suspect it was our Isabella or Dario who shot at him during an ambush."

"Of course. So, why are you here?" Strepponi asked.

"I came to Paris produce an opera," he added as their waltzing brought them ever closer to Rossini.

"I don't mean Paris; everyone knows you're here to produce an opera. What I want to know is why are you here - here in my arms dancing with me – again?"

"I truly just came to apologize."

"For what?"

"For us, for me, for the past few years. I have been horribly wrong. And scared and terrified."

"Giuseppe Verdi speaks! You? Frightened? Of what?"

"You," replied Verdi.

"Me? You're terrified of me? A broken down singer? Me?"

"Yes. You. No one in the world loves you—"

"No one?"

"No one except me."

"Really? How is it I've forgotten your great love for me."

"Are you mocking me? Have you no heart?"

"You broke it. And now I'm a free woman, free to cavort from joy to joy."

"Forgive me. It is all my fault."

"Yes, it is. When I was child, I had a vision of a man in my future, one handsome and divine. And our love made me throb like the pulsing of the universe. You, my little Verdi, first you bring me such mysterious ecstasy to my heart – I loved it and I loved you - but then you ended it with such cruel pain. Clarina's rules."

"I beg your forgiveness," he said.

They were practically on top of Rossini's piano by now. The maestro, who was resting between waltzes, looked at the couple with a bemused look upon his face.

"Would you have me fly off on the wings of desire?" Strepponi asked.

"Yes, a thousand times over, yes, yes, yes."

"Such nonsense," replied Strepponi. She stopped their dancing.

While still holding her hands, Verdi dropped to one knee and looked directly back up into her eyes. "Giuseppina Strepponi, I love you."

"Get up! Your love is just a mad delusion," she replied as they were just about to start waltzing again, "But a pleasurable time always cures my pain."

"Wait," Rossini suddenly interjected, "The good doctor left you a note."

"Ah, my physician not doubt explaining himself," Strepponi said as she reached for the letter.

Rossini shook his head. *"No, non è per la signora, ma per il signor Verdi,"* he declared as he handed the note instead to a somewhat surprised Verdi.

Strepponi was dumbfounded. "You're getting my love note? What does *Herr Doktor* Kreisler have to say."

Verdi unfolded the letter and read it aloud, "Thank Dario for the cannoli. They're impossible to find in Vienna."

Chapter Ten:

May Dawn Never Arrive in Paradise

Paris, The Next Morning, July 30, 1847

With concerns about Kreisler preying on his mind, Verdi awoke early, before even the usually noisy peacocks had stirred from their roosts. His bedroom at *Le Jardin de la Beauté Tranquille*, was pitch black but he could hear Strepponi softly breathing as she slept beside him. Slipping out from under the summer weight covers as silently as possible, he then gathered up his clothes from under her ballroom gown and tip-toed out into the drawing room. Only after he had closed the bedroom door and dressed, did he light a candle and check his pocket watch. It was just after 4:00 am.

Was the good doctor a friend or a foe? A revolutionary or a lackey? He did not know but with lives were at stake, Verdi set pen to paper. With great haste, lest Strepponi wake and interrogate him before he finished, he managed to craft two complete messages and accompanying *Canzonatini* full of warnings and questions. By 5:15 am, just as the sun rose to the accompaniment of the peacocks, Verdi put the first one into an envelope addressed to Mazzini's agents in London and the second one, well, the second one was to be sent to Isabella and me at *Casa di Trevi* with an extra exhortation for us to find out more about Kreisler through our connections not just with *Giovine Italia* but also, if possible, from her cousin Enrico Guastella, a well-connected partisan and banker with deep access to the Hebrew communities in Milan and Vienna.

Verdi brought the two letter downstairs to the hotel's concierge just as the clerk arrived for the morning shift. He then inquired about where he could find the nearest bakery at this hour – which turned out by good fortune to be around the corner. After purchasing several crème filled croissants with pistachios – Strepponi's favorite addiction - he headed back up to his suite.

As he reached the landing outside his door, he heard singing coming from inside. Yes, she was awake. It was a melody he recognized almost immediately, *Violetta's Lament*, though he had not heard Strepponi sing that Ladino melody since that day the revolution began at Ca' Dario.

"Good bye, my love, I do not want to live…" she sang.

Back then, he had fallen in love with her soprano voice which he considered exquisite; this time around, he was in love with the entire woman, madly, passionately and joyfully. He lingered on the landing and listened. And for the first time, he did not just hear her voice projecting as if she were playing a role on stage, he heard her probe the deepest wounds of a woman's soul, a woman who had suffered and endured much in loving her man. He felt her anguish, her pains, her trauma; emotions he knew he had inflicted upon Strepponi by loving her both poorly and not enough. It is these heart-wrenching passions that Verdi would capture only a few short years later on when he wrote perhaps the most enduring and beloved soprano role of all time, that of the appropriately named Violetta Valery in his masterpiece, *La Traviata*. And when that Violetta is dying at the end of the Third Act, she sings *Addio, del passato*, whose sentiment, words and melody were absolutely inspired by that original fifteenth century Ladino version of *Violetta's Lament*, *Adío Querida*. But that was still in future.

Now, on that warm summer morning in Paris, tears pooled up in Verdi's eyes as he experienced the depth of their mutual affections while simultaneously understanding that if he was ever going to capture the true essence of a woman, any woman, in his arias, the wisest, best, most passionate guide, he could ever learn from, was that beautiful wizard on the other side of that door. After wiping his cheeks, he put the key in the lock and opened it.

And as the door to the suite swung open, he found Strepponi, singing and dancing, using his cane as her partner. She wore one of his unbuttoned white shirts with his red silk scarf draped across her shoulders. Atop her head, she wore his ubiquitous black top hat.

"I'm not leaving and I am not dying," she announced as she strutted toward him, "Not now, not this morning, not ever."

"*Viva la rivoluzione*, viva Violetta," declared Verdi as he set the pastries down. He knew there was much to learn about women, especially this woman, and he was prepared to spend a lifetime so engaged.

"Pistachio! You brought me pistachio croissants! Oh, Giuseppe Verdi, your little Violetta loves and adores you."

"Come," he half whispered, as he pulled her back into his arms for a sweet lingering kiss, one they would both declare later, was akin to Paradise Found.

****

They began August as if they were honeymooning in Paris, spending every night and day together. The restorative powers of their love affair provided Verdi with all the rest and relaxation his soul required. They enjoyed leisurely breakfasts at cafés along the boulevards; afternoon strolls and carriage rides through the parks; theater, ballets and concerts in the evening; and dinners at Lapérouse, an ancient restaurant favored by the likes of Georges Sand, Chopin and Victor Hugo. He never tired of listening to her sweet soprano voice, be it to hear simple thoughts of the day or some profound insights into the depths of human nature. Her eyes, ones that proved the Shakespearian cliché of being the windows to her soul, fascinated him, nor did he ever tire of simply looking at her, gathering in her total beauty, strength and wisdom. Yes, he admitted to himself, he was totally, deeply, irrevocably in love with this woman. And best of all, her love for him made him desirous of composing again it was as if she alone had restored beauty back into his life.

And Strepponi? She was pleased beyond all measure to feel embraced by Verdi's affections for her. Yes, the man every woman would have liked to conquer, was hers. Clarina's rules be damned. Verdi's attachment to her was a dream realized. It wasn't just the way they could talk, dance, discuss life, or make love; they so naturally enjoyed the aura of the other's presence, that even sitting quietly together or reading books beside each other, felt simply grand and wonderful. And for Strepponi to be appreciated for her intellectual qualities was a novelty. What other lover had every realized that her female body came equipped with fully functioning brain? Only Verdi.

Frankly, the hardest task they both faced was not only believing their mutual joy was genuine, but that they each deserved to be happy in this life… And they were, ecstatically so…

By mid-August, after Roqueplan signed off and paid for the score, Verdi set to work composing the new music for *Jérusalem*, which he dedicated it to Strepponi. And she, when not instructing her vocal students, would often sit by his side while he composed, suggesting touches here and there that Verdi not only welcomed but trusted. Yes, he knew her worth and that meant the world to her.

Come September, Verdi surrendered even the pretense of maintaining a separate address at *Le Jardin de la Beauté Tranquille*. After bidding farewell to the Oriental garden and its muster of peacocks, he moved into Strepponi's apartment near the opera house on the *Rue de la Victoire*. There, he continued to work on the new score.

It was at the *Rue de la Victoire*, that my reply to his *Canzonatini* about Kreisler finally caught up and found Verdi. "No," I wrote him, "Stay on guard. No one in Milan knows the doctor's allegiances," but, I went on to add that neither Isabella nor I nor Guastella had heard back from our contacts in Vienna. I promised to alert him as soon as we did. I also described the rising tension between the Austrian militia and we Milanese. Early in September the police had shot at a crowd that was protesting the ascension of the detested Bishop Giuliano Giuliani as the new archbishop of Milan. The clash left a dozen dead and more than sixty wounded. Both the Hapsburgs rulers and the ghouls in the church leadership dismissed the violence as necessary, claiming the rebels were all part of the outlawed

Giovine Italia movement.

After the rioting, the Austrian Field Marshall Joseph Radetzky – nobody's fool when it came to military matters – realized that he needed to strengthen the size of his armed forces in Milan if he was to succeed in maintaining control as were his orders from Emperor Joseph. Given that funding was short, Radetzky found another solution, which we learned about from our spies. The Field Marshall had met in secret with some of the local aristocrats loyal to the Emperor and informed them in absolute frankness that the Hapsburgs could no longer guarantee that law and order would be preserved in Lombardy. All of their estates and properties would be at risk unless they helped in the creation of create private militias that would serve in support of the regular army. Those aristocrats who failed to help the Emperor in this time of need, would be viewed with great disdain. Hoping to maintain their favored status with the Hapsburgs, Cesare Briscola – now the Duke of Mantua after the death of his elderly father - and some of his closest allies, including the Trombas, the Cornettis and the Bannos, took the lead in assembling these mercenaries. However, to pay for their private armies, many of them were compelled to raise capital by selling off or mortgaging surplus properties. And although the battle lines between those royalists and we revolutionaries were being drawn ever starker, some fascinating opportunities were also appearing. Lands up for sale near Busseto alone included not only *La Corte degli Angeli*, but tracts around an enclave known as Sant' Agata that Verdi had long coveted. Was he interested? Antonio Barezzi, Verdi's father-in-law and the man who kept an eye on Verdi's accounts when he was away, was more than happy to act as an intermediary along with Enrico Guastella – whose actual job when not fighting was as a staid and conservative banker in Parma.

In October we received Verdi's reply. "Revenge is best done in secret. Have Barezzi and Guastella buy up all good lands of value using third party names and shell companies." He added that he'll be home in the new year, but left the date vague. Cleary, for the first time since the death of Margherita, Verdi had found happiness and was anxious to have a true home again.

Strepponi stayed by Verdi's side through the grueling rehearsals for *Jérusalem*, assisting him with both the principal singers and the chorus right up until its November opening. Roqueplan and Escudier were both sufficiently pleased and as a result, a slew of offers continued to flow in for new Verdi operas, seemingly here, there and everywhere. Verdi could not thank Strepponi enough for her strength and support, which continued to enrich his soul.

In December, Verdi's former father-in-law, Antonio Barezzi, came to Paris on business. Strepponi played the welcoming hostess. Rather than have Verdi's friend and benefactor, book a hotel, she instead asked Barezzi to stay at her home. He accepted. Although Strepponi was clearly the new woman in Verdi's life, she and Barezzi managed to get along quite well. For his part, Barezzi found her a more than worthy companion for his former son-in-law - a state of affairs that pleased Verdi.

Barezzi also shared with the couple the news coming out of Lombardy and Parma, some good, some ominous. First, with the help of Enrico Guastella, the land purchases were progressing under the auspices of several shadow entities Barezzi had created but the gems of the region, that is to say Sant' Agata and *La Corte degli Angeli*, were still priced too high. Negotiations would continue.

"War is coming," Barezzi said. The Austrians were continuing to build up their forces in Lombardy. In addition to the private militias, Field Marshall Joseph Radetzky had imposed a Tobacco Tax. Radetzky's intent was to use funds generated by the widespread sale of ever-popular cigars enjoyed by the Milanese to pay for his increased militarization of Lombardy.

In response to the tax, the people reacted much as the American colonialist had done when their British overlords imposed a tariff on tea: universally, the Milanese stopped smoking cigars. The tobacco boycott was on and woe unto those who were caught smoking not just by our partisans but by the everyday citizens of the city. Those who did light up – mostly supporters of the Habsburgs - were often set upon by street gangs and beaten up. Tensions grew ever higher in the city.

Barezzi left Paris for Busseto Christmas week, and it was soon thereafter that the capitals of Europe welcomed the New Year of 1848 with – as Mazzini had predicted - riots and uprisings. This Year of Revolutions began in January when angry mobs of Sicilians chased the Spanish Bourbon King out of his castle in Palermo. In February, barricades went up all over Paris as a coalition of French citizens deposed King Louis-Philippe - events Verdi and Strepponi witnessed firsthand.

Remarkably, in March rioting sprang up in the very heart of the Hapsburg Empire: Vienna. Partisans there scored a yet another major victory over the aristocracy. And Kreisler? We learned this; he had indeed been on our side. The good doctor was in the vanguard of partisans who forced Prince Klemens von Metternich, a Chancellor of the Austrian Empire into exile. Metternich was the man who three decades earlier after the defeat of Napoleon, had restored the royal monarchies of Europe to power. His flight from Vienna combined with the news that the Hapsburg's power was crumbling, led to more riots across the border in Venice. A loss there would upend the Austrian's control of the entire Veneto region.

The spark of revolution was also about to ignite Milan next… So, while Verdi and Strepponi continued to find peace and contentment with each other at her Paris apartment on the appropriately named *Rue de la Victoire,* more blood was destined to flow on the cobblestone streets outside Ca' Dario.

****

Though Verdi was content to linger with Strepponi in France, and resist the allure of home, his music and his operas, suffused with songs of rebels and revolt, surrounded and embraced Milan as a lover and nowhere more so, of course, than at Ca' Dario. There, every evening students from the conservatory would sing arias and duets from his ever popular works. These young singers, such as a teenaged Eduardo Villa, and his then girlfriend, another up and coming Italian-American soprano, also from Santa Barbara, Gianna Carradori, would enthrall diners. Rather than have our singers stay rooted to the piano in the Il Nord room, I would often accompany them on a guitar as we would wander out from *Il Nord* into the bar and then all the other rooms, including *Il Colosseo, Lo Stivale,* and *la Cucina gratuita,* the free kitchen in our Sicily outbuilding. At Ca' Dario, everyone, from the rich to the poor to the homeless and destitute, embraced Verdi's patriotic melodies.

Yes, his songs had so become the heart and soul of the *Risorgimento,* that the more the Austrians cracked down upon our ever growing resistance to their absolute control, the more his arias were embraced and exalted.

And the response to Field Marshall Radetzky's tobacco tax? Why, the Milanese would ask, should we pay for the privilege of being oppressed? Its widespread failure frustrated the Austrian commandant.

Finally, on the night of March 17th, as news spread of uprising across Europe, those two forces, one symbolized by cigars and the other by Verdi's music, came crashing together inside the Tuscany Room Bar at Ca' Dario where I was backing up Gianna and Eduardo as they were performing a variety of *canzoni* from Verdi's operas.

Even then, though Eduardo was barely 17, he had an intimidating physique characterized by that powerful barrel chest and massive arms, all of which had led to Uncle Roberto to bestow upon him that nickname, *Il Torino*. Eduardo had just launched into an aria from Verdi's *Ernani* – the one where our namesake hero hears the hunting horn that calls him to his death - at the same moment that Cesare Briscola and two of the self-appointed Colonels in his private army, Primo Tromba and Renato Giuliani, the Archbishop's nephew, entered from the street.

The three clowns and their toy soldiers, for that is what they all were, wore ornate gold braided uniforms that were pathetically more about puffery than real power. Briscola, Tromba and Renato Giuliani sat down at the bar and after ordering a round of drinks for their men, the three immediately lit up cigars – the only patrons in the length and breadth of Ca' Dario to do so.

Uncle Roberto, who had a keen eye and was always watchful for such provocations, insisted that the clowns needed to crimp and crush out their cigars.

Instead, Cesare and his allies all cried out, "All hail Emperor Joseph!"

Their shouts momentarily startled everyone around them into silence. I signaled Eduardo to stop singing and then, as a show of strength I went and stood beside Roberto.

The clowns, thinking they had won the day, thrust their fists up in the air and shouted again, "All hail Emperor Joseph!"

This time, the reaction of our customers was both universal and unsurprising. They roared back, *"Viva l'Italia. Down with the Tax! Viva la rivoluzione!"*

Now, suddenly feeling intimidated by the very crowd they had so incited, Briscola, Tromba, Giuliani and their accompanying mercenaries drew out their sabers.

In response our patrons pulled guns and knives…

Sensing the potential for grave danger, Uncle Roberto stepped between the factions. With his hands raised in a gesture of peace he positioned himself directly in front of Briscola's blade. "You best leave, he said.

"Not until I finish my cigar," replied Cesare waving his blade about. "Do you not fear me?"

"Why?" replied Uncle Roberto.

"I'll slice the strings that make the music here and your Hebrew God will not protect you."

"And your God will? Your God will do what?" asked Roberto.

Cesare laughed, "You think me vile, a wretched bastard; well, you are right, I am. I believe in a cruel God, one who created us in his image. I am God's meanest child birthed and bathed in primordial slime. And in his name, I am the evil fury that will destroy you and this rabble of yours. The deeds we do this day are my destiny's decree."

"So be it," said Roberto. "That may be your creed, but his is my restaurant. And my rules. Now get out."

"Beware the black spider web we'll weave about you and the bite that kills."

"Now," said Roberto, pointing directly from one thug to the next. "Now."

But when Cesare shook his head, "No," and sliced a button off Roberto's shirt with his blade, our *Il Torino*, Eduardo Villa, stepped forward. He positioned himself directly beside Roberto and in front of Briscola's sword. In retrospect you might say that our little bull had taking on the *Ernani* role a bit too seriously by emulating his heroism, but that would have been to underestimate Eduardo's lifelong courage in the face of death.

As tempers rose and accusations and threats bounced back and forth between the clowns and the patriots, we all feared someone's stupidity would trigger bloodshed.

Cesare sneered at Eduardo and then pointed at Gianna Carradori. "Women are fickle, my foolish friend. They flitter like feathers in the wind. She'll change her voice, her thoughts and put on a pretty face. But you, you will always be miserable if you trust her, confide in her and leave your heart unguarded."

Abruptly, our *Il Torino* began to sing *Va' Pensiero* at the top of his lungs. In an instant, all of Ca' Dario joined in and the resultant noise was as overwhelming and intimidating as the roar of lions. Our unanimity and collective defiance, so unnerved Cesare and his jesters that the mercenaries signaled retreat and thus the clown troops backed away and slunk out the door, but not before Cesare issued one last threat to Uncle Roberto, "You'll pay for this... Beware the bite that kills."

When they were gone, huge cheers of exultation rang from the rafters. "*Viva la Vittoria,* Long live Victory!" but we knew it would not last. The Austrians would be back.

And yes, what historians now call "The Five Days of Milan," began the next morning. We were prepared.

When a mixed group of Austrian soldiers and Cesare Briscola's mercenaries – some thirty strong and all smoking cigars - returned in force to the avenue outside Ca 'Dario, we met them with a crowd of Milanese twice times their number. Uncle Roberto, Eduardo and I were among them. And of course, with a hot-head like Cesare, leading the pack, trouble began immediately. With raised swords and muskets, the soldiers sought to intimidate our patriots.

But the Milanese had had enough and would not cower. We shouted back in defiance "*Viva l'Italia, Viva la rivoluzione!* Down with the Tax!" Yes, we were ready. After all, it was not for naught, that through *Giovine Italia*, we had been smuggling, stockpiling and distributing guns and ammunition; much of which now appeared in the hands of our fellow partisans. At first, we booed and mocked the Austrians. Then, rocks began to fly. As the stones cascaded down on the soldiers, one knocked Cesare Briscola to the ground. The Austrian officer in command gave the order to load and to prepare to fire.

And there's the rub that worked in our favor. Because muskets are notoriously difficult and slow to load particularly in the tight quarters of urban combat, veteran troops usually coordinate their firing in two or three ranks, that is to say, one group shoots as the others reload and aim.

Not today, though. Briscola's mercenaries – an untrained group of lowlifes and drunks – were the first to panic. They fired wildly and then, rather than reloading, they ran off, leaving Cesare and the Austrian troops alone to face a rebellious crowd, one that vastly outnumbered them.

After the Austrians fired their initial salvo into the crowd, our people surged forward before the soldiers could reload. Hand to hand combat ensued with injuries and deaths on both sides. Blood flowed everywhere, staining the cobblestones once again. I was right beside young Eduardo as our *il Torino* led the charge, saber in hand, though his only training with that weapon had been on an opera stage. To our left, Uncle Roberto fired his pistol at an Austrian musketeer and dropped him, only to have Cesare Briscola pop up from behind the dying soldier and slash at Roberto with his blade. However, it was soon clear that those remaining foreign soldiers, mostly recent conscripts, had no taste for battle. They too hastily broke ranks and fled.

News of our clash spread immediately and soon triggered a full scale insurrection. Combat between the Austrians and the Milanese rapidly transformed into open warfare. Everywhere throughout the city, our citizens took up arms using the weapons we had stockpiled.

When Radetzky's main forces tried to counter attack, our partisans hastily erected hundreds of barricades with overturned carriages, pianos, sofas, barrels and more, which made it virtually impossible for the Austrian troops to maneuver around our city's narrow streets. Our fighters then responded by attacking each of the Austrian army's check points and outposts that were scattered about the city with overwhelming force. Combat was rapidly played out in many isolated battles which was highly advantageous to us, as we Milanese, knew the streets and the terrain. On the fifth day, March 22nd, when our forces threatened to overwhelm the central Austrian garrison, Radetzky ordered his troops to evacuate Milan. They retreated over a hundred miles, all the way past the Lombardy border with the Veneto, into what Radetzky called his Quadrilateral defense, near Verona. There, the wily old commander sought to regroup his forces while awaiting reinforcements from Austria.

As the Habsburg troops fled, some of our Milanese leaders begged King Charles Albert of neighboring Savoy to join us in the war against the Austrians. And Charles Albert, an Italian who ruled from his palace in Turin, welcomed the invitation. Ever the conniving opportunist, the King decided this was the moment to solidify opposition to the Hapsburgs and thus begin the process of unifying the Italian peninsula under his rule. As Charles Albert's troops took up the battle against Radetzky's forces, our first real taste of freedom arrived in Lombardy. Yes, just like that, after centuries of foreign control, our day of liberation had come.

As I would later share in a dispatch to Verdi, the price we paid for our victories, was severe. Over six hundred Milanese died in the uprising. Among the first heroes to perish, a victim of Cesare Briscola's saber, was my Uncle Roberto who fell outside Ca' Dario. After that first skirmish had ended, our *il Torino* carried Roberto's broken body back to the restaurant with as much solemnity as if he had been Michelangelo's Nicodemus lifting Christ down from the Cross. I swore that day that I would avenge his death and deliver my own form of final justice to Cesare, but that would have to wait. Briscola and his allies had all fled with the Austrians to Verona.

And as tragic as that loss was, it also changed my life forever as responsibility for Ca' Dario immediately fell upon me, Isabella and our now eight year old son, Tre.

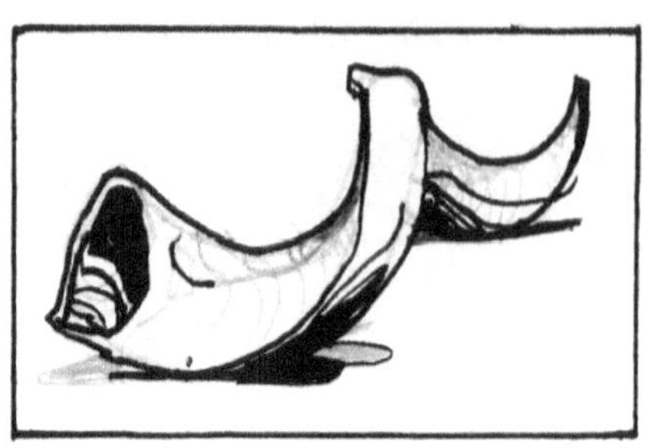

Chapter Eleven:

A Gift from Someone Among the Angels

Milan, April 1848

Will you go back to Milan?" Strepponi asked of Verdi after the two had read my dispatch about our victory over the Austrians.

"If only to stand with Dario at his Uncle Roberto's funeral." Verdi explained the debt he owed my uncle. He shared with Strepponi about how in the past, Uncle Roberto not only fed him and his family for free when Verdi was as poor as the proverbial church mouse, Roberto had always insisted that the Verdis dine on his best meals, the daily specials, and drink the best wines in his fanciest dining room, *il Nord*.

"Why there?" asked Strepponi.

"He believed in me. And he did not want me to feel self-conscious or anxious or even intimidated by his gifts. 'You deserve the best,' he would say before repeating his motto, 'Why be mundane, when with passion you can be monumental?' And when I asked him how I could ever pay him back, he simply said, '*Viva la rivoluzione*. Continue composing the music that conspires with Italians to create Italy and I will pass into heaven a happy man.'"

"Then you must go, but you better be coming back to my boudoir," insisted Strepponi. Although she expressed confidence then that Verdi would return and that their bonds were now unbreakable, years later – after an incident involving the soprano, Teresa Stolz - she confided in me that a part of her was not so sure he would return. In a small corner of her heart, she steeled herself to be dumped yet again while dreading a "Dear Giuseppina," letter. Yes, she was scared. But more on that later. In the meantime, Verdi reassured her he would be back. He left Paris for Milan the next morning, arriving later that week. We met at Ca' Dario.

Verdi's first wish upon arriving in Milan was to pay his respects to my Uncle Roberto. You can well imagine that during the insurrection we were unable to hold a traditional Hebrew funeral nor stay at home for the seven days of mourning known as sitting *shiva*. Instead, Isabella and I decided to wait until after Verdi returned and to then hold a memorial gathering at Ca' Dario.

With Verdi's wish as my marching orders, we drove out by wagon to my uncle's grave at the old Jewish Cemetery of Porta Vercellina, which, as many of you know, was around the corner from Santa Maria delle Grazie, the church that housed Leonardo da Vinci's fresco of another famous Jew finishing his final feast on a night he was betrayed by one of his own.

"Are you here to stay?" I asked him.

"Much as I would like to, no, I can't. I'm here just few weeks, maybe a month. Strepponi and I, we both have commitments in Paris to finish before we can move home."

"Together? Move home? The two of you?"

"Yes, absolutely. And if you must know, for the first time since Margherita died, I'm actually happy and content... I love her. And if I have my way, we will never be apart again."

"Truly?" I was both surprised and pleased by this declaration.

"*Si, assolutamente!* When I first reached Paris after staging *I Masnadieri* in London, I was exhausted to the core of my soul and frankly, I was ready to quit and end this maddening career. People may judge me famous, but you know my truth. I would have come to nothing without Strepponi's help, first *Oberto* and then *Nabucco*. She was the star who lifted me up when I was as low and sad and desperate as any man could be. And she did it again in Paris with *Jérusalem*. Even though we may have switched places in the firmament of stars everyone calls fame and success, she still lifts me up every day. Her love is the reason I wake each morning and bring her, her coffee and pistacchio croissants, And that love causes me to happily slide back into our bed at night." Verdi confessed to me that he had no intention of destroying his relationship with her as he had once before.

"Don't judge yourself too harshly," I said. "You did what you thought you needed to do back then. There's no blame in that."

"I wasted years," he said with a deep sense of regret in his voice, "Years we could have been happy."

"No, be kind to yourself. You were not ready. You had to learn what you needed to learn. Remember, when it comes to love, as Alessandro Manzoni once wrote, the heart is forever making the head its fool. And if there is anything of value I have come to understand in our short lives, it is this: The love we crave is no different than the Democracy we desire. Both are fragile. We must become gardeners, tending them constantly and consistently or they will fail, they will die. But if we are to succeed, if we succeed in nourishing our gardens, my friend, in the end, we will be better people in a better world."

"That is my plan," he said, "Especially if Barezzi and Guastella are able to negotiate a deal on the property I want north of Busseto at Sant' Agata. This time, for real, I am going to return to the land and become a farmer – or at least a farmer who composes occasionally."

Or at least a composer who farms a bit, I thought knowing Verdi. "I'm happy and delighted for you both, but Strepponi will come with you?" I asked. Though Verdi was in his heart and soul, a man of the earth, one who could thrive in the countryside, the Strepponi I knew and had traveled with, was an urban woman, a lady more comfortable wearing high heels at a salon than mud boots in a pig slough.

"Of course! She's already agreed, she loves the idea. She's even looking forward to having her own garden of flowers," Verdi declared, but then he changed topics when we reached the grave site, one covered with fresh soil, "Though I was delirious with joy when I read in your letter that the Austrians were gone, I cried my eyes out to learn of Uncle Roberto's death – and that it was Cesare Briscola who killed him. I loved Roberto; a true patriot. And he was my family too. Now, to think, Dario, that thanks to his sacrifice, the hour of our liberation, Lombardy's liberation has at last, arrived."

"Yes, it's wonderous but our new found freedom is almost too hard to believe," I said, "And I was there at the barricades. I saw it happen, yet every time I walk into Ca' Dario, I expect to see the Austrians playing cards in the bar. But, *liberami*, they're gone."

"We won, the people of our country won," said Verdi. "Everything we dreamed of, everything we hoped would come true, has happened. I knew it would be dangerous traveling now, but I had to be here and bear witness."

"Your right about that," I said. Throughout Lombardy there remained pockets of resistance by isolated Austrians troops who were trapped in place by Radetzky's rapid and unexpected retreat. Snipers with twitchy fingers hide everywhere, along the main highways and country roads.

"But like the good gardener you alluded to before, I had to be here to see freedom sprouting with my own eyes. Yes, risky or not, I had to be here," said Verdi. "More than ever, I am convinced that when we, the people of this land, demand our independence, no monarch that can resist. The royalists and clergy can conspire as much as they like, but they will not succeed in cheating we the people, out of our rights."

"*È vero*, it's true enough," I said. "Perhaps in a few years, maybe even with good fortune, this year, all of Italy – not just Lombardy and Savoy - will grow into a free, united country and for once, a Republic."

"What else should Italy be? There cannot be any music more welcome to our countrymen's ears in 1848 except the echo of cannons," replied Verdi. You cannot imagine the magnitude of impact upon Verdi's soul that came with his knowing all of his creative efforts had actually helped us gain our freedom and independence. For him, for us, this was a moment of true and unadulterated joy.

"All that is missing," I added, "Is the sound of that bastard Cesare Briscola begging for mercy."

"*Sì,*" said Verdi. "We will get him. Mark well my words. Nothing unavenged shall remain."

Before returning to Ca' Daro, Verdi insisted we should stop at the convent of Santa Maria delle Grazie to see da Vinci's *Last Supper*. Though the chapel where the fresco was displayed was closed to outsiders, Verdi nonetheless inquired of one of the friars if we could gain entrance. You must understand that by 1848, Verdi knew his fame was such that just his mere presence was the key that unlocked many a door, and sure enough the friar was thrilled to have the Maestro visit.

After studying da Vinci's masterpiece, Verdi turned to me and said, "If I could only compose an opera equal in genius to that, ah, that would be my dream."

"A worthy one, indeed," I replied, a goal that in retrospect Verdi certainly did achieve in the course of his long lifetime.

"But, I confess," Verdi went on to say, "That when I gaze upon da Vinci's masterpiece, I can only imagine what Uncle Roberto would have said were he here, 'It's da Vinci, his *Last Supper*, in Italy? Of course it's about the food.'"

****

A few nights later we closed Ca' Dario to outsiders for Uncle Roberto's memorial and kept the guests to a relatively small group. There was, after all, a guerilla war still raging outside the city and travel was truly difficult. Even my parents and the Barezzis who had wanted to come up from Busseto, stayed away. Though the Duchy of Parma had not been as yet involved in the fighting, travel into Lombardy from there was still far too risky. That was particularly tough on my *papà* as after all, he and Roberto were *gemelli* – twins. *Papà* later confided that they held a similar ceremony at Figaro in Busseto. How could he not?

After nearly five decades of running Ca' Dario, Uncle Roberto had amassed a fair number of friends and favored customers, many of whom insisted on attending despite the difficulties. The memorial gathering itself veered from the sacred to the profane, fueled by great food – of course – fabulous wines – absolutely – and endless stories that brought both tears and laughter.

Eduardo, our *Il Torino*, was there and it was that night I introduced him to Verdi. The two men, who both self-identified themselves as peasants from the countryside, bonded immediately. Over the course of his career Eduardo would go on to perform as the heroic tenor in some seventeen or eighteen of Verdi's operas; *Don Carlo*, *Ernani* and *Otello* being his favorites. Few were the singers who could not only match Eduardo's tenor voice, but his thorough comprehension of the subtleties of Verdi's works that enhanced his acting on stage as well.

The most significant of those guests, the ones who would play critical roles in Verdi's life and mine, were three members of *Giovine Italia*: Garibaldi, Giuseppe Mazzini and Isabella's cousin, Enrico Guastella. As a banker from Parma, our cousin's covert work had apparently helped finance the weapons used in our uprising. As for Garibaldi, I had not seen him since we both sailed out of Genoa years ago. After leading freedom fighters in South America for more than a decade, Garibaldi had returned to join the military uprising against the Austrians. And Giuseppe Mazzini, whose hat I still wore, he too had also left his exile in London as soon as he had heard the news, He had joined up with Garibaldi and his militia as they moved south from the Swiss border.

In retrospect though, the details of the party in honor of a man who had played an oversized role in our lives, were not so very important, save for a few conversations that I feel obligated to share with you. Coincidentally all but one of them involved Enrico Guastella. Though he was my cousin by marriage, until that evening I had never actually met him in person. His real name was Michele Isacco Benedetto, which he changed to Guastella in order to shield his fiancé and their daughter from retribution after he joined *Giovine Italia*. If you recall, it was a branch of the Benedetto family in Busseto that had sheltered my mother-in-law Sophia after she had been beaten up by the Briscolas.

Guastella, who grew up in the Jewish ghetto in a town of that same name, was an astonishingly talented and well connected partisan. The town of Guastella was about as far northeast of Parma as Busseto was northwest. While working as a banker, businessman and occasional journalist, Enrico served covertly as a militia officer of *Giovine Italia*. When not actually fighting, his forte as a partisan was using *lettere di credito* - letters of credit - to move money around Europe with the express purpose of purchasing weapons and ammunition. Those *lettere di credito* were written in a code akin to our *Canzonatini,* but instead of musical notes, they used the characters of the Hebrew alphabet. His work frequently brought him into direct contact with Giuseppe Mazzini and Garibaldi.

On the evening of Uncle Roberto's memorial, Guastella found himself mediating an argument between Mazzini and Garibaldi that seemed trivial if not downright insignificant at the time, but ultimately shaped the very nature of the Risorgimento and the birth of our nation. Mazzini was perturbed that the partisans of Milan had turned to King Charles Albert of Savoy to help throw out the Austrians.

"Our goal is a free, independent and democratic republic," Mazzini insisted. "What justification is there to throwing out an Austrian Emperor and allowing a king, any king to rule, even if they're Italian?"

Verdi shared his thoughts, which aligned with Mazzini's. "I may not understand politics, but why must we have a king? How can we be a true democracy when a king wielding his divine right to rule can overturn the rights of the people on a whim? Is this progress?" he asked, "Or merely the illusion?"

Garibaldi, who had spent much of the last decade in the thick of actual fighting, was ever more the pragmatist. He argued, "The enemy of our enemy should be seen as a friend and if unity between Lombardy and Savoy helps us birth an Italian nation, then I am all too happy to serve under a king whose father had once ordered me hung from the gallows."

This argument between friends grew heated until Guastella interceded. Our cousin used his diplomacy skills to keep our two most important leaders working in unison for a common goal, by pointing out that their arguments were irrelevant. "King Charles Albert's involvement is already a *fait accompli,*" he said. "To succeed you both needed to simply accept this fact and build our future strategies based on that reality." Neither Verdi nor Mazzini were pleased with the concept of freedom first and then only later, Democracy, but reluctantly agreed.

After the memorial, all three men, Garibaldi, Mazzini and Guastella, were to lead their troops south through Tuscany to Rome with the strategic hope of fomenting an uprising there that would directly undercut the Pope's civil authority. Pope Pius IX ruled as a king over the Papal States, a vast swath of the Italian peninsula that bordered the Veneto in the north and the Naples region in the south and included, most of the territory on the east of the Apennines, including Bologna, Ravenna, Ancona, Perugia as well as Rome and the surrounding regions. Though the publicists of the Vatican promoted Pius IX as a liberal concerned with the welfare of his flock, nothing could have been further from the truth. He was a die-hard conservative who reinstated the Jewish Ghettos that Napoleon had torn down fifty years earlier and his regressive polices favored no one but the aristocracy from which he had been born into.

It was Guastella's second conversation about real estate in Busseto however that had the most direct and immediate impact upon Verdi, Isabella and me. Guastella and Barezzi had succeeded in negotiating a price for Sant' Agata well within Verdi means. "All you need do is give us the final approval and it's yours."

Verdi did. The Maestro would finally have his country estate.

But Guastella had even better and more surprising news for me.

"Do you want to gain a measure of revenge against Cesare Briscola for what he did to Uncle Roberto?" he asked.

"And for what he did to *Mamma, Papà e mio Fratello,* added Isabella. "The Duke of Mantua is a murderer."

"I had not forgotten that. So, here's how we do it. With help from Uncle Roberto above," said Guastella, pointing to the heavens.

Apparently, Cesare Briscola had mortgaged *Corte degli Angeli* to the hilt to pay for his private army.

"How do you know all this?" Verdi asked.

"Duke Cesare Briscola may have fled to Verona with the Austrians, but his wife, the Duchessa, has been sharing my bed for years."

"*È vero?* Truly?" I was stunned.

"Yes. Carlotta was my fiancée, until her *papà* forced her to marry Cesare. It was a classic exchange: her father, a *Converso*, bought himself a royal title and became a Baron while the Duke of Mantua got a necessary infusion of cash to pay for his army."

"That's horrid," said Verdi, "But not surprising."

"Yes, but the last laugh comes at Cesare's expense," said Enrico, "*È impotente.*"

Isabella and I could barely contain our laughter, "*È impotente.*"

"Ah," said Gustella as he pulled a notarized document out of his coat pocket, "It gets even better. Through my connections with the leaders of the *Risorgimento*, I had Cesare and his allies all declared "Enemies of the Republic," and given death sentences in absentia."

"Brilliant," said Isabella. "Set Cesare before a firing squad, and I'll pull the trigger myself." And I had no doubt my wife would, given the chance.

"Perhaps, someday soon, but for now you need to know this: I leaned on his bankers in Parma, all of who are friends of the *Risorgimento*, to foreclose on Cesare's loan. They did."

Guastella went on to tell us that if we so desired, we could take over the loan and make it ours. Normally that would have been a stretch far too rich, but with Uncle Robeto's death, as his sole heir, I had not only inherited Ca' Dario but also his entire fortune, which was substantial.

*** * * * * * * * * ***

The last conversation of significance that night occurred just after Verdi and all of the other guests had departed. A well dressed and distinguished looking gentleman in his early sixties entered *il Nord* as Isabella and I were about to close up the restaurant. His face was familiar. Both Isabella and I had seen him before but neither of us could not place where or when.

"Forgive me for being late," he said, "But would you happen to be *Signor* Dario Conegliano, the opera singer and nephew of my friend, *Signor* Roberto Conegliano?"

"One and the same," I answered.

"And you must be Signora Isabella?" he said to my wife.

"Si?" she replied but as if asking a question herself.

"Ah, then please allow me to introduce myself. I am your neighbor from the Via Vittorio Veneto neighborhood, *Signor* Alessandro…, *Signor* Alessandro Manzoni."

His answer floored both Isabella and me, as this seemingly humble man was none other than our literary idol; the greatest writer of modern Italian; the author of *The Betrothed;* the creator of those original iconic characters Renzo and Lucia, whose portrayals lept off the page. Neither one of us could believe he had just walked into our trattoria. *Signor* Alessandro – for that is how he asked to be addressed - then reached into a satchel he carried over his shoulder pulled out a small framed document, which he handed to me.

"I thought you might appreciate this gift in honor of your uncle."

Carefully secured under glass, it was an autographed Ca' Dario menu from April 1, 1800, the day forty-eight years earlier that Uncle Roberto had first opened the restaurant.

"Please," he said, "Read the inscription," which I did.

I recognized the words straight off, *"To my new young friend, Mr. Alessandro Manzoni; Viva Italy! Why be mundane when, with passion you can be monumental?"*

"I was but fifteen when your Uncle Roberto wrote that," said *Signor* Alessandro. "His words have inspired me ever since. My parents had brought me that night and I have been returning here to dine for nearly fifty years. I confess I would not be the man, the writer, the poet nor the philosopher, people claim me to be, if not for your uncle nor Ca' Dario."

"I can't believe that," I said. "You? Our hero? Our inspiration?

The voice of our people?" I bade *Signor* Alessandro to sit at one of our tables. While Isabella made him comfortable, I raced back to the office area before returning with one of our finest wines, a twenty year old Brunello from Roberto's private collection and the original leather bound copy of *The Betrothed* that Verdi had received from Giuseppe Mazzini – code name Renzo - the night our revolution began. It's true I thought, his face was familiar as one of our frequent diners in *il Nord*, one of those quiet gentlemen who would usually sit alone off in a corner, either reading a book or a newspaper. To imagine *Signor* Alessandro Manzoni, our literary hero, the man whose very existence embodies the dreams of the *Risorgimento*, had been here all along and we never knew it or recognized him. *È strano* – it's strange how life often pulls blinders over our eyes.

"Ah," said *Signor* Alessandro as the three of us began to share that bottle, "You have one of the very first editions of *The Betrothed* here. And this is a superb Brunello."

Though Isabella was in as much awe at meeting *Signor* Alessandro as I was, she told him the story of that night; of how she had selected his novel and the code names of Lucia and Renzo; of how her brother, Piero Lusardi, was supposed to do the secret exchange and lead Giuseppe Mazzini and his lover Giuditta Sidoli to freedom; and I continued the story by telling of Piero's murder of at the hands of Field General Matteo Gaetz.

"Say no more, I was there that night with one of my daughters. *Signorina* Strepponi sang a poignant lament in Ladino about King Solomon's daughter, Violetta, and later the two of you sang *Là ci darem la mano* from *Don Giovanni* to us. Yes, I saw it all; from the storm outside raging; to Commander Gaetz and his henchmen killing that man, your brother, out on the streets. And you say it was Verdi who made the book swap with Giuseppe Mazzini?"

"Yes, it was Verdi," I said.

"Ah, a shame, I would have enjoyed meeting the man, even back then. Verdi is by far my favorite opera composer. No one has captured the spirt of the Italian people and our struggles better than Verdi, though I have never had the honor of shaking his hand in friendship. We've came close once at Contessa Maffei's salon, but, alas, he has always eluded me. Perhaps one day."

"Sadly, you missed him by only minutes tonight," said Isabella.

"Ah, my loss again. Still, could you imagine if the three of us, Verdi, Giuseppe Mazzini and I had met that night with a crystal ball in our hands? Would we have envisioned what the future held for us all? The fame, the pain, the responsibility? Would we have understood the wisdom revealing the path to Democracy? Should we have seen our glorious revolution come to pass? Could we have felt in our bones the freedom, we fought for? Would we have grasped all that?"

"Because '*that which comes next is not always progress*?'" I asked repeating one of *Signor* Alessandro most notable quotes.

"Ah," said *Signor* Alessandro, "You know my work well. But do either of you know why I wrote that line?"

Isabella and I both shook our heads, "no."

"Because sometimes, what comes next is progress. But the difference between a good outcome and a bad one, depends, collectively, on each of us in our society and the wisdom to know the difference."

Inspired, Isabella spontaneously quoted lines from the last paragraph of *The Betrothed*, "*Events come at us sometimes by our own causation and sometimes from purely external, but where they come from is less important than the fact that we must deal with them, nonetheless.*"

"Exactly," said *Signor* Alessandro. "And if we, as my heroes Renzo and Lucia, discover in the course of their respective odysseys, make the correct choices, if we, again collectively, do the right thing in each and every moment of our lives, then we increase the odds that what comes next is indeed the progress all humanity desires. And make no mistake about it, humans thrive best in a free Republic where truth, kindness, compassion, equality, justice for all, and the rule of law prevail. But if instead we fall under the spell of cruelty and corruption perpetrated by those we know to be truly evil – such as a Field General Matteo Gatz or a Duke Cesare Briscola -

and we behave counter to the best interests of humanity, progress will elude us, justice will not be had and Democracy will fail."

Isabella kissed *Signor* Alessandro on both cheeks. "I love you," she declared, a love I was not jealous of, a love I was in fact proud of and one I shared.

"But you, Dario, you know Verdi best. Why is it he has never considered making an opera out of *The Betrothed*? That would be the greatest of honors for me to have him bring my story to La Scala."

I had to laugh. "First, you must know Verdi has held your works in awe since he was a teenager composing works for the *Società Filarmonica* Busseto and back then he actually scored several pieces based on your poem, *Il Cinque Maggio* and your tragedy, *Il Conte di Carmagnola.* They were my first exposure to your writings and I recall singing them both just before leaving for my studies at the conservatory in Milan," I said to Signor Alessandro, "But - and you must know when it comes to *The Betrothed*, Verdi and I have discussed this at length – it's too long and complex a novel to squeeze into the mere two to three hours allotted to an opera."

"Perhaps, but certainly a simplified version?" he asked.

"Yes, it's possible but it requires a librettist of great skill to shrink a massive and brilliant work into something significantly shorter without losing its essence or power.

"As your cousin, the illustrious Lorenzo Da Ponte did for Mozart's *Don Giovanni*?"

"You know his work?"

"*Assolutamente!* Without Da Ponte's masterful adaptation of the *libretto* from Tirso de Molina's play, *The Trickster of Seville and the Stone Guest*, how could Mozart, an Austrian, have become one of Italy's greatest composers – after our Verdi, of course?"

"*Certo*, but that brings me to the second and more important reason Verdi would never try to adapt your work into an opera. He's mortally afraid of disappointing you."

"Me? A mere novelist and writer?"

"Yes. You. He holds you and *The Betrothed* in such high esteem -

he considers it the greatest work of Italian literature since *The Divine Comedy* and *The Decameron* – that he is absolutely terrified of ruining it."

"But he's done Schiller and Shakespeare? He puts me above them?"

"They're dead… And foreigners… You, you're alive and you're Italian and the scribe he considers closest to the Gods."

"I'm just a simple man with a pen."

"And so is our Verdi," said Isabella. "Though others consider him arrogant and aloof, you must know our *amico* is really quite shy. And I can tell you with absolute certainty that our dear friend is not only afraid of ruining your novel, he is purely petrified by the prospect of meeting you and facing your disapproval. You're his absolute idol."

"*Si, va bene*, then perhaps one day he'll allow me to shake his hand, but let me change the subject. I'm here, we're here to honor your Uncle Roberto," said *Signor* Alessandro, "One of the greatest comforts of this life is friendship; and one of its virtues is that of having someone we can trust with a secret. Your uncle was that man, for in truth, I could have never written *The Betrothed* without your Ca' Dario." *Signor* Alessandro went on to tell us that which he claimed he has never shared with anyone else ever other than Uncle Roberto. "When I first conceived of this novel, I wanted to tell a story about our Italian people and our seemingly perpetual struggle against the oppressive forces that bedeviled us, including our highly corrupted clergy and the rapacious aristocrats who hold our people in abject poverty."

"Much like Verdi's operas?" I interjected.

"Precisely," said *Signor* Alessandro, "Yes, Verdi and I are two weavers of silk pulled from the same spool. I use words, he uses music but our objectives were or are the same, to capture the emotions of the people, our people, the common people, in our dramas in such a fashion as to make them…"

"Unforgettable?" said Isabella finishing his sentence.

"Indeed, yes, unforgettable. But look at me," said *Signor*

Alessandro, "I come from an old patrician Lombardy family that lived almost entirely in the world exemplified by those diners who could never conceive of sitting anywhere but in this room, your *il Nord*. My family knew nothing about the lives of the rest of our people and very quickly my efforts at writing ended up in the fireplace. They held no truth, a thought I shared one evening years past with Signor Roberto over just such a bottle of Brunello. Your uncle laughed at me and said, 'Seek perfection, accept failure. That is to say, always do your best but accept the limitations of being human when you fall short with dignity, grace and forgiveness of yourself and others. The true revolution is to improve oneself and improve the world at the same time. If you want to learn about the people of our land, their fears, their hopes, their dreams, their struggles, their passions, go and dine with them, break bread with them, drink wine with them. Remember, the greatest secrets are hidden in plain sight, and you will find them all here at Ca' Dario, from *il Nord* to the free kitchen. Never forget that our lives are a constant striving to salve a hunger that will never be satisfied. To understand our Italy, you only need to get out of your comfortable chair and wander through each of our dining rooms and say, Good afternoon, good evening, how are you?' And so, after listening to Uncle Roberto, I conceived of a plan and setting aside some nervous hesitation, I put it into place."

Signor Alessandro Manzoni went on to describe how he borrowed the ragged clothes from one of his servants and then, night after night, he would show up with the rest of the homeless and starving at the window of the free kitchen. Though at first timid, if not downright intimidated, he gradually became comfortable with and amongst the poor who ate in our Sicily outbuilding. He'd listen to their stories, their tales of woe, the sagas of their misfortunes, and the blows that brought them to their present state of despair. This he did for many weeks, until he would recite their tragic tomes from memory and do so in the twisted tongues of the uneducated and desperate.

Next, he changed into another identity, that of a tradesman, a silk weaver, an artisan, and he repeated the process in *Lo Stivale* – the Boot. Beneath the murals depicting Mount Vesuvius, he'd hear and speak their language, that of the working poor, men and women who found relief in wine, sustenance in risotto and comradery amongst their class.

Months later, he would return again and again to *Il Colosseo* – the Coliseum - and join the families and fellowship of the burgeoning middle class; the bank clerks, the office workers, the city employees, the school teachers and the artists, all of whom had new, albeit tiny, bank accounts and dreams of a better life for their children.

After that *Signor* Alessandro took up cards and gambling while sharing shots of hard liquor with the soldiers and *bon vivants* of our Tuscany Bar Room. He admitted that at first, he was a dreadful card player, that is until he learned to stop caring. Throwing caution to the wind on the strength of those whiskey shots, he soon became a bit of a card shark.

"I came to actually enjoying it," he said, "Outwitting those Austrian cavalry officers, the same ones we had all come to fear when out on the streets."

Finally, he told us, he shed all of his previous costumes and returned to *il Nord*. Nearly a year had gone by since his initial night at the free kitchen. And for the first time, he saw his social peers – the triangle of evil he called them - in a new light. Up first were the obese bishops like Giuliano Giuliani who gorged to excess on six days of the week, only to preach restraint on Sundays to the minions stuck in the squalor of poverty. Next came the mindless Counts and Countesses who ordered plate after plate of our finest of fares, yet left enough food behind to feed a family of fifteen. And finally, the guardians of the governing caste, the Austrian Army officers who alternated between polite abstinence when on duty, to excess and abuses when not.

When Signor Alessandro Manzoni was finished, he declared, "This is what I learned through Uncle Roberto. The true revolution is to improve oneself and improve the world at the same time, thus we should never be afraid of rising up again. A single thought, be it freedom or Democracy, if it is true, is stronger than an army. And the world we live in, it's not evolutionary, it's not moving towards some better world. No, instead we have an endless dialectic where everything swings back and forth between the two polarities of human existence: the fate of the individual versus the fate of the greater community. Our human dream of harmony between lovers and of peace within and between nations, is a delicate balance between these forces and thus, it is relatively unstable. Just as each individual human exists in a balancing act between self-interest and the need for community, so too does society rachet back and forth between these conflicting but inseparable desires. Ca' Dario is Italy. It contains its heart, its soul, but most of all, its stomach. And I confess, that I would have never been able to write my novel with any sense of authenticity or honesty had I not inhabited each of these rooms here and learned to break bread with all of its people."

By now, as we had come near to the end of the Brunello, I poured each of us a last glass. After Signor Alessandro offered up a final toast to Uncle Roberto, I asked him to autograph of our copy of *The Betrothed* and this is what he wrote:

"To *Signor* Dario and *Signora* Isabella and in honor of my friend and your Uncle Roberto, *Viva l'Italia, Si tratta sempre del cibo."*

✱✱✱✱✱✱✱✱✱✱

In May, Isabella, my son Tre, Verdi and I braved the highways and returned to Busseto. Verdi wanted to inspect Sant' Agata with Barezzi and his parents who would oversee whatever renovations were necessary to make the home hospitable and the farming operations successful.

Isabella and I had other plans for the *la Corte degli Angeli.* Given that our life in Milan revolved around Ca' Dario, our intent was to turn the management of the estate over to the one person who knew it best; the one who was not only born there but grew up knowing every inch of the property as a child; and who as an adult had kept and recorded every bit of information about the farm operation, from seeding the crops each year to dividing the harvest to distributing profits to the workers who all live there: my mother-in-law, Sophia Benedetto Lusardi.

A few days after returning to Busseto, Sophia, Isabella, Tre and I rode over to *la Corte degli Angeli* in my father's old supply wagon, which was pulled by two new draft horses. Abramo and Isacco, were long gone, reminding me that I had not been back there since I was a teenager, nor had Isabella and Sophia been there since the day of their expulsion by the Briscolas. Both were nervous and apprehensive as we turned onto the long approach road that cut through a field of wheat.

I should note that even at a very young age, our son Tre was infatuated by his grandmother, by her ever evolving cookbook, *Una Festa d'Amore,* and by her use of sign language. They'd spend hours together in the kitchen whenever we visited. Sophia had long ago taught him the sign language that she had created – one that was so sophisticated that it was a precursor to modern Italian sign language – and in turn Tre would often translate Sophia's conversations for me.

When we arrived, the gate to the courtyard of the vast rectangular fort-like compound was open but we did not see a single soul anywhere, this despite the fact that at least a half dozen families still lived and worked there. I pulled the wagon through the gate and into the interior. We stopped in front of the old manor house. The courtyard, perhaps the size of four or five soccer field, was also deserted. No people, no animals, no nothing, just the sound of the wind. I dismounted and helped Isabella, Tre and Sophia to do the same. The four of us stood there, not knowing what to think.

Isabella pointed toward the barn and stable on the opposite side of the yard. "What's that noise?"

"What noise?" I asked.

And then, from off in the distance, I heard it too, the low booming sound of a shofar. We watched as one of the doors opened and out stepped Verdi in his old *Filarmonica* uniform, but instead of waving his usual conductor's baton, he brought the old *shofar* to his lips again. He played it with enough force to bring down the walls of Jericho, later claiming it was chase away the spirit of *Il Diavolo*: Cesare Briscola and his family.

A second door opened. A trumpeter, who was also dressed in a bright red Busseto *Società Filarmonica* Marching Band uniform, began playing some sort of march.

As he continued to play, I recognized the music. It was a grand processional Verdi had written as a teenager for the *Filarmonica.* Imagine it, if you will that it was a precursor to Verdi's brilliant *Triumphal March* in his opera *Aida.* Similar energy, similar orchestration, and soon, we were to discover, a similar victory to celebrate.

Another door opened, this one on the right side of the courtyard, and out stepped another trumpeter. And then a fourth door on our left opened with another horn player, a tuba; and then a fifth door and a sixth. More horn players, and then other doors opened and out came a flute player, none other than Antonio Barezzi himself, leading a procession of woodwinds… And then the doors to all the residences opened and out poured the workers, their children, their chickens, their pigs, their goats, their sheep….

And from behind us, came scores of cattle, horses, donkeys and mules, coming in from their pastures and ushered in by their shepherds.

Then Verdi, the rascal that he was, led the band members as they joined up in a formation and began to circle around us. As they continued playing, the peasant families, their children and their animals all fell into line and followed the march that was certainly as every bit as grand and triumphal as the one in *Aida*, with one key difference. In *Aida,* the march in honor of a victorious army, was filled with slaves and the spoils of war. Here at *la Corte degli Angeli,* the procession was composed of peasant families who had finally escaped from their life of near servitude to the rapacious Briscola clan. From the smiles on their faces to the sparkles in their eyes, their joy at having one of their own, Sophia, take over, was obvious and unbridled.

The procession continued until we were fully encircled. After the grand conclusion to the march, Verdi gave one last masterful blast on the shofar. Everyone assembled let out a great cheer. The doors to the manor house of the estate then opened and out walked our cousin, Enrico Guastella, with two little girls, his nieces – daughters of the women who had once cared for Sophia. The girls ran forward with bouquets of flowers that they bestowed upon Isabella and Sophia as if they were Queens, which they certainly were that day. The two women were stunned at the reception and tears rolled down both their cheeks.

I walked over to where Guastella, Barezzi and Verdi stood and embraced each one in turn. *"Grazie mille, i miei amici."*

"Haven't I told you; we would win," said Verdi, who was clearly very pleased with himself for having generated such a triumphant welcome for us.

"Grazie mille, amico," Even I had tears rolling down my cheeks as Verdi embraced me back.

"Viva la vittoria," he replied with deep and heartfelt sincerity, "But wait, there's more."

Verdi blew into the shofar one again. Upon Verdi's signal, Eduardo Villa came out of the manor house. He fell to his knees before Sophia and sang for her. Though my mother-in-law could not hear a word, her grandson, Tre, happily translated it all for her. The song, renamed *Celeste Sophia – Heavenly Sophia* - was an early work by Verdi that he had composed originally for Margherita when they were married and would find its final version in his opera *Aida* as *Celeste Aida*.

Eduardo sang, *"Oh heavenly Sophia, you reign over our thoughts and are the splendor of our lives…. We restore to you, your bright skies and the soft breezes of your native soil. We place a royal crown upon your head and raise a throne for you beside the sun…"* When our *il Torino* finished, he rose and embraced Sophia.

Verdi turned to me and said, "This is the finest accomplishment of our lives."

"Yes, I have always believed that but I never understood what winning actually meant. Now I do. Again, thank you for what you did today."

"Revenge is sweet," Guastella said, "But living a good life on the land is even sweeter."

"I cannot tell you what it means…" I started to say but was

stopped by Tre tugging on my sleeve. He wanted to translate my mother-in-law's sign language.

"Yes, it's true," Tre translated for Sophia, "That I cannot tell you what it means to be able to return to my home and to have our humanity recognized and restored."

Guastella then handed me the keys to *la Corte degli Angeli* to me and I in turn gave them to Sophia. The estate was our gift to her. She had long dreamt about this day, a day of a return to dignity. Despite her disabilities she knew exactly how to run the estate in both a profitable and humane manner, one in which every family who lived and worked there would be able to enjoy a good life and a healthy share of the profits.

We entered the manor house and wandered through the old kitchen. There we found all of Sophia's books, her entire library was still there, albeit covered with years of dust. My mother-in-law was thrilled. She was home at last. And Tre, who was fascinated with all things related to cooking, was in heaven. Oh, and those family portraits on the wall, the ones of the Briscola clan going back generations? Verdi took the one of Cesare and tossed it into the fireplace. As the flames consumed that portrait of the evil Duke of Mantua, Isabella, Sophia and Tre removed all the others, which they also consigned to the same fires that would cook our feast that night.

I could not express in words the joy of liberation we all felt that night, so instead I kissed my bride, my mother-in-law, my son, Barezzi, Guastella, Eduardo and Verdi. *Viva la rivoluzione!*

****

Unfortunately, Giuseppe Mazzini's dream of "One, free, independent, republican nation," was no more viable than a still born child. On July 24th, not long after Verdi returned to Strepponi in Paris – much to her relief - the Austrian Commander, Field Marshall Radetzky thoroughly crushed the forces of King Charles Albert at the first Battle of Custoza. Soon thereafter the Austrians marched back into Milan. Every freedom Lombardy had gained in March vanished by August. Danger lurked ahead. This time we viscerally understood what *Signor* Alessandro Manzoni had prophetically declared, *"That which comes next, is not always progress."*

Over the next few months, the armies of the *Risorgimento* were thrown back and defeated not only in Lombardy, but in Venice, Rome and in Savoy itself. Our first war for independence ended in disaster, leaving us worse off than before. King Charles Albert was forced to abdicate in favor of his son, Victor Emanuele II. Defeated in combat at Rome, Garibaldi and Mazzini fled back into exile abroad. Guastella found sanctuary in Turin, where he began working with Victor Emanuele II's future prime minister Camillo Cavour. All I could think was that line from Verdi's *Va' Pensiero* in *Nabucco,* *"Oh my country, so beautiful and lost!"*

Even from Paris, and in a last measure of desperation, Verdi joined a chorus of leaders of the uprising in pleading with the Republican government of France for support in our war against the Hapsburgs.

They wrote a letter which in part asked, *"Gentleman, can you continue as indifferent witnesses to the spectacle offered by the martyrdom of so noble and unfortunate a people? They call out to you as brothers... Every moment of delay may decide the fate of thousands of victims. Every instant lost for the freedom of Italy is a gain for despotism in Europe..."*

But to no avail. Our pleas were ignored. Once Radetzky was fully in control of Milan, the roundup of the rebels behind the revolt began with prison cells and firing squads. Duke Cesare Briscola and his mercenaries were with them, demanding vengeance and seeking revenge for their earlier defeat. For those of us who remained behind, it became a dangerous and depressing era.

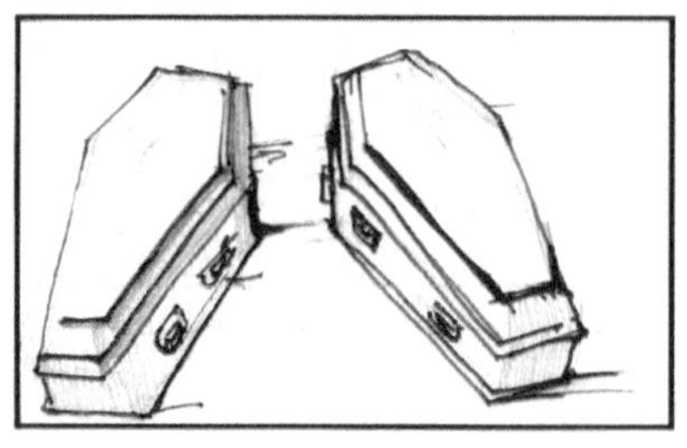

Chapter Twelve:
Farewell to the Past & All Its Dreams

Sant'Agata, Busseto, A Duck Hunt at Dawn, August 1853

Gunfire always sounds different in the fog, as if its danger and malevolence is somehow muted and dispersed. But that would be wrong, especially those," said Verdi, noting the ricochet of noise that echoed from across the far side of the River Po. "Bullets fired in anger are always meant to kill."

Over there on the north bank the Hapsburg Austrian Army maintained as tight a control over Lombardy as possible given the rebellious nature of the local population. Verdi knew that whatever partisans those soldiers were hunting there, were in as much real danger as those ducks we were after in the marsh on the south side.

The mists were so dense and chilly at this early morning hour I could scarcely see Verdi beside me, much less the others in our group as we exited the wagons that had carried us from Sant' Agata's main house. For our duck hunt that morning, Verdi had assembled a crew of ten. Verdi and I were going to be in one boat, six of his farm workers would be two-apiece in three other boats. Isabella and my now 13 year old son Tre took their guns and along with the dogs, a pack of a dozen or so retrievers, they set out on foot for the long sand bar, about a mile away, that separated the cove from the river. Verdi issued us all shot guns for the duck hunt with the exception of Isabella. An excellent marksman, she had a long rife slung on her back and a new military grade Pietta revolver in a gun belt should it be necessary to protect herself and Tre from the wild boars who loved the area's deeply tangled and unforgiving scrub brush. With a dense fog clinging to everything, Verdi quickly lost track of them. Save for the occasion bark of the dogs, they had vanished into the mists.

These were difficult times. The failure of the *Risorgimento* following the defeat of King Charles Albert's army from Savoy, weighed heavily upon Verdi. Yes, our hopes and dreams for "One independent free Republic," had been trampled under the hooves of the Austrian cavalry. Our Italian states from Milan in the north to Palermo in Sicily in the distant south, remained divided and under the control of repressive foreign empires and their clerical allies. Even the new King Victor Emanuele II of the House of Savoy in Turin had to tread carefully and appease the Austrians across the Lombard border in order to maintain a state of peace.

Although the population of the city of Milan and the surrounding regions of Lombardy remained restive and resistant to the foreign Hapsburg army, here, across the river in the Duchy of Parma, matters were a shade less oppressive but no less dangerous. Our overlords maintained their independent rule, but they were nonetheless sympathetic to the Austrians. So depressed was Verdi over the defeat that he and Strepponi vowed to avoid Milan as much as possible. Thus, they spent most of their time at his farm estate of Sant' Agata when not traveling to one of the great opera houses of Europe to unveil a new work. – and there were many.

His despair over the failure of the *Risorgimento* even impacted the very nature of the operas he continued to compose. Gone were the celebrations of patriotic heroes as in *Nabucco, Ernani* or *Giovanna d'Arco*; replaced instead by intensely personal dramas based on works of literature written by the likes of Schiller, Victor Hugo, García Gutiérrez and Alexandre Dumas, that became respectively *Luisa Miller* for the Teatro San Carlo in Naples; *Rigoletto* for La Fenice in Venice; *Il Trovatore* at the Teatro Apollo in Rome and *La Traviata,* also for La Fenice. And although most anyone who has ever been in an opera house knows that *La Traviata* is perhaps one of Verdi's greatest and most popular triumphs, its premier just a few months before our duck hunt was an unmitigated disaster, one Verdi was still trying to figure out how to reverse. The failure of a story and composition so inexorably linked to the woman he loved, Giuseppina Strepponi, still preyed on his mind. It was after all, Strepponi, who when they were back in Paris at the *Le Jardin de la Beauté Tranquille*, had bought him Dumas' book, *La Dame aux camélias – The Lady of the Camellias,* and then took him to see the play based on it.

Although Strepponi was definitely not the Camille of the story, a courtesan – a high priced whore to be blunt – she did bring the work to Verdi's attention precisely because as we all knew, she had suffered a similar ostracization from society – both high and low - due to her free-wheeling life as an opera star. When Strepponi was active in her opera career, she had openly endured the disdain of aristocratic women through her sense of humor – especially when she realized she might have slept with one or more of their philandering husbands. What caught her off guard though was the abuse she endured at the hands of self-righteous villagers in Busseto. In her first years in town, before Sant' Agata was ready to house them, she and Verdi resided at Palazzo Cavalli, an in-town estate across the street and down the block from the Barezzi residence. Many townspeople, especially those under the sway of the local priests, reviled her as if she were no better than a lowly whore. Verdi was the honored son who had made Busseto famous. Who was this *puttana* he was sleeping with? Women would curse and spit at her whenever she ventured out and at night, they threw stones at the windows and shutters of her second story bedroom. In no time she had gone from being a free, independent and distinguished woman in Paris to being a virtual prisoner of Palazzo Cavalli. Strepponi considered the home she inhabited with Verdi to be little more than a gilded birdcage of a prison for a canary who'd lost her voice.

Although *La Dame aux camélias* was not her life, it was her experience; a painful and bitter humiliation she shared with Verdi. And the novel? As soon as she read it, she knew stage dramatics well enough to know it was perfect material for an opera. And Verdi, who always appreciated her genius, agreed.

"We have to make this," he assured her after thanking her profusely for finding the novel and bringing it to his attention.

Verdi understood the pains she experienced living in town. Even the normally loyal Barezzi – the same Barezzi who had willingly accepted Strepponi's hospitality in Paris - had reproached Verdi for bringing this unmarried woman into his new home. And Verdi, to his everlasting credit, flipped the criticism back on to his onetime benefactor - the father of his first wife - and declared in no uncertain terms that Strepponi was indeed a free and independent woman of her own means who had every right to live as she did. Whether they were married or not, was their business and their business alone. Barezzi apologized, but Strepponi was only too glad when they finally moved out of town and onto the sprawling estate at Sant' Agata, where she was not only freed from daily contact with the hostile citizens of Busseto, she could spread her wings and fly unrestrained.

Verdi began composing the music for *La Traviata* in his head before he and Strepponi had even finished watching the play. He had his favored writer, Francesco Piave, draft the libretto and in it the heroine Camille was renamed Violetta and the rest, as the cliché goes, *è storia*. Now Verdi had to figure out how to reinvigorate the opera before attempting to have it staged again and in that, he was atypically stymied. He just could not put his finger on what was missing.

Sant' Agata was just a few miles north of Busseto and some of the farmlands under Verdi's control extended all the way to the ever twisting, turning and meandering Po River. In-between the estate and the river though, was what we locals called, *la Grande Palude* – the Great Swamp inside Smugglers' Cove. Any number of small streams all flowed into the swamp, an area guarded by wild boars and rife with fish and the ducks that fed upon them. Verdi's laborers maintained a rickety pier where Verdi kept a half dozen flatbottomed punts that were used both for fishing and as for today, a duck hunt. Beyond the dense reedy area of the swamp, there was an open marsh where ducks loved to nest and hide amongst the weeds. And beyond the marsh there was an open lake with a narrow outlet through a scrub covered sandbar to the Po River itself.

As the fog ever so slowly began to lift, Verdi had us slide four flat bottomed duck hunting boats into *la Grande Palude*.

The waters of the swamp were mostly stagnant channels that meandered around moss covered islets. We paddled in silence so as not to disturb the wildlife. Verdi was up front and I rowed from behind. The islands in the swamp were difficult to navigate through, but at last we passed beyond them and into the marsh area and eventually the lake, where dinner, flocks of brilliantly plumed mallards, teals and Mandarin ducks drifted on the water.

Verdi had the four boats circle silently around the sides of the lake and out toward the sand bar. As we neared it, the current picked up and flowed back toward the Po River. This "junction," or "drain," if you will, between the lake and the Po was constantly changing during the year due to the extreme variations of weather and rainfall, making access between the two treacherous and unpredictable. Only locals and thieves knew, understood and made use of these seasonal variations, which gave rise to the greater location's name of Smugglers' Cove. It was in fact the same place Verdi had been deposited oh so many years ago by the barge he had hired on the night he had helped Renzo and Lucia, that is to say, Giuseppe Mazzini and Giuditta Sidoli, escape Milan on their way into exile in Switzerland.

Verdi always directed these duck hunts, this despite the fact that Strepponi often teased him about him being such a poor marksman. Unlike Isabella and me who constantly trained with weapons, Verdi more often than not, came home from hunts empty handed. Following his plan for this morning, the four boats spread out as much a possible so as to surround the area where the ducks tended to congregate. And as the waters from the lake did ultimately drain into the Po River through the break in the sandbar, Isabella and Tre brought the dogs out there. From the sandbar, the hounds would be able to retrieve any ducks we shot down before their bodies were swept by the currents through the channel and lost out in the river.

The gunfire across the Po was consistent but sporadic, a reminder that Verdi knew that some ten thousand Austrian troops were stationed just beyond that border in nearby Piacenza and the potential for a mishap was every present.

Nonetheless we paddled out silently through the waters in our four small boats as roast duck was on the menu for dinner tonight, a feast for which Verdi had specifically asked Isabella and I to prepare. And Verdi's payment for our work? Ah, something truly spectacular and appreciated. He and Strepponi tracked down the painter, Barbarina Francini, when they were in Rome and then commissioned her to paint a portrait of Isabella. But not just any portrait. Francini had Isabella grab her gun and pose as she was when I first saw her at Garibaldi's hideout in Genoa, oh so many years ago. To this day that portrait hangs behind my desk at Ca' Dario.

After taking over the restaurant from Uncle Roberto, I retired from singing. Isabella and I stayed close to home in Milan while dodging all politics and controversy. While many of the leaders of the *Risorgimento* had been forced to flee or risk arrest and or execution, we had always been low key and working undercover – and we were determined to keep it that way and ensure that our ever popular restaurant remained afloat. In August of each year, when many Milanese left the city for the cool of the nearby mountains, Isabella and I would instead return to Busseto to visit with our family. My parents were still off the *Via Giudecca* in town while her mother, Sophia, continued to live at and manage *La Corte degli Angeli*. Tre, who loved learning from his grandmother, spent every hour he could with her in the kitchen, both uncovering her cooking secrets and helping her refine and expand her cookbook, *Una Festa d'Amore*. Verdi brought it to his publishers, the Ricordi family. They were so taken with the quality of her work that they took it on, marketing it as the first ever volume of classic Italian recipes. It sold well, a credit to Sophia's indomitable spirit and Verdi's clout.

The feast scheduled for Sant' Agata that evening was for the expected arrival – in secret - of Victor Emanuele II's new prime minister, Camillo Cavour. Our cousin, Enrico Guastella, who was now working for Cavour in Turin, was leading the prime minister on a covert journey through the central states of the Italian peninsula; a trip designed to raise support in the form of money, arms and soldiers for a second war of independence against the Austrians. Their journey was precarious both for its purpose and by its proximity to the Austrian Army bivouacked in Piacenza. The gunfire across the river was an ever constant reminder of just how much danger there was, should their mission be intercepted.

The fog continued to lift even as we four boats paddled out around the lake and toward the sandbar. The rifle fire rang out ever closer.

"Look there," said Verdi, pointing across the sand bar to the River Po. "What do you make of that?"

There was a good-sized rowboat with four people aboard, two men and two women that was apparently trying to outrace and escape from a much larger single masted scow sporting an Austrian battle flag. Riflemen in the sailboat were taking aim at two partisans in the back of the smaller craft; one of them was rowing the boat frantically, the other was firing back with hand guns. In the front of the smaller boat two women cowered as low beneath the gunwales as they could while reloading the men's guns.

"Anyone fleeing the Austrians must be a friend. We need to help them escape," said Verdi to me. "Anything less would make us paper patriots."

I agreed.

As the rowboat headed for the opening in the sand bar that would allow them to reach Smugglers' Cove, the noise of gunfire panicked all of the ducks in the marsh. The birds all flew up air and fled, taking our dinner feast with them.

But right now, that was the least of our concerns…

Verdi signaled our hunters to race toward the sandbar to lend assistance, but it appeared we might be too late. Just as the rowboat entered the channel between the river and the lake, the Austrian sharpshooters killed the oarsman. In a panic, the surviving partisan pushed the body of his compatriot overboard and took over the oars. Despite rowing as fast as possible, he could not prevent the sailing scow from gaining on them.

The remaining partisan was then shot repeatedly and when he collapsed dead and tumbled into the water, the rowboat floundered in the middle of the channel. The Austrians, seemingly secure in their victory start singing and unbelievably enough, it was one of

Verdi's own works from *Rigoletto, La donna è mobile, "Like a feather in the wind, she changes her words and her thoughts! Always miserable is he who trusts her, he who confides in her his unwary heart!"*

Suddenly, Isabella screamed "NO!" at the top of her lungs, and then Tre leapt out from behind from the covering scrub growth. Oblivious to the gunfire, my impetuous son, who was tall and muscularly built for his age, dove headlong into the channel toward the two panicked women in the rowboat. Most of the dogs followed him into the water.

The Austrians continued to sing as they stepped up their firing. I was horrified. Bullets pinged the water all around Tre as he swam toward the rowboat. Two of the dogs paddling beside him were hit and died immediately. I couldn't believe my only son was there in the water dodging gun fire.

"We've got to do something," I shouted toward Verdi, but what? Our shotguns would be ineffective at that range, little more than bee stings.

As Tre neared the stranded rowboat, one of the women threw him a rope from the bow, which he grabbed onto. Tre then turned in the water and swam toward the lake, trying to pull the boat out of the channel currents and into the still water.

"Aim for the rigging!" Verdi yelled to all his workers. "Shoot at the sail!"

Verdi fired first and the rest of us followed. Our double barreled blasts from all of our guns ripped into the canvas. Verdi's tactic worked. Our bird shot tore the sail with hundreds of holes and the wind rising off the river did the rest, shredding the canvas into confetti. Deprived of wind power, the scow was pushed by the current back into the main channel of the river.

One of the Austrians aboard the scow, a man we recognized as the new Duke of Mantua, Cesare Briscola himself, grabbed a long rifle from one of the soldiers on board and took one last aim at the women in the rowboat.

Two rifle shots exploded simultaneously. Cesare's shot knocked over one of the women in the rowboat; the second, fired by Isabella, blasted the rifle right out of Cesare's arms. Isabella tried to reload her musket for a second shot, but it was too late, the Austrian scow was pulled downstream and out of range by the currents. The last we heard of it was Cesare singing, *"Women are fickle, Like a feather in the wind."*

Isabella cursed aloud that she missed killing Cesare. The rage and anger my wife felt towards the Duke of Mantua for what he did to her family knew no limits.

Our duck boats quickly converged around the rowboat and brought it to safety on the sandbar. The wounded woman was bleeding profusely from a shot that had passed through her stomach; and the other woman, a girl of thirteen actually named Gilda, was trembling with terror. Tre, soaking wet himself, hugged her until she stopped shaking.

As I unwrapped the blue and white silk scarf Rabbi Spinoziano had once gifted me, from my neck and used it to staunch the woman's wounds with, Verdi immediately took charge with the practiced mastery of a veteran conductor. He ordered his men to bring the one of wagons around so as to be able to transport the woman back to the estate. He instructed them to unhitch one of the horses from the second wagon and ride back into Busseto in order to have Elia Segré, the Cantor at the Jewish temple who was still the town's only physician, meet us at Sant' Agata. The poor woman's blood stained my scarf a deep scarlet. Verdi glanced down at me, feverishly working on the woman, and then at my beloved scarf. Having known each other since childhood, I could sense what he was thinking and so I said, "If my scarf serves to safe this woman's life, then these blood stains will make it ever more beautiful."

Verdi nodded. He understood.

"Liberami," exclaimed Isabella when she glanced at the now unconscious woman, "That's Cesare Briscola's wife, the Duchessa Carlotta. I remember her from the night we saw the *Marriage of Figaro* when General Radetzky closed the theater. The Duchessa and I were both pregnant and bumped into each other with our enormous bellies," she added while looking back and forth from Tre

to Gilda. "Was that you, yes?"

"*Si,*" said the girl, "The Duchessa is my mother. And yes, the Duke of Mantua wants us dead."

****

But as if the violence of the morning was not already enough, more trouble came upon us as our hunting party was carefully loading the wounded Duchessa into the back of one of our wagons. No doubt disturbed by all of the commotion and gunfire, a wild boar, a strapping young male with huge tusks, charged Verdi as he was the harnessing the horses to the wagon. The horses reared up defensively and would have bolted away if not for Isabella. To Verdi's relief, she quickly dropped and wounded the beast with a single shot from her musket. As the boar lay flopping and squealing on the ground near the horses, Isabella with great calm and intent walked over to the struggling creature and spit at it.

"*Il Diavolo,* I curse the day you were born," she sneered. And in what I quickly realized was an expression of her anger and frustration at missing a kill shot at Cesare, Isabella pulled out the Pietta revolver from her belt. She fired away, one shot at a time, until the squealing stopped and all that was left was a bloody carcass.

On the ride back to Sant' Agata in the wagon, Tre continued to console Gilda. After wrapping a blanket around her, he coaxed Gilda into sharing with us the tale of their escape. Though the story the traumatized girl revealed to Verdi came out in fragmented bits and pieces, I can summarize its essence thusly: This nightmare for Gilda and her mother began when Cesare and the Austrians regained control of Milan and Lombardy. The Duke, she said, was furious about the rumors that his wife – Gilda's mother's – had an affair with a partisan and a Jew no less. Cesare wanted them all dead, but even he knew that the Austrians would not sanction him murdering his wife and child. Still, Cesare reasoned that an ex-wife was different. After first having the Duchessa and Gilda exiled to one of the Briscola estates near Cremona, Cesare then demanded of his cousin, Pope Pius IX, that the church annul his marriage of nearly fourteen years. Although Pius IX considered Cesare and the Briscolas his close family, he was none too fond of the Duke. He judged Cesare a hothead and unstable, which was a polite way of saying that which was obvious: the young Duke of Mantua was a ruthless and narcissistic psychopath who would stop at nothing and say anything to get his own way. When Cesare upped the pressure on the Pope to do his bidding by threatening to reveal certain confidences of a sexual nature, Pius IX relented but he made it a condition of the annulment that Cesare publicly confess that he was impotent and that the woman he married, *un'ebrea*, was a Jew and a heretic who had given her vows under false pretenses. Thus, it came out that Gilda, his purported daughter and one who bore zero resemblance to any of the red-haired Briscolas, was not of his issue.

"Michele Isacco Benedetto, the man you know as Enrico Guastella is my real father," said Gilda, who had the classically color dark hair and complexion of an Italian Jew. "He and my mother had been secretly engaged when my grandfather traded her to Cesare in exchange for being awarded a baron's title. My mother did not know she was already pregnant with me when the wedding occurred."

Gilda went on to say that initially, Cesare, being impotent, was all too happy to pretend that she, baby Gilda, was his daughter. But once the annulment came through from the Pope, Cesare was ever more determined that his former wife and child, both Jewesses, should be wiped from the face of the earth. Others had died on both sides during the *Risorgimento*, why not these heretics, reasoned Cesare.

Fortunately, Guastella got wind of Cesare's intentions and he sent a squad of six partisans to attempt a rescue from the Briscola estate near Cremona. The plan was to get the two women out of Cremona and across the Po River to Sant' Agata, where Guastella – on his way from Turin with Cavour – would meet up with them. Four of the partisans died trying to get the women out of the estate – the gunfire we heard - and the other two perished on the rowboat.

Doctor Segré arrived at Sant' Agata not long after we did.

Strepponi, who was so moved by Duchessa Carlotta's plight that she sacrificed her room – the most comfortable of the ground floor suites - and insisted we put the half conscious woman in her bed. It was there that Doctor Segré tended her wounds as best he could with Strepponi assisting as his nurse. Throughout the day, as Carlotta waivered in and out of consciousness, Strepponi refused to leave the wounded woman's side.

"How are you feeling," Strepponi asked Carlotta when she opened her eyes.

"Will I live?"

Strepponi smiled at her but said nothing.

"Rest," said Doctor Segré. "Have courage. You'll soon be well again."

"And my Gilda?"

"I'm here, mama," Gilda said from across the room where she sat with Tre, the two teenagers clearly having found comfort in each other's presence.

"And Enrico, is he here yet?"

"Not yet, but soon," promised Strepponi, who could not help but see in Carlotta a poor victimized woman who reminded her of *La Traviata's* Violetta on her death bed.

"Rest," repeated Doctor Segré, "I will be back tomorrow. Rest until then."

"Oh, you tell me there is hope, but your pious lies are a physician's prerogative, aren't they?" Carlotta asked rhetorically.

"Adio, adio querida," sang Doctor Segré back to her in Ladino, which brought an ever so slight smile to the injured woman's face. "I will see you tomorrow. You have my word."

"Non dimenticarmi - Don't forget me," half whispered the Duchessa.

"Domani, tomorrow," said Doctor Segré before walking over to Verdi and pulling him aside. "She has only a few hours to live." Carlotta's loss of blood, he told her was so great and her wounds so severe, that she had little chance of surviving through the night.

As for the rest of us, we returned to making plans for Cavour's visit that evening, hoping as well that Guastella arrived before poor Carlotta took that turn for the grave. And as you might have imagined, *cinghiale* - wild boar - instead of duck was on the menu for the night, a tragic night that none of us felt like celebrating.

****

The coach carrying Camillo Cavour reached Sant' Agata just before sunset. Following the briefest of greetings, Verdi led the Prime Minister into his study, leaving Isabella and I to break the news about Carlotta to Enrico. He was devastated. We took him to the Duchessa immediately where Strepponi continued to hover along with Gilda and Tre.

Although both of these meetings were of great significance, I will share with you the essence of Verdi's conversation with Cavour first as it was fairly simple. The Prime Minister understood that the people supporting the *Risorgimento*, such as Verdi, were depressed and discouraged about the prospects of unification, but he – Cavour – was not. Lessons had been learned he told us about why the initial uprising had failed. Those mistakes would not be made again. Cavour reasoned that for the *Risorgimento* to succeed, they would need the popular support of all the Italian people – not an easy task as each class had distinctly different interests, needs and desires. To gain such support, leaders of the independence movement needed to make their cause simple and easily comprehendible by all. Giuseppi Mazzini's ideas, he said, however brilliant, were far too complex for most peasants to grasp – much less care about. Simplify, simplify, simplify, was Cavour's model. In calling for freedom, change society as little as possible while touting the benefits of self-rule. "No, to succeed, like it or not, we must keep revolutionary change as simple cooking dinner. The food we offer up as sustenance to Italians, needs to be easy to digest and as tasty as that on mama's table."

"Would you keep the Pope and his Cardinals in power?" Verdi was aghast at this possibility.

"No, Democracy is incompatible with a theocracy," said Cavour. "We absolutely need to end both the church's dominant influence over local governments and the judiciary as well as Pope Pius IX direct control over Rome and of the Papal States in central Italy. Without Rome as our heart, how can there be an Italy?"

"But you'd keep parish priests and churches knowing most are simply shills and spies for the aristocracy? This troubles me."

"*Assolutamente*! We cannot empty the churches of Italy and erase two thousand years of history and culture. If we try, the *Risorgimento* fails. Whether you and I believe it or not, parish priests comfort the populace and, in that way, religion brings relief from their sufferings."

Verdi rolled his eyes and shrugged his shoulders. "Why not just admit Marx was correct, religion is the opiate for the masses?"

While Cavour acknowledged the shortcomings of their approach, he pushed forward and insisted that his covert trip across Parma, Tuscany and Bologna was essential. Should war break out again, Cavour needed to reach out to many of the aristocrats and leading citizens of those areas, including those who had previously backed the Austrians to lend support instead to King Victor Emanuele II and our cause. The King's Army of the Piedmont had been strengthened and trained. New generals had been appointed; men equal to the task of challenging the Austrians. What Cavour needed from Verdi and others were private commitments of money, weapons and when necessary, public support. He also wanted Verdi and the others friendly to our cause to run for their local assemblies and use legislative powers to ally with the King when the right moment arrived.

"But why me?" asked Verdi. "Though I support the battle for our freedom and democracy, I am not a leader, I'm not a politician, I'm not an army general, I am just a simple composer."

"But your music is Italy," insisted Cavour. "Your operas are more powerful than an infantry brigade. Your songs are on the lips of every Italian, from Milan and Turin to Naples and Palermo. Your stories of heroism are known from Calabria to Bolzano. Do you think anyone in Bari or Catania or Palermo has ever heard of King

Victor Emanuele II? Yet everyone recognizes the name of Verdi. And is so doing, every Italian recognizes the single simple theme of freedom that underlines all of your compositions. And that is how we will win. Your presence will contribute to the dignity of the *Risorgimento* in and beyond Italy. Your name will lend credit to the great national party that wants to build a new nation on a solid foundation of liberty and order. And the passion of your music has a greater chance of convincing our colorful colleagues from the south of Italy – most of whom are more susceptible to the wisdom of your artistic genius than they are to our philosophy – to join our revolution better than any prattling on of politicians from our cold and far away Po Valley."

Impressed by Cavour's intellect and intentions, Verdi remained concerned that Victor Emanuele's revolution would probably change nothing except the name of the ruling family. Cavour actually agreed but insisted that this was the only way the Italians would ever discover democracy: one small step at a time. When the conversation ended Verdi said openly that he had many misgivings about the direction the *Risorgimento* was taking, but nonetheless he let Cavour know he would do all he could to support these efforts, covertly now and openly whenever Cavour thought the time appropriate.

****

Concurrent with that conversation was the reunion of Enrico Guastella with the Duchessa Carlotta and their daughter Gilda.

As soon as Gilda saw Isabella and I lead Enrico into the room, she lept up from the couch she was sitting upon with Tre and hugged her father.

"Mama," she called out to Carlotta, "Papa's here."

"Oh," Carlotta half-whispered, her voice so weak she could barely speak, "You've come back to me."

Enrico slide in next to her on the bed. He then took her hand and placed it on his own heart. "It is only beside you that my life is worth living."

"Forgive me," she whispered in a strained voice, "I'm dying. How strange a feeling. But now that you are here, I can say goodbye."

"Blame love, for this was my fault," replied Enrico. "Marry me, my love and be my bride." Enrico took a ring from one of his fingers and slide it onto Carlotta's left ring finger.

"*Si*," she replied, "I am yours, eternally yours." Carlotta's body was rocked by a spasm. She grimaced in deep pain as she spoke, "*Addio*, my loves. Look… there…, an angle of death approaches… Already… the heavens open up… our every grief shall cease... Farewell… this valley of tears… fly… fly on golden wings… wings of eternity." She then called to her daughter, "Sing it…, sing it again…, please. I know… I am dying…, sing it again…"

Gilda knew exactly what her mother meant. Swallowing hard and gathering her courage, Gilda began to sing *Violetta's Lament, Adio Querido*, first just softly in a little girl voice while stifling the tears in her throat; "*Farewell my love, farewell to the past and all its dreams.*"

Startled by the pathos in Gilda's voice, Strepponi could not let the girl suffer alone. She immediately joined her on the first reprise and together they strengthen their song, "*Adio Querido…*"

Equally inspired by the painful sincerity of the moment, Isabella joined in, blending her voice with the other two. Tre immediately stood beside Gilda and he too sang. I followed. All of us could not help but be touched by the tragedy unfolding before us.

Enrico kissed Carlotta's forehead as we all merged our voices to sing the lament as powerfully and loudly as possible.

Verdi, hearing our voices and no doubt grasping the true and painful pathos of our lament, entered from the study with Cavour and they too joined our chorus, "*Adio Querido…*"

Spontaneous and pure, our singing was unlike any performance of any opera anywhere ever – and somehow, we all knew by looking into each other's eyes that what we were experiencing and witnessing was beyond the grasps of anyone of us… the ultimate expression of love, pain, life, death, the war, the *Risorgimento* and all of those painful letting goes and those departures, those departures to eternity that last forever… We continued to sing the refrain over and over again, no one wanted to stop for fear of what came next.

Finally, Carlotta raised her hand ever so slightly to signal us to pause. Marshalling the last of her strength, she pursed her lips and with a last breath, she blew a kiss toward Gilda.

Enrico then kissed those lips now gone still. And as the heavens opened to embrace Carlotta, Enrico, closed her eyes for the last time…

****

The next morning at the Hebrew cemetery outside Busseto we lowered not one, but two, coffins into two graves dug side by side. Changing roles, Doctor Segré became Cantor Segré. In his deep bass voice, the cantor recited the *Kaddish*, the mourners' prayer, which Verdi followed with a recitation of the *Twenty-Third Psalm*. Afterwards, Strepponi and Isabella reprised *Violetta's Lament* while we each, in turn, tossed flowers into the graves. Even Cavour and the cavalry officers in his security detailed participated in this gesture of respect.

Verdi had the Duchessa Carlotta's name was inscribed on one casket and Gilda's name was on the other. Unbeknown to anyone outside our inner circle, there was no corpse in that second coffin, only rocks equal to the weight of a thirteen year old girl. Given that we all knew that the Duke of Mantua would not rest until his ex-wife and daughter were wiped off the face of the earth, the notion of two coffins was to create the appearance that he had succeeded in doing just that. Gilda would be safe only so long as Briscola thought her dead. Gilda's fake death and burial were Verdi's suggestion, a secret we all swore to keep.

Wisely Enrico Guastella realized that if he took Gilda with him on his diplomatic mission, Cesare would eventually learn of her existence. And so, collectively, to effectively sell the lie in order to keep Gilda safe, Verdi kept her away from the ceremony. Instead, before dawn, he had Tre hitch up one of his carriages and drive Gilda directly to *La Corte degli Angeli* where she would assume a permanent new identity. Thereafter, the girl once known as Gilda Briscola, became, under the care and watchful eye of Sophia, her "new" niece, "Luisa," a name the young girl plucked from the title of a Verdi's opera, *Luisa Miller*, that she loved, so as to honor him for rescuing her at Smuggler's Cove.

In turn, Luisa's presence in our lives, inspired Verdi. His having participated in singing *Violetta's Lament, Adio Querido* with everyone in response to the death of a woman well-loved, was enough of an emotional jolt to trigger Verdi into reworking subtle bits and pieces of the score he had composed for *La Traviata*. His soul and heart had grasped the pain of suffering, a pain he himself had not felt since deaths of Margherita and his children and he was able to tweak his music and his arias to reflect those emotions with ever greater subtlety, power and resonance. And that did it. When Verdi had *La Traviata* restaged in Venice the following spring, it was universally applauded, as it still is to this day.

****

As the fates of politics and history would have it, Cavour's strategy worked. A year after Field Marshall Joseph Radetzky, the Austrian's only effective army general, died, Cavour signed a secret alliance with Napoleon III of France. Cavour then provoked the Austrian into attacking and thus, our Second War of Independence began in April of 1859. The combined forces of France and the Piedmont faced off against the Austrians. Their battle cry, *Viva Verdi,* would soon echo from Bergamo in the north to Siracusa in the south. Although Cavour, ever the astute politician, did not invent the acronym of *Viva Verdi, he* quickly capitalized upon the slogan as it masked the spelling out of the initials for *King Victor Emanuele re d'Italia* behind the Italians' universal adoration of Verdi and his operas.

Hampered by poor leadership, the Austrians were crushed by our forces. By July the defeated Hapsburg armies were forced into negotiations. Soon after the armistice was signed the regions of Parma, Piacenza, Tuscany and Modena merged with the Piedmont and Sardinia to become the united Kingdom of Italy. Not long thereafter Garibaldi invaded Sicily, Naples and the Papal states and they too became a part of the new Kingdom. By the end of 1860 most of the Italian peninsula except for Rome, Venice and the surrounding Veneto region, were part of our new nation.

And though Verdi was thrilled with the success of *Risorgimento*, the dangers we had faced did not end. Not at all. The Duke of Mantua, Cesare Briscola and all of his allies were among the very many members of the old aristocracy – the ones who had supported the Hapsburgs – who accepted Cavour's offer to join his new government of unity under Victor Emanuele II. Yes, Duke Cesare Briscola, *Il Diavolo,* was back.

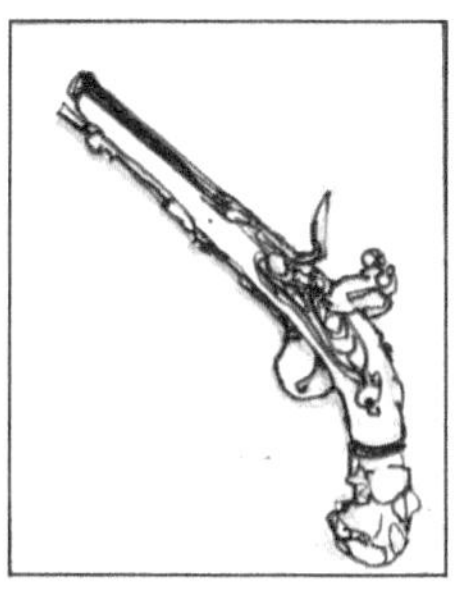

Chapter Thirteen:
I Want to Redeem Her Pride

Parco Valentino, Turin, At Dawn, June 7, 1861

Last week when Verdi took his seat in the chamber hall where the first ever Parliament of a united Italy was meeting, he said to me, "We must be approaching the fourth and final act of our opera." We were both delegates, he, from the region surrounding Busseto, and me, representing my neighborhood district in Milan.

"Whatever do you mean, our fourth act?"

"Wasn't it your cousin, Lorenzo Da Ponte, who wrote in his autobiography, 'It's a dogma of theater that a finale is a little operetta all by itself, one in which the librettist must connive to have every singer in the cast on stage, be they three or three hundred?'"

"Yes," I said, "But what's that got to do with our Parliament?"

"Look around," Verdi had replied, "They're all here, everyone in our little drama."

And he was right. Cavour had insisted on a big tent to cover Italians of all stripes and so, here we were at the beginning of our nation with Deputies from across our land taking their seats. Up on the dais sat King Victor Emanuele II, with his Prime Minister Cavour beside him. Directly behind the Prime Minister was Enrico Guastella, his ever present deputy. Liberals and progressives held down one side; conservatives populated the other. Mazzini and his many allies sat off to our left. Among them was the well-respected Milanese writer, Carlo Tenca, who had succeeded Verdi as Clarina Maffei's longtime lover. Garibaldi and his people situated themselves even further left. And although Garibaldi and his army had chased the Bourbons and the old guard Sicilians from power just a year earlier, Sicily was nonetheless represented by, yes, the old guard, in the persons of Prince Salina and the Count of Lampedusa, aristocrats whose only concern was to remain on the winning side.

Verdi trusted Cavour and took his lead from him, always voting as the Prime Minister did. At a dinner before the session began, Cavour told Verdi in no uncertain terms, "Economics and politics are merely two sides of the same coin. If you want to understand the motives behind anyone's politics, you simply needed to follow the money and see who benefits. And in Europe, for centuries, the ones who grew fabulously rich were the aristocracy, who as a mere one percent of society control ninety percent of our wealth. And the church? It exists merely to justify and perpetuate history's greatest myth: that kings and the aristocracy had a God-given divine right to rule over the rest of we poor peasants. If we intend to change our political structure and move from a dictatorship of the aristocracy to a democracy of the people, we also had to change and control the economic system that continually funneled money away from the people who created it and into the people who hoarded such wealth and used it to impose their control over society."

"In other words," Verdi asked, "You are telling us that the end result of the unrestrained greed of capitalism is Fascism?"

"Yes," said Cavour, "And we must be eternally vigilant against an aristocracy that truly believes in their entitlement to rule."

"And one they will never give up, eh?" remarked Verdi. "Unless we stop them, right?"

"Yes. And I am counting on you and every like-minded citizen to stand up against their constant pressure to impose that presumption and subvert our *Risorgimento* for their own purposes," concluded Cavour.

"You have my undying support," said Verdi. "You lead and we will follow."

As expected, the southerners, including the Neapolitans and those Sicilians, Salina and Lampedusa, all huddled on the right side of the hall with the conservatives from central and northern Italy, this despite the fact that their dialects were nearly incomprehensible to each other. For many aristocrats, their only *lingua franca* was the courtly French spoken by most of the ruling families throughout Europe. This included members of the Borgia family, the Farneses, the Orsini clan, the Medici, the Visconti, and the Sforzas. Not lost to us was that their leader was none other than our arch foe, the Duke of Mantua, Cesare Briscola. He was there with his cousin, Dino Briscola, and his closest allies, Primo Tromba and Renato Giuliani, the Archbishop's nephew, whom we suspected of being a not so secret agent in the employ of the Vatican.

Although the Pope, Pius IX at the Vatican were opposed to and fought the union of the Italian states from his bastion in Rome, the Pope too – just like the Sicilians - always wanted the Church to be on the winning side. And although he refused to allow any of his Cardinals or Bishops to participate, he nonetheless secreted his allies inside every part of the assembly with the clearly covert attempt to shape and mold legislation and policy to his liking. In fact, Pius IX not only refused to recognize the new Italian kingdom, which he denounced as an illegitimate creation of revolution, he went so far as to excommunicate all of our new nation's leaders, including King Victor Emmanuel II. The Pope claimed the king was "forgetful of every religious principle, and whose reign over Italy was therefore "a sacrilegious usurpation."

Although the joy of the general population at finally reaching a state of independence and national unity was palpable throughout the chambers, Verdi could not shake this fear that with Cavour's compromises, that we Italians had simply traded one monarch, Franz Joseph I, the Hapsburg ruler of the Austro-Hungarian Empire, for another, our new king, Victor Emanuele II.

I won't trouble you with any of the details of our deliberations that week, except to say that we heard a lot of speeches, we took a lot of votes but in the end, we approved very little real or progressive legislation in the course of that first session. One might ask, why? Despite the fact that Cavour led a majority on the strength of his personality and wisdom, his margin of victory was at best razor thin. His concept of having a parliament representing Italians of every economic class, including peasants, farmers, shopkeepers, artisans, and office workers, had been easily co-opted in the elections that sent deputies to the assemble. The affluent, be they from the great landowning aristocrats of the countryside or the new and growing business class who dominated the cities, won most of the seats. And almost all of them, including many who counted themselves as liberals or progressives, all preferred to maintain the *status quo,* the same *status quo* that had given them their wealth and exalted positions in society.

As the Duke of Mantua, Cesare Briscola, declared in one speech that generated thunderous applause from the conservative wing, "I say 'no,' to letting fools and knaves control our land. You expect us to voluntarily abandon the policies and laws that which has produced wealth for generations for our country and our families in favor of the ignorant and illiterate swine who haul manure out of our stables? Never!"

So, to preserve what clout he could, Cavour and his alliance had to constantly creep back toward the middle with compromises that denuded his policies of any real transformative power. What basic legislation that did get passed were those designed to get our new country up and running, such as forming Tax and Treasury Departments, authorizing the construction of railroads to link the far corners of the land together, creating a national army and civil service and reapproving a variety of bills and rulings dating back to conferences in Milan after the first war of independence. With the aristocracy and the Church still pulling the strings of power, albeit from behind the scenes, our hopes for a true Democratic Republic where each citizen had an equal vote, remained a mirage. Needless to say, Verdi was none too pleased with this sandbagging of our freedoms and our future as a country.

Verdi's cynicism however was not felt on the streets of Turin. The old capital of Savoy was filled with the excitement that came with birthing a new nation. Local parties, parades and celebrations were everywhere. During the weeks Verdi was away from both home and his wife, we enjoyed the sights and delights of Turin. And, oh, yes, I'd be remiss if I failed to tell you that Verdi and Strepponi had in fact finally consecrated their love and married two years earlier when he was first elected to the local assemble. That wedding band, that golden ring that bonded Strepponi to the man she loved so totally, was the one piece of jewelry she had always craved and I could not have been happier for my dearest friends whose commitment to each other remained unbroken.

Verdi's hotel, the Savoy Grand, was in the center of town and just around the corner from both the assembly hall and the Teatro Regio opera house. Occasionally Garibaldi, Giuseppe Mazzini and cousin Enrico Guastella would join Verdi and me for dinner, drinks or an evening of entertainments. Given the notoriety of my companions, it was often difficult to actually eat and drink in peace. Both reporters and members of the public would often feel free to just stop at our table to shake hands, seek an autograph or if a journalist, ask some pointed questions about the progress of the assembly. Mostly Verdi tolerated these distractions as the price of fame and freedom, but if it ever grew too oppressive, Garibaldi would just simply stare at the intruders and growl. Usually that sent them scurrying off in a panic.

Our old friend, Eduardo Villa, *Il Torino*, was starring at the Teatro Regio as Manrico in a revival of Verdi's *Il Trovatore*. His co-lead as Leonora was a heretofore unknown twenty-seven year old Czech opera singer, the blue-eyed, Teresa Stolz, and therein lies yet another story that arrived just in time to bedevil Verdi. The principle cast of *Il Trovatore* as well as many of the assembly delegates and the newspaper reporters covering the new parliament were also staying at the Savoy Grand. And so it came to pass that for their performance on the evening of June 5th, Eduardo Villa invited Verdi, Enrico and I to see him on stage. Again, given Verdi's celebrity, he thanked our *Il Torino* but declined to attend – that is, unless our little bull could find Verdi a booth where he could sit unseen so his presence would not be a distraction from the performance. Eduardo Villa did just that. He managed to secure Verdi the perfect seats at the Teatro Regio in, of course, our preferred Box 13. Still given Verdi's fame, we did not enter the theater until after the opening chorus of *Il Trovatore,* when the audience was fully engaged with the performances on stage.

Though Verdi had never heard Stolz perform previously, from the moment she appeared in Act One, he was immediately taken with her voice.

"Her tones are as fine and clearly cut as a diamond," said Verdi, "And as sweet as a silver bell."

Verdi was particularly impressed by her range, which extended from a G to a C# and with her ability to sustain notes. "Listen to this woman. Her modulation and bearing are remarkable, most remarkable. Just when you think she reached the end of a breath, you realized, no, she's just begun. That's the soprano I need for *La Forza Del Destino*," Verdi added, referring to a libretto by Piave that he was presently orchestrating for Czar Alexander II of Russia and the Marinsky Theater in St. Petersburg.

But her voice was just the first of that evening's surprises. When in Act Three, Eduardo as Manrico waved his sword to his followers and made that famous cry, *"To Arms!"* one of the stage hands directed a lantern spotlight onto our box. The beam landed directly on Verdi. Of course, when the audience realized the Maestro was in the hall, they all began to applaud, and that quickly turned into a standing ovation that stopped the show. The delay went on for at least ten full minutes as cries of "Viva Verdi," and "Viva l'Italia," filled the air.

When at last, Verdi acknowledged the crowd with a wave of his hat and a polite bow, the conductor, Angelo Mariani, had the orchestra switch gears entirely and perform *Nabucco's Va' Pensiero*. And, as you might expect, after Eduardo Villa and Stolz starting singing the lyrics, the entire audience joined them, *"Fly, thoughts, on golden wings."* It was a display of affection for my friend, Giuseppe Verdi, the likes of which he had never experienced before.

Although Verdi publicly disdained being the focal point of such expressions, he secretly relished the passion audiences demonstrated for him and his compositions. Even more importantly, he had achieved what Uncle Roberto had wished for him so many years earlier, that his music would touch the very heart of the Italian people and lead them to the promised land of the *Risorgimento*.

****

After the opera, Verdi, Enrico Guastella and I accepted Eduardo Villa's invitation to join the cast and crew at the Savoy Grand Hotel for a cast party. Normally Verdi would have politely declined such a request, but admittedly he was intrigued by Stolz. "Her voice is the finest I have heard since Strepponi sang Abigaille in *Nabucco*," he declared when we entered the party. Verdi insisted upon meeting her and so Eduardo Villa made the introductions to both Stoltz and her fiancé, that evening's conductor, Angelo Mariani. And thusly, Verdi, now solidly middle-aged and married, was presented to and enchanted by Teresa Stolz, for the first but definitely not the last time. Did the young singer, anxious at that age to climb the ladder of opera success, have Verdi in her sights? And did Verdi gush over this most charming and curvaceous soprano half his age. Who knows?

All I can tell you of that evening, is that while Verdi was engaged in an animated chat with the young chanteuse, I soon completely lost track of them both. My cousin Enrico had pulled me aside to discuss the upcoming marriage of our two children; Tre and Luisa. Both were now twenty-one and they had been enamored with each other since that day at Smuggler's Cover. Their ceremony was scheduled to take place at *La Corte degli Angeli* in August and there was much planning to be done.

Admittedly I did not see Verdi until the next morning. I was on my way to the dining room for breakfast, when I passed through the hotel lobby. There I found Verdi engaged in a furious and highly animated argument with the concierge.

"My wallet is gone! Stolen! Along with the fifty-thousand *Lire* I had inside of it." Verdi was shouting. He was certain that someone in the housecleaning or hotel staff had snatched it from his room. The discussion got so heated that many in the lobby took notice, including some of the reporters who had been covering the assembly. The House Detective and staff were immediately put on alert to search for Verdi's wallet and round up whatever suspects were deemed necessary.

Nothing I said to Verdi could calm him down as we ate a spread of *cornetti*, fruit and espresso, that is until Eduardo Villa came downstairs and joined us.

In *Il Torino's* hand was Verdi's wallet.

"Where did you find this?" Verdi demanded as he examined the contents and found all of his money was still there.

Eduardo leaned over towards Verdi and whispered very softly, "*Signorina* Stolz asked me to be very model of discretion and to return this to you. Apparently one of the housekeepers found it in her suite this morning. It was between the couch cushions."

Verdi turned beet red before either of us could even ask how his wallet ended up in Teresa Stolz's room.

"It's not what you think," said Verdi. "For God's sake, the girl's engaged. Nothing bad or inappropriate happened. I'll tell you both now, we left the party to go to her suite – which has a piano. Her fiancée, Angelo Mariani, was with us." Verdi went on to explain that he had wanted her to sight read the role of Leonora di Varga from the new score he was writing for, *La Forza Del Destino*. And apparently, when he pulled the copy of the score out of his coat pocket, his wallet must have fallen out.

We trusted Verdi implicitly and let the matter slide, but the gossips among the press did not. That afternoon, as Verdi was leaving parliament, he was confronted by the headlines in several of the local newspapers' late editions. *"Verdi loses wallet in love nest,"* and *"Did the Soprano seduce our Saint?"* Further readings had stories of *"The virtuous Verdi, the spiritual father of our country, dallying with an opera star who was not his wife and losing his wallet while no doubt wrestling amorously on her hotel couch."*

Verdi was aghast, not only at the falsity of the story but also for the impact and terror it would render upon Strepponi when those rumors of an affair spread all the way back to Milan. And remember with all those new rail lines going in, Milan was only a few hours away by train and with telegraphs becoming more common, vicious gossip traveled even faster. Verdi knew that when Strepponi saw the headlines in *Corriere della Sera* she would be horrified and humiliated and left wondering who was this woman, this soprano who suddenly threatened the sanctity of her relationship with her man… one in which they'd both been monogamous and secure for over fifteen years.

The afternoon of June 6th was clearly not a good day and it was about to get worse. First off, Cavour ended the day's parliament session early, with Enrico Guastella telling us later that the Prime Minister was not feeling at all well and had gone back to his home to rest. His physician went with him. Never a good sign.

Next, upon leaving the hall we found Cesare and his clown car companions, Primo Tromba and Dino Briscola, waiting outside the hall with trouble on their minds. All three were wearing their puffed up soldier boy costumes. Our notion was to simply ignore them but Cesare changed all that by intentionally shoving me hard, knocking me into Verdi and Guastella.

"So, you're the bastard that stole *La Corte degli Angeli* from us!" shouted Cesare. "You will pay for that, *Ebreo*!"

"Turnabout is justice." I said, letting Cesare know that I was only able to buy it legally with the money I had inherited from the very man he killed, my Uncle Roberto.

"He deserved to die, that *feccia ebrea* - Hebrew scum. Know this, revenge is my creed. No one crosses the Duke of Mantua without tasting my brand of justice," was his reply.

"Beating up defenseless women, murdering old men and raping young girls? No, you're done," said Verdi.

"Yes, you are done. Justice will carry you to the gallows," Enrico quickly added.

"Oh, you actually imagine that your laws can touch me?" Cesare snapped back at Guastella and in that moment I realized that the Duke had no idea that Guastella, the Prime Minister's advisor, was actually Michele Isacco Benedetto, the Jew whose fiancée, Duchessa Carlotta, he had once bought, married and murdered.

"Yes," said Verdi. "Your time is up."

"You are all fools. Do you think for a moment, that I'm going to leave you and your little *puttana ebrea* alive – and in my home? Didn't your Isabella tell you how much she loved it when my brother and I would fuck her behind the barn?"

My response was instantaneous. Without thinking or hesitating, I walloped Cesare so hard with the back of my hand that it knocked him to the ground.

"*Porco Zio*," said Cesare. He wiped the blood from his lips as his buddies lifted him back up. "You dare to strike me, you piece of scum. Tomorrow, dawn, *Parco Valentino*, bring your second. We duel to the death or you'll be branded a coward for eternity."

"*Certo! Assolutamente!* I will redeem her pride," I said.

At that point Enrico interceded. "It's not Dario you want, it's me?"

"You?" sneered Cesare, "Cavour's lap dog? No, I want him."

"No, you want me. I am Michele Isacco Benedetto," said Enrico.

The use of his birth name instantly froze Cesare. "I am the one you want; And you're the bastard who will pay for killing my fiancée and my daughter."

"All the more fun," said Cesare, rubbing his hands together with relish. "I'd love to kill the bastard who fucked my wife and produced that worthless child... And then I will kill you, Dario, afterwards. Two bullets, two deaths. Tomorrow, dawn. All of you, prepare to die. You too, Verdi. Your celebrity does not make you immune from my rage."

With that last threat, Cesare and his clown car companions left.

"Damn," I said to my friends, "He was planning that trap all along, and we bit the bait, didn't we?"

"Yes, we fell for his ruse and walked right into his snare," said Enrico. "But dignity demands a fight."

Verdi clapped us both on the back. "What are you going to do? Duel with that killer?"

"No doubt the bastard's been wanting his revenge upon all of us for years now," I added.

"Are either of you up for this?" Verdi asked.

"Do we have a choice? Someone has to rid this earth of that walking cancer, and it appears we're elected," I said.

"True enough. He does mean to kill us all and reverse everything we have fought for, eh?" commented Enrico.

"Yes, all the more reason to stop him tomorrow, once and for all. If we do not, who will?" asked Verdi. "Do we let this thug and his mobster allies terrorize everyone all over again. No. I have to believe that for justice to prevail, righteous people must always act and take nothing for granted."

"We will not fail," I said, blind to any other possible outcome.

"But what if he's the better shot? You're not a natural born killer, he is," said Verdi.

"I'll need a second, if I am going to save Italy," I said. "You are coming?"

"Of course," said Verdi, "But it will cost you."

"Name your price?"

"To save Italy? What else but another giant platter of your *Sacchetti al Tartufo* and a bottle of your best Brunello when we get home."

"Deal," I said.

"Deal," replied Verdi, "But don't get yourself killed. If you die, the deals off. I only eat from the plate of victors."

****

Yes. Strepponi was terrified, absolutely terrified when she saw those headlines in Milan's *Corriere della Sera*. It wasn't that she did not trust Verdi, she absolutely did. Those news stories, however foolish or inaccurate they were, triggered for Strepponi flashbacks of the worst moments in her own life, including of the disappointments she had endured throughout her career, the men who proved unreliable or dishonest, the children she gave up for adoption, the scorn she endured for being considered a *puttana* and of being dumped unceremoniously by Verdi the first time he fled back to Milan to observe Clarina Maffei's rules of sex and relationships. Her fears — as irrational as they might be - were uncontrollable.

Not knowing what else to do Strepponi left their apartment in

Milan and went to Piazza Belgioioso to introduce herself to of all people, Verdi's former lover, Clarina Maffei. The two women had never met before yet they spent the next hour sharing such laughter and tears as neither had ever experienced before. Clarina made several confessions: first, after the failed Revolution of 1848, she went into exile with Carlo Tenca. She admitted that she had abandoned "Clarina's rules," that she had let guide her life until then, for a serious and profound monogamous relationship with the liberal journalist, a man who has been her sole lover ever since. Furthermore, she admitted possessing zero wisdom or illumination about love and life, but that her good friend, *Signor* Alessandro Manzoni certainly did. Clarina immediately brought Strepponi to see Manzoni at his home just a few blocks away.

And so Strepponi finally met the man, the saint, Verdi was too intimidated to meet himself. And as you might imagine, *Signor* Alessandro was both humble and self-effacing. He entertained Strepponi and Clarina in his study and after listening to her concerns and fears, *Signor* Alessandro admitted that he too knew nothing of life's mysteries.

"The Human Heart is a font of endless tears," he told Strepponi. "I am someone who firmly believes in the ambiguous nature of the world. That is to say, I am neither pessimistic or optimistic. But certainly, when my heart speaks to me about the future, I try to hear what it says. But what does our heart actually know? More often than not, mine has had me seeing the world as I wish matters to be, instead of seeing them as they really are."

"And my Verdi," asked Strepponi, "What do I do with this man? Can I depend upon him?"

Signor Alessandro Manzoni shrugged, "I only know your husband through his art, though his operas. Of the man himself? What can I tell you? Remember that our life is a constant striving to slake a thirst that will never be satisfied. And love? It's akin to a tree: one that grows from a seed and roots itself deeply in our being. Verdi saw a pretty girl and perhaps fell under her sway. Yes, we all know that there is that other love, infatuations actually, that are born from sight, and which makes use of appearances as their sole means of nourishment. But real love, the deep affection of which your Verdi writes and composes, is another kind of attraction, which even at birth is totally blind to others, and which can only be sated by a spiritual attachment that outsiders cannot see. Only you. Never forget, you are that tree, that oak, in Verdi's life and he in yours. The inexplicable fact is that the blinder love is, the more tenacious it becomes. It is never stronger than when it is completely unreasonable. Such love is a frail air that does not flower except in the fullness of time. But we shouldn't be afraid of failing And that's why in love we have no choice but to be passionate and faithful. Both of you."

****

At dawn on the morning of June 7th, 1861, Verdi and I meet Enrico outside the Savoy Grand Hotel. His face and expressions, normally strong and determined, are uncharacteristically glum, full of sadness and despair.

"Cavour is dead," he tells us. "He died at his home last night of a heart attack. And I will swear to anyone who asks, it was birthing the *Risorgimento* that killed him."

We are in shock – and with duels still to fight.

"Our Prometheus is gone, and guiding star extinguished." Verdi shakes his head.

"What now?" I ask. "Our enemies in Parliament will run the table in favor of the aristocrats. We cannot let our Democracy be still born."

"Not if we stop Cesare this morning," says Enrico.

"What choice do we have?" asserts Verdi. *"Andiamo!"*

As we walk over to the dueling grounds at *Parco Valentino,* Enrico Guastella, an experienced and battle-hardened partisan at his core, insists on a bit of strategy. "The Duke of Mantua will cheat and we need to be prepared."

"I'm ready," I declare as I open my coat and reveal a Pietta military revolver on my belt. Guastella does the same. Verdi? He does not carry a weapon, nor would we allow the Maestro, a notoriously bad shot, to do that.

Guastella reiterates, "Remember. I don't trust Cesare. If he cheats, shoot to kill. Do not hesitate."

"*Certo,*" I nod agreement as I touch the revolver on my belt, "I'm ready."

"Good," says Enrico. "Our Lady of Democracy definitely needs us to defend her ever more today. But should we fail," he says as he hands some papers to Verdi, "Bring these to the authorities as soon as possible. It's our final trump card."

Verdi examines at the documents and comments, "Warrants for the arrest and execution of Cesare Briscola, Primo Tromba and Dino Briscola? Signed by Cavour? How did you get these?"

Enrico quickly explains that last week Cavour had added a rider into one of the few pieces of legislation that actually passed. None of the conservatives have noticed that in the details of the bill, the rider reauthorizes all warrants issued by the Milan provisional government back in 1848 when the Austrians were first thrown out. This includes the death warrants for the Duke of Mantua and his allies. Verdi tucks the papers into his coat pocket, yes, the same pocket where he keeps his recently recovered wallet.

We arrive at Parco Valentino. A steady breeze coming off the river stirs the trees on what is otherwise a beautiful morning in June. Birds, oblivious to our drama, fill the air with their songs.

Cesare, Tromba and Dino Briscola, wait in an otherwise empty field, Cesare's first comment is meant to rattle us, "I did not think *i maiali ebrei* – the little Jewish pigs – had courage enough to show," but we expect his vitriol and ignore it.

Tromba opens a wooden gun case holding two ivory handled single shot flintlock pistols. Verdi, who does have an eye for such weapons, insists on inspecting both guns. We let him. Both are loaded with gunpowder and a single round shot. Verdi, who will act as the judge and call out the count of ten, has Guastalla select his pistol first. Cesare grabs the other.

Guastella and Cesare line up, back to back.

Verdi begins, "I will slowly and steadily count from one to ten as you each walk away from the other. Only when I reach the number ten, will you both turn and fire. Do you both understand?"

"Yes," says Guastella.

"Oh, get on with it already," says Cesare, "So I can kill these bastards and then go home for breakfast."

Verdi starts his count and the combatants walk, "One…, two…, three…, four…"

Cesare does not disappoint. Instead of waiting for the count of ten, the Duke of Mantua instead pivots on "five" and pulls the trigger. His two allies lift their pistols as well to fire.

I scream at Guastella, "Shoot!"

He hears me, turns and fires…

And although everything seemingly happens at once, when death approaches, it arrives as if in slow motion…

As I draw my revolver, I see the smoke that belches out from the barrel of Cesare's pistol and the little round bullet that emerges from the gun metal as it hurtles toward me. Similar puffs of smoke come from pistols wielded by Primo Tromba and Dino Briscola. And I hear every one of the six shots from Gustella's revolver as he repeatedly squeezes the trigger.

Cesare's first bullet burns into my hip with a searing pain and as I collapse, I fire back into the smoke. I keep shooting until I crumple to the ground. A second bullet blows a hole in my blue fedora and knocks it off my head, and a third rips through my coat sleeve.

And then suddenly, it's quiet, totally quiet except for the wind blowing off the river and the sparrows singing.

Verdi hovers over me. I see his face, then Guastella's. They speak to me, lips move, but I hear nothing. My eyes close… My mind drifts off. I fly on golden wings. All pain vanishes. Am I dead? Am I dreaming? I know not. My only realization is that I am at peace, profoundly at peace as if all the troubles of the universe have been lifted from my shoulders and Isabella is caressing me in her arms. Yes, I could sleep for a thousand years. … Peace…, *pace…*, peace…. Is this our final act?

Chapter Fourteen:
Nothing Unavenged Remains

The Church of San Marco, Milan, May 22, 1874

Verdi begins the *Introit* and *Kyrie* of his *Requiem Mass* with low and warm harmonics emanating from the cellos. The sound quickly rises through the violas to the violins until finally it is picked up by the choir, *"Grant them eternal rest, O Lord; and may perpetual light shine upon them."*

I sit in the first row, the first pew actually, resting my hands on my cane. Strepponi sits beside me, her eyes focused on her husband. For this somber occasion, she wears a satin jacket and gown, a greyish-silver in tone but edged with a violet trim that only our Violetta could pull off with such elegance and poise. We watch together as her Verdi conducts the hundred-piece orchestra and choir of one-hundred and twenty voices, situated in the transept and choir loft of Milan's Church of San Marco. There are four soloists: two men, a tenor and a baritone; and two women, a mezzo and the woman who had become Verdi's favorite soprano, Teresa Stolz.

All of the other pews in this, the second largest cathedral in the city, are filled with a vast array of mourners and dignitaries as well as admirers and friends of our maestro. With Cavour now long gone, his allies including the new Prime Minister Minghetti, fill the left side of the church. Minghetti, who struggles to maintain progress forward in Parliament, was compelled into a coalition with the conservatives. They are represented at the Church of San Marco by the new Deputy Prime Minister, Renato Giuliani, a Briscola family ally and cousin to Archbishop Giuliano Giuliani. They sit in the first row on the other side of the aisle.

In the calculus of our lives, that is to say for Verdi, Strepponi and me, it is our long held conviction, that the revolution to birth our republic begins the night we all meet at Ca' Dario in July of 1833, and that the *Risorgimento* ends, forty years when *Signor* Alessandro Manzoni exits Milan for eternity. Verdi considers Manzoni a saint and a founding father of our nation, To celebrate the life of the *Signore* and to mourn all of our beloveds who have died during those four brutal decades of wars of independence, Verdi creates his Requiem Mass to be performed this day, the first anniversary of Manzoni's death.

The revolution is over. Rome, Venice and the Veneto have been joined to the Kingdom, but the price of Italian unity is paid by the long list of those whose memory we shall not forget. Yes, of course, Verdi leads our mourning of *Signor* Alessandro Manzoni death as well as the departure of our first Prime Minister Camillo Cavour. But Verdi composed his *Requiem* to mourn everyone, from my own parents, Liliana and Jacopo, and Uncle Roberto; Margherita, Verdi's first wife and their two children, Virginia, and Icilio; Isabella's brother, Piero Lusardi, her father, and her step parents, Beppo and Aurora; as well as Guastella's fiancé, the Duchessa Carlotta; and more, many more of our family and friends as age and time exact their tolls.

And although the *Requiem* is far more operatic and theatrical than the typical Catholic mass, Verdi insists that it be premiered here at the Church of San Marco, a mere hundred yards from the canal towpath where a bolt of lightning roasted Father Abbondio and Field General Matteo Gaetz as crisp as Roman artichokes and forever altered the course of both our personal and national histories. Although Verdi considers the quality of sound at San Marco to be vastly superior to all the other churches in the city, including the Duomo, for him it is the Malediction, the curse, the lightning strike and the proximity that night to the birth of the *Risorgimento* that ultimately makes his choice easy. Remember for Verdi and every Italian of our generation, these wars of independence define our lives. We come full circle. Just as the Hebrews of old wander in the desert for forty years, so too have we come to this, as Verdi declares, to a *Requiem* for the *Risorgimento*. When we were young, we began with the pleadings of *Va' Pensiero,* where our thoughts as exiles once flew on golden wings to the Promised Land along the sweet banks of River Jordan; and then we arrive at today as his *Requiem's* offers up *"A hymn in Zion..."* and a debt paid *"in Jerusalem."* Spiritually, we, the exiles of *Nabucco,* are home. The unification of Italy is the substance of our existence and what better way is there to honor all the blood on the tracks of our century than a *Requiem.*

But why a church at all? The Verdi we all know is anti-clerical. He could have easily gone secular and premiered it at La Scala as. Has Verdi suddenly found religion? Does he have second thoughts? Is he changed? Is this some sort of retreat? Is he embracing the church?

"Hear my prayer, to Thee shall come all flesh," intones the choir.

No, no, no, not at all. Verdi is always Verdi. And when he speaks, his best, his most powerful works, they are always in the vernacular. His music, his operas, his songs, emerge from the passions our people who work our native land and the good earth that grows our food. You hear them, his arias, his choruses, his marches, his duets, and how they always sound at once new yet familiar, as if they have always been here. His songs are birthed from a musical devotion our people understand through their very flesh. So, to mourn the end of an era, an era that took down so many of our beloved friends and family, and it is indeed mourning – we also mourn the death of our dream, the dream and vision of the *Risorgimento* that a new Italy will be born, one that is a free and independent republic, along with all that those ideals a Democracy stands for. To do this, to engage a nation in a global act of reflection and prayer, Verdi uses the vernacular and in Italy, for two thousand years that language is the language of the church. So, he creates his *Requiem* for the *Risorgimento,* which commemorates our greatest national dreams, hopes and aspirations and he links it all, to all of us, by invoking the name of one man, *Signor* Alessandro Manzoni, who also similarly seeks to unify Italy behind one common language and heritage.

"Grant them eternal rest, O Lord and let perpetual light shine upon them."

And here in lies yet another irony. As great a man as *Signor*

Alessandro Manzoni is, Verdi only meets him once. How was it he is so inspired by that occasion to go completely outside the genre of opera to even consider such a work as the *Requiem*? The answer, as always, originates with *Signora* Strepponi, the woman who sits still beside me with an enigmatic smile upon her lips such as only seen in da Vinci's *Mona Lisa*. She is wise and brilliant and somehow the magic in those hands now crossed in her lap, have always illuminated, enriched and inspired everything Verdi undertakes. But the route behind that passion is a circuitous one indeed.

Yes, Strepponi's inner fears about Teresa's Stolz's intrusion into their lives do terrify her, but she grows to admire this young woman who has certainly caught Verdi's attention. In Stolz, Strepponi sees a vision of herself, but one twenty years younger, twenty years more energetic and twenty years more attractive. Here are two smart, intelligent, talented women of different generations. Are they competing against each other for Verdi? And does Verdi tip the scales one way or the other? When Verdi had returned from Turin, Strepponi not only confronted her husband directly and without hesitation, she told him of her visit with Clarina and *Signor* Alessandro.

Verdi has expected her words of reproach but he has not expected that she has dared to visit the great man, Italy's living literary saint, before he has. And so, as a humble penitent, he visits *Signor* Alessandro Manzoni himself. And when the author of *The Betrothed* simply asks Verdi, "What are you doing with this soprano that so terrifies your wife? Do you understand that to want what you do not own, is to heap scorn that which you do possess? Such behaviors represent a lack of virtue, a lack of humility, a lack of gratitude. Remember, the greatest secret of life – love – is often hidden in plain sight. And know, the people we share it with are akin to sunsets: they will disappear in a blaze of glory all too soon. Death always arrives sooner than we desire. Therefore, the most terrible mistake we can make is to not breathe in harmony with another while we live."

Verdi goes deep inside himself before responding to *Signor* Manzoni, "The last two decades with my Violetta have been the most magical and special of my very existence. The strength of our union is more powerful and more wonderful than any other life I could have ever imagined when I was but a boy growing up in Busseto. And yes, I confess, Stolz, yes, I was tempted to, as you say, to want what I did not have…"

"But why would you ever do anything ever to jeopardize your Violetta?"

"Have I? No, but I need Stolz for my art. She is a superb soprano who fits perfectly into the tone and texture of my operas," says Verdi of the woman who has now song the lead in his *Don Carlo, La Forza Del Destino* and last year's *Aida* premier.

"Do you share these thoughts with your wife?"

Verdi shakes his head, "no," admitting he has all too often taken that magic and passion Strepponi brought into their lives for granted.

"If there is anything I have come to understand," says *Signor* Manzoni, It is this: The path of life and love is fragile. We must always be as gardeners, passion gardeners, tending our affairs constantly and consistently or they will fail, they will die. But if we are to succeed, if we succeed in nourishing our gardens with love and respect, my friend, in the end, we will be better people in a better world. So, to achieve that result, you must not try to convince Strepponi of your virtue with words, you must live your convictions. That alone will not guarantee success but it will give you a gambler's chance to save your marriage… And your life."

Inspired by *Signor* Manzoni, Verdi attacks the traditional structure of the Requiem Mass and remolds it with such genius into a most personal gut-wrenching and soul-searing operatic libretto, one that pays homage to the existing liturgy while simultaneously transcending it with such brilliance and artistic unity that those of us who sit in those pews at the Church of San Marco are all held in awe once more by his utter and complete mastery.

"Lord have mercy, Christ have mercy, Lord have mercy."

****

Verdi begins the next section of his *Requiem*, the *Dies Irae, the day of wrath, that day will dissolve the world in ashes,* with a degree of musical violence that is perhaps the most terrifying depiction of the Last Judgment ever composed. Booming bass drums; voices that wail and spin in a torturous descent of sounds that carry us all into the depths of hell itself. It is the Malediction itself, conceived in a maelstrom of sound that strikes fear into all who listen. And for those of us who know Verdi, we experience the nightmares of his own life and the tragic deaths of so many he loved.

"How great will be the terror, when the Judge comes who will smash everything completely!"

And Verdi's message is simple, where as in the *Introit* and *Kyrie* we mourn the departure of those we love; in the *Dies Irae*, we feel the fires and witness the fate of those who fight against justice and humanity and are damned for eternity. In those screaming, wailing torturous voices of the choir we experience passion in reverse, the anguished cries of a Father Abbondio, a Commander Matteo Gaetz, and of course the worst brute of all, the Duke of Mantua, Cesare Briscola.

Yes, in the *Dies Irae,* Verdi not only captures the hell of our wars of independence, he transports us right through the violence our blood spewing duel at Parco Valentino. I feel Cesare's lead shot shatter my hip and in turn I hear the devil die as my bullet pierces the Duke of Mantua's heart, black as it is, and ends his reign of terror. Cesare is gone.

"Nothing Unavenged Remains."

Primo Tromba fell as well that day and cousin, Dino Briscola was wounded and arrested for treason. But alas, before he could be hanged, he was pardoned by a conservative judiciary. Dino, who took on the mantle of corruption shed when his deceased cousin Cesare fell, now reigns just as dangerously as the new Duke of Mantua. History repeats itself. This Briscola sits beside Renato Giuliani, the Archbishop's nephew who as Deputy Prime Minister calls his shots from the dark shadows of hell.

No, we have not won. Not yet. Our aspirations for a free and independent Italy fall short and remain stymied under the rule of a king and the old guard. The coalition's cabinet is filled with Princes, Dukes, Counts and a new class of tyrants, business tycoons who quickly come to dominate our economy. Poverty and the plight of the peasants remain unchanged and justice, justice for the people, where is that, you ask?

"The trumpet, scattering a marvelous sound through the tombs of every land, will gather all before the throne. Death and Nature shall stand amazed, when all Creation rises again to answer to the Judge."

****

The seventh and final movement of the *Requiem*, the *Libera mi – Deliver me*, is surrendered to the soprano, Teresa Stolz. She sings as Verdi instructed. Her final *"Libera mi,"* is as if we are all without hope. She begs God for an answer, for salvation, for hope.

"Libera me - Deliver me - O Lord, from eternal death on that awful day, when the heavens and the earth shall be moved: when you will come to judge the world by fire."

Yes, Verdi's *Requiem* is a street fight between us and God. When it ends on that chord of C major, one that sounds so pessimistic, Verdi leaves us a path to the future that is nothing but a question mark.

****

After the applause, applause as thunderous as that lightning strike forty years on, Strepponi turns to me and asks, "What's next?"

"Dinner with your husband at Ca' Dario awaits," I say.

She smiles at me.

Together we stand and walk over to Verdi, who is a portrait of exhaustion overlayed with deep, deep satisfaction.

Channeling the overwhelming passion of the *Requiem*, Verdi takes his wife in his arms and together they share a kiss that will last the length of eternity.

After, when they pull apart, I embrace my friend, my Busseto brother from another mother and whisper, "We made it and you have made Uncle Roberto proud, very proud. Viva Verdi."

"*Grazie mille. Sei un vero amico*, you're a true friend," He says. Verdi in turn looks at Strepponi and says, "*Viva* Violetta."

She looks at me, "*Viva l'Italia*, Dario! Now what's for dinner?"

"*Sacchetti al Tartufo?*" Verdi asks with plaintive hope in his voice.

"*Si,*" I reply, "And *La Zuppa della Mamma.*"

"*Va bene*," says Strepponi. "*Libiamo!*"

The three of us lock arms, and in step we exit the Church of San Marco and the past. At Ca' Dario, the future, an uncertain future, awaits the answers to our questions and prayers, "What's next?"

Epilogue:
What Came Next

Ca' Dario, Dawn, February 28, 1901

On the morning after we laid Verdi and Strepponi to rest at the *Casa di Riposo per Musicisti*, I sit alone at the bar of Ca' Dario in quiet reflection. Before me are several freshly baked *cornetti* and my usual double espresso. The sun is coming up and yes, it is the dawn of a new day, a new era at Ca' Dario, one without Verdi. The floor, I notice, needs repainting, and not for the first time. The map of Italy beneath our feet is over a hundred years old, as is the framed menu that Uncle Roberto once signed for *Signor* Alessandro Manzoni which hangs on the wall. Why be mundane, when with passion you can be monumental?

Toscanini, Eduardo Villa, Enrico Guastella and all of the other guests have gone home, their questions, hopefully answered. It has been a long night, one best memorialized by the vast quantity of bottles of wine consumed and the platters of *salumi* that came full to our table and departed empty. We filled the length and breadth of my little trattoria, my little piece of Italy, with stories of the Maestro's life and the *Risorgimento*; and with a passion inspired by Verdi, we sang his *canzoni* deep into the night. The last singer and the last song, being the most poignant, Luisa reprising, *Violetta's Lament, Adio Querido. "Farewell my love, farewell to the past and all its dreams."*

Today we awake to a different world, the start of the Twentieth Century, and I too wonder, "What comes next?" Oh, that I had a crystal ball and the power to see into its mysteries.

Finishing my coffee and pastries, I carry my dishes into the kitchen with a tap, step, step. tap, step, step - the ever present reminder that while the Duke of Mantua is dead and gone, the bullet from his pistol remains inside my hip.

Tre and Luisa are the only ones still there and they're busying straightening up. I wish them, "Good night," and then "Good morning." The dawn is here. They respond in kind. I grab my coat, my top hat and my silk scarf – yes, the same one I used to try to save Duchessa Carlotta oh so many years ago – and put them on. Milan is icy cold in February, especially at dawn.

I blow a kiss to the portrait of Isabella, the one Verdi commissioned Barbarina Francini to paint of *mia moglie* waving her pistol at me back in Garibaldi's hideout in Genoa. There was my beloved, captured for eternity as a remarkably beautiful young woman with waist length raven black hair and hazel eyes, almond shaped and set above high cheekbones My gun toting partisan, my guiding star and the absolute love of my life, passed away peacefully three years ago. She left us content to have been a wife, a lover, a daughter, a mother, a grandmother thrice over and as a partisan fighter for freedom until the end. It is always at dawn, when a new day, resplendent with wonder and fresh opportunity arrives, that I miss her the most.

Now, ready to head home to *Casa di Trevi* and catch up on sleep, I open the back door of the kitchen, the one that leads to the inner courtyard and step out. Only then do I see a young man poking around the windows and doors of the Sicily Free Kitchen.

"Can I help you?" I call out.

The young man, who's probably not more than seventeen or eighteen, turns and looks my way. He has a brutish face and a somewhat disheveled overall appearance. He's also shivering and is clearly underdressed for the cold weather.

"I was told there was a free kitchen here. I haven't eaten in two days."

I wave him towards me, "Come," I say. "We'll feed you here. The free kitchen was closed for Verdi's funeral."

"I missed the funeral?" he asks as he walks over to me.

"Yes," I said, "Come inside and warm up. The funeral was yesterday."

"*Porco Zio*," he swears with a defeated attitude. "I left Forli three days ago trying to catch a train here but they never run on time."

As I usher the young man back inside Ca' Dario, I again use my fingers to kiss the ancient brass mezuzah on the door post. He notices and gives me an odd look.

"You're Jewish?'

"Yes."

He grabs my top hat and lifts it up off my head. "Where are your horns?"

"Horns?" I take my hat back.

"Yes, where are your horns? The priests at the school where I was studying to be a teacher, claim all Jews have horns."

"Church propaganda, not to be believed. Have a seat," I tell him.

"I wanted to hear Toscanini conduct. He's Italy's greatest conductor, yes?"

"You just missed him. He left here not ten minutes ago."

"Damn trains," he mutters.

In moments Tre has a hot bowl of *La Zuppa della Mamma* and a plate of *Sacchetti al Tartufo* with a garnish of fresh basil and finely chopped bits sweet red peppers that echo the tricolors of our national flag, in front of the young man. Lusia drapes his shoulders with some of the tri-colored bunting she had used to decorate Ca' Dario. It's wool and it's warm.

He scarfs down the *sacchetti* with all the grace of a wild boar shredding a carcass.

"You're studying to be a teacher?" I ask as he hardly looks the type.

"Well, I was, until they threw me out for getting into a fight with one of the lecturers."

"Oh, too bad. I am sorry to hear that. Italy needs good teachers, ones that know Jews do not have horns. What's your name?"

"My name?" he asks, "Benito, Benito Mussolini."

237

THE END

Acknowledgements:

There are a number of other friends whom I would also like to thank for their contributions to and assistance in completing Viva Violetta & Verdi. First, for being my essential teacher of all things Verdi, and the man who pointed the way to Mary Jane Phillips-Matz's biography of Verdi, composer and musicologist, Robert Greenberg. For help with my Italian language usage and translations, our dear friend in Rome, Barbara Francini. For assistance with the history Italy, the Risorgimento, and even the weapons used during that era, Gaja Kabaretti, a mezzo-soprano, music teacher and attorney, originally from Firenze. For sharing their deep knowledge of Verdi's operas and the Requiem, Simon Williams, retired Professor of Theater at UC Santa Barbara and Nir Kabaretti, Artistic Director and Conductor of the Santa Barbara Symphony. For their assistance with reading, reviewing, editing and publishing my manuscript: Fredric D. Price, Founder & Publisher of Fig Tree Books LLC.; novelist and historian, Julian De La Motte Harrison; theater & arts impresario George Konstantinow, Ph.D.; and my wife, Patricia Dixon. And finally for his stunning artwork that graces the pages of this novel, my son, Zak Smith. *Grazie mille a tutti!*

About the Author:

Howard Jay Smith is an award-winning writer from Santa Barbara, California. VIVA VIOLETTA & VERDI, is his third novel in his series on great composers, including BEETHOVEN IN LOVE; OPUS 139 and MEETING MOZART: FROM THE SECRET DIARIES OF LORENZO DA PONTE. His other books include OPENING THE DOORS TO HOLLYWOOD (Random House) and JOHN GARDNER: AN INTERVIEW (New London Press). He was recently awarded a Profant Foundation for the Arts Fellowship for Excellence in Writing. Smith is a former two-time Bread Loaf Scholar and three time Washington, D.C. Commission for the Arts Fellow, who taught for many years in the UCLA Extension Writer's Program and has lectured nationally. His articles have appeared in the Washington Post, American Heritage Magazine, the Beethoven Journal, Horizon Magazine, Fig Tree Press, the Journal of the Writers Guild of America, the Ojai Quarterly, and numerous trade publications. While an executive at the ABC Television, Embassy TV, and Academy Home Entertainment he worked on numerous film, television, radio and commercial projects. He serves on the board of directors of the Santa Barbara Symphony and is a member of the American Beethoven Society.

WWW.HISTORIUMPRESS.COM

www.ingramcontent.com/pod-product-compliance
Lightning Source LLC
Chambersburg PA
CBHW061124310726
48974CB00002B/671